*Duties, Pleasures, and Conflicts*

# Duties, Pleasures, and Conflicts

*Essays in Struggle*

Michael Thelwell

Introduction by James Baldwin

The University of Massachusetts Press

Amherst

Chapters in the present work first appeared in the following publications:

"The Organizer" in *Story: The Yearbook of Discovery 1968*, edited by Whit and Hallie Burnett (New York: Four Winds Press, 1968). Copyright © 1968 by Scholastic Magazine, Inc.

"Bright an' Mownin' Star (1)" in *Massachusetts Review* 7, no. 4 (1966). Copyright © 1966 by The Massachusetts Review.

"Bright an' Mownin' Star (2)" in *Okike: An African Journal of New Writing*, no. 6 (December 1974), ed. Chinua Achebe. Copyright © 1974 Okike Magazine.

"The August 28th March on Washington" in *Présence Africaine* 21, no. 49 (1964). Copyright © 1964 by Présence Africaine, Paris.

"Fish Are Jumping an' the Cotton Is High" in *Massachusetts Review* 7, no. 2 (1966). Copyright © 1966 by The Massachusetts Review.

"The Politics of Necessity and Survival in Mississippi" was published in two parts in *Freedomways* 6, nos. 2 and 3 (1966). Copyright © 1966 by Freedomways Association, Inc.

"Toward Black Liberation" in *Massachusetts Review* 7, no. 4 (1966). Copyright © 1966 by SNCC. Reprinted by permission of The Massachusetts Review.

"Negroes with Guns," as "Black Studies and White Universities," in *Ramparts* 7, no. 12 (May 1969).

"Black Studies: A Political Perspective" in *Massachusetts Review* 10, no. 4 (1969). Copyright © 1969 by The Massachusetts Review.

"James Baldwin: Native Alien" in *Motive Magazine* 24, no. 8 (1964). Copyright © 1964 by the Board of Education of the Methodist Church.

"Baldwin's New York Novel" in *The Black American Writer: Fiction* (London: Everett/Edwards, 1969). Copyright © 1969 by Everett/Edwards, Inc.

"Mr. William Styron and the Reverend Turner" in *Massachusetts Review* 9, no. 1 (1968). Copyright © 1968 by The Massachusetts Review.

"The Turner Thesis" in *Partisan Review* 35, no. 3 (1968). Copyright © 1968 by The Partisan Review.

An earlier version of the first two letters of "Contra Naipaul" was first published in *The New York Times Book Review*, June 24, 1979, copyright © 1979 by The New York Times Company. Reprinted by permission.

"The Gods Had Perished" was published as the introduction to Amos Tutuola, *The Palm-Wine Drinkard* (New York: Grove Press, 1980); copyright © 1980 by Grove Press.

"Modernist Fallacies and the Responsibilities of the Black Writer" was first published by the Institute for Advanced Study of the Humanities, University of Massachusetts, Amherst. Copyright © 1983 by Michael Thelwell.

*For Roberta, Chinua and Mikiko*
  *and*
*in memory of*

  *Ralph Featherstone*
  *David M. Sibeko*
  *Walter Rodney*

*Three of the most principled and*
*committed black men of my generation.*
*Among the most effective and admirable of us,*
*they were murdered in the struggle.*

# Contents

## A Contemporary Perspective

# Preface

## "The Lizard That Jumped from the Iroko Tree"

T HAT a collection of pieces written over many years, in varied circumstances, different genres, and addressing very distinct—albeit related—issues and campaigns could benefit from a retrospective synthesizing overview is a simple, even obvious, editorial proposition.

However, the cheerful good grace with which I accepted the assignment was as innocent as it was short-lived. I have discovered that the writing of this preface is attended by ambivalences and difficulties quite absent in the writing of any of the original pieces. Why this should be so I find quite interesting. And not for the obvious reason that of the mediations of time and distance with their inevitable erosion of certitude and fervor. There was remarkably little of that in the rereading. Of course I encountered a few passages that appeared intemperate and a few judgments that I would not make today in the same way, but nothing sufficiently excessive or unfair as to require changing. So finding little that demanded moderation, I changed nothing. The ambivalences are of a different order.

For one thing, the only possible justification for such an undertaking is as a service to readers: it should establish for them, with

economy and clarity, whatever by way of context and provenance is necessary in order to make the meaning and relevance of the whole more
accessible, and sensibly be finished.

As I discovered, this is far easier said than done when, as in this case,
one's relationship to the work is burdened not only by the usual subjective
proprietorship, but also by passionately held political views, intellectual
commitments, and a history of public battles. This investment—at once
emotional *and* political—delivers itself of an impulse toward endless explication. Almost nothing encountered in the rereading seems less than
transcendently significant, fully deserving extravagant amplification and
commentary. And distinguishing what is objectively important and interesting from what is rendered in that guise only by the sentimental nostalgia
of memory is not so easy as it would appear. What once seemed a simple
task is further complicated by my own impatience with writers unable to
curb an unseemly tendency toward self-absorption and revelation when
addressing their own work, usually at far greater length than is necessary.
This is a question not of modesty so much as of restraint and of a decent
regard for the reader's time and intelligence.

Instead of working, therefore, I was complaining loudly about these
ambivalences to an African friend who shares my appreciation of the
proverbial wisdom of the ancestors. He listened patiently; then, with an
ironic twinkle of the eye, to which I should have given more attention, he
asked, "Remember the Ibo story of the lizard who jumped from the tall
*iroko* tree?" I nodded. "Well, then," he said with *finality*, "you know what
you must do." Greatly edified, I did as instructed. But later I shall have
more to say of that lizard and the layers of irony and subtlety which so
delighted the ancestral mind, and my friend.

The fundamental and legitimate question attending such a collection is, of
course, Why? What considerations justify the resurrection and drawing
together of scattered pieces, most of which have been previously published? Happily, the most common and unassailable reason—that of the
loyalty of the author's friends given stimulus usually by his death—does
not apply here. What does apply is my feeling, subject always to correc-
tion, that in this case, and for a number of reasons, the whole indeed is
greater than its parts. The first of these reasons is related to the genesis of
the project. This came about from a chance meeting in an Amherst café
with Bruce Wilcox of the University of Massachusetts Press. To his inevitable editor's question, "Do you have a manuscript?", instead of the
usual "no," I answered "maybe," and this book is the result.

At the time, I was associated with a group of colleagues in a large Five-College course on the Civil Rights Movement which was led by James Baldwin. In some twenty years of teaching, I, for some reason, had never thought to offer such a course, having, I think subconsciously recused myself from the subject for reason of previous involvement.

The course was instructive. For one thing it forced me to retrieve the experience and to engage it critically in a systematic way. It also caused me to examine much of the extant literature. Which led to the introduction into the course of several of the pieces presented here. It was the student responses—those of a new generation of Americans—to these pieces that prompted my response to Mr. Wilcox's question.

It may very well be that those students—black and white—who were attracted to the course were not typical of their allegedly narcissistic Reagan-loving generation. But, for the most part, they seemed no less intellectually curious, socially questioning, morally concerned, and politically venturesome than was our generation. What they lacked was opportunity, confidence, and as clear and obvious a sense of mission as was given us by history. They professed amazement—and envy—that people their ages could have had such centrality in, and effect on, national policy. They felt strongly, indeed resented, that the "antihistorical biases" of the society had somehow conspired to keep them ignorant of any clear view of this period.

Particularly they responded to the pieces precisely because they were not "historical" writing so much as artifacts of history. That is, rather than post-facto reconstructions and analyses, they were of the time: engaged, purposeful, polemical, and, as it were, with an immediacy that reeked of the stench of struggle. They conveyed—so the students said—a good sense of how my generation perceived itself and its circumstances and what it was struggling for, with, and against. They regretted that the pieces were not collected and generally available. Now they are. And, as I have indicated, as they originally were written.

The temptation to update the material to conform to changed political perceptions and fashions was almost nonexistent. In only one case—the essay on the March on Washington—was there temptation to reevaluate. The essay is accurate in its detail and honest in its portrayal of our sense at the time of betrayal and co-optation. But one wonders in retrospect just what the consequences for us and the Movement would have been had we been allowed to engulf the Congress and White House—the symbols of national government—with the confrontational, aggressive (albeit nonviolent), massively disruptive demonstration of which we were then capable. An interesting question. Would there have been violence, deaths? Excessively long jail sentences? Certainly, a confrontation of that nature could never have been presented as the triumph for democracy and victory for the system that the United States media, both private and official, projected the March as being. The air of national relief and self-congratulation would have been replaced by what? Outrage, racial polarization, and the oft-threatened, much-to-be-feared white backlash? Certainly the image of the Kennedy administration and the history of the Movement, therefore the nation, would have been different. . . . In any event, the center held in 1963 and we were justly angry. This may be a rare case of old men *not* sending the young into battle—the right deed for the not so right reasons. But, looking at South Africa's daily headlines, we should perhaps, in retrospect, be grateful.

Most of the essays are of necessity polemical and combative. Consequently, there is an incivility of tone, an absence of kindness in some references to certain political figures, some of whom are now dead. This gave rise to an impulse to moderate at least the more cutting of these references. But they are judgments out of a particular time and were the result not merely of political differences, but frequently of great provocation. I concluded that they should stand.

Of the political essays there is, mercifully, not too much that need be said. They are occasional pieces called forth by the necessities of the Movement in particular times and circumstances. Thus they represent neither a history of the Movement nor my own political "autobiography," although elements of both might be inferred from them. They should more accurately be seen as signposts at some of the important stations in the political and intellectual passage of one generation of black people in this country.

As Dr. King might have put it, the train left the station marked Segregation in the valley of racism for the urban landscape of civil disobedience and popular mass demonstrations. Then south through the cotton fields and piney woods of Dixie and the grim struggle there for the vote, and the right of independent political organization. This track led directly to the thorn bushes of congressional and national party convention politics. From there the track turned sharply up the steep slopes—yet unscaled—of self-determination and Black Power. This pointed us toward the deceptively pleasant but mined fields of academe and Black Studies—the search for intellectual autonomy and cultural self-definition. A long layover there with an exploratory excursion into presidential politics and the track still stretches before us. [It may be noticed that this train does not venture into the siding marked "Detour: Vanguard Parties, Urban Warfare, and Revolutionary Suicide." Those tracks took an erratic course toward a dubious destination on rails poorly laid over treacherous terrain. A few coaches took that turn off, but since no useful discourse was possible or permitted, my only response was silence.]

For many of my generation that was the itinerary. And what an improbable, unprecedented, and surprising journey it has been: frightening and exhilarating in turn, it has always been instructive. Profoundly grateful to have made the trek, my soul looks back in wonder.

There are those who will say, have said, that these stations are merely testaments to futility and defeat. Where, they ask, are the victories? So many of the engineers are dead. So many organizations defunct. So many hopeful initiatives dissipated without apparent trace or effect. So much suffering unredeemed.

But they are wrong. These are not monuments to defeat. They are testaments to a struggle that was bold, honorable, and principled. We need make no apology for what we dared. And if we did not win, neither did we lose. To the extent that there is defeat or failure here, the dishonor, the loss is not ours, it is the nation's. You have only to look around you.

Of the fiction there is even less to say, save that I regret that there is not more of it that, like "The Organizer," is directly rooted in the day-to-day grittiness of the Movement. There was a moment in the South—a uniquely American moment—in which the very texture of reality intensified. A brief circumstance, which can never return or be repeated, in which major and disparate themes of American history—politics, culture, race, and sex—rang together in clamorous dissonance and creative tension. Its unpredictable configurations into which elements of character, culture, fear, courage, faith, doubt, love, and bigotry were woven were the very substance of great fiction. We have let it pass insufficiently explored.

One point regarding the fiction may be of interest. One of the pieces shares a title with a famous, earlier, very powerful story by Richard Wright. This has raised on occasion the kind of question having to do with intention and subliminal literary influence so dear to the heart of critics of the psychological tendency. Subliminal factors may indeed have dictated this choice, in which case I would have no way of knowing. But what I do know—or imagine I do—about this is more interesting than speculations issuing out of a certain tradition of academic Lit. Crit., because it is related to a quite different tradition which concerns and interests me more.

In ways I could not possibly have anticipated, the experience of the South was for me a profound and transforming one. Inevitably the ways in which this experience was apprehended were mediated by Art. One aspect of which was more or less expected. I knew that for someone black and twenty-one, who had read William Faulkner and Richard Wright, it would not be possible to go to Mississippi without receiving graphic confirmation of the way literature can inform and define one's perceptions of reality. Not completely unexpected, this surprised only in extent and degree.

What I was totally unprepared for was the effect of black southern culture. Its extraordinary power, pervasive style, sensibility, and sense of tradition resonated—in a way inexplicably evocative of *recognition*—against the most distant, half-forgotten memories and impressions of a childhood in a different country. The encounter with the oral tradition—musical, religious, literary—led, among other things, to a different and heightened understanding of my native culture; but that's another matter.

Particularly I developed a fascination with the song-sermon, which I still believe to be the only major original poetic form to have developed in this country. At first I was merely overwhelmed aesthetically—at the originality of its complex combination of poetic image, language, harmony, rhythm, and movement into an organic form. Then I began to appreciate elements of structure, the way in which the form embraced and combined the traditional and the innovative, the communal with the individual. Gradually I recognized the existence of a collectively held repertoire of images, metaphors, and motifs: rhymed couplets, quatrains, biblical verse, proverb and parable, folk poetry and blues lyric to which the individual composers had recourse. Also, I saw the extent to which each sermon was a new composition retrieved from the communal resources of this oral tradition and assembled into a pattern dictated by the inspiration and intention of the particular preacher—a process reminiscent of the dynamic of improvisation in the musical tradition known as jazz.

At the time it was new, wondrous, and fascinating. And I found myself becoming, if not quite a pillar of the church, at least a regular face in the congregation.

One of the most skillful and versatile exponents of the form was Ed Brown, a close friend and SNCC colleague from Louisiana. I fear I must have made quite a nuisance of myself with my constant cajoling for performances out of his seemingly inexhaustible repertoire. But Ed was good-natured and must clearly have loved the material to have achieved such virtuosity.

One of his favorite lyrical fragments that would constantly be interwoven into the text follows. Anyone familiar with West African praise songs will recognize the ancestry.

*I was feeling kinda sad, feeling kinda low*
*That Little Man Jesus came riding by.*
*He made me want to laugh,*
*He made me want to cry.*
*Made me feel my time was nigh . . .*
*He planted a mighty sword*
*In my right hand.*
*Bid me go down to the field to fight*
*Fight til every foe that would not yield*
*Lay down amid the field of slain . . .*

*A thousand devils may tangle your feets*
*But none shall hol' you fas' . . .*
*For, He my lily of the valley,*
*My bright an' mownin' star*
*The dearest of ten thousand to my soul.*

It is, of course, oral poetry set in a musical and dramatic frame. Reduced to print, it loses everything, and it is not really possible to suggest the haunting allusive quality that used to—and still does sometimes—resonate in my head. But when I needed a title, I went through and tested each line for sound and evocation, and "Bright an' Mownin' Star" beat out "a mighty sword, etc." I like to think that many years earlier from cold Chicago, Richard Wright, also, had reached back into the communal inheritance and borrowed what he needed for his particular purposes.

The literary essays and engagements will be seen to have recapitulated the direction and movement of the political odyssey. As we engaged, in turn, each evolving issue exposed in the struggle toward political liberation, organic and fundamental questions concerning the politics of culture and the role of literature—and the literary establishment—therein, took their effect. Hence, the critical essays are no less polemical than the political ones. And if their direction is away from the frame of reference, critical concerns, and point of view of contemporary literary fashion and endeavor among white folk, that is natural and necessary. We in the black world have too many exciting challenges and imperatives within the untended business of our cultural and literary patrimony and these are far too attractive, insistent, and laden with promise, for one to be still looking into alien fields through borrowed glasses.

Oh; what of the proverbial lizard? After he jumped successfully (so he claimed) from the tall *iroko* tree, what he said was, "*If there is no one else to do so, I must sing my own praises.*" In contemporary discourse the proverb is a great favorite of Nigerian politicians, who evoke it as an

excuse for the inexcusable. What is lost on these politicians—and on occasion some writers—is that in the values and sensibility of the traditional
culture, the proverb is a wickedly clever, sharply ironic rebuke to exactly
the behavior it pretends to sanction. For, no man of worth would ever have
thought of associating himself with either the transparently graceless behavior or the pathetic isolation of that feckless figure of constant and
earned misfortune. For the record, neither do I. I believe that, unlike the
lizard, we have kinfolk and a community capable of singing whatever song
is appropriate.

Inasmuch as the work collected into this volume represents the issue of
many years and different places and circumstances, a great many people
bear a hand either in its creation or in its survival. Certainly, the most
influential or instrumental of these should be acknowledged—if for no
other reason than to distribute responsibility. All of which may be of no
great general interest, but is important to me.

I am indebted to my professors Sterling A. Brown and Owen Dodson of
Howard University for inspiration and encouragement. Whit and Hallie
Burnet of *Story Magazine,* B. J. Styles of *Motive,* Percy Johnstone of
*Dassein,* and Hoyt Fuller, Jr., of *Negro Digest* offered the most tangible
and essential encouragement a young writer needs—that of publication.

Almost everything is owed to the Movement and all I met there. More
specifically, my brothers Stokely Carmichael of the Student Nonviolent
Coordinating Committee and Lawrence Guyot of the Mississippi Freedom
Democratic Party who collaborated on two of these pieces. Alan Schiff-
man and Tom Kahn also contributed in less obvious but equally significant
ways.

In Amherst, the debts are legion. Joseph Langland, the chairman of the
writing program, was very helpful, as were Richard Kim and Andrew
Fetler. Many of the pieces were commissioned and first published by
Sidney Kaplan and Jules Chametzky of the *Massachusetts Review.* Some
were translated into French by Odile Hellier and most were produced in
manuscript by Meline Kasparian. I am greatly indebted to all of you. And
for assistance with this collection, very special thanks are owed to my wife,
Roberta Uno, and Sidney Kaplan, mentor and friend.

For years of inspiration and encouragement by example, and for engaging the issues of the book so seriously and eloquently in his introduction,
I am deeply indebted to James Arthur Baldwin and truly honored by the
association.

# Introduction

THERE is a photocopy of a press photograph on my desk before me. I have just returned to my home away from home, in France, and don't remember or perhaps never knew who sent it, or for what reason. It is a photograph of five black men hanging from a tree—they seem, still, to be turning in the wind—and it was taken in Sabine County, Texas, on June 15, 1908. It is accompanied by a poem which I beg the reader's indulgence to quote in full:

*The Dogwood Tree*

This is only the branch of the Dogwood tree;
An emblem of WHITE SUPREMACY!
A lesson once taught in the Pioneer's school,
That this is a land of WHITE MAN'S RULE.
The Red Man once in an early day
Was told by the Whites to mend his way.

The negro, now, by eternal grace,
Must learn to stay in the negro's place.
In the Sunny South, the Land of the Free,
Let the WHITE SUPREME forever be.
Let this a warning to all negroes be,
Or they'll suffer the fate of the
DOGWOOD TREE.

I quote the poem to pose a question which the bulk of the white citizens of the United States of America have rarely, if ever, confronted and which they have certainly not resolved. I am far from convinced that either the poem or the photograph is behind us. The question, furthermore, is now a global one, with the most dangerous and devastating domestic implications: What, precisely, are the black people of this country to make of a "foreign policy" which not only appears to be the enemy of most of the nonwhite people in the hemisphere but which may require their sons to die for the freedom of Nicaragua while this same foreign policy refuses even to recognize the horror of the black South African slavery? Black people are not all—as Langston Hughes is no longer here to tell you—"second-class fools." (Not everyone—indeed, no one I know—believes that Qaddafi had any reason to bomb a Berlin discotheque, frequented, according to people I have talked to who live there, by black GIs and Turks. Black and white GIs do not, as *I* know, in the generality, spend any more time together than they must.) Black freedom, in the land of the free, now, as always, is the last item on the agenda—if, indeed, as Thelwell's book suggests, it is to be found on the agenda at all.

Incredible pressures combined to delay these notes. I was working, on the road, in America, and it is simply not possible to concentrate on writing anything between planes, lectures, classes, and the public pressures surrounding publication.

Yet, now that all that has begun to subside and I am in sight of my worktable once again, I am not certain that this was all that hindered me. I took the book with me on my travels, intending to "study" it. I didn't study it. I opened it and closed it. I think I was afraid to read this book.

It is a partial record of a terrified and terrifying, noble and ignoble time. (No record of this moment in our history can be complete.) It is the record of a monumental betrayal: but, the moment I say that, I check myself; I wonder. I am not sure, that is, with that 20/20 vision called hindsight, that I can say that what I will, here, arbitrarily (but, I hope, usefully) call "Martin's dream" was betrayed. I think it was manipulated, as were we, and that it was never intended that any promise made would be kept. That, after all, is the history and the morality of the Republic. It may even be considered as its most important skill.

In any case, and incontestably, we are certainly no better off in 1986 than we were that day in Washington, in 1963. I was privy to—part of—the original plans, or plan, for the March on Washington. Reading Thelwell's account is like reliving a specific nightmare—which is, indeed, what he calls it: it is also like facing someone who has, in his hands, some crucial sections of the jigsaw puzzle of which you have, in *your* hands, some other sections.

The official and semi-official opposition to *any* kind of March on Washington was terrified and profound. I had absolutely nothing to do with the March as it evolved, but I was asked to do whatever I could do to prevent it. In my view, by that time, there was, on the one hand, nothing to prevent—the March had already been co-opted—and, on the other, no way of stopping the people from descending on Washington. What struck me most horribly was that virtually no one in power (including some blacks or Negroes who were somewhere next door to power) was able, even remotely, to accept the depth, the dimension, of the passion and the faith of the people.

This says something arresting concerning their real relationship to (and responsibility for?) the people they allegedly represent—throws a scarchlight, as it were, on what my countrymen take to be democracy.

And, indeed, every page in this book does that. I find it arresting, furthermore, that the Thelwell sensibility has its roots, not in Harlem, like mine, but in Jamaica. Because I am nearly twenty years older than Mike Thelwell, I am much impressed by the fact that this book was written by a very young man. And this unspoken inheritance is suggested, if not revealed, in a certain arrogant openness of point of view—the candid viewpoint of the stranger—and a corresponding attempt at veracity most clearly revealed in the passionate effort to convey the subtlety and depth of what is known as Negro dialect. "Bright an' Mownin' Star," although reminiscent of Wright and bearing the same title as a Wright short story, could not have been written by Wright, especially not the second episode in the General Forrest Hotel. One senses an artist testing his ear, his capacity to interpret. For the same scene did not occur in quite the same way in Jamaica.

Therefore, I find, throughout these studies, a striking note of embattled isolation. None of these scenes—the dynamic of these scenes—is unprecedented for the narrator: and, yet, in detail, each is new. This is true of the factual studies and interpretations of the situation in Mississippi. Our narrator is not deterred by great expectations: or, in other words, he is insufficiently American to have in his closet charred remnants of the American dream.

What he *does* have, and not in his closet, is the vivid memory and awareness of the price and meaning of black community. I hazard that he was able to endure and function in Mississippi because he immediately recog-

nized that bitter, blood-drenched and beautiful country as his own. The
artless beginning of "Fish Are Jumping an' the Cotton Is High" is, if one
knows the weight and meaning of the British presence in "the islands,"
a devastating déjà vu:

> There is an immense mural in the Hinds County Courthouse in Jackson,
> Mississippi. On the wall behind the judge's bench is this mansion. White,
> gracefully colonnaded in a vaguely classical style, it overlooks vast fields,
> white with cotton which rows of darkies are busily (and no doubt, happily)
> picking. In the foreground to the left stands a family. The man is tall, well-
> proportioned, with a kind of benevolent nobility shining from his handsome
> Anglo-Saxon face. He is immaculate in white linen and a planter's stetson as
> he gallantly supports his wife, who is the spirit of demure grace and elegance
> in her lace-trimmed gown.

And, here, again, the intense precision of the listening ear: "Ah tell yo'
that man wuz *shock,* he wuz *confused.* I want to know, what is we gon'
do?"

The pages written with Guyot concerning the Mississippi Freedom
Democratic Party are central to this book and to any study of the era. The
liberal betrayal—Humphrey et al.—was trivial because foreseen. It was
not a betrayal, it was an inevitability. These liberals were not about to confront the complex legal machinery responsible for the absence (or the
manipulation) of the black vote, the complex legal machinery required to
keep the Negro in his place; they were not about to confront, much less
attack, the North-South collusion (so that, whatever party wins, blacks
lose). They were not prepared to confront American history—or, for that
matter, history—and their apprehension of the "color question" was both
benevolent and demonic: *I weep for you,* the Walrus said, *I deeply sympa-
thize:* Hubert Humphrey's song, precisely.

I was fairly young then, too, and I sensed this moment coming, smelled it
on the wind. I was young enough—I was at the end of my youth—to have
hoped to prevent that moment. This is why I was labeled, at all the literary
cocktail parties, the "angry young man." I was not angry, I was anguished,
and I should have been upon being forced to recognize that that so vaunted
liberal, the Negroes' "friend," would never be present at roll call.

Long before Birmingham, liberals discovered that they had other fish to
fry, and, by the time Mrs. Fannie Lou Hamer and the other members of the
Mississippi Freedom Democratic Party arrived in Atlantic City, the liberal
had washed his hands, and dried them, and is, now, indistinguishable, in

action, from the sheriff in these pages, or from the stunning lucidities issuing presently from the White House.

Which brings us, abruptly, to *Nat Turner,* Bill Styron, and me.

I do not at all regret the position I took concerning Styron's *Confessions of Nat Turner* nor has my position changed. My position was, and is (a) I am not about to tell another writer how and what to write, for too many people have tried to tell *me.* And (b), if you don't like Styron's *Nat Turner,* write yours.

That seems to me fair enough and Styron, in any case, is not a liberal. He is a product of the South, tormentedly enough; he was born in the neighborhood of the Turner insurrection, and it is not romantic to point out that this event is also a part of *his* past, his torment, and his identity. Furthermore, when I distinguish Bill Styron from a liberal, I am merely saying that white liberals risk absolutely nothing in their journeys to the New Jerusalem for they assume that their alabaster motives have already placed them in the center—or, rather, on the height—of that city.

But Southerners come to awareness surrounded by the presence, the stink, and the reality of those mutilated charred corpses, some living and some dead, which are the history of their region, the history of their country, and the history of their lives. Furthermore, it is far more difficult for them to be removed from them: the "inner city" is a Northern creation and is described and defended in the liberal jargon.

It is true, as Thelwell points out, that Styron's novel departs vastly from fact or distorts some and abolishes others: but this is one of the prerogatives, or, indeed, necessities of fiction. The only question properly to ask is whether or not the novel succeeds according to the terms of the novel—whether or not the novelist "cheats." To this question there are as many answers as the novel has readers and the judgment which time will deliver no writer can possibly live long enough to hear.

The real question, as concerns this book, is a vexed and vexing one. But it is an important question.

The subtext of Thelwell's book, and nowhere more clearly than in the chapters on Mississippi and especially on the MFDP, is not so much an indictment of American history—which would be easy: it is instead a study, both lucid and tormented, of Americans' refusal to accept that they are a part of history and that history is a part of them. After all, the situation in the South, until today, is both illegal and immoral. The history and the situation of black people in this country is totally immoral and totally illegal. It is perfectly clear that the whites of this country do not have—

and, now, will not find—the will, the stamina, or the grace to recognize themselves in their victim or their victim in themselves. The career of a Senator Eastland is not merely a moral abomination; it is also a crime committed by the State against the citizens. The citizen is defined by the State as white and the justification for these crimes is the presence of the nigger—the nigger, who has never been, and is not now, conceived of as a citizen.

But the citizen in whose name these daily and hourly crimes are being committed has every right (and may take whatever means) to distance himself from them. He will do it, inevitably, in the language which has formed him and will, inevitably, reveal the assumptions on which the language is based. So much the better, and *sauve qui peut*.

For, in Styron's novel there is a very deliberate attempt to mock the pious attempt, to reveal this piety as slavery, and to suggest that the only possible end of slavery is slaughter.

This is not a minor perception. Bishop Tutu said, the other day, in response to a speech repudiating sanctions against South Africa made by a friend of some former friends of mine, "The West can go to Hell!"

I wonder what Martin, my younger brother, would have to say right now.

Here is Mike Thelwell's book. A most valuable book. Turn off the TV set and read it. Then, have your children turn off the TV set. Persuade them that Qaddafi is not responsible for *all* the evil in the world (and neither is Russia); that we need not turn Libya into a parking lot; that our lives, our fortunes, and our sacred honor are redeemable only by the depth of our commitment to the power and the glory and the limitless potential of every human being in the world.

JAMES BALDWIN
*July 20, 1986*

# Southern Movement Fiction

# The Organizer

■  ■  ■  ■  ■

T HE river of that name cuts in half the town of Bogue Chitto, Mississippi. All of importance is east of the river—the jail, the drugstore and Western Union, the hotel, the Greyhound station, and the Confederate memorial in the tree-shaded park. West of the river one comes to a paper mill, a cemetery, a junkyard, which merges with a garbage dump, and the Negro community.

Perched on a rise overlooking the dump and cemetery on one side and the Negro shacks on the other is the Freedom House. A low, unpainted concrete structure with a huge storefront window, it had been built for use as a roadhouse in expectation of a road that had turned out to be campaign oratory. When the road failed to materialize, the owner left the state feeling, with some justification, that he had been misled, and the building remained unused until the present tenants moved in.

It is reported that when Sheriff John Sydney Hollowell was told of the new arrivals he said, "Wal, they sho' chose a mighty good place—ain't nothin' but trash nohow, an' mighty subjeck to needin' buryin'."

This sally was savored, chuckled over, and repeated, rapidly making its rounds out of the jailhouse, to the bench sitters in the park, the loungers in the general store, to be taken home and repeated over the supper table. Thus by ten o'clock that same night it had filtered up by way of the kitchens to the tenants of the Freedom House.

"That peckerwood is a comical son-of-bitch, ain't he?" Travis Peacock asked, and the thought came to him that perhaps the first thing to be done was to board up the big storefront window. Either he forgot or changed his mind, for when the other members of his project arrived they painted "BOGUE CHITTO COMMUNITY CENTER, FREEDOM NOW" on the glass in huge black letters. Two weeks later, while everyone was at a mass meeting in the Baptist church, someone demolished the window with three loads of buckshot. Peacock boarded it up.

Time passed.

Peacock lay on his back in the darkness listening to the clock on the town hall strike eleven. He turned on his side, then sat up and unsnapped the straps of his overalls. "Too damn tight, no wonder I can't sleep," he muttered, reached under the cot for the pint bottle that Mama Jean had slipped to him at the café that afternoon, laughing and cautioning him, "Now doan go gittin' yore head all tore up, honey."

He had no intention of getting his head "tore up," but the fiery stump likker was a comfort. He jerked to a sitting position, listening. It was just the creaking, rusty Dr. Pepper sign moaning as the wind came up. He made a note to fix the sign tomorrow: "Damn thing run me crazy soon."

He lit a cigarette and sat in the darkness listening to the squeaking sign and shaking. He had never before spent a night alone in the Freedom House. Maybe I do need that rest up North, he thought. At the last staff meeting when Truman had hinted at it, he had gotten mad. "Look, if you don't like the way I'm running the project come out and say so, man." And Truman had muttered something about "owing it to the movement to take care of our health." Maybe he did need that rest.

He thought of going down to Mama Jean's or the Hightowers' and spending the night there. He pulled on his boots to go, then changed his mind. The first rule for an organizer, and maybe the hardest, was never to let the community know that you were afraid. He couldn't go, even though the people had all tried to get him to stay in the community that night. That afternoon when he was in the café Mama Jean had suggested that he stay in her son's room.

"Shoot, now, honey," she beamed, "yo' doan want to be catchin' yo' death o' cold up theah on thet cold concrete by yo'se'f."

Raf Jones had chimed in, "Yeah man, we gon' drink us some stump juice, tell us some lies, and play us some Georgia Skin tonight." But he had declined. And Old Mrs. Ruffin had met him and repeated her urging to come stay a few nights at her place. But that was above the call of duty. A standing joke on the project was that the two places in Bogue Chitto to avoid were, "Bo Hollowell's jail, and Ol' Miz Ruffin's kitchen. She a nice ol' lady, but she the worse cook in Mississippi. Man, that ol' lady burn Kool-aid."

As the afternoon progressed and he received two more invitations, he realized that the community knew that the other three staff members were in Atlanta for a meeting and they didn't want him spending a night alone in the office.

By his watch it was nearly midnight. He took a drink and lit another cigarette. Maybe they'd skip tonight. He was tempted to take the phone off the hook. "Hell no," he muttered, "I ain't going give them that satisfaction." But what did it mean if the phone didn't ring? At least when they on the phone you know they ain't sneaking around outside with a can of kerosene.

He got off the cot and went into the front room, the "office." It was the big public part of the building with a couple of desks, a table, chairs, mimeo machine, and a few old typewriters, and in one section a blackboard where small meetings and literacy classes were held. He sat at a desk with the phone, staring at the boarded-up window.

"Ring, you son-ovva-bitch, ring. You kept me up, now ring." He calmed himself down by reading the posters. A black fist holding a broken chain. "Freedom." Goddamn you, ring. Another poster, "Pearl River County Voters' League: One Man One Vote." Would it be a man or a woman this time? It was five after midnight. They were late. That was unusual.

Maybe they wouldn't call tonight. They always seemed to know what was happening. Maybe they thought that everyone was gone to Atlanta. Suppose they thought that and came to wreck the office? Peacock was still, listening. He was certain that he heard the sounds of movement outside. He went into the storeroom, tripped over a box of old clothes and swore. He came back with the shotgun just as the phone rang, piercingly loud. He dropped the gun and jumped for the phone.

"Pearl River County Voters' League, can we help you?" His voice is steady and that gives him some satisfaction.

There is a low laugh coming over the receiver. "Heh, heh, heh."

"Hey, you late man," Travis says.

"Nigger," the voice asks, "you alone up theah, ain'tchu?"

It's a man's voice. Good. The women are hysterical and foulmouthed.

"You alone up theah?" The voice persists. Travis's nervousness has become anger. He starts to say, "No Charlie, I ain't alone, yo' Momma's here with me." But restrains himself.

"I'm not alone, there are three of us here." He says and laughs, yeah me, Jesus, and mah shotgun.

"Ah know you alone. Thet pointy-head nigger an' the Jew-boy gone to Atlanta. Heh, heh."

"If you think so, come up and find out." Peacock invited in an even voice. "Why don't you do that?" There was a pause.

"We comin' direckly, boy, an' you can sell the shithouse, cause hit's going to be yore ass." Peacock doesn't answer. He stands holding the phone listening to the hoarse breathing from the other end. "Heh, heh. Nigger, yo' subjeck to bein' blowed up." Click. The phone goes dead and Peacock, shaking violently, stands listening to his own breathing.

Somehow that final click is the most terrifying part. As long as you can feel that there is a human being on the other end, despite the obscenity and the threats, you have some contact. Peacock broke the shotgun and loaded it. The phone rings. Briefly he debates not answering it, but he knows he has to. With Ray and Mac on the road, he has to; they could be in trouble. He picks up the phone.

"Hello." That demented chuckling.

"Knowed yo' wasn't sleepin', Nigger. Ain't nevah goin' sleep no mo'."

"If I don't, neither will you, brother."

"Boy, yo' subjeck to bein' blowed up." Click.

Well, hope that's over for the night. But it isn't. They're going to take turns calling. He went to get what was left of the bottle wishing he could remove the phone from the hook. They must rotate the telephone duty, everyone volunteering to give up a night's sleep on a regular basis. Damn.

Peacock began to regret his decision not to go to the meeting. It would have been nice to see everyone again and find how things were on other projects. In Alabama, things looked pretty mean. But so were things here. That was one of the reasons he had stayed. As project director he thought that he should stay with the community in case some crisis broke. Where did his responsibility end?

Sitting there waiting for the phone to ring, he began to leaf idly through the progress report that he had sent to the meeting. He had done a damn good organizing job. The community was together, and had really strong local leadership, whose skill and competence were increasing rapidly.

Morale was high. They had formed a voters' organization and elected

Jesse Lee Hightower chairman. He was a good man with real leadership potential for the entire state. And every act of intimidation seemed to increase his determination and that of the community. After the deacon board of the New Hope Baptist Church had been informed that the insurance of the church would not be renewed, they had met and voted to continue to hold meetings there. A week later the church was a total loss. The sheriff attributed its destruction to a mysterious and very active arsonist called Faulty Wiring who had been wreaking havoc with other Negro churches in the state.

Then Mama Jean's café came under fire. She had been publicly displaying posters and announcements. The merchants in town cut off her credit, and refused to sell her supplies for cash. She had been selling beer and wine for fifteen years with the approval of three sheriffs, although the county was allegedly dry. Now she was charged with the illegal sale of alcohol and a hearing scheduled for the purpose of canceling her license.

When the news reached Peacock, he had been worried. The huge, loud, tough-talking woman was a leader and a symbol in the community—it was Mama Jean and Jesse who had been the first to go across the river to try to register to vote—Mama Jean wearing her floppy, terrible flowered hat, gloves, and long black coat in the summer heat. They had been met by the sheriff and three deputies.

"This office is closed till four o'clock."

"We come to register, Sheriff Hollowell."

"This office is closed."

"Why, thass all right, honey." Mama Jean's gold teeth were flashing. "Usses done waited a hunnerd yeahs, be plumb easy to wait till fo' o'clock." And she swept into the hall, marched to the only chair available, and composed herself to wait. Hollowell and his deputies, obviously not prepared for that, had remained muttering veiled threats and caressing their guns. All knew the office would not open that afternoon.

Without her and the Hightowers, Peacock could never have gotten started in the community. If she broke, the community would crumble overnight. So he had been very worried when he ran to her café that afternoon. He was somewhat surprised to find her behind the bar laughing and joking.

"Mama Jean, what are you going to do?"

"Whut ah'm gon' do? Do 'bout whut, honey?" She was looking at him as though surprised at the question.

"Didn't they cut your credit? I heard. . . ."

"Oh shush now, take mo'n thet li'l bitty ol' sto'keeper to stop Mama

Jean. Jes' doan yo' fret yo'se'f none, heah. Ah be keepin' on keepin' on like ah always done." And she had. No more was heard about the illegal sale of liquor, and twice a week she got into Jesse Lee's pickup truck and drove into Louisiana to buy supplies. She claimed it was much cheaper.

Then the county tripled the tax assessment on her café. Peacock got her a lawyer, and she was challenging the assessment, even threatening to file a damage suit.

"Damn," Peacock muttered, "if that lady was thirty years younger I swear I'd ask her to marry me." Thinking of Mama Jean cheered him. Some of the people in that poverty-stricken, hard-pressed community were so great, like the Hightowers and the Joneses, he felt warm with pride and love; it was as if he had returned to a home he had never known, but always missed.

He had lived with the Hightowers at first, while he met the people and learned the community. He felt closer to them than to his natural family who now seemed to him shadowy figures leading barren and futile lives in their northern suburb.

He thought of Miss Vickie, Jesse's wife, a small fragile appearing woman always hovering around her burly husband, expressing her support by small, thoughtful acts. And the two kids, Richie and Fannie Lou who was extremely bright and curious beneath her shyness. Peacock loaned her books and had long talks with her, constantly being surprised at the range and breadth of her curiosity. The Negro school only went to the ninth grade, and she had long surpassed her teachers. She had finally quit, and was now a full-time volunteer, doing the typing and running the office.

His favorite was eight-year-old Richie, like his father a leader and a born organizer. He had created an organization of children to blanket the community with leaflets. Then he had badgered and begged until Miss Vickie bought him a denim jacket and overalls "like Travis's." A hell of an organizer he will be when he grows up, Peacock reflected.

Peacock noticed that his bottle was almost empty. He could feel the effects of the liquor, particularly potent after his recent tension.

"Hell, no wonder, you sittin' here getting so sentimental. A sixteen-year-old girl has a crush on you, her kid brother thinks you are Jesus, and your leader complex runs away again." But he felt easier now and tired. He went into the back room and streched out on the cot, feeling his limbs relax as he gave in to exhaustion. But his mind wouldn't turn off.

He was in that halfway zone between sleep and wakefulness in which thoughts disguise themselves as dreams when he heard the sound. That is, he sensed it, a kind of silent, dull reverberation, that reached his mind before the sound came to him—the heavy, somehow ponderous boom of dynamite. Silence, then a yapping, howling chorus as every dog in town began to bark.

Peacock froze on the cot. *Oh God. Oh God. Let it be a church, not anyone's house.*

He wanted to pull on his boots but was paralyzed. His stomach felt empty and weak. He retched and puked up all the hot acid liquor. His fear returned and he began to shake violently. Somebody's dead. They killed someone. Mama Jean. I don't want to know. I can't go. He sat there smelling his vomit, until he heard the pounding on the door. "Travis, ho, Travis!"

He stumbled into the front room, going for the door. Then he returned for the shotgun. His voice came as a hoarse whisper and it took two efforts to make himself audible. "Who is it?"

"Us, Raf Jones and Sweezy. We alone."

Peacock knew the men. They had both been fired from the paper mill after attempting to register. When there was money in the project he gave them subsistence, other times they helped Mama Jean in the café in return for meals. He opened the door. Jones and Sweezy were carrying rifles. They didn't know what had happened, either, having been outside the Freedom House when they heard the noise.

In a few moments they were running down the hill, past the edge of the cemetery toward the town and the café. Peacock was sure that the night-riders had tried for the café, but when, panting and gasping, they reached there, they found it intact. So was the little church that was now being used for meetings. Where was the explosion? A car turned into the road, going fast and raising a cloud of dust. The headlights picked them out, and they dived into the ditch. The car roared past.

"Hit's the sher'f," Raf said. "Trouble taken place fo' sho'." They set out running in the car's dust. It passed two side roads, then turned. Peacock had no doubt where it was headed now.

"Good God Almighty." He half moaned, half shouted, and stopped. The two men ran on without him, then stopped and turned.

"Yo' awright?"

Peacock nodded and waved them on. His eyes and nose were filled with dust. His chest heaved. He coughed. Whatever had happened wouldn't change before he got there. He even had a momentary urge to turn back, to run somewhere and hide, certain that something terrible and irrevocable had happened. He stood bent double in the road, clutching his sides, coughing, eyes streaming water, no longer gut-scared but filled with dread. He couldn't go on.

Wait, maybe no one had been hurt. A house can be rebuilt. He personally would go North to raise the money. He would gouge it out cent by cent from his family and their affluent and secure neighbors. If it was only the house! Then he was running again. He could smell burnt powder now. It seemed like the entire town was crowded in the road before him. He recognized faces, people, everyone was talking.

"Wha' happen? Wha' happen?"

"Whole family daid?"

"Two white fellers in a car."

Pushing his way through the crowd, Peacock realized that he was still carrying the shotgun. He didn't know what to do with it. The people would be looking to him, and if he had a gun. . . . Besides it'd be in every lousy newspaper in the country that the local representative of the organization had arrived on the scene carrying a weapon.

He pushed his way to the front of the crowd, no one called his name. Was it his imagination or were they stepping away from him? Oh God, were they blaming him?

The sheriff's car was right in front of the house, its searchlight beaming into the living room. The front of the house was a shambles, porch completely gone, the front wall torn away. A pair of deputies stood facing the crowd carrying tear gas guns, cumbersome, futuristic looking weapons that seemed to belong in a Flash Gordon kit. "Y'awl keep on back now. Sheriff's orduhs."

Clutching the shotgun, Peacock darted out of the crowd toward the house. One deputy turned to face him.

"Wheah yew going?"

"I'm kin," Peacock said without stopping. The deputy turned back to the crowd which had surged forward.

Peacock ran around the house and came up to the back door. The smell of burnt powder lingered strong. At the kitchen door he stopped, looking in; the kitchen was filled with people. Mama Jean turned to the door and saw him.

"Oh Travis, Travis, honey. They done hit. They done kilt Jesse." The people gave a low moan of assent. It seemed to Travis that they were looking at him accusingly, the stranger who had brought death among them. Then Mama Jean was holding him. He clung to her without shame, comforting himself in her large, warm strength. He was sure now that there was hostility in the room. The people gathered there had kept aloof from the Voters' League, explaining that they had to avoid commitment so that they could keep their position flexible and talk with the white community. He recognized the school principal, the minister from the big Baptist church, and the undertaker. No one spoke. Then Mama Jean was leading him into the bedroom. "The fam'ly bin askin' fo' yo', Travis."

Their heads all turned to Peacock as they entered. Fannie Lou was holding Richie, their eyes big, black solemn pools in their young faces. Miss Vickie huddled on the bed, leaning forward, her back sharply curved, hunch-shouldered, clutching her clasped hands between her knees. Her face seemed set, polished from smooth black stone. When she turned her head to the door her eyes showed nothing.

"See, he come. He all right, nothing happen to him." Mama Jean's tone was soothing, meant to reassure them. But for one second Peacock heard only a reproach for his own safety and survival. *You must say something. You have to tell these folks something.*

From the next room he heard a low wailing hum. They were half humming, half singing one of those slow, dirge-like songs that was their response in times when no other response was possible. *"Shiine on Mee, Oh, shiiine on Meee . . ."*

Peacock crossed to Miss Vickie. His limbs felt heavy, as though he were moving through some heavy liquid medium, but his footsteps sounded loud. He bent and took her hands. They were limp at first, then they imprisoned his in a quick fierce grip. He was looking into her eyes for some sign of warmth, life, recognition, but most of all for some sign of absolution, forgiveness.

Jumbled phrases crowded through his mind. Trite, traditional words, phrases that were supposed to bear comfort, to move, to stir, to strengthen, and ultimately to justify and make right. But the will of which God? Whose God, that this man, this husband. . . . *I am not to blame. I didn't do it.* Silently Peacock looked at her. She returned his look blankly. Then she pitched forward and her head rested on his arms.

"We will do everything . . . we must keep on . . . brave and good man . . . do what he would want us to do . . . death not in vain."

*Which voice was that spewing out tired political phrases we hear too often. It couldn't have been me, please it was someone else. What hard hands she has.* "Miss Vickie, I'm sorry," Peacock said, "I'm sorry."

"Hush chile. T'aint yore fault." Mama Jean's deep voice cracked. "T'aint none of us heah fault, cept we shoulda moved long time ago. Hit's a long time they been killin' us, little by little. . . ."

"Ahmen," Miss Vickie said. Richie started to cry. Peacock picked him

up, surprised at how light he was. The boy threw his skinny arms around
Peacock's neck and buried his wet cheeks in his neck. Hugging him tightly,
Travis felt his own tears starting for the first time.

"Who is comforting who?" he asked himself.

There was a soft knock on the door, and the elderly unctuous minister
clad in his black suit glided in from the kitchen.

"Miz Hightower, hit's the sher'f come to talk to you." Miss Vickie sat
up, a mixture of emotions crossing her face.

"Thet 'Bo' Hollowell have no shame. Effen he did. . . ." Mama Jean
began as Sheriff Hollowell strode into the room, accompanied by a man in
a business suit. "Seems like some folks doan even knock fo' they come
bustin' into folks' houses," Mama Jean snorted.

The sheriff stood in the center of the room. He ran his glance over the
group, fingering his jowl. He was a big, solid man, heavy-boned, thick-
waisted, and with enormous red hands. He was wearing his khaki uniform
and a planter's Stetson. He stared at the floor just in front of Miss Vickie,
and his jaw moved slowly and steadily.

"Ah just come to git a statement from the widow." His voice must have
sounded subdued and apologetic in his own ears for he paused briefly and
continued in a louder voice. "So theah ain't no need fer anyone else to be
saying nothin'." Mama Jean snorted. Then there was dead silence in the
room. Rev. Battel who had been standing in the doorway made a sidling
self-effacing motion and was frozen by a glare from Mama Jean.

"Well, which a yew is the widow?" the sheriff asked.

"Ah'm Mrs. Hightower," Miss Vickie said and pulled herself up erect.
She looked at the official with an expression of quiet, intense contempt
that seemed to be almost physical, coming from a depth of outrage and
grief beyond her will. Peacock would swear that Miss Vickie had no
knowledge of what was in her eyes. His own spirit shrank within him.

"Sheriff Hollowell," he said softly, "there's been a death in this house."

The second man flushed and removed his hat. The sheriff gave no sign of
having seen or heard anything. "Yew have another room where ah can git
yore statement?" He could have been addressing anyone in the room.

"We used to," Miss Vickie said. "Anythang need to be said kin be said
right here. These my husband's family and friends."

Hollowell produced a notebook and flipped his Stetson back on his
head. The second man was also holding a pad. "Wal, whut happened?"
Again there was a pause.

" 'What happened? What happened,' Jesus God Almighty." The words
flashed through Peacock's mind, and he only realized that he had spoken
when Hollowell said, "Ah'm not gon' tell yew to shut up again, boy."

Miss Vickie's voice was calm and low, without inflection or emphasis. "Ah wuz sleepin' an' then ah woke up. Heard like a car drive up in the road going slow like. Hit drive past three times like they was lookin' fo' something. Ah see that Jesse Lee wun't in the bed. Ah listen fo' a spell an' didn' heah nothin' so I call out an' he answer from the front.

" 'Hit's allright, go to sleep.' But ah knew hit wuz somethin' wrong and ah started to get up. . . . Then, then like the room light up an' ah feel this hot win' an' the noise an' hit was nothin' but smoke and ah heah mah daughter scream. . . ." Her voice broke off and she began to sob softly. The two children began to sob too. Mama Jean turned and stared at the wall.

"Is this necessary, Sheriff?" Peacock asked.

"Boy, yew not from round heah are yew?"

"You know who I am," Peacock said. Miss Vickie began to speak.

"An' thass all. Evrah thang wuz like yo' see hit now, only the children wuz cryin' and Jesse Lee was lyin' on the floor in the front room. Ah nevah seen no car."

"Jes' one thang more, Miz Hightower." Hollowell's voice was almost gentle. "Yew know any reason fo' anyone to dew a thang lak' this?"

Peacock stared at the sheriff incredulously.

"Same reason he got arrest three time for drunk drivin' when evrahbody know he nevah did drink," Mama Jean said.

"Ah doan know why some folks do whut they do," Miss Vickie said.

"Wal, ah'l sho' let yew know soon as ah find out anything." Hollowell snapped his book. "Mighty sorry myself. Only one thang more, this gentleman heah, be wanting to ask yew a few questions." His companion seemed uncomfortable, his Adam's apple bobbing jerkily in his thin neck. His cheek twitched and he passed a hand quickly over his thinning hair. "I think I've got all I need," he began. Hollowell looked at him. "Well maybe just one thing. I'm from the Associated Press in New Orleans, happened to be passing through." He darted a quick look at the sheriff, and spoke more rapidly. "I want you to know how sorry I am. This is a terrible, terrible thing. I want you to know that you have the sympathy of every decent person in the state, Mrs. Hightower. I hope . . . I'm sure that whoever did this will be found and punished. I was wondering if there is anything that you would like to say, any kind of personal statement. . . ."

"Why can't you leave the family in peace?" Peacock was on his feet. "What more statement do you want, isn't what happened statement enough? For God's sake, what more do you want?" But Peacock's anger was not at the timid little man, but at what he knew was to come for the family—an ordeal that would be as painful as the night before them and in

its own way more obscene than the brute fact of death. He was lashing out
at that future and the role that he could neither escape nor resolve.

"Now ah've warned yew." The sheriff was advancing toward him.

"Mist'r Hollowell, come quick before something happen." A deputy
was standing in the door. "Hit's the niggers, yew bettah come." The
deputy disappeared, followed by Hollowell and the reporter.

"Preacher," the sheriff called over his shoulder, "mabe yew better come
on." The old man followed silently, and then Peacock heard the crowd.
Waves of boos and shouts came in spurts, and in between shouted angry
words.

"Thet sho' doan sound good," Mama Jean said. "Them folks is mad.
Them peoples is afixin' to turn this town out an' ah swears thet in mah
heart ah doan blame 'em."

"Ain't that the truth," Peacock said, "but I'd blame myself. You know
the Safety Patrol is coming, and maybe even the army. Them peckerwoods
will shoot us down like dogs. And we gotta do something. The only people
can stop them is right here in this room." He looked at Miss Vickie. She
rocked back and forth and wouldn't look at him. He thought for a while
that she hadn't heard. Then she spoke very softly.

"Travis, ah jes' doan know no mo'. Seems like either they gits kilt
tonight or one by one nex' week. Maybe this is what hit had to come to. Ah
jes' ain't straight in mah own min'."

Peacock sat down silently on the bed, his head bowed. He understood
how she felt. He too longed for the swift liberating relief of wild, mindless,
purging violence, ending maybe in death. But survival, what of that? Suppose he was one of the survivors. It was a nightmare that had hovered in
the back of his consciousness ever since he had joined the movement—yet
he saw himself limping away from the burning town, away from the dead
and maimed, people to whom he had come singing songs of freedom and
rewarded with death and ashes. The organizer is always responsible. That
was the second rule.

"Miss Vickie. You know how much I loved Jesse, more than my natural
father. I ain't got to tell you how I feel, but you know Jesse would feel this
way too. If you won't come with me to speak to the folks, lemme give them
a word from you." Miss Vickie did not answer immediately. There was a
new frenzy of shouting outside, louder, more hysterical than before.
Peacock couldn't wait for an answer, and Mama Jean followed him as he
ran out into the shouting. . . .

"Look at them peckerwoods. Look at them. See who them guns pointing at. We din' kill nobody. We din' bomb no house. Hit wuzn't us, but

who the guns pointing at? Why ain't they go find the killers? Why? 'Cause they knows who they is, they brothahs an' they cousins, thass who!"

Peacock recognized Raf Jones. Himself and Sweezy and some of the younger men were grouped in front of the police car. They were armed. "Look at thet Raf, fixin' to get hisse'f kilt too," Mama Jean muttered. "Yo' right Travis, now whut is we gon' do?" They walked over to the car. Hollowell began to talk through a bull horn, his flat, nasal voice magnified and echoing through the night.

"Awright, awright. This is Sher'f Hollowell. That's enough, ah want yew to cleah these streets." Angry shouts from the crowd. "Yew good collud folks of this town know me."

"Yo damn right we does," Raf shouted back.

"Yew know me, and ah know most of yew. Ah know yew're good, decent folk that don't want no trouble. An' this town din' have no trouble till them agitators pull in heah to disrup' and destroy whut we had. Now a man was kilt heah tonight. Ah wanna ask yew, yew all sensible folk, ah wanna ask yew. Was theah any trouble fore these trouble-makers started hangin' round heah?"

"Allus bin trouble," Raf screamed. "Allus bin killin's." The crowd roared agreement.

"An' ah want to tell yew, ah have mah own feelin's 'bout who done this terrible thang heah tonight. Ah tell yew, yew got evrah right to be mad. Why, hit could'a jes' as easy bin a white man got blowed up. Yew're decent folk, ah know thet. Ah know hit wasn't none o' yew did this thang. We got a good town heah. But ah want to ask yew this. Dew yew *know* anythang 'bout these outsiders yew bin harboring? What dew yew know 'bout them? Tell me, dew yew thank thet these race mixahs an' agitators mean this town any good? Wheah dew they come from? Right now ah only see one ov 'em. Where's the othah two raht now? Ah want yew to go home an' thank 'bout thet. Yew will git the true answers, you cain't plant corn an' hit come up cotton. Y'awl go on home now an' thank 'bout whut ah said."

The crowd was silent, shuffling sullenly. No one left. "Ah want yew to go now. Ah'm ordering yew to break this up. Stay and yew break the law. Ah've called the Safety Patrol barracks an' troopers is on the way. In ten minutes they be heah. Anyone still heah goes to jail. Yew heah me?" Silence.

"Awright, awright. Ah got someone heah yew all know. He is one of yew, a fine collud gentleman. He got somethin' to say, then he goin' to lead yew in prayer, an' that'll be awl. Step up heah, Preacher Battel." Before the old man could move Mama Jean stepped in front of him, one hand on her

hip, the other wagging in his face. Peacock heard her saying, ". . . . Swear
'fo' Gawd, effen yo' git up now an' start in to Tommin' fo' thet cracker,
ah'm gon' run ye outta town myse'f. Yo' heah me, Charlie Battel, ah'm sick
an' tard of bein' sick an' tard of yo' selling the folks out." Battel backed
away before her fury. Hollowell came over fingering his gun.

"An' as fo' yo' Bo Hollowell, the onliest true thang yo' say wuz thet we
knows yo'. An' ah knows yo' pappy befo' yo'. Yo' wuz none o' yo' any
good. No mo' good than a rattlesnake. Whoa now, Bo Hollowell, yo' lay
a han' to me an' hit's yo' las' living ack. Me 'n' Travis gon' git the folks to
go home, but hit's gon' be our way. We gon' do hit cause we doan want no
mo' peoples kilt, an' thass whut you fixing to do. But if hit's mo' dying
tonight, t'aint only black folks gon' die."

She turned her back on him and marched over to the car, walking past
an immobilized Hollowell as though he were not present. The passionate
power of the fat, middle-aged woman was awesome even to Peacock,
against whom it was not directed. He followed her automatically.

"Gi'mme a han' up," she demanded. She balanced herself on the fender
of the car, holding Travis's shoulder for support. Silently she surveyed the
crowd, her broad chest heaving, hair unkempt and standing out on her
head. "Lookaheah. Hit's me, Mama Jean, an' ah ain't got much to say. But
yo' all hear that rattlesnake talking 'bout outside agitators. Yo' all knowed
he wuz talking 'bout Travis. Wal, maybe he is a agitator. But yo' seen the
agitator in yo' white folks' washing machine. Yo' know what hit do, hit git
the dirt out. Thass right, an' thass what Travis gon' do now. Listen to him,
he got a message from Miss Vickie. An' he gon' git out all the dirt thet
Hollowell bin asayin'." She jumped down. "Go on, son, talk some sense
to the folks. Ah'm jes' too mean mad mese'f, but yo' kin tell them lak
hit is."

Hollowell stepped up. "Don't look like ah got much choice." He drew
his pistol from its holster. "So yew say yore piece, but remember ah'l be
raht heah behind yew. Yew git them to go home now. Say one wrong
word. . . ." He waved his pistol suggestively.

Travis climbed onto the bonnet of the car and waved his arms for
silence. The skin of his back crawled, sensitive to the slightest pressure of
his shirt and waiting for the first probing touch of Hollowell's bullet. He
closed his eyes and waited for the crowd's attention.

"Friends. Friends, you got to be quiet now, cause I ain't got no bull horn
like Hollowell, an' I want you to hear every word." That's right, keep your
voice low so they have to calm down to hear. "You all can see that house
right there, least what the crackers left of it. There's a lady inside there,

a black lady. And her husband's dead. They killed her husband an' she grievin'. You know she grievin'. Seem like thass all we black folk know to do, is grieve. We always grievin', it seem like." Peacock shook his head and bowed his head as though in grief or deep thought. A woman gave a low scream, "Jesus, Jesus," and began to sob, deep, racking sounds that carried into the crowd. Peacock waited, head bowed, until he heard a few more muffled sobs from the crowd.

"Yes, some o' us cryin'. Thass all right, let the good sister cry, she got reason. Will ease huh troubled heart. Lady inside thet bombed-out, burned-out house cryin' too. She cryin' right now but while her soul cry for the dead, her min' is on the livin'. She thinking 'bout you. That's the kind of lady she is. She say to tell you the time for weeping is almost over. Soon be over. She say she cryin' for her man tonight, an' she don't want to cry for her brothers and sisters tomorrow. She say they already kill one, don't give them a chance to kill no more. She say to go home peacefully."

"Why?" Raf shouted, "so they kin git the rest o' us when we lyin' up in the bed? Ah say, GIT ON WIT THE KILLIN'!" There was a roar from the people, but Peacock judged that it came mainly from Raf's little group. Raf, shut up, please. Every time you say something like that, I can just feel that cracker's finger jerking. He had to find something to divert the people. "Miss Vickie say to go home, it's what Jesse Lee would want." A deep murmur of rejection came back.

"Jesse Lee was a fighter!" Raf yelled. This was greeted with cheers.

"Lookaheah," Travis said, raising his voice and adopting the accent of the folk. "Lookaheah, y'awl heard the sheriff." I sure hope Hollowell doesn't lose his cool. I got to do this now. A small muscle in his back kept twitching. "Yeah, ah'm talkin' 'bout Bo Hollowell, that ugly ol' lard-ass, big belly, Bo Hollowell." Peacock held his breath. No sound came from behind him. There was scattered laughter in the crowd.

"Yeah," Peacock continued, "look at him. Ain't he the sorriest, pitifullest thang yo' evah saw? Ain't he now? Looka him. See him standing there holdin' thet gun. He scared. Yo' heard him say he called fo' the troopers. Wal, he did. Yo' know he did, cause he scared as hell. Hit's too many angry black folk heah fo' him. He scared. Look at him." Peacock turned and pointed. Hollowell was standing in front of his deputies. His Stetson was pulled down to hide his eyes, but Peacock could see the spreading black stain under his arms, and his heavy jaw grinding as he shook with barely controlled fury. But there were cheers and laughter in the crowd now.

"He scared lak a girl," Peacock shouted and forced himself to laugh.

"Why ol' bad-assed Bo Hollowell standin' theah shaking jes' lak a dawg tryin' to shit a peach stone." That cracked the people up, real laughter, vindictive and punitive to the lawman, but full, deep and therapeutic to the crowd.

"Yessuh, lak a dawg tryin' to shit a peach stone," Peacock repeated, and the people hooted. Jesse, I know you understand, Peacock apologized. I got to do this. He waved for silence and got it. His voice was soft now.

"But looka heah, very close now. Sho' he scared. But he scared jes' lak them peckerwoods whut blowed up this house. An' yo' knows whoevah done it ain't even folks. They scared, they sick. Thass right. Whenevah peckerwoods git scared, niggers git kilt. Ahuh, thass lak hit is, whenevah white folks git scared, black folks git kilt. Yo watch 'at ol' big belly Bo. He scared right enough to kill me right heah." Peacock was sweating in the night breeze. I have to do it just right, one word too much and he' goin' break, he warned himself.

"See," he said, "an' when them othah crackers git heah, they goin' be scared too. They gon' start whuppin' heads an shootin' folks lak we wuz rabbits."

"Thass right."

"He right."

"Tell the truth."

"See. An' they's a lot of women an' chillun, beautiful black chillun out heah. What's gon' happen to them? Now yo' men got yo' guns. An' thass good. If Jesse Lee hada had his'n he might be alive this minute. So we gotta be ready. But whoevah stay heah now, bettah be ready to die. Thass right, *be ready to die.*"

"We dyin' right now," Raf shouted.

"That wuz true. An' hit still is. But not no mo'. Hit's a new day comin'. Hit's gotta come. A new day. Thass whut scared them peckerwoods, why they kill Jesse Lee. 'Cause Jesse was a free man. He didn't take no mess. Y'awl know that? An' he was tryin' to git y'awl to come with him. That's what scare them folks. He was a free man. His min' was free. He was not afraid."

"Tell it."

"Right. Thass right."

"Yes, brothahs an' sistuhs, thass whut scare 'em. Black folks wuz fixin' to be free. Ahuh. See, an' ol' Bo knew thet. Them peckerwoods is mighty tricky. Yo' gotta study 'em, they *awful* tricky."

"Yes Jesus, they sho' is."

"So now, lookaheah very careful now. Inside that house is this black lady, an' she mournin' fo' her husband. An' she say, Go home. She say, Go home, 'cause she love yo', an' she cain't stan' no mo' grievin'. Then out heah, yo' got Bo Hollowell an' his gun. He say, Go home, too. Now why would he say that? 'Cause he scared? Thass part of hit. But mostly, yo' know why he say thet, 'cause he know we sick an' tard. He know we sick an' tard o' bein' whupped." Peacock was now chanting in the singsong cadence of the ecstatic sermon with the full participation of the people.

"Sick an' tard o' being starved."

"Oh yes, oh yes."

"Sick an' tard o' being worked to death."

"Oh yes, yes Jesus."

"Sick an' tard o' bein' cheated."

"Jesus Gawd, yes."

"Sick an' tard o' bein' kilt."

"Yeah, mah brothahs an' sistuhs, that cracker know we sick an' tard, thet we sick an' tard o' *bein' sick an' tard.*"

"Tell it, tell it."

"Yeah, that cracker sure do know thet so long as we live, *we gon' be free.* He know that if he say go home, yo' gon' stay. An' yo' know somethin', even though he scared, he mad too. An' cause he scared he want yo' to go home. An' cause he mad, he kinda hope yo' gon' stay. An' yo' know why? Yo' know why that cracker, yeah look at him, yo' know why he want yo' to stay? SO HE CAN KILL SOME MO' BLACK FOLKS. Thass right. Evrahone heah know he bin sayin' he gon' come down heah an' clean the niggers out. Yo' know he say thet evrah time he git drunk."

"Thass right, an' he *stay* drunk, too!"

"The gospel truth."

"Yo' right, man."

Peacock waved his hands for silence. He spoke softly and clearly now as though he were revealing a great secret. He tried to inject into his voice certitude and calm authority. Yet he was tired and the slowness of his speech was not entirely for effect. His dripping body was lethargic, relaxed, and a peacefulness crept over him. For the first time he did not care about Hollowell's gun at his back.

"So whut we gon' do, mah brothers? We are going to go home like Miss Vickie say do. We going to trick ol' Bo Hollowell this time. No more black folk going to die tonight. We men with the guns going to get the women and kids home. We going to get them there safe. And then we going to stay there. When those troopers come, there ain't going to be no folks standing around for them to beat on, all right? And we are going to stay home so that if any more bomb-toting crackers come we can defend our children an' our homes, all right?"

The crowd shouted assent.

"But that's only tonight. We aren't going to let Jesse Lee Hightower jes' die like that, are we? No. Uhuh. Tomorrow night we going come back to a meeting. Tomorrow night at eight o'clock, we all going to come to a meeting an' plan and decide just what we going to do."

"Yes, we is!" the crowd roared.

"An' we going to do it all together. Us folks gotta stick together. And you know where the meeting is going to be tomorrow night? In Rev. Battel's church, that's where. Rev'ren' say he done seen the light, an' out of respect fo' Jesse Lee, he gon' let us have the church."

Peacock listened to the cries of surprise and approval from the people. They all knew that Battel had kept himself and his church apart from the activities of the movement. Glancing behind he could see Mama Jean rocking with mirth at a thoroughly unhappy looking Preacher Battel.

"All right, so we going home now. Raf an' Sweezy, will you get everything all straight so that folks get home safe? But before we do that, one more thing. Rev'ren' Battel will give us a prayer. An' we not going pray for no forgiveness, we going to pray for justice, an' for the soul of our brother."

Battel stepped forward. "Let us bow our haids an' ask the Almighty. . . ." he intoned.

"Wait," Peacock shouted. Battel stopped. Bowed heads were raised. Peacock pointed to Hollowell and his deputies. "Folks, I didn't mean to interrupt the prayer. But remember what happened here tonight. A man is dead, murdered. And I know that Sheriff Hollowell and his men don't mean no disrespect. But I believe we should ask them to remove their hats. Even if *they* don't believe in prayer."

The crowd stood stock still for a moment, a low murmur growing and thickening. The officers made no move. Peacock could not see Hollowell's face which was shaded by the brim of the Stetson.

"Jesse Lee Hightower is one black man they had to respeck in life," Mama Jean boomed, "an they bettah respeck him in death too."

Slowly the crowd was closing the distance between itself and the lawmen. It had become very quiet, the only sound that Peacock heard was the soft hum of feet on the dusty road. The people were no longer a diffuse crowd, but had become a single unit.

The click of Hollowell's pistol cocking was sharp and clear. Peacock cursed himself; it had been such a close thing and now he had torn it.

"Take them off, take off the damned hats!" He thought that he had screamed, but apparently there had been no sound. The deputy on the left took a half pace backward. Hollowell's lips moved stiffly. "Hope the bastard's praying," Peacock murmured, but he was sure that Hollowell was only threatening the deputy. But the man's nerve had broken. Peacock saw his hand moving, stealthily, unbearably slowly in the direction of his head. It sneaked up, tremulously, then, faster than a striking rattler, streaking up to snatch the hat from the head. . . . The other deputy looked at Hollowell, then at the crowd. He made his choice. Hollowell was the last. Peacock did not see it happen. But the sheriff's hat was suddenly cradled against his leg. The crowd let out a great moaning sigh, and Battel resumed the prayer in a quavering voice. Peacock felt an arm on his shoulder. He slumped onto Mama Jean's shoulder putting his arm around her neck and they stood watching the people disperse.

"Yo' donc jes' great, Travis, hit was beautiful. But yo' know them crackers jes' ain't gon' take the way yo' done them tonight. Careful how yo' walk. Like ef that Hollowell should stop yo' on the road by yo'se'f. . . ." Her voice trailed off.

"I know, Mama Jean." Peacock squeezed her shoulder. "An' I'm gonna be watching him. But ain't nothing he can do for the next few weeks." And that's the truth, Peacock reflected. Come tomorrow this town is going to be so full of newsmen and TV cameras that Hollowell won't be able to scratch his balls without a national audience.

"Yeah, but yo' know he ain't nevah gon' forget. He *cain't.*"

"Surprised to hear you talking like that, Mama Jean. Way you light into him an' Battel, jes' like a duck on a June bug. Don't you know you gettin' a little old to be doing folks like that?"

"Who ol'?" she growled. "Long as ah keeps mah strength ah ain't nevah gon' be too ol'. Ef they want to stop me, they gon' have to kill me. An' ah ain't sho' but whut the ones thet gits kilt ain't the lucky ones. Whut 'bout those thet lef'?" She looked toward the broken house.

Yes, Peacock thought, what about them? Us? He watched the police car drive slowly down the road behind the last group. What about them? He wondered if the family in the house had heard him. Jesse wasn't four hours dead, and already he had cheapened and manipulated that fact. He had abstracted their grief and his own, used it, waved it in front of the crowd like a matador's cape and this was only the beginning.

Inside the house, Mama Jean took charge, bustling around collecting whatever she felt the family would need next morning. She was taking them to spend the night at her place. They still sat in the bedroom, as though they had not changed position during the time Peacock had been away. Looking at his watch, Peacock discovered that the incident outside had taken less than forty minutes. He looked up to meet Fannie Lou's eyes, big and dark with grief, staring at him. What was she thinking? Of her father? Or of him, the stranger who had come to live with them like the big brother she never had? How did they feel now? Miss Vickie used to call him her son, to introduce him to visitors that way. And he had felt closer to this family than to the family he never saw and rarely thought about. But there was nothing he could say. Everything that came to him sounded weak and inadequate, incapable of expressing the burden of his feeling. Unless he could find new words that would come fresh and living from his heart, that had never been said before, he could not say anything.

When Raf and the men came back, they left for the café, Peacock walking between the mother and daughter and holding a sleepy Richie. He felt Fannie Lou's light touch on his arm.

"Travis, yo' gon' stay?" Peacock looked at her uncomprehendingly. She bit her lower lip and said quickly, "I mean tonight at Mama Jean's." Her eyes filled with tears.

"I'll be back later, but I have to go to the office first." But he knew she wasn't asking about tonight. They knew that he came from another world, and one that must seem to them far more attractive, to which he could return.

He had not told them his reason for wanting to go back to the office. He had to call the national office with a report of the evening's events, and he did not want them to hear him reporting and describing their loss to unknown people.

Before he had begged and pleaded to be put on the organizing staff, he had worked on the public relations staff in the national office. He had written hundreds of coldly factual reports of burnings, bombings, and murders. And the "statements," how many of those had he written, carefully worded, expressing rage, but disciplined controlled rage, phrases of grief balanced by grim determination, outrage balanced by dignity, moral indignation balanced by political demands. Every time it was the same, yet behind those phrases, the anger and the sorrow and the fear were real. So we become shapers of horror, artists of grief, giving form and shape and articulation to emotion, the same emotion, doing it so often that finally there is nothing left of that emotion but the form.

He reached the Freedom House and placed the call. Before it was completed, Raf called through the door. Peacock let him and his companions in.

"The womens said we wuz to come stay with yo'," Raf explained. "We got some mens watching the café." Peacock watched them file into the office, gaunt men roughly dressed in overalls and army surplus boots, as he was. One of them, an older man with thinning gray hair and a creased face, came up to him. Peacock did not know him. The man took his hand in a horny calloused grip.

"Ah knows ah ain't bin to the meetin's. Ah call myse'f keepin' outta trouble. Ah says them Freedom folk, they mean to do good, but they ain't from roun' heah, somethin' happen they be gone an' lef' us'ns in the mess. Ah wuz 'fraid, ah ain't shame to say hit. But ah seen yo' wit the laws tonight an' ah says, let the fur fly wit' the hide. Ef thet young feller kin do, ah kin do too. Ah's heah to do whatevah is to be did." Peacock was like an evangelist suffering from doubt in the face of a convert. He had heard those words before. Each time it had been a new and moving experience to see a man throwing off his burden of fear and hesitancy and finding the courage to step forward. But this time the responsibility seemed too much. What was the man expecting? Reassurance, praise? The phone temporarily rescued him.

The connection was a bad one, and it was as though his voice and not another's, echoed hollowly back into his ear. "June 16th, Bogue Chitto, Miss. . . ." Peacock was staring into Richie's shock-glazed eyes. ". . . A Negro civil rights leader was killed in the blast that destroyed his home. His wife and two children were unharmed. . . ." Peacock saw Miss Vickie's rigid sleepwalker's face. . . . "Resentment is high in the Negro community. A crowd formed in front of the house, but the local representative of the Nonviolent Council persuaded the crowd to disperse peacefully. . . ." The voice went on and on. Raf and the other men were watching him as though he had stepped into a new identity that they did not recognize.

"No," Peacock said, "I have no statement."

"But we should have something from the local movement. You are project director."

"Look, if you want a political statement, write it, that's your job. All I can say is I'm sorry." Peacock hung up the phone and sat cradling his head in his arms. He knew the office would call back. Tomorrow the networks would be in town, so would politicians, leaders of various organizations. For a few days the eyes of the country would be focused on the town and everyone would want to be included. He wanted no part of it. The secret fear of every organizer had become reality for him. How do you cope with the death of one of the people you work with?

The phone rang again. Peacock knew before he answered it that it would be Truman. Big, shaggy, imperturbable, bearlike Truman. He was the chairman and was always scrambling to keep the organization afloat, to keep the cars running, the rent paid. Before he had become administrator, he had worked in the field. He would be calling with a program to "respond" to the bombing.

"Hey, Travis, how you doing, you all right?"

"Yeah, Truman, I'm all right."

"Look, in the next couple days you are going to need help. Would you like me to come down?"

That was a normal question, but Peacock suddenly felt a need to lash out. "What do you want to come for, the publicity? To be in all the pictures, to project the organization?"

"I know you are upset, man, but I think you should apologize."

"I'm sorry, man. You know I don't mean that." No, he couldn't afford to mean it because it was too close. God, they were forcing us to be just like them. Then Truman started outlining the program. Peacock listened silently. Then he interrupted. "Stop, Truman, stop. You want to stage a circus. I can't ask the family to subject themselves to that."

"Look, Travis, I know how upset you must be. But we have to do it. Where is the money to come from to build back the house, to educate the kids? We've gotta launch a national appeal and the family must be there."

"Yes, I'm upset. If I hadna come here. . . ."

"He might still have been killed. He was organizing before you came."

"But it was me who told him to go register. I went to that courthouse with him, not you."

"Travis, I know it's tough, but it's what happens in this kind of a struggle. We've got to live with it. You got to keep telling yourself that we don't ask anyone to do anything that we don't do ourselves. You gotta remember that. You or Ray or Mac could have been in that house."

"For God's sake, Truman, don't lobby me. I know the line."

"Listen. . . . You say you want to respect the family's privacy. So do I. But what's your responsibility? The only way to stop these bombings is to make them public. Yeah, we gotta exploit it. Yeah, we gotta have the family crying on national TV. The cat's dead and nothing can undo that, but we have a responsibility to use his death against the people that killed him."

"I don't want to argue politics. That's not the issue," Peacock said.

"Travis, how can you say that? It is already an issue. And we, whether we like it or not, have to take it from there."

Peacock agreed with Truman, but he could no longer respond to that category of practical, pragmatic realities.

"Besides," Truman was saying, "even if we wanted to keep everything simple and pure, we can't. If you think that the other organizations won't be in town tomorrow morning, then you are crazy. You call it a circus; well, it's going to be one with or without us. Just came over the wires that Williams is calling for a hero's burial in Arlington, a mourning train to Washington, all under the auspices of *his* organization. We can sit aside and refuse to participate or get in there and fight. . . ."

"Yeah," Peacock said. "fight for the corpse. Fight for the corpse and raise some money?"

"Yeah, Peacock. That too." Truman was angry now. "You know how many folks been fired that we are carrying on the payroll? When those people off your project got arrested two weeks ago, where did you call to get the thousand dollars bond? You know people only send us money when they feel guilty. And that's the same as saying when someone gets killed. What the hell do you expect us to do?"

"It's true, but it's not right. Man, all I can see now is that little house blown to hell. And that lady just sitting and staring . . . Man, I just don't know."

"Look, I know what you're going through, but if you feel that you can't organize in the situation right now, I understand that. If you want to go someplace for a while. . . ."

Peacock saw what was coming. He would go off to "rest" someplace, and someone else would come in. Someone who, without his guilts and hesitations, could milk the situation for the most mileage. He was furious precisely because something in him wanted to leap at the chance. "You really think I would do that? Run away now? Screw you, Truman!"

"It may be wrong. In fact it is. . . ." Peacock heard a weary sigh, ". . . but man, I don't see how else we can operate. Get some sleep, man. Tomorrow you will feel different about what has to be done when the vultures swoop down. You decide then how to operate."

"Thank you," Peacock said.

"One last thing, man. Maybe I shouldn't even say this but . . . ask yourself this question. Suppose it was you who had got it, what would you want us to do? What would you expect us to do? Then ask yourself if Jesse Lee Hightower was a lesser man than you. Freedom."

"Freedom," Peacock said and hung up.

•

Peacock crossed over to the door, opened it, and stood looking down on the sleeping town. Later today it would be overrun. Camera crews, reporters, photographers, dignitaries. Across the country guilty and shocked people would be writing to congressmen. Some would reach for checkbooks. And the checks would go to the first name they read in the papers, the first face they recognized on the screen. Some labor leader would announce a Hightower relief fund and kick it off with a munificent contribution. Others would follow, even unions which somehow managed to have no black members. And the churches would send collections. Some conscience-stricken soul would make the rounds of his suburban community where no black folk lived. The resulting check would somehow reflect that fact. In Washington, Jesse Lee's fate would be officially deplored and an investigation ordered. And in the middle of all this, the meaningful thing would be to try to get enough to keep going for another six months. He was known and trusted by the family and the community. They would be asking his advice on every proposal, at every development. He could stage-manage the entire proceedings for maximum effect, package the pain and the loss to ensure the greatest "exposure."

They were talking about a hero's burial. Well, he had seen the last one. He remembered the fight about which organization had priority, whose leaders would have the right to walk on the right of the bier where the cameras were set up. He remembered the night before the funeral. The "hero" lay in state, his coffin set up in the center of the room draped with a wrinkled American flag smelling of mothballs. At a table by the door, an old woman sat selling memberships, buttons, and pamphlets to the people who filed in. Outside, proselytes of all kinds sold or gave away their particular version of the truth. The people bought their memberships and filed past that rumpled, dingy flag.

Somehow a man's life should be reflected in the final ceremony at his death. Jesse had been a simple man, and honest. That had been his way in the world and that was how he should go out. Peacock turned and walked back into the room.

"Travis, Travis. Whut happen?" Raf sprang to his feet and was peering at him anxiously.

"I . . . I'm all right, what's the matter?"

"Wal," Raf said, "effen yo' seen yore own face jes' now hit woulda set yo' back, too. Yo' bettah take a taste." Peacock drank deeply, the hot liquor bringing tears to his eyes.

"We wuz jes' figurin'," Raf said, "whut is we gon' do now, Travis? Ah mean the movement heah in Bogue Chitto?"

Peacock sat down and shook his head. He passed his hands over his face, massaging his eyes. He shook his head again. But when he looked up the men were still looking at him questioningly.

"Well," Peacock said, "be a lot happening real quick during the next few days. Here's what I think . . . We got to start with that meeting tomorrow. . . ." Peacock talked, the men listened, nodding from time to time. He kept looking at his watch. When morning came he had to go back to be with the family. Funny he hadn't thought of it before, but Miss Vickie had a great face. Be great on a poster or on TV. . . .

*1966*

# Bright an' Mownin' Star

T RAVELING south from Memphis on Highway 49, you cross over the last rolling hill and the Mississippi Delta stretches before you like the sea, an unbroken monotony of land so flat as to appear unnatural. So pervasive is this low-ceilinged, almost total flatness that one loses all other dimensions of space and vision. An endless succession of cotton and soybean fields surround the road.

A few weather-grayed shacks, stark, skeletal, and abrasively ugly, perch in a precarious oasis hacked out in the narrow, neutral strip between the road and the encroaching fields. Contemptuous of weather, time, and gravity, they stand apparently empty, long-abandoned and sheltering nothing but the wind. Then some appear, no different in point of squalor and decrepitude from the others, except that people stand before them.

At one point a single huge tree, off in a cotton field a distance, breaks the horizon. It is the first tree of any size that has appeared. This tree is an oak that bears small, gnarled acorns so bitter that there is no animal that will eat them. Its wood is very hard, but is knotty, faulted, and with a grain so treacherous and erratic that it cannot easily be worked. It is used for nothing more durable than a weapon. In this region they are called blackjacks, from the sootlike darkness of the bark, and find utility mainly in conversation as a metaphor of hardness, "tougher'n a blackjack oak."

This one is unusual beyond its mere presence and size, having both name and history. Its appearance, too, is unusual. The trunk and lower limbs are fire-charred to a dull black. These limbs are leafless and dead, but the top-most branches in the center of the tree continue to grow. In a strange inharmony the living oak flourishes out of the cinders of its own corpse. White folk call this tree the Nigger Jack, while Negroes speak of it hardly at all, save on those Sundays when the tree becomes the central symbol in some hell-fire sermon, for it is widely known that the flames that burned the oak roasted the bodies of slaves judged dangerous beyond redemption or control.

Once, it is said, some young black men from the county, returned from defeating the kaiser, resolved to fell and burn the tree. On the night before this event was to take place, a huge and fiery cross was seen to shine at the base of the tree, burning through the night and into the next day.

For many years—the space of three generations—the land around this tree has lain fallow, producing annually only a tangled transient jungle of rabbit grass and myriad nameless weeds, for no Negro could be found who might be bribed, persuaded, or coerced into working there.

Lowe Junior grunted deep in his chest as the heavy, broad-blade chopping hoe hit into the dry black earth. He jerked it up, sighted on the next clump of wire grass and weeds, and drove the hoe-blade into the furrow just beyond the weeds, and with the same smooth motion pulled the blade toward his body and slightly upward, neatly grubbing out the intruder in a little cloud of dust without touching the flanking cotton plants.

"Sho' do seem like the grass growin' faster'n the cotton." He leaned on the hoe handle and inspected the grubbed-up weed. "Hit be greener an' fatter'n the cotton evrahtime. Heah hit is, middle o' June, an' hit ain't sca'cely to mah knee yet." He ran his glance over the rows of stunted plants, already turning a dull brownish green, then squinted down the row he was chopping, estimating the work left. He saw much "grass" wrestling its way around and between the cotton. "Finish dishyer after dinner," he said, noting that the sun had already cleared the tip of the blackjack oak which stood some ten rows into the middle of the field. Dragging his hoe he started toward the tree's shade.

Lowe Junior was tall, a gaunt, slightly stooped figure as he shambled with the foot-dragging, slightly pigeon-toed, stiff-backed gait that a man develops straddling new-turned furrows while holding down the jerking, bucking handle of a bull-tongue plow. His boots and the dragging hoe raised a fine powder of dust around his knees. When he reached the tree, he leaned his tool against the trunk and stretched himself. He moved his shoulders, feeling the pull of the overalls where the straps had worn into his flesh during the morning's work. Holding the small of his back, he arched his middle forward to ease the numb, cramping ache that hardly seemed to leave the muscles in his back. Then he straightened up and stood for a while looking out over his cotton.

Then Lowe Junior turned to the tree and took a pail which hung from one of the broken stubs. He touched the blackened trunk, running his hands over the rough cinders. "Thet fiah oney toughed yo' up, thass all . . . an' there ain't nothin' wrong with thet." There was something familiar, almost affectionate, in his voice and action. When he first started working this section, he had carefully avoided the tree, sitting on the hot earth in the rows to eat and rest. But he had become accustomed to the tree now, was grateful for its shade, and he found himself accepting it as the only other living thing he encountered during the day. After all, he assured himself, "Hit cain't be no harm to no tree, fo' a certain fack."

He eased himself down ponderously, almost painfully, like a man too old or too fat, and began to eat. In the pail were butter-beans boiled with country peppers, wild onions, and slabs of salted fatback. This stew was tepid, almost perceptibly warm from the midday heat. The coating of pork grease that had floated to the top had not congealed. Lowe Junior briefly debated making a small fire but decided against taking the time. He ate quickly, stirring the stew and scooping it into his mouth with a thin square of cornbread, biting into the gravy-soaked bread, then chewing and swallowing rapidly. Finishing his meal he drank deeply from a kerosene tin filled with water and covered with burlap (wet in the morning but now bone dry), which stood among the roots of the tree.

He stretched himself again, yawned, belched, spat, and braced himself firmly against the tree. He lay there limply, his eyes closed as though to shut out the rows and rows of small, drying-out plants that represented the work of his hands, every day, from can see to can't, since early in the spring.

"Ef hit would jes' rain some . . . seems like the mo' a man strain, hit's the harder times git. Li'l rain now, an' the cotton be right up, but soon'll be too late." Weariness spread in him and the effort even of thinking was too great. He just lay there inert, more passive even than the tree, which at least stood. Even if by some miracle this cotton in the section he was "halfing" for Mr. Riley Peterson survived the drought, rains coming in August or September would turn the dust into mud and rot whatever cotton was ripening in the bolls—or else wash it into the mud.

A sudden panic came upon Lowe Junior, stretched beneath the tree. He could hardly feel his body, which was just a numbness. He felt that he could not rise, could not even begin, for his body would not obey him. For a brief moment he was terrified of making the effort lest he fail. Then he sat up suddenly, almost falling over forward from the violence of his effort. "Better study out whut t' do. No profit to layin' here scarin' m'se'f. Quarter section be a lot o' farmin' fo' a man. Sho' ain't be able to keep t' grass outen the cotton by myse'f."

This was a problem for him, had been ever since he had asked Mr. Peterson to give him this quarter section. He was young but a good worker; still Mr. Peterson might not have given it to him had it not been for the fact that no other tenant would take it. Lowe Junior did not want to ask for help with the chopping because, in "halfing," the cost of the seed, fertilizer, ginning, and any hired help came out of the tenant's half. Already most of his half belonged to Mr. J. D. Odum, the merchant in Sunflower who had "furnished" him. He knew that he would have to have help with the picking, and did not want to hire any help before then, when he would at least have an idea of the crop's potential. "Man can en' up with nothin' thet way," he muttered. "Hit'll happen anyways, tho. Figured to put in eight mebbe even nine bale fo' my share come the crop . . . now be the grace o' the good Gawd ef ah makes fo' . . . man doan feel much even t' keep on . . . Lawd, hit be better t' die, than t' live so hard." He found little comfort in those grim lines from the old blues to which his grandmother was so partial. She was always incanting that song as though it had a special meaning for her.

After his father died, and his mother went off to the North to find work, it was the old woman, pious and accepting, who had told him the old stories, raised him in the Church, and interpreted for him the ways of their world. He remembered her story of how God had put two boxes into the world, one big and the other small. The first Negro and the first white man had seen the boxes at the same time and run toward them, but the Negro arrived first and greedily appropriated for himself the larger box. Unfortunately this box contained a plough, a hoe, a cop-axe, and a mule, while the smaller box contained a pen, paper, and a ledger book. "An' thass why," the old woman would conclude, her face serious, "the Nigger been aworkin' evah since, an' the white man he reckon up the crop; he be sittin' theah at crop time, jes' afigurin' an' areckonin'; he say:

> Noughts a nought,
> Figgers a figger,
> All fo' us white folks,
> None fo' the Nigger."

He had been fifteen before he even began to doubt the authenticity of this explanation. Now the old lady was ailing and very old. But she had not lost her faith in the ultimate justice of the Lord or her stoic acceptance of whatever He sent. It was a joke among the neighbors that when the good sisters of the Church went in to see the old lady, now failing in sight and almost bedridden, her answer to the question, "How yo' keepin', Miz Culvah?" invariably was "Porely, thank d' Lawd." Lowe Junior chuckled, got up, dusted off his clothes, and went out into the sun.

That evening he stopped work early, just as the sun was setting, and started home, trudging slowly over the flat dusty road past fields, a few as parched and poor as his own, and large ones where elaborate machinery hurled silvery sprays over rows of tall lush plants. A wind swept the fine cool spray into the road. He felt the pleasant tickling points of coldness on his face and saw the grayish dust coating his overalls turn dark with the moisture. Minute grains of mud formed on his skin. He looked into the dazzling spray and saw a band of color where the setting sun made a rainbow.

> D' Lawd give Noah d' rainbow sign,
> No mo' watah, d'fiah nex' time.

"Thass whut the ol' woman would say, an' tell evrahbody thet she seen d' Lawd's sign. Be jes' sun an' watah, tho." He did not look at the green fields. Looking straight ahead into the dust of the road, he increased his pace. He wanted only to get home.

Just where the dust road meets the highway, at the very edge of a huge field, was the shack. Tin-roofed with gray clapboard sides painted only with the stain of time and weather, it had two small rooms. As Lowe Junior came up the road, it seemed to be tossed and balanced on a sea of brown stalks, the remains of last year's bean crop which came up to the back door.

In the front, the small bare yard was shaded by a pecan tree already in blossom. Small lots, well-kept and tidy, grew okra, butter-bean, and collard green plants on both sides of the yard. Lowe Junior walked around the shack to a standpipe in back of the stoop. He washed the dust from his head and arms, filled his pail, and drank. The water was brown, tepid, and rusty-tasting. He sprinkled the okra and bean plants, then entered the shack. The fire was out, and the huge pot hanging over the fire, from which he had taken his dinner that morning, had not been touched.

"Mam, Mam," he called softly, "Yo' awright?" There was no answer, and he went into the old woman's room. The room was stifling-hot as the tin roof radiated the day's heat. The air was heavy with the smell of stale urine, old flesh, and night sweat. The old lady lay against the wall, partially covered by an old quilt. A ray of sunlight beamed through a small knothole and lighted up the lined and creasing skin pattern on one side of her face. A single fly buzzed noisily around her open mouth and lighted on the tuft of straggling white hairs on her chin. Her eyes stared at a framed picture of the bleeding heart of Jesus, violent red and surrounded by a wreath of murderous-looking thorns and a hopeful glow, which hung on the opposite wall above the motto, "The Blood of Jesus Saves."

Lowe Junior searched his pockets slowly, almost absently, for two coins to place over her eyes. His gaze never left her face and, as he looked, the ray of sunlight gradually diminished, seeming to withdraw reluctantly from the face, finally leaving it to shadow.

Failing to find any coins, he straightened the limbs, pulled the quilt over the face, and went to tell the neighbors.

When he returned, the thick purple Delta darkness had descended with a tropical suddenness. He added more beans, fatback, and water to the stew, and started the fire. Then he lit a kerosene lantern and took it into the yard to a spot beneath the pecan tree. He hung the lantern on a branch and began to dig.

The neighbors found him still digging when they began to arrive in the little yard. The first small group of women was led by Sister Beulah, a big, imposing, very black woman with a reputation for fierce holiness. She stood out from the worn and subdued group not only because of the crisp whiteness of her robe and bandanna but also in her purposeful, almost aggressive manner. She led the women to the side of the hole.

"Sho' sorry t' heah 'bout Sistah Culvah, but as you knows. . . ," she began.

"She inside," Lowe Junior said without looking up, "an' ah thanks yo' all fo' comin'."

Interrupted in mid-benediction, Beulah stood with her mouth open. She had failed to officiate at buryings in the community only twice in the past twenty years, and then only because she had been holding revivals at the other end of the state. She had never quite forgiven the families of the deceased for not awaiting her return. She resented Lowe Junior's thanks, the first she had ever received for doing what she thought of as an indispensable service. May as well thank the grave.

"Thet boy sho' actin' funny," she murmured and swept into the shack to take charge of preparations.

More neighbors straggled into the yard. Another lantern was brought and hung in the tree, widening the chancy and uncertain perimeter of light in the otherwise enveloping blackness of the Delta night. Each man arriving offered to help Lowe Junior with the digging. Some had even brought tools, but Lowe Junior stonily refused all offers.

"Ah be finished time the box get heah," he answered without looking at the men. "Sho' do thank yo', tho."

So the men sat and smoked, speaking only in murmurs and infrequently. The women passed out steaming plates of stew and tins of coffee bitter with chicory. Lowe Junior declined all food. The plates in the shack were emptied and rotated until all were fed. After a muttered consultation, one of the men approached Lowe Junior. He was old, his hair very white against his skin. He was very neat and careful of himself, moving with great dignity. His faded overalls were clean and shiny from the iron. He stood quietly at the side of the hole until Lowe Junior stopped work and looked up at him. Then he spoke, but so softly that the other men could not make out his words. The yard was very silent.

"Brothar Culvah. The peoples ain't easy in min'. They come to he'p yo' and heah yo' takin' no he'p." Lowe Junior said nothing.

"In time o' grief, praise Jesus, folks, they wants t', an' mo'n thet, they needs, t' he'p . . . they come t' pay respeck t' the daid an' share the burden an' sarrow o' d' livin'. Thass how hit's allus bin . . . Son, when folks offer comfort an' he'p, a man mus' accep' hit, 'cause hit's mebbe all they got."

Lowe Junior looked at the old man.

"Yo' unnerstan' what ah'm asayin', son?" he asked gently.

"The peoples doan feel like as if they got anythang t' do heah, anythang thet they needs t' be adoin'."

Lowe Junior looked into the darkness. His voice was low and without inflection. "Hit ain't no he'p to give, ain't no sarrow t' share. Hit's jes' thet the ol' woman was ol', an' now she daid. . . . Ain't no sarrow in thet."

They became aware of a sound. It came from the shack and at first did not seem to intrude or in any way challenge the dark silence. It began as a deep sonorous hum, close in pitch to the sound of silence. Then it grew,

cadenced and inflected, gathering power and volume until it filled the yard
and was present, physical and real. The men picked up the moan and it
became a hymn.

hhhmmmmmmmmmMMMay the Circle . . . be Unbroken
Bye and bye, Lawd . . . Bye annnn Bye

"Peoples can sang," Lowe Junior said. "Praise Jesus, they can allus do
thet."

The old man walked away, silent. He sat on the stoop ignoring the questioning looks of the others. He hunched over, his frail body gently rocking back and forth, as though moved against his will by the throbbing
cadences of the singing. He sat there in isolation, his eyes looking into the
darkness as at his own approaching end, his face etched with lines of
a private and unnamable old man's sorrow. Deep and low in his chest he
began to hum the dirge.

Lowe Junior chopped viciously at the earth. The people intoned the old
and troubled music that they were born to—the music which, along with
a capacity to endure, was their only legacy from the generations that had
gone before, the music that gathered around them, close, warm, and personal as the physical throbbing of their natural life.

When the hole was to Lowe Junior's chin, the Haskell boys came into
the yard carrying the coffin. It was of green pitch pine, the boards rough-
planed so that all depressions on the surface of the boards were sticky with
sap. The men also brought two boxes so that the coffin would not rest on
the ground. The Haskells stood by the hole, wiping their gummy hands
on their overalls.

"Yo' reckon hit'll be awright?" Ben Haskell asked.

"Shol'y. Sho', hit'll be jes' fine. Yo' done real good; hit's a coffin, ain't
hit?" Lowe Junior still had not looked at the coffin, which was surrounded
by the neighbor men. The Haskells stood silent, looking at him.

" 'Sides, ol' woman . . . allus was right partial t' scent o' pine. Yassuh,
hit'll be right fine," Lowe Junior said. Ben Haskell smiled, a diffident
embarrassed stretching of his mouth. "Yo said cedar, but see, quick as yo'
needed hit, pine wuz all we could git."

"Thass right," his brother assented.

Leastwise, Lowe Junior thought, Mist' Odum wouldn' give yo' all cedar
fo' credit. He repeated softly, "Yo' done good, real good." The Haskells
beamed, relieved, and expressed again their sympathy before moving
away.

·

The yard was now full, some twenty persons stood, hunkered, or sat around. Set on the boxes in the center of the group, the raw white coffin dominated the scene like an altar, filling the air with the pungent odor of crude turpentine.

Lowe Junior walked around the coffin and approached the steps of the shack. The neighbors' eyes followed him. Sister Behlah met him at the door. He saw the faces of the other women peering down at him from behind her. All conversation ceased.

"Brothah Culvah, this yer ah'm agonna say ain't strictly mah business. Some would say hit rightly ain't *none* o' mah concern atall." She paused, looking at Lowe Junior and the men in the yard. Nothing was said, and she continued. "But lookin' at hit anothah way, hit what ah'm gonna say, *is* mah business. Hit's bin troublin' mah min', and hit's lotsa othah folks heah, what ah knows feel d' same way." When she paused again, there was a faint assenting Ahmen from the people.

"So ah'm agonna say hit . . . Now, yo' all knows me, bin apreachin' an' aservin' the Lawd in these parts fo' thutty year, an' live heah thutty year befo' thet." Murmurs of "Thass right" came from the group.

"Yas, thass the Lawd's truth, an' ah knows Sistah Culvah, Miss Alice we used t' call her, from she fust come off t' plantation an' nobody evah had a word o' bad to say 'bout her, praise Jesus. Yas, an' ah known yo' po' mothah, an' yo' se'f, Brothah Culvah, from evah since." The murmurs from the neighbors were stronger now. Encouraged, Sister Beulah continued. She was now speaking louder than anyone had spoken in the yard all evening.

"She wuz a good woman, a go-o-d woman, she knowed Jesus an' she wuz saved. Hit's true, towards the las' when she wuz porely an' gittin' up in age, she couldn' git to meetin' to praise her Gawd, but yo' all knows she *lo-oved* the Church." She took a deep breath. "Now, ah knows thet back then, in slavery times, when the ol' folks could' do no bettah, an' had to hol' buryin's an' Chris'nin' an' evrah-thang at night. But, thank Jesus, them days is gone. They's gone. Hit ain't fittin' an' hit ain't right an' propah t' hol' no buryin' at night, leas' hit ain't bin done herebouts. The body o' the good sistah, now called t' Glorah, ain't even bin churched. Yo' knows thet ain't right. Ah knows thet, effen she could have somepin t' say, she'd want hit done right at the las'! Ah *kno-o-ows* in mah heart she would."

"Yas, yas, ahah, praise Jesus." The neighbors agreed.

"An Brothah Culvah, yo' a young man, yo' a Gawd-fearin' man, an' ah knows yo' wants t' do right. 'Cause . . . yo' know hit says . . . the longes' road mus' ha' some endin', but a good name endureth fo'evah." On this dramatic and veiled note of warning the huge white-draped woman ended.

Everyone was quiet, but there was a faint expectant shuffling of feet as the people looked at Lowe Junior.

" 'Tain't no call t' fret yo'se'f," he said. "Ol' woman wuz ol' an' now she gone. Ah be aburyin' her tonight." There was a quickly stifled murmur from the people. No one spoke, and Lowe Junior continued more softly.

" 'Tain't thet whut yo' say ain't got right to hit, Sta' Beulah, 'cause hit do. But hit's no law say thet effen yo' got buryin' t' do, hit cain't be done in the night."

"Yas, Brothah Culvah, effen yo' *got* t' do hit. Doan seem like t' me hit's no hurry. . . ." Beulah said.

"Yas'm, hit is a hurry. See, ah feel like ah should take care o' this thang personal. Ol' woman raise me from when ah wuz young, ah wants t' take care o' the buryin' personal."

"Whut's wrong with t'morrow? Yo' answer me thet."

"Be no tellin' jes' where ah'll be t'morrow," Lowe Junior said, lifting one end of the coffin and asking Ben Haskell to help with the other end. They took it into the shack to receive the body.

"Hey, Lowe, yo' sho' nuff fixin' t' leave?" Ben could not keep the excitement out of his voice.

"Thass right." Lowe Junior's first knowledge of his decision had come when he heard himself telling Beulah, a moment before.

"Yo' mean yo' ain't even gon' stay t' make yo' crop?"

"Any one o' yo' all wants t' work hit is welcome t' my share. Ah'll sign a paper so Mist' Peterson and Mist' Odum'll know." Temptation and fear struggled in Ben's eyes, and finally he said only, "Ah'll tell d' other'ns . . . but supposin' no one wants t' take hit?"

"Yo' mean 'bout Mist' Peterson . . . well, he got mo' cotton. Fack is, he got 'bout all theah is."

"Lawd's truth," Ben agreed, and went quickly to share the news with the men in the yard. There the women were grouped around Sister Beulah who was threatening to go home. After what she judged to be sufficient entreaty to mollify her hurt dignity, she agreed to remain and conduct the burial, but only because "hit's mah bounden duty to see to hit thet the pore daid woman gits a propah Christian service." She led the women into the shack to put the old lady into the coffin.

After everyone had taken a last look at the corpse, Ben Haskell nailed the lid on and the coffin was brought out and placed on the boxes. During the singing of "Leaning on the Everlasting Arms," two of the women began to cry. Lowe Junior stood a short distance off under the shadow of the pecan tree and looked out over the darkness. He took no part in the singing until the lines of "Amazing Grace,"

> Ah wunst wuz lost but now ah'm Found,
> Wuz blind but now ah See.

In a loud but totally uninflected voice, he repeated "Wuz blind but now ah See."

This unexpected voice, coming as it were from behind her, distracted Sister Beulah who had begun to "line out" the succeeding lines for the benefit of any backsliders who might have forgotten them. She stopped, turned, and glared at Lowe Junior, then continued in the joyful and triumphant voice of one whose seat in the Kingdom is secure beyond all challenge.

" *'Twuz Grace thet taught mah heart t' feah*," she exulted; "*An' Grace mah feah relieved*." Her face was illuminated, radiant with the security of grace.

When the coffin was being lowered and was a quarter of the way down, the rope under the head slipped, and it thudded into the hole, almost upright. The people stood in momentary shocked silence. Sister Beulah at the head of the grave raised her massive white-sleeved arms to the sky as though appealing for divine vindication of this sacrilege, the result of Lowe Junior's stubbornness. Lowe Junior quickly lay flat on the edge of the grave, and shoved the high end of the coffin with all his strength. He grunted with the effort and the box slid into place with a heavy thump, followed by the rattle of dirt and pebbles from the sides.

At that moment the sky lightened. They all looked up and saw the risen moon peering from behind a wall of dark clouds that had not been there when the sun set.

"Glorah, Glorah!" a man shouted hoarsely, and the ritual resumed. Sister Beulah had thought to preach her famous "Dead Bones Arisin" sermon, capped with a few well-chosen words on the certain doom of impious children, but recent events had lessened her zeal. Almost perfunctorily, she recounted the joys and glories of Salvation and the rewards awaiting the departed sister. Then they piled dirt on the coffin, patted down the mound, and departed.

∎

Lowe Junior sat on the steps. Barely acknowledging the final murmured consolations, he watched the neighbors leave. He realized that he was not alone when the old man approached the stoop.

"Ah heah yo' is leavin', Brothah Culvah. Done any thankin' on wheah yo' goin' an' whut yo' gonna be doin'?"

Lowe Junior did not answer. He in no way acknowledged the old man's presence.

"Thass awright, yo' doan have t' answer 'cause ah knows—yo' ain't! Jes' like ah wuz when ah wuz 'bout yo' age. An' ah lef' too, din' know wheah ah wuz agoin' nor whut ah wuz lookin' fo'. Effen yo' doan know whut yo' seekin', Brothah Culvah, yo' cain' know when yo' fin' hit."

Now Lowe Junior was looking at the man; he seemed interested in what he was saying. It was the first interest he had shown in anyone else that evening.

"See, Brothah Culvah, ah travelled aroun' some when ah wuz yowr age, and heah ah is now. Ah never foun' no bettah place nowheahs." He shook his head. "Fo' usses, theah wuzn't none, leastways not thet ah could fin'."

"But at leas' yo' looked," Lowe Junior said.

"Thass why ah'm asayin' to' yo' whut ah is. 'Cause ah did. Brothah Culvah, yo' a good worker, yo' knows farmin' an' cotton, but whut else do yo' know? Ah disbelieves thet yo' even bin so far as Memphis."

"Well," Lowe Junior said, "t'morrow thet won't be true. But ah 'preciates yo' kin'ness."

The old man hobbled into the darkness, shrouded in his own ancient knowledge.

Lowe Junior sat on the steps and watched him leave, until finally he was alone. He went to the tree, blew the lamp out, and sat in the darkness. . . . When the sun came up next morning, he had not moved. The astringent pitch-pine smell still hovered in the still air. Lowe Junior saw that the morning sky was covered by a heavy, metallic-gray cloud that had come swirling up from the Gulf in the dark. He entered the shack and looked about him for something to take. In the old woman's room, he found nothing. He returned, picked up his hoe, turned around in the small room, saw nothing else that he wanted, and started to leave. On the steps he changed his mind and reentered the house. In the old woman's room, he took the picture of the Sacred Heart from the frame. Then from a small wooden box he took a Bible which he held by the covers and shook. Three crumpled bills fluttered to the floor. He gave the book a final shake, tossed it into the box, then picked up the bills and carefully wrapped them in the picture. He placed the package in the long deep side-pocket of his overalls.

He picked up his hoe from the steps and started out. At the dirt road he turned, not toward the highway, but east toward his section. Soon he could see the top of the oak in the thin dawning light.

"Sho' nevah put no stock in all thet talk 'bout thet tree," he mused. "Burned like thet on the sides an' so green t' the top, hit allus did put me in min' o' Moses an' the burnin' bush. But ah wager a daid houn', ain't no Nigger agoin' t' work thisyer lan' now."

He stood for awhile looking at the tree, at the lean runted plants. "Sho' do feels like ah knows yo' evrah one, evrah row and clump o' grass like hit wuz the face o' mah own han' or mah own name."

He strode up to the tree, set his feet, and swung the hoe against the trunk with all the strength of his back. The hickory handle snapped with a crack like a rifle in the early morning. The blade went whirring into the cotton rows. He felt the shock of the blow sting the palm of his hands, and shiver up into his shoulders. He stepped away from the tree and hurled the broken handle as far as he could into the field.

"Theah," he grunted, "yo' got the las' o' me thet yo' is gonna git—the natural las'."

He started back toward the highway at a dead run. There were tears in his eyes and his breath was gusty. He tired and slowed to a walk. He saw the first raindrops hitting heavily into the thick dust of the road, raising sudden explosions of dust and craters of dampness where they struck. Before he reached the cabin, torrents of water were lashing the face of the Delta. When he reached the highway, he turned once to look at the mean little house, gray and forlorn in the storm. He saw a pool already spreading around the roots of the pecan tree.

The dry earth gave off an acrid smell as the water dampened it. "Be nuff now fo' evrah one, white and black," Lowe Junior thought and laughed. "Sho' doan mattah now effen they takes ovah mah fiel'. Hit be all washed out, evrah natural one."

The rain swept down with increased violence. He was completely drenched, streamlets ran down his face, washing away the dust. "Ah nevah seed the like. Sho' now, be hongry folk heah this year. Even white folk be hongry in the Delta this winter." He walked steadily down the highway stretching into the distance.

*1966*

# Bright an' Mownin' Star

*(2)*                    ■  ■  ■  ■  ■

T HE driver stopped the bus at the brightly lighted intersection of Galveston
Avenue and Jefferson Davis Boulevard. Lowe
Junior alighted leaving the bus empty. Waiting for the light to change, the driver watched ,
Lowe Junior as he crossed the intersection in
the direction of the hotel.

"Wouldn't want that boy amessing round
mah do-er when ah'm sleepin'. Nigger big as
thet'n, wonder what he do in thet hotel. Them
quiet ones, they the worse kin' too."

Lowe Junior crossed underneath the GEN-
ERAL FORREST HOTEL sign. In smaller letters under the name it said, "The Pride of Old
Dixie and the Home of the True Southern
Comfort." The hotel was named for a favorite son of the region, ex-slave dealer turned
General Officer of the Confederacy and later
guerrilla leader and grand dragon of a later
less honorable army. Bankrupt by the advent
of war, he had traded his tainted, not quite
respectable wealth for a commission and a
fame that would endure as long as the memory of that war endured fiery and present in
the minds and even the faces of the people, so
that now not only the hotel but the county itself bore his name, "Forrest County, named
for one who never quite surrendered."

Oblivious to the history embodied in the sign under which he passed, Lowe Junior went quickly to the back of the building, to the door under the sign "Employees Colored." He had been working there for nearly a month, but still he could not rid himself of a feeling of jeopardy and uncertainty whenever he entered the building. He followed a long dim corridor to the big metal door behind which he changed into his working clothes. His working clothes—a mismatched combination of shiny silver-buckled pumps, bright blue form-hugging pantaloons coming to the middle of his calf, and a long, hot, red and blue coat with innumerable brass buttons, ruffles of lace at neck and sleeve. In this attire—for which he felt a vague unexamined hatred, sensing that it was somehow meant to mark him off, to reduce his presence to something comfortable and acceptable in the eyes of the patrons of the place—he would stand until eight the next morning at the big glass doors, opening doors and carrying bags. It has been impressed on him by the assistant manager who hired him that he was never, "nevah fo' any reason atawl" to come upstairs in his street clothes. He wondered why that above all else was so important.

He paused outside the door. He could hear a dim hum of activity inside the door. He knew he was early and thought briefly of going back into the streets until it was nearer time to go on duty. The muffled shouts and laughter of his fellow workers made him uneasy. He did not understand them. It had been hard to recognize the boisterous, aggressive men who gathered in the furnace room each night, as the same neuter and impassive figures he met gliding ghostlike about their duties upstairs. But the thought of the streets, where he felt so exposed and vulnerable caused him to open the door. All sound and movement ceased. About seven men were in the room; when they saw Lowe Junior alone the activity resumed. It was a huge room, brightly lighted with whitewashed walls and a high ceiling. Apart from a few metal cabinets, a metal shower stall, with a sign ordering all employees to shower before donning their uniforms, the only other furniture in the place was a long bench. On one side of the room was a row of giant electrical furnaces also painted white. The harsh light bounced off the white walls and stung his eyes. Blinking he entered and muttered quickly, "Evening All." He always felt that one night there would be no answer, and afraid of that embarrassment he always muttered.

"How yo' making hit Culver?"

"Easy theah, now man."

The answers always came, but perfunctorily. He was clearly not included in the group. He went quickly to his locker and poked around inside. He was immediately aware of the smell of corn whiskey struggling with the sharp stifling smell of the hospital antiseptic with which the windowless room was doused each week.

Glancing covertly over his shoulder, he looked at the group dwarfed by the giant furnaces and towering white walls. They made a strange picture. Tireiron, a big waiter who was something of a leader, was still fully attired in the purple swallowtailed coat and red pantaloons in which he worked. One man was in his street clothes, and between these poles, the others ranged through every possible absurd combination of dress, even as they represented every possible shade of skin color, from one called "Whitey" because of the marvelous and total blackness of his skin, to a young boy called "Roosie," almost white who was wearing a plum-colored coat and nothing else.

The group was centered around Whitey who was shaking the dice.

"Com'on Mothuhfuckahs, com'oon li'l sistuhs, ain't ah allus bin good teryo'? This yer is ol' Whitey, yo' sweet evah-humping ol' daddy. Yeah, thass hit. Com'oon Mothuhs." Whitey released the dice, covered his eyes. "Ah cain't bare to look, yo' all tell me hit's a six."

Lowe Junior noticed that he left enough space between his fingers to be able to peer through.

"Six mah ass, yo' done crapped to hell out," someone howled gleefully and signaled a general rush for the stakes.

"Shieet," Whitey said and walked over to the bench and observed the game silently. Then his glum expression brightened and he produced a pint bottle from his locker.

"Whooee Lawd, did yo' all niggers see that parade today. Wun'it somethin'? Ah swear yo' shoulda seed them white gals, man, with spangles an' bangles, they bare ass jes' ashakin' and atwinklin'. Put me in min' o' thet Texas ho-house ah used to work at."

Roosie stood up from the circle of gamblers and looked at Whitey.

"Hear at this nigger," he said scornfully, "Ugly as yo' is an' black as yo' is—an' yo' knows yo' blacker than midnight in a cypress swamp—hit ain't no white folks be lettin' yo' watch no bareassed white gals. Shit, Nigger, yo' ain't seed no parade, someone *tell* yo' 'bout hit."

Lowe Junior could tell from the response to this jibe that a good deal of drinking had been done before he arrived. The game broke up, and the players gathered around Whitey whooping, shouting, and urging him on. He knew what was going to follow, but he did not understand it. What did the strident vulgarity and the gratuitous abuse of each other mean? It was Whitey's turn.

"Who yo' callin' ugly," he blustered. "Roosie, ah swears 'fo Gawd, effen ah had a mangy ol' dawg an' his face ugly as yours ah'd shave his ass an' learn him to walk backways."

"Whoo Lawd."

"Whoowhee, Roosie, yo' gonter take thet?"

Roosie clearly wasn't. He strutted up until he towered over Whitey.

"Damn ef ah ain't surprised to hear you say that, Whitey." He shook his head in puzzlement, " 'cause hit sho' ain't whut yo' *Mammy* say."

It seemed to Lowe Junior that the game was going against Whitey tonight. Roosie's last sally was greeted with a frantic glee.

"Whooee, ugh."

"Man can thet be yowr *mammy* he talking 'bout so bad?"

"Nigger tell me that ah'd cut his black ass fo' Gawd git the news."

"Yassah, sho' would. Cut me a cracker too."

"Ahuh, wide, deep, an' often."

Tireiron, who had been watching the proceedings passively, egged Roosie on.

"Jes' whut *do* his mammy say?" he asked. Before Roosie could answer—Lowe Junior was not sure that he would have answered because to the extent that he understood the rules of the game, it was Whitey's turn—the little man moved up to the grinning Roosie. Whitey moved slowly stiff-kneed, his hand reaching slowly and menacingly into his back pocket.

"Nigger," he sneered, "effen ah had mah razor an' half a notion, ah would calubrate yowr yella ass. . . ."

"Mercy Jesus," someone asked, "Whut do thet word mean Whitey?"

"Mean ah'd cut him from his eyebrow to his appetite, an' from his asshole to his bellybutton, and some mo' after that. Thet's what hit mean."

Tireiron jeered. "Shit thet doan even scare me, an' I'se a stone coward."

"Whitey gotta come better'n thet."

"Yeah man, that some weak-ass ol' shit he talking."

Roosie was encouraged by Whitey's failure.

"Damn boy, yo' sho' bettah respeck me. Yassuh, 'cause fo' yo' could evan say 'cornpone' ah wuz crawlin' ovah you naked ass to get next to yo' mammy."

That was so absurd that Lowe Junior had to repress a smile. Roosie was at least ten years Whitey's junior.

"Ooh, now. Damn, thet Roosie he a bad man."

"Lawd yes, thisyer a b-a-a-d nigger."

They surrounded the victorious Roosie who was fairly dancing with glee, slapping his back, head, and outstretched hand. Whitey took his defeat with a shrug.

"Onliest reason ah doan cut him, is the nigger owe me money, man, an' he ain't pick up his pay yet."

"Yeah, no sense to killing a nigger owe yo' money, man. Sho' ain't no way to git paid."

"Yeah, but white folk is different. Then yo' knows yo' ain't gittin' paid nohow," someone amended.

"Specially," Tireiron put in, "a *Mississippi* white man. 'Cause even if he pay yo' some, yo' knows sho' as cotton ain't black, thet he gon' fin' some way to jug yo' outta the res'."

"Thass because yo'all niggers ain't got no heart, nor no sense neither," Whitey said.

"Yeah? An' yo' has huh?" Tireiron asked, "an' thass why yo' doan have to leave half yo' tips upstairs with thet peckerwood mothahfucker, eh?" Whitey spread his hands palms outwards against the jeers.

"Shiyit, man, thass different. He the headwaiter ain't he?"

"Yeah, he sho' is," Tireiron said softly, "an' he white ain't he? An' he ain't do shit but walk up an' down, do he? An' y'awl gives him half yo' tips don't yo'? Yeah, an' grin like hell while yo' doin' hit too. *Wal don't yo'?* Yeah, y'awl does, an' yo' know why, 'cause like Mr. Charlie say, *'niggers ain't shit.'* "

Lowe Junior watched as though he too were hypnotized by Tireiron's anger. The men were silent, sullen before Tireiron's contempt. He looked from face to face and they all looked away. He seemed to be coming in Lowe Junior's direction so Lowe Junior turned and pretended to be looking for something in his locker.

"Wal *shit,* Ir'n, *yo'* gotter give up yowr tips too."

It was Whitey who broke the silence. There was a murmur of assent from the others.

"We all does," Tireiron said, his voice gentler as though he were talking to himself, "an' we allus done, all kin's o' ways. Ah recolleck thet mah mothah, raht heah in this city, bought her thisyer li'l phillco raddio one time. Li'l bitty ol' thang hit wuz too, en do yo' know, that po' lady paid the man fo' that thang fo' five years. Paid thet man, three dollars an' fifty cents evrah month the good Lawd sen'."

Heads nodded silently. The men stared away from each other at the walls, as though each was remembering a private story of his own. For a while the silence was unbroken as they concentrated on drinking. To Lowe Junior they seemed up tight, stiff, no longer drunk. Then Roosie broke the silence. Loudly.

"Shiyit, but thet parade today wuz somethin', wu'nt hit?"

"Hell yes," another agreed.

"Hey Culvah, see the parade man?" Roosie asked.

"No. Ain't see no parade," Lowe Junior muttered and bent to remove his shoes.

Whitey got up and swayed a few steps in Lowe Junior's direction.

"Who ask the man thet?" he demanded. "Don't yo' know ol' Lowe heah doan need to see no parades? Muh man heah, why he jes' goes to church. Thass right, an' thass better'n any parade. Shiyit, man, when thet ol' spirit gits next to them good sistuhs, an' they gits to feeling good and throwin' up them ol' skirts, an' pitchin' out them big fat laigs, ahollerin' Jesus, Jesus." Whitey threw his hands in the air and rolled his eyes simulating religious ecstasy. "Yeah man, an' muh man Lowe Junior heah, man he jes' cool, jes' a-watchin'. Man effen his min' set on Jesus, his eyes sho' somewhere else. Ah swear, be enough raw pussy waving roun' them meetings to make yo' haid swim."

Lowe Junior kept his head down as waves of jeering laughter swept the room. Finally Whitey had scored. He heard someone, it sounded like Tireiron, say to Whitey.

"Nigger that's according to how light yo' head is."

More laughter.

"Yeah, yeah," Whitey was saying, "an' then there be that ol' chicken-eater Johnson up theah befo' the flock, snortin', fartin', an' abellerin' loud as he can, watching them ol' fat laigs, with his eyes turnin' to blood, jes' awatching them fat sistuhs. 'Chilluns,' he sayin' to hisse'f, 'yo' soul may belong to Jesus, but yowr ass belong to the pastor'."

Whitey was strutting around, triumphant.

"Yeh," Roosie gasped wiping his eyes, "yeh, thass whut, haw haw, Lawdy thass whut they calls, ha haw, *sharing the crop with Jesus.*"

Hardly knowing when or how he came to be there Lowe Junior found himself standing over Whitey. His big hand trembled in Whitey's face.

"Now lookaheah, yo' had no call to say thet Whitey."

"Ah wuz only playin' man," Whitey protested, "git outa mah face."

"Wal ah ain't playin' an' ah ain't jokin' worth a damn. Don't yo' *nevah* do hit no mowr."

Silence in the room. Whitey stepped backwards, staggered, and almost fell. Someone laughed. Tireiron said, "He right Whitey, an' yo' wrong. This man is serious an' yo' shouldna said hit."

"Yeah, like yo' wuzn't laughin' too, Ar'n. Yo' wuz, y'awl wuz. Sides he din have to jump all salty over thet. Ah ain't scared of no plantation nigger nohow."

No one answered Whitey, and he stood apart, mumbling and scowling.

His eye began to twitch, Lowe Junior noticed, and he looked angry and mean.

"Wal anyways," he said very loudly, defiantly, "way ah feels raht now, had me a piece o' white ass, ah'd . . ."

"Yo'd *whut* Nigger," Tireiron asked as heads turned quickly toward the door, "Yo'd *whut?* Shiyit, yo'd be so scared yo' wouldn' know wether to miss hit, kiss hit, or tell hit good mawnin."

"What *ah'd* do? Nigger effen ol' as yo' is yo' doan know, hit sho' ain't fo' me to tell you."

"Guess ah do know," Tireiron said. "Yo'd be arunnin' so fas' yo'd be in Memphis 'fo the sun come up. That's effen yo' got good sense."

"Uhhuh, Ar'n, yo' got the wrong nigger. Me? Ah'd stretch hit so outa shape, yo' could use hit fo' a cotton sack. Thass right."

"Listen heah at thisyer runty nigger," Roosie scoffed. "He wrong fo' fair. He so ugly, black, an' wrong thet the las' time he see any pussy is the day he born."

"Whoo lawd, ugh."

"Yeah man," a waiter called Seven-Eleven put in, "an' hit wuz so dark then he never even see that good."

"Hey Whitey," they shouted, "Leben say yo' din' even see hit good that time, haw-haw."

Whitey tried to shout over the laughter. Finally he was able to have himself heard.

"Oh yeah?" he was saying. "Oh yeah? Wal yo' better believe, ah doan needs to see hit, jes' so hit's hairy, hot, an' wet. . . ."

"An' black yo' mean," Tireiron taunted, "Nigger yo' bettah hush, member who yo' talking to."

"They say," Roosie jibed, "thet thisyer Whitey so dumb thet he . . ." He was overcome with mirth but managed to continue, ". . . doan know the difference between skunk cabbage an' pussy willow."

"Yo' jokin' Roosie. But lookaheah y'awl bettah not encourage this nigger. Nex' thang yo' knows the sonnabitch he believin' hisse'f. Man this nigger so simple hit's a shame."

Then Tireiron turned to Whitey.

"Damn nigger, effen Charlie jes' ketch yo' *thankin'* thet mess, he turn yo' po' black ass evrah-which way but loose. Yo' sho' bettah hush now."

"Ah ain't simple, ah ain't jokin', an' ah sho' ain't scared," Whitey blustered. "Ah'm a man ain't ah? A man ain't got no business to be scared o' no pussy. Y'awl Mississippi niggers ain't got no heart."

"Whoah now. Y'awl heah that?"

"Yeah thisyer nigger *mus'* be serious."

"He *say* he serious, din' yo' hear him?"

"Damn but he *bad*," Roosie simulated awe. "This *mus'* be the baddes' nigger Gawd's got."

"Yassuh, the baddes' one he evah got too," Seven-Eleven agreed.

"Wal, he say *he* ain't scared o' nuthin' an' thet we ain't got no heart. Thet whut yo' say Whitey?" Tireiron asked.

"Yo' heard whut ah said."

"Yo know ah allus figured yo' wuz simple . . . but ah nevah took yo' for a damn fool. Now hit's a big difference twixt bein' 'fraid an' bein' scared, an' only a gawddamned fool gon' stan' heah an' say he ain' nevah scared o' them crazy mothahs. Only a damn fool nigger go lookin' fo' white folks' trouble. Now hush, yo' heah me."

Tireiron glared down at Whitey. He was a massive frightening figure in his purple coat, with his bullet head shining.

It seemed to Lowe Junior that Whitey would have liked to "hush" but just then Roosie said, "Yeah Ar'n, but Whitey's bad, Charlie be scared to mess wid him."

Goaded, Whitey launched into a long passionate almost incoherent diatribe announcing that he was not only serious but shonuff serious, gawddamned serious, an' wu'nt he a man, and that he was gittin' ready to go find him that ass, white, black, or striped, the first one he met willing or otherwise. His speech was punctuated by jeering cheers from the others.

"Y'awl damn right ah is serious," Whitey concluded and started for the door. Tireiron stopped him.

"Hey nigger whoa now. How come yo' so badass now. Yo' wuzn't las' year when we wuz workin' thetyer dinner party, huh?"

Whitey stopped, reeled around, and stared at Tireiron. His eye twitched furiously, but he said nothing.

"So tell me, how come? How come yo' so bad now?"

"Thass a lie, Ar'n," he said. "Yo' know hit nevah happen. Ain't yo' tired o' tellin' thet lie?"

"*Goddamn hit ain't no lie*," Tireiron roared, "an' ah nevah told hit befo', but sence yo'awl gettin' so fuckin' bad an' all, I thanks I will." He was staring at the little man, a funny little grin on his sweating face.

"Ar'n, yo' bettah don't. Ah'm warning yo'." He waved his bottle threateningly. Then he said, "Why yo' wan' to do thet to me, Ar'n, ain't we bin frien's?"

Whitey was almost sobbing.

"Thass why, 'cause we frien's," Ar'n said. The men were very silent, watching the big man whose eyes never left Whitey's face. Whitey was himself moaning, staring at Tireiron like a rabbit at a rattlesnake. Lowe Junior felt that something was going to happen. He wanted to leave, but did not want to call attention to himself. Besides he wanted to hear whatever it was Tireiron would say.

"No Ar'n, no Ar'n," Whitey whimpered.

"Sheddup. Yo' so damn bad. Now yo' kin jes' sheddup."

Tireiron's roar seemed to blow Whitey backwards from sheer volume. It was very hot and bright in the room. Whitey looking at Tireiron looking at Whitey. Lowe Junior felt as though he was stifling in the silence. Tireiron was like no one he had seen before. Purple coat. Sweat shining round head. Big tall and big fat, his voice just a deep rumble. Everyone silent. Whitey sorta rolling from side to side like he was slipping blows, but not moving.

"Ohyeah, ohyeah," Tireiron said, "here's whut happened. Hit wuz las' year, night o' the parade an' the big ballgame. Wuz a convention heah too, a big un. Which wuz hit again Whitey, seem to slip muh min'?"

"Not true a lie," Whitey said sullenly.

"Ohyeah hit wuz the Templars—yo' know, folks dress up sorta like the kluxers, but ain't the same? Wal, they wuz heah for some kinda meetin' and the hotel was full. Like now, only worse. Hit seem like evrah room had leas' two people who shoulda bin somewheres else and wit someone else. All kinda funny thangs happening. Lotsa drunk folks, lotsa calls for bootleg whiskey an' womens.

"Yeah, that's the kind o' time hit was. Wal, me an' ol' badass Whitey heah was sent up to do this dinner party. 'Bout twenty-fi thutty men, no women. We serve dinner, an' they was doin' some kin' a drinkin' too. We had jes' clear off the dinner things an' settin' up the bar fo' the after dinner drinkin' when the doer open and jes' whut yo' thank come in?"

Tireiron stopped. Took a drink. Looked at the men. Looked at Lowe Junior as if to say yo' hearin' this boy? Looked at Whitey and resumed.

"Yeah, ah wuz in the back o' the room an' off to the side afixin' up the bar, an' ol' Whitey heah wuz handin' out the drinks an' takin' orders. Then these two women come in. They sorta look like they wuz sisters; hot as it wuz they had on some long fur coats, could'a been rabbit or possum. Both with ginger-colored hair and real white with lotsa red stuff on they face. Tell the truth ah nevah studied them real close til they takes off the coats, 'cause they sho' din' have much on then. Ah wuzn't sho' what wuz comin' nex' but ah could guess. Ah kinda look outa the side o' mah eye to see how ol' Whitey wuz takin' hit, an' ah swear the nigger had done turned plumb white, his eye commenced to jerkin' same like hit doin' now. Ah kept lookin' fo' them men to member we wuz theah, and say we wuz to go, but it wuz like they plumb forgot evrahthang but them two gals. Ah even drop one of the empty whiskey bottles on the floor but hit pears like the only person in that room who hear it wuz Whitey, an' he nearly drop his little tray. But this time they playing some funnysoundin' music an' the gals call theyse'f dancin'. Ah tells yo' ah wuz sho' nuff asweatin' hit out, fo' fair. Ah wanted outta theah so bad, effen ah'd opened mah eye an' fin' thet I wuz back in the cotton fiel's at Parchman ah'd said Praise Jesus. An' them men. All thet ol' red whiskey was talkin' to 'em an' they wuz higher'n any ol' georgy pine. Some o' whut they wuz callin' to them gals man, shame any man that had a mothah. Yo' ain't *nevah* seed nothin' like hit. Uhhuh."

He shook his head and seemed lost in the memory.

"See, ah knowed ah wuz too big an' too black to hide in thet room. But ah figured bes' ah turn mah back to the whole thang. Ain't shame to say thet ah wuz watchin' hit though, in the little mirror on back o' the bar. Yassuh, ah wuz watchin' mighty close. Evrah time them drums would go 'rhudum, rhudum dum dum' an' them ol' ginger-haided gals roll they belly-skin an' shake they ass, muh heart gave a jerk. An', they *wuz* frisky too, bettah believe hit. Like they lean back, way back, moanin' an' shakin' them ol' fat hips, showin' all they got an' then some. Hit wuz a powerful bad feelin'; evrah time them gals give one o' them deep georgy roll an' them men give a shout ah'd be scared all over again. Wu'nt nothin' fo' hit, but to place mah trust in the whiskey—Lawd sho' couldn't he'p then, fact is *he* ain't supposed to be in a place like thet—an' hope thet them men wuz drunk nuff to forget me an' Whitey."

He paused and his big belly shook with soundless laughter. Whitey seemed in a trance.

"Ah wuz spyin' out the men kinda close too. One particular one. All evenin' he roun' an' roun' acheckin' this acheckin' thet. Want to know wuz the food alright, wuz the drinks alright an' like that. Like hit wuz his party. Big summabitch he wuz too, damn neah big as me."

"Oh gawd, Ar'n." Whitey's voice was very low.

The men shushed him.

"From way he talk, up in his nose an' kin' a high like he wuz from Georgy. An' ah wuz watchin' him, cause from the way he so concern that evrahthang be alright ah figured him to be sorta in charge. So ah wuz sorta watchin' him quiet like. His face were red from the gitgo but hit steady git redder an' redder. Seem like he breathin' so hard thet yo' could heah hit, an' the sweat jes' shinin' on thet ol' red face. He keep lookin' at the gals, an' at the mens to see how they takin' hit. He seem a mite worried. But hit din' seem like to me he had nothin' to fret 'bout. They wuz *a-w-l* lookin' an' lickin' they lips like they wuz dry, an' sweatin'.

"Fin'ly them gals din' have awn a livin' stitch o' nothin' but skin, *noplace,* an' them men jes' sittin' theah an' blowin' with they face up tight like they in pain. The big 'un ah bin tellin' yo' 'bout he sittin' theah, his eyes gittin' smaller an' smaller an' mean lookin'. Funny eyes he had too, sorta like they wuz wunst blue, an' were bleach out like ol' overhalls. . . ."

Lowe Junior wanted to leave. Yet he wanted to hear the end. And it seemed to him that the other men, even Whitey, were feeling the same way. They kept moving, muttering under their breath, but never interrupted Tireiron.

"Yo' know," he was saying, "lookin' back on hit ah believes some a them men wuz kin' a uneasy too. Way they keep studyin' each othah quiet-like, some lookin' to the door quick an' secret like . . . But anyways, all of a sudden. . . ."

Tireiron stopped and rubbed his eyes as though he were tired. He looked at Whitey a long time. Neither man spoke.

"Then whut?" Roosie asked.

Tireiron motioned him to silence.

"Yo' done started. May as well finish," Whitey said, " 'cause ah'm gon' kill yo' anyway."

"Shiyit," Tireiron said. "An' all of a sudden one o' the gals stop dancin' and start to cryin'. The othah one keep on dancin' an' sorta pull on the othah one, like 'come on' but she shake her off an' scream as to how she din' like the way Whitey wuz lookin' at her an' she nevah knowed she wuz to dance fo' no niggers. She pointin' straight at Whitey who holdin' the li'l silver tray like he tryin' to hide behind it, staring straight back at the gal like he freeze. All the time his eye jerkin' like hit doin' now, like his whole face tryin' to close up roun' the eye.

"Then it like them men seein' us fo' the fust time. Mad as hell but like they not quite sho' whut to be mad at. Some starin' at Whitey, some at me, an' some at each othah. Then the big red one he outta his chair an' holdin' Whitey up gains the wall.

" 'What the fuck yew starin' at Boy?'

"Po' Whitey stammer but cain't git nathin' out but,

" 'Ah'm, ah, ah, ah.'

" 'Ah say whut yew winkin' at. Yo' think the lady dancin' fer yew?'

"Whitey tryin' to say that he wu'nt lookin' or winkin' but he shakin' too bad. Two o' the younger men come rushin' up to the bar an' ah still doan know what they had a min' to do, 'cause ah stand there holdin' this bottle kin' a quiet like an' they sorta standin' fo' me. None o' us say nothin'.

" 'Yew callin' the lady a liar, Boy?' an pitch him up against the wall again. Then thisyer ol' man, he come up to the one that got Whitey an' say somethin' to him real low. He shake his head an' beller how he gonter 'barbecue the black bastid,' an' the ol' man say, 'Yew always wuz a damn fool Pritchard' and tell him to let Whitey go. An' some o' the others when they hear thet, they sorta pull Whitey away an' one a them shout,

" 'Leave him be, black sonnabitch done wet his pants anyhow.'

"An' sho' nuff there was Whitey with this big wet mark creepin' down his pant. Then they start to laugh. Me'n Whitey started out an' ain't nobody stop us. As we leavin' ah heard the ol' gentleman assayin' as how 'we must make amends to these ladies' and reachin' into his pocket. All the while we waitin' fo' them to leave Whitey cryin' an' mutterin' how he gon' kill all of 'em some day."

No one said anything. Lowe Junior finished dressing quickly. He felt a deep dull anger and shame. He wanted to be out of there but the thought of going upstairs made him sick. He wanted to say something to Whitey, but did not know what it was he wanted to say. He could see the anger and shame in the others. They were finishing changing their clothes, not talking save an occasional curse. Not looking at each other. Whitey stood glowering, looking quickly at the other men whenever they moved. No one would look at him.

"Hey Whitey, yo' wanna kill this?" It was Roosie approaching Whitey with his bottle. Whitey snatched it silently and drained it. Then he turned away from Roosie and began to pick up empty bottles from the floor. He threw the first one against the wall over Lowe Junior's head. Shards of glass whizzed past his ear. The next one broke a light and sparks and glass fragments rained down. He wasn't saying anything. He didn't seem to be aiming at anyone. Each exploding bottle made loud noises in the enclosed room.

"He gone plumb crazy," Lowe Junior thought, "he gon' kill someone sho'."

Everyone was still watching the bottles crash against the walls. The last bottle shattered against the metal door. Whitey lunged about looking for things to throw. Tireiron, face bleeding from a glass cut, moved very fast for such a huge man, his big fist catching Whitey on the side of the jaw once. It did not seem like a powerful blow to Lowe Junior but Whitey crumbled.

"What the hell's going on heah?" The hotel detective was standing in the doorway.

"Ah asked a question." He surveyed the broken glass, Whitey lying on the bench where Tireiron had placed him.

The white man took two steps into the room.

"Ah am not goin' to ask agin." He put his hand inside his coat and looked at each man in turn.

"Hey yew," he pointed to Tireiron, "what happened to thet boy?"

Faces hard, stubborn, sullen, the men looked at Tireiron. He said nothing, just stood wiping the blood from his cheek.

"Dammit Nigger, yo' deaf? Ah wanna know whut happened."

Tireiron rubbed his cheek, looking at the man, face impassive but his eyes hard.

"Oh lawd, Ar'n gon' kill him. Why'd thet white man have to come in heah now, callin' Ar'n outta his name like that. Lawd, git him outta heah," Lowe Junior thought.

"Yew gittin' smart with me Nigger?" There was silence, the men watching Tireiron for a sign. He was rigid, showing nothing.

"Who me?" Tireiron asked; then his face broke open suddenly. He seemed to slump, to loosen up, his eyes crinkled up with good humor, his teeth flashed white against his skin. He chuckled deep in his chest, his belly juggled.

"Din' know yo' was talkin' to me cap'n. He he, ain't nothin' rightly wrong with thetyer boy; ol' man whiskey done hit him kinda hard, hee hee."

He winked at the man.

"Me 'n the boys jes' gettin' ready to tidy the place up, ain't we boys?"

He laughed again.

"Was you niggers fighting? Yew sho' thet boy jes' drunk? Ah'm warnin' yew don't lie to me."

"Lawsy, he he, sho' now take more than a little moonshine to hurt a nigger, cap'n. Usses ain't gon' lie to yo' cap'n. Us jes' fixin' to clean up an' go. Ain't no need to fret yo'se'f. Nah suh."

The man was looking at Tireiron suspiciously when Whitey groaned and sat up.

"Yew, what's the mattah with yew?"

Whitey moaned and shook his head.

"Ah'm asking yew something boy."

Whitey saw him and his face fell with surprise.

"Sho' beats me, Boss," he said and smiled, "jes' sittin' heah an' next thing ah knows I'se stone asleep. Hee hee."

There was a chorus of laughter from the others.

"See, cap'n," Tireiron chortled, "Nigger jes' lighthaided." He slapped his thigh and guffawed.

"Niggers." The man laughed and shook his head. "See yo' clean this place up an' be out of heah in ten minutes. Yo' heah me?"

"Wal c'mon. Y'awl heerd the cap'n," Tireiron boomed, "whut yo' waitin' fo'?"

He started toward the broom, grinning.

*1966*

# On Politics

# The August 28th March on Washington

*The Castrated Giant*

THE now historical March on Washington for Jobs and Freedom was in many ways a social phenomenon that could have taken place, as the *Readers' Digest* is fond of saying, "only in the United States." The true significance of what happened in Washington on that day defies any simple definition. What *really* happened on the tortuous road that the March took to Washington will probably never be made public. This is unfortunate because somewhere along the twisting road that stretched between the first ideas for the March, and the abortion of those ideas that was finally delivered in Washington on August 28, lies the corpse of what could have been a real step forward in the struggle for Negro rights in this country.

It would be useful, especially to Negroes involved in this struggle, to know just who was responsible for what happened to the March, and to know what forces were at work, what kinds of pressures and bribes were tried and by whom. It would be important to know what deals were made, and who made them. Which of the many compromises were the results of inevitable social pressures, and which were forced by the power machinations of the Kennedy administration? Which decisions were sincere mistakes of timidity and of judgment, and which were deliberate attempts to reduce the whole operation to impotence? It would be useful to know, for example, what the real role of the middle-class Negro organizations was in this event, and whose interests they imagined themselves to be representing, and whose interests they did, in fact, end up representing. It would help to know these things, but for understandable reasons, the people who have the information that would indicate these things are silent. But there were some things that are public, like what happened—this the whole world saw, and some of these leaders *did* make public statements that said more than the words spoken.

On the day itself, as the far-flung tentacles of the sprawling organization that had materialized around the idea for the March came together, it was clear to observers that something significant was happening before their eyes. The nature of what was happening was not then, and is still not, clear. On the one hand, there was an undeniable grandeur and awesome-ness about the mighty river of humanity, more people than most of us will ever see again in one place, affirming in concert their faith in an idea, and in a hope that is just. And on the other, there was an air of grotesquery as in some kind of carnival where illusion is the stock-in-trade, an impression given sustenance by the huge green and white striped carnival tent and the hordes of hucksters peddling gaudy March pins, pennants, tassels, and similar items more readily associated with sporting events than with seri-ous social protest. It was a day of contrasts, a day of platitude and rhetoric juxtaposed with genuine passion and real anguish, a day of bitterness and disappointment for some, and of hope and inspiration for others.

One looked into the black face of a southern sharecropper, weathered and marked by privation, yet on this day filled with hope and pride, and the belief that a new day was indeed coming. Then one looked at his son, sixteen years old, fresh from the brutality of a southern jail, who did not need the abstractions about oppression and intimidation because his own body bore their marks, and one could not but share in the bitterness in his eyes. And if one looked from these two, to the small army of propagan-dists, wheeling cameras and masses of equipment around, intent on recording this day as some kind of triumph for the system that has op-pressed these people, one could not escape the feeling that somewhere there had occurred a subtle and terrible betrayal. Because, this day that had promised so much was too sweet, too contrived, and its spirit too amiable to represent anything of the bitterness that had brought the people there. And, while the goodwill and amiability of the marchers surmounted race and class and was a heartening thing, there was an overhanging atmosphere of complete political irrelevance.

As originally conceived, the March was to come as the climax of the most tumultuous summer of Negro militance in the history of the country, and was to have been the largest single demonstration of social discontent that this government had known.

When I heard the plan articulated for the first time, and it was still embryonic then, I was told that waves of nonviolent demonstrations of civil disobedience were planned to completely immobilize the Congress. The militant student group—the Student Nonviolent Coordinating Committee (SNCC)—was already thinking out stratagems to get huge numbers of demonstrators into the halls of Congress. This is forbidden by law, and the plan was to replace the demonstrators with another wave as soon as the first was removed, and to keep this up until the jails of Washington were filled. Simultaneous with this action there were to be sit-ins in the offices of the Justice Department protesting that agency's failure to protect the constitutional rights of Negroes in the South. Similar sit-ins were planned for the offices of certain politicians from southern states where the constitutional and legal rights of Negroes were being, and are now being, violated each day by local authorities as a matter of official policy. All these activities, which were to be done by the same people who were then manning the lines in demonstrations all over the country, were to be auxiliary to the huge body of the March which would break no laws, but would come to Congress and present to it a petition for the redress of three hundred years of wrongs. The civil disobedience aspect of the demonstrations were intended to dramatize the situation of the Negro: Negroes were there offering their bodies to the jails because in this country they *are* in a jail, because they are not citizens and are not really represented by Congress, because they have no voice in the decisions that govern their living and their dying, and because they have been traditionally and deliberately excluded from full participation in the social processes of the country in which they were born.

Civil disobedience was central. Laws are for those who make them, and who give their consent to them and are protected by them. On this basis, Americans, white and black, fought one revolution, and the Negroes, by symbolically defying the laws, as they have been doing in small communities throughout the South, were again affirming that "government without representation is tyranny." And the attack was to be directed to the seat of government as that is the symbol and residence of power and represents the entire system that persecutes us.

The goal was social dislocation without violence. This is the underlying technique that informs all direct action projects in the movement toward justice for America's disinherited blacks: it is one of rendering the institution under pressure inoperable by the presence of determined black bodies. When demonstrators descend on any establishment, the purpose is to so disrupt its functioning as a segregated institution that it will become non-functional and be forced to close and reopen on an integrated basis. So in one sense the demonstrations are aimed at destroying institutions that function unjustly, and replacing them by a different institution, in the sense that the same restaurant once integrated has become a new entity in terms of its function. This was not the idea for the March, since the goal was not to attempt a permanent dislocation of the Congress, but merely to use this kind of pressure for one day. This was in May, and planning was geared toward having this action during the congressional debate on the civil rights legislation that President Kennedy had decided to introduce, largely because of "Ole Miss" and Birmingham.

Certain questions were still to be resolved at this time. The penalty for disrupting the function of the Congress is a sentence of up to five years in jail. Could, from among the thousands of Negroes who were at that time involved in demonstrations all over the country, a sufficiently large number be found who were willing to risk this long sentence? Was it justifiable to ask them to do this? Where would the money come from to stage the kind of complicated and expensive legal battle that would be required to free these demonstrators afterwards? Would the authorities use force to break the demonstrations up? This is the pattern in the South, but not in Washington. But neither is it the pattern to allow demonstrations aimed at Congress. In 1961, when 120 students from Howard University attempted to picket on the steps of the Capitol, the police broke the demonstration up with the threat of the five-year sentence. On the other hand, there was a question of whether Kennedy would risk the kind of adverse publicity that would result if the demonstrators were forcibly removed from the halls of Congress. It has been this administration's posture abroad that it is committed to equality for all Americans. The reality is that it is committed to political expediency and to containing the Negro militance by conciliation. Would it have risked giving the lie to its official image by a picture on the front pages in Africa and Asia, showing ten resisting Negroes being dragged from the steps of the Capitol—the American symbol to the world of democracy and justice? The other alternative would be either to head off the March by making real concessions to Negro demands, or else to allow civil disobedience without any police action that might have triggered off violence. The demands of the March were to be:

"Full employment for all Americans of both races, and an appeal for a massive federal program to train all unemployed . . . in meaningful and dignified jobs at decent wages.

"Integration of all public schools by the end of this year.

"A federal fair employment practices law, outlawing all job discrimination.

"Passage of the Kennedy administration's legislative package . . . without compromise or filibuster."[1]

As it turns out, the administration was spared having to make this decision. I remember leaving the conversation where the original plan for the March was told to me. I said to my friend who was to play a central role in organizing the March, "I've told you that when the 'revolution' comes it will be the Negroes who begin it." This was a joke between us, but only partially so, because we were agreed that at the time when the Negro succeeded in forcing the power structure of this country into revising its practices and this society into amending its traditional attitude of exclusion and exploitation toward him, its effects would be so far-reaching and profound as to completely remake society. It is still my conviction that this is so, because no one can look at the deeply entrenched tradition of racial injustice in America and imagine that any gradual evolution of justice is possible. It will take traumatic action of various kinds to wrench society out of the deep channels of segregation in which it moves, and which causes this evil to re-create itself. Early this year, a group of Negro students was told by a Negro official of the federal government that the latter could do nothing to enforce fair employment on one of its contracts, because the kind of extreme action that this would require in the face of the long

1   The latter is particularly interesting, since this legislation has had an unusual history. Kennedy called it the "most pressing business" of the Congress during the summer's racial turmoil. He recently made the statement that his tax cut is the most necessary, and now that the demonstrations have slowed down, and the polls say that white opinion is that the Negro "is pushing too fast," he and his brother Bobby have indicated that the civil rights legislation needs to be "watered down" to ensure that it is passed. A strong bill at this point would not pass they say; what is already an inadequate bill must be further diluted. It is not difficult to see where the two Kennedys are looking—at the presidential elections of '64.

Yet despite this clear betrayal, Kennedy is still supported by his favorite "responsible" Negro leaders. Roy Wilkins and Whitney Young came out this week with statements that sounded alarmingly like Kennedy's, and as though they were saying that the Negro was pushing too hard. It is not difficult to understand why Malcolm X calls Wilkins "Kennedy's Nigger."

history of exclusion would disrupt too many of the established socio-economic patterns and affront too many powerful groups within the society. That bureaucrat really meant that the federal government *could* take this action, but that it *would* not. But this illustrates why any meaningful integration of the Negro will be accompanied by social tension, chaos, and will result in the restructuring of the extant social patterns. In this sense it will be "revolutionary" in the deepest sense of that term.

Every Negro leader, except Roy Wilkins and Whitney Young, who has felt the burden of this systematic cultural policy of exclusion, knows that he cannot integrate into this society but into a new and decent one that will have to be created from energy that must be initiated by the Negro people. For this reason, the language of every Negro leader, even those that are incredibly conservative on all other political issues, is couched in the idiom of revolution whenever he talks about integration.

Minister Malcolm X, the fiery and witty leader of the Black Muslim movement, which bases much of its social ideology on the impossibility and undesirability of integration and appeals for complete separation, sums up the totality of the Negro's exclusion in these terms: "Martin Luther King says that we are second-class citizens. That is not true, we are not citizens at all. The fact that we were here before 1776, and that we are born here does not make us citizens. A cat can have kittens in an oven, but does that mean that they are biscuits?"

It was this entrenchment of discrimination that led me to speak in terms of the "revolution." And this is why I favored, and still do favor, the tactic of disobedience to the civil law on the March, and the use of aggressive nonviolence. If these original plans had not been abandoned, a crisis might have been forced. The mere threat of using five thousand veteran demonstrators who had known jails and police brutality from demonstrations in cities like New York, Birmingham (Alabama), Cambridge (Maryland), and Danville (Virginia), and Negroes from the Deep South where the state quite literally represents a monopoly of violence against the Negro, may well have been enough to pry some action from a reluctant Congress. The history of the United States Congress over the last one hundred years is a history of racism. It has never acted in the interests of the Negro unless it was forced into doing so by political pressure. Like any other institution, its reactions are geared to practical considerations and self-interest and not moral imperatives; therefore, its actions tend to ride on the coattails of public opinion, which means in this country, white opinion and national prejudice. As a body, it will do nothing for the Negro that is likely to move against the mainstream of social momentum. This unwillingness to act for integration is compounded by the structuring of that body, which places southern politicians, who represent areas in which Negroes are effectively disenfranchised, at the head of influential parliamentary committees. Thus Congress is in great measure controlled by men who derive their power from segregation and to whom integration on a political level means the end of the system that brought them to power. The presence of these "Dixiecrats" in the Democratic party, and the essentially schizophrenic and bastard nature of that party within which an allegedly liberal president must live with the most reactionary forces in this country, is one more indication why the Negroes' posture toward the political establishment must be one of attack. It also indicates why no meaningful legislation can be induced out of a Congress with its present political composition, and why the March was originally conceived not as an appeal to conscience, but as an expression of strength.

Such a demonstration as was outlined would not have attracted anything like the 250,000 people who attended on August 28, but there can be no doubt that it would have received widespread support. This was the Negro mood at that time. Newspapers and TV news programs were filled with the story of the "Negro uprising." Demonstrations were erupting in the streets of cities across the nation, North and South. Within a period of two weeks after the March was first mentioned to me, upheavals were recorded in cities as far apart as Albany and Americus in Georgia, Greenwood, Goldsboro, Jackson, and Oxford in Mississippi, and in cities in Florida, Alabama, Louisiana, the Carolinas, California, and the "border" states of Virginia and Maryland. Before the summer was over, outbreaks of varying degrees of violence were to shatter the northern complacency of cities like Chicago, Philadelphia, New York, and Boston.

In Cambridge, Maryland, some of the most critical confrontations took place, and the possibility of a racial war was sufficiently present to warrant the imposition of martial law. In Danville, Virginia, the tactics used by police to break up nonviolent demonstrations were more savage than in Birmingham. On the 10th of June, of sixty-four demonstrators, forty required medical attention after club-wielding police and deputized garbage collectors followed blasts of water poured from fire hoses into the group, clubbing women and children indiscriminately and strewing the street with bloody, soaked bodies. One result of this was that three days later, the demonstrations included 250 Negroes. These two instances illustrate the all-pervading nature of the oppression of Negroes here. I chose them because they are both located within a few hours drive of Washington, D.C., but similar instances of this nature can be found all over the land.

After the much-publicized Birmingham demonstrations, the Negro mood hardened perceptively and became more abrasive and determined. There was more bitterness and less patience; there were also more demonstrations. On these mornings, a glance through the newspapers, which generally subdue their reports of racial unrest, revealed that Negroes, like the spring, "were breaking out all over." Even from the relatively neutral reports, it was evident that the mood of these demonstrations was changing. Incidents of Negroes facing up to the police and to white mobs were more frequent. In the streets, the bars, the homes, the churches, the mood ebony was clearly one of indignation and open anger. The landlady of a friend of mine, a lady of some sixty-five years, and up until then, a veritable stereotype of the respectable, religious, and passive older generation of lower-middle-class Negro, began to seriously investigate the possibilities of purchasing a revolver.

This new mood did not escape the white press, nor did the politicians miss it either. Great concern was expressed about the possibility of a major race riot, or a series of race riots sweeping the country.

President Kennedy had publicly affirmed the right of peaceful demonstrations earlier in the spring. Now, moved as much by the southern and conservative charges that he was encouraging anarchy, as by the possibility that the Negro people would retaliate in kind to their attackers, he took the position that, although legal, demonstrations were irresponsible and that Negroes should return their battle to the arena of the courts, which was, among other things, less visible. The position of the student demonstrators was that there was nothing to be gained by keeping the illusion of "peace." There is no real peace where there is no justice, and the white man's peace is for us a slave's peace. The demonstrations did not stop.

In this position Kennedy was supported by the National Association for the Advancement of Colored People (NAACP), whose national secretary, Roy Wilkins, publicly questioned the effectiveness of street demonstrations. There are two important considerations which militate against this position. One, the simple fact that the white establishment's wish to stop demonstrations is the best possible brief for their continuance; if it becomes sufficiently threatened, it will remove the causes of the demonstrations. The other factor is that discrimination does not exist because of any absence of law affirming Negro rights. It exists, in spite of such laws and the Constitution, because the federal administration *has never acted to enforce these laws* which are blatantly broken and ignored, unless some kind of crisis seems imminent. Therefore, it is not more laws that are needed, but more pressure.

The 1954 Supreme Court decision on segregated schools directed the integration of the entire school system "with all deliberate speed." Nearly ten years later, there has been little more than token observance of this ruling in the South. One answer is direct action, and even with the schools this is possible. In Englewood, New Jersey, Negro parents took their children out of the Negro kindergarten and into the white school where the children had not been permitted to enroll. The teachers attempted to ignore these illegal infiltrators, but the white infants did not, and after three days the teachers found it simpler to include the "demonstrators" in the class activities. In Boston, Negro citizens set up "freedom schools," and withdrew thousands of Negro children from the official high schools in protest of the inferior facilities given to Negroes. The "freedom schools" included in their curriculum classes in the theory of civil disobedience, social responsibility, and Negro history. The Boston school system hastily came to terms with the Negro community.

The plans for this March were evolved by Bayard Rustin, a Negro militant and pacifist; Tom Kahn, a white student in a Negro university who was a young man with a long history of civil rights activities, and Norman Hill, an executive of the Congress on Racial Equality (CORE), a militant direct action group.

Rustin is one of the most colorful characters in the civil rights movement. In addition to being an astute tactician, and extremely politically sophisticated, he is one of the few real intellectuals that is active. He is essentially not a "leader" figure, but there is no one person who has had more direct effect in defining the direction that the struggle has taken in recent years. He was executive assistant to A. Philip Randolph in planning the March on Washington for the integration of war industries during World War II. He was Martin Luther King's adviser during the Montgomery bus boycott, the director of the Youth March on Washington for integrated schools in 1954, and has organized nonviolent demonstrations in Tanganyika and in England, and, three years ago, led a party of Africans into the Sahara in protest against French nuclear bomb tests. One of the reasons that he is not a publicly acknowledged leader in this struggle—and this does not speak too well of the courage of existing groups—is his association with the American Communist party during the depression, but he is certainly the person with the most realistically radical approach to the struggle, and one of the few adult voices that the students in the struggle respect and will listen to. Another such person is the novelist James Baldwin.

Main opposition to Rustin as organizer of the March came from Roy

Wilkins of the NAACP, that huge, middle-class based and essentially conservative Negro organization. Wilkins is the "Negro leader" most appreci-
ated by the middle-class Negro and white liberal community as being
"responsible." He is roundly rejected by the students as a tool of the white
power structure. It is difficult to understand how anyone can be naïve
or nearsighted enough to demand sweeping changes in the area of Negro
rights, in a country where any meaningful demand on behalf of the Negro
is radical and yet hold conservative attitudes toward all other areas of
society.

When I left Washington in June, the plans for the March were not yet
made public, and it was my understanding that the first steps were already
under way. A. Philip Randolph was approached, and was willing to call on
the other five civil rights groups to participate. Since the appeal was for
jobs and freedom, it was felt that organized labor should be involved.

Martin Luther King's Southern Christian Leadership Conference
(SCLC), which had spearheaded the Birmingham demonstrations, committed itself to the idea eagerly. CORE, another militant organization, and
the one responsible for the 1961 Freedom Rides, and the Student Nonviolent Coordinating Committee, which is a student organization which spe-
cializes in working only in the deepest South, were also eager to support
the March in its unadulterated form. However, the heads of the NAACP
and the Urban League, the two most affluent of the civil rights organizations, withheld their support on the basis that it did not appear to be worth
the effort or the money. It should be pointed out that the support of these
two organizations was considered essential for reasons of politics and
finance.

From this point on, the March plans were subjected to the bewildering
succession of changes, disputes, and distortions that resulted in the final
fiasco that took place on August 28. One meeting of these leaders was described to me in these terms: "Well, we finally pinned Wilkins (of the
NAACP) down and finally wrung a commitment from him." By this time
he had held up the campaign for several weeks, but the support of the
NAACP and the Urban League was on the condition that civil disobedience
be abandoned. The first compromise was made: there were to be no sit-ins,
pickets, or aggressive activity of any kind. The next issue was a strong
objection to Rustin as the deputy organizer. Randolph and King were adamant on this point, and Rustin's services were retained.

My next information was to the effect that although the March was not
officially announced, the Kennedys knew about it, and it was in the wind
that the administration was against it. The committee was having diffi-

culty getting support or money. "You would be surprised," my informant concluded, "how liberal doors close in your face when Kennedy is opposed to a project." Shortly thereafter, there was a public announcement, and Kennedy publicly disapproved of the idea. A Negro clergyman in New York declared that there were going to be "massive acts of civil disobedience, prostrate bodies on streets and airport runways and railroad tracks, massive and monumental sit-ins at the Congress." The white community was unanimously horrified. It then became a matter of public discussion that SNCC and CORE were preparing for "nonviolent civil disobedience, all day sit-ins at the Justice Department, in Senator Eastland's (of Mississippi) office and in the Congress." The country's reaction was, as nearly as I could observe, one of apprehension, if not open fear. The events of the spring and early summer, especially those in Birmingham, had convinced them that the Negro community was about ready to retaliate in kind. Bloodbaths were predicted, should the March take place.

The Committee for the March, and the leaders of the Urban League and NAACP singly denied any plans for direct action, and CORE and SNCC were chastised for "irresponsibility." I was told that "the Kennedy administration was putting up unbelievable opposition," and that administration maneuvering was "fantastic." I was not told, nor did I ask, the nature of this opposition. However, after the official rejection of any kind of civil disobedience, public opinion began to veer. The entire idea of the March was no longer condemned as un-American, and groups not normally active in the Negro cause began to hint at support. Liberal columnists began to remember that the Negro had the force of morality and a history of persecution behind him. But the powerful labor federation, the AFL-CIO, still refused, and never came out in support.

Shortly thereafter, the announcement came of the rerouting of the March. Instead of going to the Capitol legally and petitioning Congress, the March would now proceed from the Washington Monument to the Lincoln Memorial and listen to the speeches of the leaders. The leaders alone would *visit* the politicians. Plans to include two unemployed Negroes in the meeting with the president were quietly forgotten. I do not know that they were ever officially changed, but I do know that no unemployed persons made that visit.

With this new announcement, President Kennedy underwent a sudden and dramatic change of heart, and publicly welcomed the March as an expression of support for the legislation that the events of the summer had convinced him to introduce. From this point on, the March became more of an expression of faith in the Kennedy administration. The changing of the route had guaranteed that the whole proceedings would be as unobtrusive as possible and that it could be isolated to one small and relatively unimportant section of Washington.

It was the second week of August before I was able to get to New York. Despite severe doubts about having anything to do with this March, I found myself being pulled, possibly by curiosity, to its headquarters. There the truth of the assertion that "Americans Love a Parade" was made evident. There was great willingness to support the project. The phones buzzed with supporters of this "social revolution" to complain "that the bus that my bridge club has chartered has no air conditioning" or that "our buses have no reclining seats." One group wanted to know if they could carry signs bearing talmudic inscriptions and whether their leader could make a speech or see the president. Others wanted to know if they would lose a day's pay by attending. . . .

In the New York headquarters, I found many students whom I knew. Their attitude was one of expectant excitement. They were all veterans of the struggle; most had prison records as a result, and were sufficiently aware as to have few illusions about what their relationship as young Negroes was to their environment. Knowing this, I had difficulty determining how they could lend their support to what the project had become. That question is still largely unanswered, but I suspect that the answer has much to do with a personal loyalty to Rustin, and the manner in which any activity can generate around itself a force and an energy that completely immerses anyone who is in too close proximity to it. For those students, the problem became one of obtaining six more buses, trying to get a train, or getting letters out, and in the solution of these individual problems, the validity of their total meaning passed unnoticed.

The scene at Washington's March headquarters ranged between irony and absurdity. The entire town buzzed with activity and speculation; the newspapers were filled with little else. In the office, the volunteers of both races, by some queer coincidence, became divided into what appeared to be racial groupings, whites to the North, Negroes to the South. This proved to be the result of coincidence and a personality conflict between two organizers, rather than any racial tension.

Quite obviously, the March was the best thing that had happened to private enterprise and small business in Washington. Three days before the event, private entrepreneurs started selling the March pins, pennants, and other assorted souvenirs that they had had the foresight to have made. It was a triumph of American ingenuity, and I calculate that the March Committee lost many thousands of dollars to these opportunists who undersold the official March prices for these items.

Very clearly, the agents of the government were under orders to co-operate with the workers. One student volunteer—Stokely Carmichael—received a traffic ticket while driving a "March" car; the police captain promptly tore the ticket up. This apparently insignificant incident represents a fraudulent inversion of normalcy which can be understood if you know that the student had seen a companion assaulted two months before by a Washington policeman when they protested against brutality in the arrest of a Negro. He was arrested off a picket line a week before in Washington because of the "intimidating" nature of the sign he carried.

The cooperation of various groups was, to say the least, surprising. Huge, luxurious, and air-conditioned cars were loaned to the committee. Two of these came from a firm that had been picketed by CORE that summer because of alleged discrimination in their hiring policy. So much sweetness was generated, in fact, that one woman's conscience was moved. She wanted to help, although her attitudes toward Negroes had not been of the best in the past. She had this huge house so she decided that she'd take in marchers. She phoned the housing committee: "Yes, that's right. I can give housing to twenty marchers. Yes, that's right, twenty. Anything to help a good cause. But, one thing . . . would you please see that you only send me white marchers please?"

But it was most nauseating at the headquarters tent that was pitched by the Washington Monument. White tourists forsook the tour of the monument to photograph and gape at the volunteers at work making signs. The government photographers shot miles of film; they often interrupted the work to pose the volunteers, so as to "integrate" the work teams. "Now smile," they said, "this is going to Africa." So it happened that Negro students from the South, some of whom had still unhealed bruises from the electric cattle prods which southern police use to break up demonstrations, were recorded for the screens of the world portraying "American Democracy at Work."

The sweetness and light was so all-pervading, and the smiling official faces so numerous, that one student volunteer remarked to me: "It's incredible! Look how cooperative they are. When the 'revolution' comes, the government will be cooperating with the revolutionaries."

He was wrong. Whenever it appears that Negroes are about to change the shape of things, and to effect a more equitable distribution of power and privilege—and this is what any kind of Negro freedom in America will require—the real racism will emerge in the form of guns, clubs, police dogs, and the violent suppression that happened in Danville and Birmingham. The March no longer had pretentions of doing that. However, amid this ocean of goodwill, one or two local whites maintained their perspectives. On the night of the 26, the telephone cables into the headquarters tent were cut. On the morning of the 28, some of the buses en route to the demonstration were stoned. The American Nazi party contributed their usual racial abuse until one of their number was arrested. On that morning, a young Virginian was arrested while driving toward the crowd, carrying a sawed-off shotgun. One was almost grateful to these people for reaffirming reality.

Little needs to be said of the events of the day itself. One white marcher gave this account:

"From the headquarters tent they began passing out the placards. They must have had ten thousand of them all neatly lithographed, each bearing one of five officially approved slogans such as 'We March For Jobs For All.' 'If you want a sign please step up,' said a young woman, and the people who had come so far stepped up and were given their officially approved signs.

" 'Do you want a program?' asked a busy lady in white, and she made sure that the people who had come so far each had a mimeographed program, showing them which way to march, and telling them how to behave properly.

"And afterwards, through the long hot afternoon, we stood in front of the stolid Memorial while they sang at us and spoke to us of equality and justice; all, it seemed, in officially approved words. And through diligent organization and scrupulous planning, they managed to stage a mass protest against injustice *without offending anyone.*

"I suppose that this is necessary, but I am sad. I had high hopes and I came away sad. I find it sad to live in a society where a man demanding individual freedom must march into battle carrying a mimeographed map, and under a lithographed banner showing an officially approved slogan. And, I feel deeply, that in some way I don't fully understand, the people who had come so far had been betrayed."

These are sentiments that are quite understandable, but suppose the writer instead of being a white Californian, had been a Negro student out of a Mississippi jail? There are two events from the day that are illustrative. James Lee Pruitt is an eighteen-year-old Mississippi Negro. He worked on voter registration for SNCC; his job was to organize Negroes to make the attempt to register. It is dangerous and frustrating work. One student, Jimmy Lee, was shot in Mississippi for doing this two years ago. At the March, Pruitt was stopped by one of the marshals whom the committee had provided to keep the peace.

"Has that sign been approved?" asked the marshal.

"It's my sign," Pruitt said.

He was led silently to the chief marshal for judgment to be passed on his sign which simply said "STOP CRIMINAL PROSECUTIONS OF VOTER REGISTRATION WORKERS IN MISSISSIPPI." This was something that young Pruitt understood since he had recently spent four months in a five by eight foot cell along with fourteen other SNCC workers. In jail they had been kept without any clothes for forty-seven days, and had the fans trained on their small cell. Pruitt had been placed into a tiny zinc cubicle set in the Mississippi sun until he passed out after twelve hours, with a reported temperature of 104 degrees. When one of the group fell ill and the services of a doctor were requested, the guard said only, "Sure, Nigger, after you are dead."

During his trip to Washington to carry that sign, the car that he was traveling in developed mechanical trouble. No garage in the town would touch the car and it had to be abandoned. Pruitt was one of those who "had come so far" and at great price. It could not have been much consolation to him that the chief marshal, after hearing his story, decided that he had a right to carry the unofficial sign. And this story, while extreme, is symbolic of a great many who had come a long way and at great sacrifice, whose stories were not told and whose anguish was not expressed on that day. There is a small footnote to the Pruitt story. Yesterday, November 15, I heard from a SNCC field secretary that Pruitt was again in Parchman Farm, the Mississippi penal farm of folk song and legend.

The other story concerns another young Negro whose name is John Henry Lewis. He is the twenty-five-year-old national chairman of SNCC, the outfit to which Pruitt belongs. He has been arrested in the South more than twenty-five times and the day of the March was one of the few times that I have seen him without some kind of bandage on his head. He was listed on the "mimeographed program" as a speaker, and, when he spoke, he would tell some of the truth, and at least the stories of the Pruitts would be heard. Of this we were sure.

However, a copy of his speech was seen by the Catholic archbishop of Washington, Patrick O'Boyle, who decided that the speech was "inflammatory" and refused to give the invocation unless it was revised. Over the strong objections of Lewis, supported by Rustin, pressure of the other leaders carried the day and the speech was changed. The final chapter in irrelevance was written. The people who had come so far were to get dreams and visions and rhetoric. Here is some of what Lewis was to have said:

> Listen, Mr. Kennedy! Listen, Mr. Congressman! Listen Fellow Citizens!
> The black masses are on the march for freedom and for jobs. We will march

through the South, through the heart of Dixie, the way Sherman did . . . we
shall pursue our own scorched earth policy.

We shall take matters into our own hands to create a new source of power
outside of any national structure, to splinter the segregated South into
thousands of pieces and put the pieces back in the image of democracy.

So there is much to be sad about as regards the magnificent abortion of
August 28. It is sad that at the end of so much activity, the best and worst
that could be said is that "it was orderly and no one was offended." It is
much sadder and a little obscene that if anyone gained from the day's
activity it was the U.S. Department of State which converted the proceedings into a great propaganda victory. When the Telestar broadcast of the
March was suddenly and inexplicably canceled by Russian TV, this was
hailed by the American press and by the State Department as evidence that
the "Russians were afraid to show their people this example of democracy
in action." But even if this is true, who does this help? Could they not
afford to allow their people to see this mammoth crowd of "free" people in
a "free society" petitioning their government for the redress of wrongs?
No explanation has been offered as to why a free people should need to
march for freedom, or why, if the government is really theirs—i.e., really
represents them—it has made no move to redress these wrongs. This
exploitation of so many angry and sincere people, whose indignation was
misrepresented as some kind of testimonial for the system that had oppressed them, and against which they were protesting, must qualify as one
of the greatest and most shameless manipulations of recent years.

But the real political waste was that the March became a symbol and
a focal point in the minds of Negroes during this explosive summer of our
discontent, and in many communities where the Negro temper was right,
and where there had begun meaningful protest activity, the militants were
diverted into mobilization for the March. In one community the local student group was told in June that the most important activity they could
undertake was to make the March preparations their summer project. This
was before the emasculation process had begun, and these students decided to set aside their local program and to work toward this end. This
happened in too many areas; local action slowed down, and we all looked
to Washington for the climax that never came. In this way, much energy
and much anger were wasted on the spectacular. Ironically, what was to
have been our day of protest served a similar function to the "bread and
circuses" of the Roman emperors—it drained the anger of our people into
irrelevant channels.

*1964*

## POSTSCRIPT

Like most Americans, I watched the event on television. A group of activist students—
SNCC folk mostly—had been, by default and accident, left in possession of the headquarters
tent when the March began spontaneously without the leadership. There being no possible
way to stop that sea of humanity, the assembled dignitaries had to scramble rather un-
ceremoniously to overtake the masses they perceived themselves to be leading. A spectacle we
found symbolically appropriate and funny.

Because we had just learned of the sanitizing of John's speech, as it turns out, for remarks
critical of the Kennedy administration's civil rights agenda, our mood was not celebratory.
Which is why we were quite ungracious when a messenger appeared with several large boxes
of leis sent by sympathizers in Hawaii. The refrigerated garlands were accompanied by a message of heartfelt support and the hope that the leaders on the platform would wear them.

It was a touching gesture of solidarity, but in that moment it seemed entirely too festive.
Besides which none of us, even were it possible, was in the mood to chase after those leaders to
festoon them with the petals of orchids. So far as I know, the present was never acknowledged
and the donors, watching from Hawaii, never saw their gifts on TV, nor learned what happened to them. (If they looked closely when the camera panned the crowd, they *may* have
noticed that a number of attractive young women and some small children were indeed
bedecked with bands of orchids.)

When the telecast began, the mood in the tent was mixed. We were respectful when the
venerable A. Phillip Randolph opened the program. "We are gathered here in the largest
popular demonstration in the history of this nation . . . we are not an organization . . . not
a pressure group . . . we are not a mob. We are the advance guard of a moral revolution. . . ."

But with each succeeding speaker, the mood in the headquarters tent grew grimmer and
more sullen, all the more so because of the inescapable and confusing ambivalence we all
felt—our deep-seated sense of co-optation and irrelevance in conflict with the sheer numbers
and unprecedented size of the operation. So we hid our confused anger behind a screen
of sarcasm. We mocked and jeered the "bullshit and rhetoric" so roundly that the few
journalists who wandered in in search of "background" seemed visibly surprised and left
hurriedly. Clearly they had expected jubilation.

Then something unforgettable happened. Martin Luther King, Jr., began to talk. We
greeted him with crude witticisms about "De Lawd." Then that rich, resonant voice asserted
itself and despite ourselves we became quiet. About half-way through as image built on stirring image, the voice took on a ringing authority and established its lyrical and rhythmic
cadence that was strangely compelling and hypnotic. Somewhere in the artful repetitions of
the "Let Freedom Ring" series, we began—despite our stubborn, intemperate hearts—to
grunt punctuations to each pause. "Ahmen, Waal, Ahhuh."

By the time the oration triumphantly swept into its closing movement—an expression of
faith and moral and political possibility, delivered in the exquisite phrasing and timing of the
black preacher's art—we were transformed. We were on our feet, laughing, shouting, slapping palms, hugging, and not an eye was dry. What happened that afternoon in that tent was
the most extraordinary, sudden, and total transformation of mood I have ever witnessed.

Then drowning the electronic sound from the set, like an eerie counterpoint, came the
booming, indescribably deep and visceral roar of the real crowd—some 250,000 souls—half
a mile away.

Seventeen days later, after I had mailed off the above, four young girls in Sunday school
were murdered when their church was bombed. Two months later, in Dallas, Texas, John F.
Kennedy was gunned down.—*M. T. (1986)*

# Fish Are Jumping an' the Cotton Is High

*Notes from the Mississippi Delta*  ■ ■ ■ ■ ■

THERE is an immense mural in the Hinds County Courthouse in Jackson, Mississippi. On the wall behind the judge's bench is this mansion. White, gracefully colonnaded in a vaguely classical style, it overlooks vast fields, white with cotton which rows of darkies are busily (and no doubt, happily) picking. In the foreground to the left stands a family. The man is tall, well-proportioned, with a kind of benevolent nobility shining from his handsome Anglo-Saxon face. He is immaculate in white linen and a planter's stetson as he gallantly supports his wife, who is the spirit of demure grace and elegance in her lace-trimmed gown. To the right, somewhat in the background to be sure, stands a buxom, grinning, handkerchief-headed Aunt Jemima, everyone's good-humored black Mammy. In this mural, progress is represented by a work gang of Negroes, building, under the direction of a white overseer, what appears to be an addition to the great house. Although this painting is not wired for sound—a concession, one imagines, to the dignity of the court—it requires little imagination to hear the soothing, homey sound of a spiritual wafting on the gentle wind from the cotton fields. The general tone is certainly one of orderly industry, stability, and a general contentment. "Take a good look at them," Len Holt, a Negro lawyer said to me, "because they are the last happy darkies you are likely to see here."[1]

Actually this mural is so inept in technique and execution, that at first flush one is inclined to mistake it for parody. But Mississippians, especially the politicians, have never demonstrated the sense of security or humor that would permit them consciously to parody themselves, although they seem incapable of escaping self-parody in their public utterances. That this mural, consciously or not, is a burlesque of a parody of a stereotype which has never had historical or social reality goes without saying, but the mere fact that the mural exists and is intended to be taken seriously, or at least with a straight face, is equally important. Because, despite the fact that the Deep South is an area of as vast geographic, economic, and even sociological differentiation as any region in the nation, it is this plantation image of the South that persists in the sentimental subconscious of the American popular imagination. It is this image, or some derivative of it, that people tend to see when the Deep South is mentioned.

In point of fact, the area in which the huge cotton plantations of *Gone With The Wind* popular fame existed, and to an extent still do, is limited to a relatively small, specific geographic region. This is a narrow band of very level, fertile black earth which runs erratically south, then west from the bottom of Virginia through parts of the Carolinas, central Alabama, picks up in southwest Georgia, and runs through northwestern Mississippi and into Arkansas. This very generally describes the region known as the "Black Belt," where the institutional replacements of the huge antebellum plantations exist, and where the descendants of the slaves still greatly outnumber the descendants of their masters, and where the relationship between these two groups shows only a superficial formal change. In Mississippi, this area is called the Delta, a term which, in its precise geographic meaning, refers only to the wedge of land between the Mississippi and Yazoo Rivers, but which extends in popular usage to most of the northwestern quarter of the state. The area of the Delta coincides almost exactly with the Second Congressional District of Mississippi, the home of Senator Eastland, the Citizens' Council, and of the densest population of Negroes in the state. It is here, were it to exist anywhere, that one would find the image of the mural translated into reality.

1 Len Holt—the legendary "snake doctor"—is a brilliant and fearless young lawyer who is one of the few black lawyers handling civil rights cases in the state. He is greatly admired for his courtroom style, which is proud, abrasive, and uncompromising toward expressions of racism from officers of the Mississippi courts.

■

What can be said about this place that will express the impact of a land so surrealistic and monotonous in its flatness that it appears unnatural, even menacing? Faulkner comes close to expressing the physical impact of the region: "... *Crossing the last hill, at the foot of which the rich unbroken alluvial flatness began as the sea began, at the base of its cliffs, dissolving away in the unhurried rain as the sea itself would dissolve away."*

This description suggests the dominant quality: a flatness like an ocean of land, but within that vast flatness, a sense of confinement, a negation of distance and space that the sea does not have. And there are the rivers—in the east the headwaters of the river called Big Black, and sluggish tributaries, the Skuna, Yalabusha, and Yacona, which flow into the Tallahatchie, which in turn meets the Sunflower to become the Yazoo which was called by the Indians "the river of the dead." The Yazoo flows south and west until it meets the Mississippi at the city of Vicksburg. These rivers are, in Faulkner's words, "... *thick, black, slow, unsunned streams almost without current, which once each year ceased to flow at all, then reversed, spreading, drowning the rich land and subsiding again leaving it even richer."*

I once entered the Delta from the west, from Arkansas, over a long, narrow old bridge that seemed to go for miles over the wide and uncertain Mississippi. It was midsummer and a heat that seemed independent of the sun rose from the land. The slightest indentation in the road's surface became a shimmering sheet of water that disappeared as you approached it. The numbing repetition of cotton fields blurring in the distance wore on one's nerves and perceptions. This has been called the richest agricultural soil in the world. So it may have been, but it also is tough and demanding— no longer boundlessly fecund, it now yields its fruits only after exacting disproportionate prices in human sweat and effort. An old man told me, "for every man it enriches it kills fifty," and some folks joke that "the Delta will wear out a mule in five years, a white man in ten, and a nigger in fifteen."

For long stretches of highway where the fields are unbroken by any structure or sign of habitation, one might be in another century, except that a few things serve to place you in time. Even if tractors are not visible they are suggested by the certainty that there could not be, no, not in all the Southland, enough Negroes and mules to have planted all this. And there are the airplanes. On smooth strips next to the cotton, these toylike little craft, fragile and buoyant as children's kites, are tethered to the ground.

The gentlest wind causes them to rear and buck against their moorings like colts. At times they are seen at absurdly low levels, skimming the top of the crops they are "dusting" against the boll weevil. They are used increasingly on the large plantations. One pilot, unnecessarily reckless, you think, crosses the highway *underneath* the telegraph wires and directly over your car. You remember, in that moment, the outdoor rally in Indianola that was bombed from one of these planes one night.

The billboards along the highway are also indexes, not only of time but of place. They exhort you to support your Citizens' Council, to save America by impeaching Earl Warren, and challenge you to deny that "In Your Heart, You Know He is Right." "KILLS 'EM FAST, KEEPS 'EM DYING" is the message of another, and it is only when you are nearly abreast of the sign that the small print reveals that an insecticide is being advertised, and nothing larger than a boll weevil is the proposed victim.

But the combination of plane and grisly advertisement reminds you of a report from Panola County, in the heart of the Delta. The SNCC worker who wrote the report is distressed by the fact that many small Negro children in that area are plagued by running, chancrelike sores on their faces or limbs. These lingering and persistent ulcers are attributed by the community to a side effect of the "pizen" sprayed on the cotton. Children of all ages pick cotton in the Delta, and apparently this insecticide enters any exposed break in the skin and eats away at the flesh like an acid. "What can we do," the report asks, "isn't there some law. . . ?" Perhaps, you think, it may be this particular brand of pesticide that "keeps 'em dying."

This is "The Heart of Dixie"—as numerous signs proclaim—the very center of the myth and the image, but what is its reality? For you right now, its only reality is heat, and an almost unbearable cumulative discomfort, sweat burning your eyes, oven blasts of dusty air when you open the window, the metal edge of the window that keeps scorching your arm, and all around a punitive white glare that is painful to look into.

For the SNCC workers who are your companions the reality seems to be a certain tense caution. They work the Delta and know the road, but in curious terms. Their knowledge is of the condition of the jail, idiosyncrasies of the lawmen, and the make, model, and color of the cars they drive. They choose a route, not necessarily the most direct, but one that avoids certain towns and the jurisdictions of certain local officers. They watch the background intently for the car that may be the sheriff, the highway patrol, or one of the new radio-equipped prowl cars of the Klan. A car or pickup truck filled with youngish white men, stripped of license tags, is always ominous, especially if they keep passing and inspecting your car. Often, because it is legal to carry openly displayed weapons here, the cars will be fitted with racks on which rifles and shotguns are conspicuous. This should not suggest that violence is an inevitable consequence of using the highways. But the tension is always present, for when a car follows you for a few miles, passes you a number of times, then streaks off down the highway, you have no way of knowing their intentions. "Man, watch for a '63 Chevy, light gray, no plate on front an' a long aerial. See anything that look like it shout."

The tension in the car draws to a fine edge. All know the car, and the reputation of the patrolman who polices the next fifty or so miles of highway. Two of the young men in the car have been "busted"—arrested—by him, and as one says, "Once is enough. That man would rather whup yore head than eat shrimp . . . an' he's a seafood lover."

This trooper is regarded with a mixture of fear and contempt by the Negroes in the county. He is reputed to stop every Negro he encounters, driving or on foot, to check their licenses and to find out where they are going and why. He is particularly fond of "interrogating" adolescent girls. As your companions talk about him, a sort of grim, parodic humor attaches to him. His first statement, they say, is invariably, "All right Nigger, pull to the side, take off your hat, spit out your gum, an' lemme see your license." It makes no difference if you are hatless and have never chewed gum. And because, for SNCC workers anyway, the response is either silent compliance or a denial that their name is Nigger, his next utterance is usually "Dammit Nigger, don't you know to say Sir?" But this day he does not appear.

On another occasion I saw him making an arrest. Like most things in the Delta, he verges on being a caricature, drawn with too heavy a hand. He is not tall, but blocky and heavy. His hair is thinning, his face is round, full-cheeked, cherubic save for small pale blue eyes behind absolutely innocuous gold-rimmed glasses. In the heat his complexion could not be called merely florid; it was red, deeply and truly red. His khaki-colored military-style uniform was too tight and stained with damp circles at the armpits and the seat of his pants. His ponderous, hard-looking belly sags over the belt which slopes down almost to the junction of his thighs. Most striking are his hands: blunt, stubby, very wide—with the skin of the fingers stretched tight, like so many plump, freckled and hairy link sausages. Two images stay with me: one of a boneless, formless, shapeless face; another of the chunky figure, standing spraddle-legged and tugging at the cloth of his trousers where it bunched in tight wrinkles between his thighs. I often wonder about this man. From all accounts he is a sadist, and one with entirely too much opportunity to indulge his impulses, but there is also present a pathetic, somehow pitiable, banality about him. Besides, he represents the most easily solved of the problems in the Delta.

Driving along the highways in the Delta, you occasionally pass people walking—a single man, two, or sometimes what appears to be an entire family. Usually the man is in front, in overalls or blue denim pants and jacket, and with a wide-brimmed straw hat against the sun. The children follow behind in single file, with the woman usually at the end. They often carry tools, but more often cardboard boxes and newspaper-wrapped bundles tied with string. These little caravans become visible while you are some distance down the highway. If they have shoes, then they walk on the hot but smooth asphalt; if they are barefoot, they take to the weeds. When they hear your car approaching, they step off the highway and face the road, motionless, waiting with a quality of dogged, expressionless patience to resume their plodding journey. Sometimes, but rarely, a child will wave, a vague and tentative motion of the arm somewhere between greeting and dismissal, and that is the only sign. No smiles. Often you find such a group miles from any house, village, side road, or anything that might be called a town. One wonders where they sprang from, where they hope to go, and why. They are almost always—I cannot remember seeing any white families walking—Negroes.

Indianola is the capital of Sunflower County, a county distinguished because it contains the 4,800-acre plantation of u.s. Senator James O. Eastland, the state prison farm at Parchman, and is the home of Mrs. Fannie Lou Hamer, the ex-plantation worker who has become the symbol of the resistance.

Although this is your first time there, you recognize when you have come home. When the pavement runs out—the streetlights become fewer or nonexistent and the rows of weather-textured, gray-grained clapboard shacks begin—you experience feelings of relief, almost love. This chaotic, dilapidated shantytown represents community, safety in numbers, friendship, and some degree of security after the exposed vulnerability of the highway.

Even if you wanted to, you could not escape the children of all sizes and shades who abandon their games in the dusty streets or weed-filled lots for the excitement of a new arrival. Noisy with impatient curiosity and quick vitality they surround you, shooting questions. "Is yo' a freedom fighter? Yo' come for the Meeting? Is yo' start up the school? Have any money?"

Or proudly, "We does leafletting, yo' want us to give out any?" Big-eyed and solemn they await the answers, ignoring their elders' warnings, shouted from the porches, "Yo' all don't be botherin' that man now, heah?" They must have some bit of information so that they can go scampering importantly up the porches to inform the old people. The community grapevine.

And on the porches, the people are almost always old, at least no longer young. Frequently they are the grandparents of the children because the true parents, the generation in between, are at work, or have left the state in search of work. This gap between generations lies like a blight on every Negro community, and especially in the Delta. You see it in any kind of meeting, in the churches—any gathering of Negroes in Mississippi consists predominantly of teenagers and older people.

So the old people on the porch rock and fan and listen politely, perhaps too politely, expressing a cautious, noncommittal agreement that is somehow too glib and practiced. And their eyes flick over your shoulder to see who may be watching. It may be the Man. The quiescent, easy agreement is another aspect of the mask, and one has no right to judge the only practical response that they have fashioned, the only defense they had. For if they survived yessing the white man to death, why not you? "Thou seest this man's fall, but thou knowest not his wrasslin'."

The motion and energy, the openness and thirst to know of the children in the road forms a tragic counterpoint to the neutral caution of the porches. So short a journey and symbolically so final. The problem comes clear: to create within the community those new forms, new relationships, new alternatives that will preserve this new generation from the paralysis of fear and hopelessness.

In all the shantytowns that cluster at the edge of every Delta city and town, the population steadily increases as increasing numbers of Negroes are driven off the plantations and off the land. Everywhere you get the impression of hopelessness and waiting. Large numbers of human beings in a kind of limbo, physically present and *waiting*. And what they wait for is the cotton. At planting time, chopping time, and picking time, buses and trucks come into the shantytowns before the sun is well up. The people—men, women, and children—file on in the numbers needed and are taken to the plantations where they work a twelve-hour day for $2.50, or thirty cents an hour. Each year fewer and fewer people are needed for less and less work. If the fall is unusually wet, then it is a little better. The dust becomes a black and adhesive mud miring down the ponderous cotton-picking machines. Then, for a few hectic weeks almost the entire community can find work getting the crop in before it rots. Still, denied education and the skills that would give them mobility, these waiting people are superfluous, the obsolete victims of a vicious system that depended on large numbers of human beings being kept available in case they were needed. One plantation owner in the county is quoted as saying "Niggers went out like the mule."

One way to understand this primitive and haunting place and the gratuitous human misery that it breeds, is to figure out who is in charge. Two forces rule the Delta: racism and cotton. Though the white folks put up a great show of control and dominance, they are at the mercy of both. It is cotton—not even Anglo-Saxon, but an immigrant from Egypt—that determines how the society is organized. And as a ruler, it is as ruthless, capricious, and sickly as the final issue of some inbred and decadent European house. Delicate, it must be protected from more vigorous hybrid weeds, and from a small beetle from Mexico. Drought will burn it out, water will rot it. Extravagant and demanding, it has—in alliance with human cupidity—all but exhausted a land of once incredible fertility which must now be pampered and fertilized excessively before it will produce. This process is so expensive that the final, grudging yield must be bought by the United States government which alone can afford it. The federal government has a surplus at present of some fourteen million bales. This spring the federal cotton allotment has been reduced by one-third in the Delta. Even fewer Negroes will have work of any kind. The millionaire planter Eastland and other landlords, however, will still profit handsomely from their federal subsidy. While awaiting a federal check that runs into hundreds of thousands of dollars, the senator will, if he maintains his average, make three speeches deploring the immorality of government handouts and creeping socialism, by which he must mean the distribution of food surpluses to starving families in his county.

At suppertime the "freedom house" is full of bustle, the local kids pass in and out, a couple of carloads of SNCC workers from other parts of the state have stopped by on their way through. The shouted laughter and greetings are loud, the exchange of news marked by a wry humor. A young man from the southwest corner around Natchez tells stories about a local judge, nicknamed by the lawyers "Necessity," because in Horace's observation "necessity knows no law." But this judge is a favorite because his records invariably contain so much error that although he never fails to convict, the higher court hardly ever fails to reverse him. Frequently, they say, his mind wanders, and he interrupts the proceedings of his own court with, "Your Honor, I object."

Another worker just down from Sharkey County, which is very rural and contains no city of any size, complains loudly about conditions. "Even the mosquitoes threatening to leave the county. They organized and sent Johnson a telegram saying that if the Red Cross didn't come down and distribute blood, they weren't staying." He wouldn't be surprised, he adds, to find when he returned that they had gotten relief.

The meeting is called for eight, but will not really get started much before nine, as the women must feed their white folks their suppers before going home to feed their own families. But folks start gathering from seven. They use the time to "testify": to talk about whatever troubles their minds—mostly the absence of food, money, work, and the oppressiveness of the police. They talk about loss of credit, eviction, and voting, three things which form an inseparable unity in the Delta. Some young men are there from Washington County. They say the people over there got together and told the owners that they wouldn't work anymore for thirty cents. After the evictions they started a tent city, have a "strike fund" collected in the community, and are planting a "freedom garden" for winter food. Everyone cheers. What they want is cooperation. "If they sen' buses from Washington County don't go. Be workin' gainst us if you do."

"Thass right. Nevah. Freedom."

In the clapping, shouting, stomping excitement, there is brief release from tension and fear. But over it all hovers an unease, the desperation of the unanswered question, "Whut *is* we gon' do?" Winter is coming. *"Whut is we gon' do?"*

A lady wants to know. She is from "out in the rural" she says and two nights ago was awakened by what sounded like people crying. A man, his wife, and seven children were coming down the road carrying bundles. The children were crying and tears were in the man's eyes. They had no shoes. He said that evening the owner had given him twenty dollars and told him to find someplace else. He had worked that plantation all his life, had less than three years of school, and had never been outside the county. "Ah tell yo' that man wuz *shock,* he wuz *confused.* I want to know, what is we gon' do?"

A portly, middle-aged lady answers her. This lady is known for a tough nerviness, an insouciant streak of daring best characterized by the Yiddish word *chutzpah,* or by the sheriff in the term "smart nigger." She also has a heart condition of some fame and strategic value. (As she gets up, you recall the time she was in jail and convinced the jailor, after two minor attacks and a constant and indignant harangue, that she was quite likely to die, and that he was certain to be held responsible if she were not allowed to have her "heart prescription." And she got it, too. You remember her, dramatically clutching her ailing heart, breathing laboriously, and accepting with a quick wink the druggist's bottle of sour mash bourbon.) There were two little boys walking down the road, she says. They were throwing stones at everything they met. They came upon a chicken which the larger boy sent off with a well-placed stone. He does the same for a pig, a cow, and a mule. Then, they come to a hornets' nest. When the bigger boy makes no effort to hit that target the other asks, "Ain't yo' gonna pop that nes'?" "Nope, sho' ain't." "Why ain't y' gonna hit thet nes'?" the smaller asks. "Well, Ah ain't gonna hit thet nes',"—she pauses, looks at the audience, winks, shakes her head—"I ain't gonna hit thet nes' *because dey's organized.*"

They like that story, even if it is only a partial answer, saying *what,* but now *how.* So they nod agreement and murmur that "we'uns gotta be *together,* an' we gotta keep on, keeping on, no matter how mean times git." There is in these Delta communities a great spirit of closeness and cooperation. When a family is evicted, the children may be absorbed into the community, two here, one there. Or an entire family that finds itself suddenly homeless (landlords aren't required by any law to give notice) may be taken in by another family whose home is already too small. Without these traditions the folks could not have endured.

In the meetings, everything—uncertainty, fear, even desperation—finds expression, and there is comfort and sustenance in "talkin' 'bout hit." A preacher picks the theme up with a story of his own. "Wunst times wuz very bad fer the rabbits."

"Fo' the *Whut?*" comes a chorus. The old man smiles, "Fer the *rabbits.* Yes Sir, Ah tells yo' they wuz bein' hard *pressed.* Them ol' houn's wuz runnin' them *ragged.* Got so bad it seem like they couldn't git down to the fiel's to nibble a little grass. It looked like they wasn't gonna be able to make it."

"Yeah, Yeah, Tellit," the people shake their heads in sympathy.

"They wuz *hard pressed* fo' a fack. So fin'ly, not knowin' what else to do, they calls a meetin'. Yessir, they call a *mass meetin'.*"

"*Ahuh, Freedom.*"

"So they talked an' talked, discussed it back an' fo'th, how the houn's wasn't givin' them space even to live."

"*Thass right, tell it.*"

"But they couldn't meet with no solution. It jes' didn't seem like hit was nothin' they could do." The speaker shakes his head. "No, it didn't seem like they could make it. So fin'ly thisyer ol' rabbit, he wuz ol' anyways an fixin' to die anyhow, he sugges' that since they wuzn't making it *nohow*, they should all jes' join together an' run down to the *river an' drown theyself.*"

Everyone in the church is listening very closely. There is the beginning of a low murmur of rejection.

"But since nobody said any better, they put hit in the form of a motion, an' someone secon' hit an' they take a vote. It passed [pause] *unanimous*. So on the nex' moonlight night, they all git together jes' as the motion call fer, link they arms and start fer the river, fo' to drown theyself. Hit wuz *a-a-l* the rabbits in the county, an' thet wuz a long line, jes' hoppin' along in the moonlight to go drown theyse'f. It wuz somethin' to see, chillun, it sho' wuz. An', yo' know, they hadn't gon far befo' they come upon the houn's, out looking fo' rabbits to chase. Them ol' houn's be so surprise at seein' all them rabbits commin' towards them steady, *they thought they time had come.* They be so surprised they turn roun' and run so fas' they was outen the county, befo' sun come up. Rabbits had no mo' trouble."

"*Talk 'bout Freedom.*"

There is little of subtlety or delicacy here; it is a region of extremes and nothing occurs in small measure. All is blatant, even the passing of time. Night in the Delta is sudden and intense, an almost tangible curtain of blue-purple darkness that comes abruptly, softening and muting the starkness of the day. The moon and stars seem close, shining with a bright yellow haziness like ripe fruit squashed against a blackboard. The wind is warm, very physical and furry as it moves with suggestive intimacy over your face and body. Like the sea, the Delta is at its most haunting and mysterious in the dark. The air is heavy with the ripe smell of honeysuckle and night-blooming jasmine, at once cloying and aphrodisiac. A woman's voice, deep-timbered, husky, and *Negro* is singing an old plaintive song of constant sorrow with new words. The song becomes part of the rich-textured night, like the tracings of the fireflies. In the restless and erotic night you believe. For the first time you can believe the blues, tales of furtive and shameful passions, madness, incest, rape, and violence. Half-intoxicated by the night, by its sensuous, textured restlessness, it is possible to believe all the secret, shameful history that everyone seems to know and none will admit except in whispers. It is easy to believe that the land is finally and irrevocably cursed. The faceless voice singing to the darkness an old song with new words, *"They say that freedom . . . is a constant sorrow."*

Just off the road stands the shack. There is a quality of wildness to the scrubby bush around it, and because it is set on short wood piles, it appears to have been suddenly set down on the very top of the carpet of weeds around it. The grayed wood siding has long since warped so that a fine line shows between each plank, giving the shack the appearance of a cage. Crossing the porch you step carefully, avoiding the rotted holes. The woman inside turns dull eyes toward where you stand in the doorway. She is sharing out a pot of greens onto tin plates. The cabin is windowless and dim but is crisscrossed by rays of light beaming through the cracks in the siding and from gaps in the roof where the shingles have rotted and blown away. This light creates patterns of light and shadow on everything in the room. As the woman watches you, at least inclines her head in your direction, her children sidle around her so that she is between them and the door. You see that there are only five—at first it seemed as though the cabin was full. None of them is dressed fully, and the two smallest are completely nude. As the mother gives you the directions back to the highway, she ladles out the greens and each child seizes a plate but stands looking at you. They are all eyes, and these eyes in thin tight faces blaze at you. The full, distended bellies of the children contrast with the emaciated limbs, big prominent joints, narrow chests in which each rib stands out, the black skin shiny, almost luminous. You cannot leave, so you stand gently talking with the mother, who answers your questions with an unnatural candor. She seems beyond pride. As you talk, she sits on a box and gives her breast to the smallest child even though he seems to be about five. This doesn't surprise you unduly for you have learned that in the Delta, Negro mothers frequently do not wean their children until the next one arrives. What will substitute when there is not enough food?

You find out that she is twenty-four, was married at fifteen, had seven children but two died, the father is in Louisiana chopping pulpwood, the nearest work he could find. He sends money when he works. She lives in this abandoned cabin because it was the only rent-free house she could find after they were put off the plantation. As you leave, you see them framed in the doorway, the mother in unlaced man's shoes, one brown, the other black, holding her smallest child with the unnaturally big head and eyes.

You wonder how they are to survive the winter in a cabin with walls that cannot even keep the dust out. But this is Tallahatchie County, where thirty-three percent of all Negro babies die in the first year of life, where Negroes live, grow old, and die without ever being properly examined by a doctor, and children die of cold and hunger in the winter. One reason given for the high infant mortality rate—you meet women who admit to having birthed ten children of which three or four survived—is that in this completely agricultural county, families survive the winter, when there is no work for the men, on the ten or twelve dollars the mother makes working as a cook or maid. When her time of labor approaches, she dares not stop working.

But all of this was some time ago. All I know of the Delta now is what I hear. I am told that snow blanketed it in January and I am glad I was not there to see it. I am told that in December two hundred and fifty families were given notice to be off the plantations by January 1. This means that some 2,200 human beings are without home or livelihood, and none of the programs of the federal government—social security, unemployment compensation, or job retraining—affects them. By spring, they say, some twelve thousand people will be homeless. I am glad I was not there to see the ghostly silent caravans trudging through the snow at the side of the highway. A lady in Sunflower County told me on the phone that families were at the tent city asking to be taken in.

Throughout the Delta the plantations are automating, driven by the dual pressure of cutting costs and the potential effect of the 1965 Voting Rights Bill in a region with a Negro majority. The state of Mississippi wants its Negro population thinned out. They make no secret of it. Governor Johnson has said in praise of his predecessor that under Ross Barnett's regime "116,000 Negroes fled the state." And the state has still not been able to find any way to use the 1.6 million dollars appropriated by the Office of Economic Opportunity to be used to finance the distribution of surplus food in the Delta. Before this grant, it had been Mississippi's position that they simply could not afford the cost of *distributing* the free food. I am just cowardly enough to be glad I am not there to see.

*1966*

# The Politics of Necessity and Survival in Mississippi

*With Lawrence Guyot*
Chairman, Mississippi Freedom
Democratic Party

■ ■ ■ ■ ■

R ECENTLY much national attention has been focused on the state of Mississippi. Voluminous commentaries have appeared on the Summer Project of 1964, the murder of Cheyney, Schwerner, and Goodman, the challenge of the Mississippi Freedom Democratic Party (MFDP) delegation to the Atlantic City National Democratic Convention in August of 1964, and on the 1965 Congressional Challenge to the seating of the five "representatives" from Mississippi also conducted by the MFDP.

It is perhaps indicative of the conditions of the American press and politics at this time, and of the condition of the society that tolerates both, that so few of these commentaries speak directly and clearly to the real issues and conditions that surround the MFDP and dictate our actions. It has been easier, and in some cases more expedient, to attempt to dismiss the MFDP as either an incongruous coalition of naive idealists and unlettered sharecroppers without serious political intent or possibility—a kind of political oddity embodying simply a moral protest—or else hint ominously at sinister, alien, and, of course, unidentified influences, which find expression in an intransigent and unreasonable "militancy." It is difficult to assess which of these two well-touted fictions is more prevalent, or the more misleading, but it is clear that the persons advancing them cannot all be the victims of simple ignorance. They range through a curious and wholly unprecedented assortment including: old line civil rights leaders, the Mississippi white Democratic politicians, LBJ "liberals," labor movement leaders, and hack journalists allegedly "close" to the administration.

It is not particularly useful to speculate, as intriguing as that may be, on precisely what it is in the prospect of Mississippi's Negroes organizing themselves politically to end almost a century of systematic exploitation and suppression, that so confuses and threatens so many within the establishment. Clearly it is time that the MFDP gives some kind of comprehensive public expression of its necessities and goals so as to relieve these overly willing commentators of that obligation.

There is nothing inherently unique in the idea and operation of the MFDP. We are a political organization of people in Mississippi. Our purpose is gaining and utilizing the greatest possible measure of political power and influence in the interest of our constituency, *as that constituency expresses its interests.* There is no radically dramatic mystique or visionary political insight attendant on the MFDP's functioning—unless one considers as new political insights the idea that Mississippi's Negroes can and must gain political representation in proportion to their numbers, that the entire community must be encouraged to participate in the decisions governing their lives, and that vote must be used as an instrument of social change.

We are the political organization of a community, which, if it is quite literally to survive, must win for itself those political rights which white Americans take for granted. As we will show, the decisions taken, the policies and programs pursued, and general strategy of the MFDP, to the extent they are unique, derive not from a tendency toward abstract political philosophy, but from a practical response to the primitive conditions of political life in Mississippi, and the experiences that unless we in Mississippi save ourselves politically, there is no source of salvation in the country to which we can look.

The experience of the movement for Negro rights in Mississippi indicates very bluntly that we cannot look to the office of the presidency, the Democratic or Republican parties as presently constituted, the redemptive force of love, public moral outrage, the northern liberal establishment, nor even to the Congress with its "Great Society" legislation. We are not saying that these institutions and groups are necessarily hostile or can be of no practical assistance to the Mississippi Negro in his struggle for survival and political freedom. This is not so. But it is true that the political and legal rights of the Negroes of Mississippi, even when guaranteed by the Constitution and enforced by civilized morality, will continue to be subject to the self-interests of these institutions unless reinforced by political power. This can be clearly illustrated by examining the historical record of Mississippi's illegal actions against its Negro population, and the national record of tolerance and indifference to these policies. And it is a fact (despite the much-vaunted "progress" in the area of civil rights), there has been no effective change, on any significant political or economic level, in the policy of tolerance on the part of those who hold national power, toward the systematized degradation of the black population in Mississippi by the state.

### The Old Mississippi Plan

To understand present realities in Mississippi, it is necessary to grasp clearly certain historical facts because nowhere are the effects of history so present and so real, as in Mississippi today. It must be understood that during the past 150 years, *the overwhelming political concern of the white power structure of Mississippi has been, and is, effecting and perpetuating the subjugation of the black population.* Historically the policy of the state toward the Negro community has been one of war, and this warfare has been conducted with the placid acceptance of the rest of the nation. This must be stressed, because despite the fact that constitutionally speaking there has been no legal government in Mississippi for ninety years, the state of Mississippi has enjoyed full political rights and complete acceptance from the nation. Conditions in Mississippi today—the grinding poverty, lack of education, absence of legal rights—which affect its Negroes are not accidental or the results of private prejudices, or blind emotional racism on the part of some of its citizens, as is widely projected by the American press, but are the result of deliberate and systematic policies of the state's government, and must be understood in that light.

Today, the smallest political subdivision in the state is known as a beat. This terminology comes from the 1840s and 1850s when Mississippi was one of the wealthiest states in the Union, with a large proportion of that wealth deriving from the value of its slave population. This "wealth," however, constituted more of a threat to the peace of mind of its owners than more traditional forms of capital. It represented the danger—which haunted and still haunts the southern mentality—of a violent uprising. In order to secure this "wealth," it became necessary for the owners to organize the state as though it were an occupied territory. Every evening at sundown, in every town and city in Mississippi, a military exercise could be observed. A mounted militia, composed usually of every able-bodied white male, would parade to the rolling of drums, after which it would disperse to assigned "beats," which were patrolled during the night to prevent the movement of slaves between plantations, an activity necessary to the planning of any organized uprising. Negroes without passes were, as a matter of course, denied the streets between the hours of six P.M. to six A.M. (Curfews which apply only to Negroes are still a mainstay of Mississippi police activity.) These "beats" were divisions according to population and were utilized in setting up political precincts. What is important, however, is the fact that this military garrison psychology is still present in the state's attitude toward the Negro community.

After the Civil War, the Negro population, rather than diminishing, increased substantially as a result of the creation within the state of a number of centers for the reuniting of Negro families scattered by slavery and the war. Many of the freedmen who were drawn to these centers remained in the state and became registered voters under the Reconstruction constitution of 1869, creating by 1890 a Negro voting majority. The full political effect of this majority was never realized, however, because of terroristic activity and election fraud on the part of the whites. After the elections of 1873, in which large gains were made in the number of Negro elected officials, Mississippi's whites were determined that the congressional elections of 1875 were to be white dominated. The *Yazoo City Banner* (July 31, 1875) declared editorially that "Mississippi is a white man's country, and by the eternal God, we'll run it." Another newspaper, the *Handsboro Democrat* (April 10, 1875) called for "a white man's government, by white men, for the benefit of white men." This hysterical fear of an incipient Negro takeover is still reflected in the public statements of Mississippi's white politicians. It is at this point that Mississippi's white minority evolved the first of many "Mississippi Plans" not so much by the agency of the eternal God, as by rewriting the constitution in 1890, to disenfranchise the Negro electorate.

This first plan was many faceted, and was designed to promote a number of purposes which have been fairly consistent until the 1950s, and which need to be understood.

The simple expedient of driving the Negro majority from the state was not possible, since Negro labor was necessary to the economy. Negroes had to be kept in the state, but they could not be permitted participation in politics since that endangered the new "Mississippi Way of Life," and would eventually remove the Negro from his condition of serfdom. Education for the Negro was also unthinkable since educated people do not pick cotton, do the washing, or sweep the floors.

Consequently, any policy adopted by the state had to accomplish a number of tasks: it had to disfranchise the Negro, keep him uneducated, economically dependent, and psychologically manageable, and, at the same time, *prevent him from leaving.* By a combination of organized terror and violence, reinforced by the new constitution of 1890, and a succession of discriminatory voting laws, the first purpose was accomplished; the following figures reflect how well. In 1890, when the constitution was rewritten, there were 71,000 more registered Negro than white voters, and a total Negro majority of population. By 1964, after some seventy-five years of the "Plan," the Negro majority had declined to 45 percent of the total population, and only 5 percent of the 450,000 voting age Negroes were registered voters.

The agent of this disfranchisement was, of course, the Democratic party, which then enjoyed seventy-five years of unbroken control of the state as the political expression of "white supremacy." It also gained increasing national power and influence through the congressional seniority system, and the longevity of the congressmen it sent to Washington.

Once the political goal of Negro disfranchisement was achieved, the other items of policy followed easily.

To limit Negro education the simple expedient of building few or no schools for Negroes was followed. It is a fact that there are counties in Mississippi where the first high schools for Negroes were established in 1954, *after* the Supreme Court decision calling for desegregation in education (65 percent of all schools in Mississippi have been built since World War II, and of those schools 75 percent are Negro).

The economic reorganization of the state centered around the introduction of sharecropping, and the reestablishment of the plantation under a system of labor only slightly more sophisticated than outright slavery. One advantage of this new credit work system was that in the event a Negro died or was killed, the plantation owner was not out-of-pocket to the extent of a slave's value.

Theoretically, Negroes could leave plantations, and some did. As a practical matter, however, many remained because of immobility, coercion, or the rather prevalent ploy where the owner informed the worker at the end of the year that he had not earned enough to cover the expenses of his family's keep, and was thus obligated to work another year, thus getting deeper in "debt." Workers who left despite this warning were frequently jailed for evasion of debt and "paroled," for the duration of excessive sentences, to the very same plantation. This plantation system exists today with labor conditions virtually unchanged, which violate every federal child labor and condition-of-labor law which has been passed. The national responsibility here is very clear, since it is the federal government, through its cotton subsidy laws, that subsidizes these plantations.

The police machinery of the state continues to operate precisely as though its primary function is the protection of the white society from Negro uprising. The state highway safety patrol is, like the slavery-time militia, a paramilitary organization. However, the concept of the militia survives most obviously in the ever-present "posses" of deputized and armed whites which are selected at random to be utilized against civil rights activities.

Despite the conditions just described, the formal ending of slavery did result in the emergence of a small Negro middle class of businessmen, independent farmers, and a number of professional persons who, for some reason, did not escape to the North with their education. The exploitative economic conditions, and repressive social and political system forced a steady trickle of Negroes northward, and the absence of adequate medical facilities and the resultant high infant mortality rate served to erode the Negro majority of 1890, to the present figure of 45 percent.

This, very briefly, is the *old* "Mississippi Plan," representing the full legal, economic, and military resources of a state being consciously directed toward the systematic oppression of a segment of that state's population.

### The New Mississippi Plan: Gradual Depopulation

The posture of the government of Mississippi toward the Negro population did not change significantly from 1890 up to the 1950s. At this time, the rumblings caused by the Supreme Court school decision and the spreading wave of Negro demands for justice caused the state to rethink its plan. One extremely significant change had taken place since the end of the Second World War. Whereas, in the past, it had been necessary, even to the extent of violence and fraud, to keep Negroes in the state for economic reasons, technological changes in the cotton fields were beginning to make large concentrations of Negroes unnecessary.

In the early sixties, the first modern voter registration drives, which is to say, the first signs of sustained political activity in the Negro community, were begun. At that time, there was an attitude prevalent in the older civil rights groups, notably the NAACP, that Mississippi had to be changed from outside pressure. Inherent in this attitude was the belief that it was not possible for Negroes in Mississippi to organize for political action without a disproportionate cost in human life. What was established, under fearsome conditions, by Bob Moses and that first small group of SNCC organizers, and the local Negroes, is that it was possible to organize politically and to survive. And, as farfetched as this may sound today, the right to organize politically in Mississippi was really in the balance during those violent months in 1962. That the MFDP exists today is due to the determined heroism of the small group who fought and won that first battle.

It is at this point, when even the most hidebound racist could recognize that the movement in Mississippi was not to be driven out by violence and economic reprisal, that the change in the state's policies began to be evident. This change focused on the fact that there were just too many potential voters in the Negro community, and that Mississippi had the highest percentage of Negroes of any state in the Union. (Later, during the debate over the 1964 Civil Rights Bill, the Dixiecrats were to express this fear of the large Negro population, by their advocacy of a program of "equalizing the proportional Negro population of all states," in which they challenged the nation to undertake a program of relocating the Negro population so that each state would have the same proportion of Negroes.)

In Mississippi, the state began a program which can best be characterized as one of gradual genocide, the goal of which was to effect the dispersal or extinction of the Negro population.

The White Citizens Councils were organized and, in Mississippi, received financial support for their programs from the state through the Sovereignty Commission. Richard Morphew, public relations director of the councils, admitted to receiving $90,000 from the state. In communities touched by the movement, the Citizens Councils launched counter programs designed "to make it impossible for Negroes involved in agitation" to get work or credit, in short, to remain in the community.

This was particularly true in the Second Congressional (Delta) district, where the densest concentrations of Negro population are to be found. It is in this area that the huge plantations are located and that the large reservoir of Negro labor had to be maintained. In this area, the Negro population is predominantly agricultural laborers, who either live on plantations, sharecrop a small "section," or else are herded together into tar paper and clapboard shantytowns from which they are fetched in trucks and buses to their work on the plantations. To a person going through one of these towns, the dominant impression is of large numbers of people who are *waiting*. That is precisely their condition; they have been *kept* available, in a kind of perpetual waiting for the times when their labor would be needed on the plantations. So long as they were needed, they were given credit, welfare, or some form of subsistence during the winter months. Even in the best of seasons, families that worked a full season in the fields—an increasingly rare occurrence—would be forced as a matter of course to go on welfare during the winter. It was in this manner that their economic dependence was maintained, as a matter of political and economic policy.

However, with Negroes clamoring for the ballot, and the mechanization of the cotton fields rendering Negro labor more and more unnecessary, an entirely new situation came into being in Mississippi.

These changed conditions precipitated a kind of grim race between the Negro community and the state. It has been our necessity to militate for the franchise before the new conditions forced so many Negroes out as to render the franchise meaningless in the depleted community. The state's policy was to delay and obstruct Negro voting until the community had been thinned out. There have been specific acts that the state has taken against the Negroes which are illustrative of this warfare.

Welfare payments to entire communities, and particularly to persons who have attempted to register, have been severely cut back. In these same communities, the welfare agency has distributed leaflets extolling the generosity of welfare and wage rates in northern cities like Chicago.

The state has steadfastly maintained that it is unable to afford the cost of distributing free federal surplus food to needy Delta communities. This, despite the fact that it can afford to subsidize Citizens Council propaganda broadcasts; appropriated $50,000 to lobby against the 1964 Civil Rights Bill; has undertaken the cost of the legal defense of any county clerk indicted under the 1957, 1964, or 1965 Civil Rights bills for failing to register Negroes; and was able in 1964 to afford to double the manpower of the highway safety patrol and purchase thousands of dollars worth of military weaponry to use against the Summer Project.

In 1961, the congressman from the Delta, Jamie H. Whitten, in his capacity as chairman of the House Subcommittee on Appropriation of the Agriculture Committee, killed a measure that would have provided for the training of three thousand tractor drivers in Mississippi. Two-thirds of the applicants for this program were Negro.

These actions by the state represent essentially a changing of the rules, an alteration of the economic arrangement in which winter credit and subsistence to agricultural workers were central. Viciously effective, it leaves thousands of Negroes with the alternatives of starving or leaving. It poses a serious crisis to the Negro community, especially since those affected have been deprived of all opportunity to develop skills which would enable them to adjust to the requirements of an industrial society.

As 1966 opens, the economic interests in Mississippi have moved against the Delta population with a new ferocity. What appears to be the beginning of an organized wave of evictions has begun and some 250 families—about 2,200 human beings—have already moved or have been informed that there will be no work for them this spring. It has been estimated that between ten thousand and twelve thousand persons will lose their homes and livelihood this current season. These families are not eligible for social security, unemployment compensation, or any state or federal welfare program. The plantation owners are not required to give prior notice or compensation to those displaced. On one plantation in Bolivar County, the owner gave notice to nearly one hundred workers by giving them ten dollars each and advising them to go to Florida. Many of the evictees are active in the MFDP and the civil rights movement, but the evictions represent the bulk dismissal of unskilled workers on the large plantations. Only skilled workers—tractor drivers, cultivator and cotton-picking machine operators are being retained. This situation is aggravated by the actions of the Mississippi Economic Council, an association of planters and businessmen which has been campaigning for the rapid mechanization of cotton production as a means of spurring the Negro exodus, and by the fact that this year, the Federal acreage allotments for cotton production have been cut by 35 percent.

The economic squeeze is undoubtedly the most effective and cruel of the state's weapons, but the full force of the "embattled minority" neurosis, that guides the actions of white rulers of Mississippi, was most fully reflected by the legislation introduced, and in many cases passed, in the legislative session in the spring of 1964.

When SNCC announced the plans for the Summer Project of 1964, a special session of the state legislature was called, and the legislative record shows clearly that Mississippi's attitudes toward the black population has remained remarkably free of change since the 1840s. Introduced and passed were a bill outlawing economic boycotts and two bills outlawing the picketing of public buildings (courthouses are the scene of registration attempts). Both bills were almost identical, but the second was to be used in the event the first was declared unconstitutional by the federal courts. A series of police-oriented bills was introduced; these provided for extra deputies, for security and patrol personnel for public institutions, for placing the safety patrol at the disposal of the governor and doubling its man-power, providing for a curfew which could be enforced at the discretion of local police authorities, providing for the sharing of municipal police forces during civil disturbances, providing for juveniles arrested for civil rights activities to be treated as adults, and finally a bill to prohibit the summer volunteers from entering the state.

On the question of education, bills were passed to prohibit the establish-ment of freedom schools and community centers and to revoke the charter of the integrated Tougaloo College. The pattern of the "Old Plan" of con-trol by military force and restriction of educational opportunities can be clearly recognized in these legislative proposals.

Two pieces of legislation introduced in this session deserve special com-ment as they are symptomatic of a species of desperate hysteria which is completely unpredictable and therefore dangerous.

The first provided for the sterilization of persons convicted of a third felony. This was introduced by Representative Fred Jones of Sunflower County, in which there is a Negro majority. Jones was then a member of the executive committee of the Citizens' Council. While not specifically mentioning Negroes, the bill contained a clause placing the ordering of sterilization at the discretion of the all-white trustees of Parchman Peniten-tiary; since Negroes are more subject to criminal conviction in Mississippi courts, the intent of the proposal was clear.

A similar bill was introduced and *passed*, though with amendments. This bill provided for the sterilization of parents of the second illegitimate child, with the alternative of a prison sentence of from three to five years. In introducing this, Representative Meeks of Webster County clearly indi-cated that it was intended toward the black population. After passing the House, the bill went to the Senate, where it passed with amendments delet-ing sterilization and making the birth of the second illegitimate child a mis-demeanor rather than a felony and lessening the sentence. When it came back to the House for ratification, the proponents of sterilization argued for its inclusion, Representative Ben Owen of Columbus saying, as re-ported by the *Delta Democratic Times* of May 21, "This is the only way I know of to stop this rising black tide that threatens to engulf us." The bill finally passed as amended by the Senate.

We have been at pains to delineate this background of social, economic, and political attitudes, actions, and conditions in some detail. It is only from this perspective—not one of individual and irrational acts of racism, but one of rational, organized, and programmatic oppression on the part of the power machinery of the state, that the plight of Mississippi's black population, and the M F D P response to it can be understood.

## The Political Movement in Mississippi

In the light of the conditions we have outlined, the movement in Mississippi recognized the need for effective and speedy political changes in the state before most of the Negro population had to face the choice of starvation or migration. The answer to the prevalent northern question, "Why stay?" is simply, where is there for untrained plantation laborers to go?

It was evident that the resources of education, training, medical facilities, housing, food, and employment that the community needed could only come from massive government programs in which the state was not prepared to participate. The federal government, while possessing these resources, was not inclined to initiate any such programs in Mississippi for a number of reasons, foremost among which is its traditional and scrupulous respect for the right of the state government to conduct the affairs of its concentration camp as it sees fit. There is hardly one federal program, including the Poverty Program, which does not require the approval of the state governor. The obvious answer is to change the composition and thus policies of the state government.

However, in 1963, this kind of thinking was the most rarified and remote kind of theory. What kind of effective political participation and what kind of organization was possible for a people whom the entire apparatus of government operated to exclude and disperse. The concept of parallel elections or "freedom ballots" provided a partial solution. Its operation was simple. While most Negroes could not vote, a Negro could stand for election, and the Negro community could unofficially cast their votes in a parallel election.

The strategic advantages of this device were many. The entire community could be involved in these campaigns and a people who had been without political exposure for three generations could in this manner be introduced to the mechanics, at least, of political action. At the time that these campaigns created a tradition of political involvement in which indigenous leadership could develop, the vote itself would be an effective refutation of the curious southern contention that people who were daily risking their lives and livelihoods to attempt to register were really not interested in voting. But, most important, the "Freedom Vote" was a means of taking politics to the people, *where they were.* For example, when in 1963 Dr. Aaron Henry and Rev. Ed King ran as Freedom candidates in the gubernatorial elections, the people in churches, led by the choir, lined up and marched singing past the ballot boxes to cast their votes. Six thousand ballots were mailed out to more violent areas, to be returned by mail, and organizers traveled around the rural areas in "vote-mobiles" to encourage participation. Over 80,000 votes were cast in the Negro community for Dr. Henry for governor and Rev. King as his lieutenant governor.

Even from this first freedom election, it must be noted, the underlying concept of challenging the illegal state structure, from outside that structure, was present. Our intention was to file a suit calling for the voiding of election results on the basis of the voting section of the 1957 Civil Rights Bill and a Reconstruction period statute, providing for the challenging of state elections for reason of racial discrimination. Although this particular challenge never materialized, the challenge *concept* persisted. This was based on a need to demonstrate some kind of political effectiveness which could not be accomplished inside a state where you could not vote and on the fact that the government of Mississippi and all elections it conducted were and had been since 1890 in clear and indefensible violation of the Constitution.

In retrospect, this represented a confidence in the ultimate morality in national political institutions and practices—"They *really* couldn't know and once we bring the facts about Mississippi to national attention justice must surely be swift and irrevocable"—which was a simplistic faith somewhat akin to that of the Russian peasants under the czars. Caught in the direst kind of oppression and deprivation the peasants would moan, "If the czar only knew how we suffer. He is good and would give us justice. If he only knew." The fact was that he knew only too well.

Although the "challenge" to the gubernatorial elections of 1963 never materialized, perhaps the most significant practical consequence of the King-Henry campaign was the statewide nature of the campaign. It took the movement, for the first time, beyond activities affecting a single town, county, municipality, or electoral district, and placed us in the area of statewide organization. This consideration is now a basic tenet of MFDP organization and operation, that the entire Negro community, all 45 percent of the vote it represents, must be united in an independent, radically democratic organization so as to be able to act politically from a position of maximum strength. Without this kind of solid community organization the vote, when it comes, *will be* close to meaningless as an implement of necessary social change. It is the beginnings of this organization that emerged from that campaign, and in the summer of 1964, the statewide organization was formalized by a series of precinct, county, district meetings, culminating in a state convention of the Mississippi Freedom Democratic Party. This convention also selected the racially integrated delegation that challenged the all-white Mississippi delegation at the national convention in Atlantic City.

Toward Independent Political Power

It is not possible here to go into the machinations of the leadership of the national Democratic party which managed to avoid any vote of the convention on the issue. The important fact that emerged was that the leadership of the Democratic party—which is to say the political leadership of the nation, at this time—was not prepared to end or even amend its relationship of fraternal coexistence with Mississippi racism. The public relations gesture of offering the MFDP delegation two seats "at large" was at best a slap on the wrists of the "regulars" and a pat on the head of Mississippi's Negroes. It made no pretense of meeting the claims of the MFDP delegation for representation of Mississippi's black population.

One side effect of the MFDP delegation's rejection of the token offer should be mentioned. This is the response of truly surprising vindictiveness—and scarcely disguised contempt for the members of the MFDP delegation—with which "liberals" in the national Democratic party greeted our rejection of the compromise. Inherent in the charge that the delegation was "manipulated" to reject this gesture is the notion that the members of the delegation, who were present at the risk of jail, loss of livelihood, and even life, were somehow unable to recognize that they had been deprived of a vote by the full convention and were being asked to accept a meaningless gesture that meant no change in the conditions that had brought them to Atlantic City in protest.

Back in Mississippi, people across the state were watching on every available television set and saw that the "system" was vulnerable. That week of TV coverage did more than a month of mass meetings in showing people that there was nothing necessary and eternal about white political supremacy, and that they—who had been told by the system that they were nothing—could from the strength of organization affect the system.

Of equal importance was the fact that we emerged from the campaign with *a statewide network of precinct and county organizations* and an executive committee representative of all five congressional districts. It is possible that despite all the national furor caused by the convention challenge this legacy of grass-root, structured organization on a statewide basis will prove to be the most lasting, effective product of that challenge.

From November 4, 1964, the date of general federal elections in Mississippi, until September 16, 1965, the major resources and energies of the MFDP were directed toward the challenging of the elections of the five representatives to the U.S. House of Representatives. Again, it is not possible here to give a detailed report and analysis of the events—in Mississippi and in Washington—surrounding the final disposition of these challenges which served to maintain the five Mississippi representatives in Congress.

The issue was brought before the House of Representatives under the section of the Constitution which authorizes the House to be the sole judge of the credentials and qualifications of its membership.

Illegally Elected Congressmen

Our position was that no elections held under conditions which by reason of race deliberately and systematically excluded nearly half of the population could be *legal*. We asked the Congress not to seat the members from Mississippi and to require that new elections open to all citizens be held. After a vote on January 4, in which the Mississippi congressmen were seated pending further investigation, the issue did not come before the House again for nine months.

During these nine months between votes on the challenge, two facts became public knowledge. The first was that the Democratic party leadership of the House was determined at all costs to avoid any vote on the issue of the Mississippi elections. While not wanting to unseat the Mississippi delegation, the House leadership did not wish to appear contemptuous of the Constitution, which is, after all, the source of their authority. Any vote in favor of the Mississippi delegation could not help but appear to be the most cynical disregard for that document. No satisfactory device for evading this issue was found, and another vote was taken.

The second fact that emerged was that, despite the fact that these challenges were theoretically "a congressional issue," the illegally elected delegation received the full support and protection of the Johnson administration, which quietly put the word out to potential supporters within the Congress and outside that the White House was opposed to the unseating of the Mississippians.

By September, when the House voted for the second time, the members of Congress had available to them an overwhelming volume of evidence—

if any were needed—that the five Mississippians were fraudulently elected. In addition to three volumes of sworn and notarized statements taken in Mississippi by lawyers for the MFDP outlining the ways and means of Negro disfranchisement, there was the evidence presented by the Department of Justice in the case *U.S. vs. Mississippi,* in which the department argued that Mississippi's electoral laws were unconstitutional and discriminatory, and the report of the U.S. Commission on Civil Rights entitled *Voting in Mississippi,* which also concluded that 94 percent of the black population was systematically disfranchised by terror, violence, economic intimidation, and deliberate policy of the state.

Despite this evidence, neither the full membership of the House nor any of its committees ever debated the issue of the constitutional validity of the contested elections. In fact, at the same time that the House voted to dismiss the challenge on grounds that the people bringing the challenge had no legal standing to do so, it also rejected a conclusion that the Mississippians were "entitled to the seats." So the House of Representatives, like the national Democratic party, while drawing the line at publicly endorsing Mississippi's racism, found itself unable to take political action to renounce it. Both groups, Congress and the national party, also made strong public statements concerning the future. If there is discrimination in future elections or in future convention delegations, they said, the Mississippians will not be accepted. We intend to take them at their word.

Until the final House vote, the disposition of the challenge was never a foregone conclusion. In Mississippi the leadership of the state was at no pains to conceal its anxiety. At strategic times, the congressmen were commuting to Mississippi weekly to prepare their defenses. They sent letters to all law enforcement agents and registrars in their districts asking for a moratorium on violence related to voting. For the first time in seventy-five years, Negroes in Mississippi received routine communications from the congressman from their district. Governor Johnson, as early as last January, began calling for a new image of "moderation." He publicly appealed to "all elements in the state" to refrain from violence, then added the realistic if transparent qualification, "at least for the next six months." He also refrained from calling the usual spring session of the legislature. This was explained by the Jackson press as being caused by a fear of the possible effect on the challenge that a rash of racist and inflammatory legislation, such as was produced by the 1964 session, might have.

When the legislature was called into session in June, it was for the purpose of ratifying a series of "liberalizing" amendments to the state's voting laws. The good faith of this move was somewhat tarnished by the arrest of some 1,400 demonstrators in Jackson while the legislature was in session. Also, one proponent of the changes in the voting laws, state Senator William Pittman from Hattiesburg, in campaigning for the revision assured the white electorate that the state had received assurance from the Johnson administration to the effect that if they revised the voting requirements only a token number of federal registrars would be sent to Mississippi under the Voting Rights Bill. It is possible that he might have invented or exaggerated the commitment given in Washington, but it is a fact that there are at present a scant nineteen federal registrars in the state. This token implementation of the new legislation is particularly ironic, since one of the major arguments advanced for not unseating the Mississippi congressmen by the liberal establishment, in and out of Congress, was the notion that the new law would consign Negro disfranchisement to the dustbin of history.

Thus the need for some effective political action, coupled with the total exclusion of the state's black population from any local political activity, dictated the strategy of national challenges. Our hope was to bring the moral pressure and political strength of the national liberal community—inside and outside Congress—to bear in an effective and direct way on Mississippi's feudal political system. We had looked to the progressive wing of the national Democratic party for this relief. The results were instructive. Neither "challenge" succeeded in changing any of the basic power relationships between the racist state structure of Mississippi and the national structure. But, if nothing else was accomplished, a clear picture of the nature of political power in the nation and Mississippi's relationship to that power complex has emerged.

### Hypocrisy of State Efforts

Without abandoning the concept of the "challenge" in the future, we now turned our attention to activities within the state. While the state has not retreated from its general policies toward Negroes, it has seen the need to project an image reflecting apparent reform. Mississippi has heard the warnings given by the national Democratic party and by the Congress about future exclusion of the Negro population. Frantic efforts on the part of the state leadership to project the new facade of moderation, however, are constantly offset by actions which indicate the shallowness of this image.

In spite of an admitted need to present an apparently integrated delegation at the next national convention of the Democratic party, thereby avoiding another challenge, Governor Johnson was recently quoted in the Jackson *Clarion Ledger,* declaring fervently that "no Negroes were, nor were likely in the foreseeable future, to occupy any position of influence in the state Democratic party structure." The new moderation also reflects itself in defiance of the Voting Rights law. State Attorney General Patterson instructed all county clerks that *federally registered* persons are not to be added to the voting lists unless they meet "Mississippi's standards for voting." We know what those are. The new moderation is reflected in a redistricting scheme which was pushed by Governor Johnson and has now been enacted, the purpose of which is to eliminate the Negro majority in the Second Congressional District by gerrymandering. This is being contested in a suit filed on behalf of the M F D P. We have already seen another expression of this new moderation, also aimed at the Negro majority in the Delta, in the wave of evictions now in progress.

As Mississippi managed in the past to exclude Negroes totally from political representation and activity, it now conspires to deny us representation and power in proportion to our numbers. The first and most obvious way is to reduce these numbers as the present economic upheavals in the Delta are doing.

How often have we seen situations where Negro communities after great struggle and sacrifice have won the right to vote, only to find that the true potential of their voting strength is never reflected in real political change because the *ancient regime* has speedily redistricted predominantly Negro subdivisions so as to lessen the effects of the franchise?

## White Power Structure Tries Tokenism

Just as often the effective political organization of the Negro community has been aborted by tokenism—the time-honored practice of "giving" certain offices to selected Negroes. This assimilation of the emerging Negro politicians on the bottom of the old political structure means that these men serve as adjuncts of the very same power block that the community had struggled with for the vote. These "leaders" become vote deliverers, more responsive and responsible to the old line leadership of the white power structure than to the community they allegedly represent. By this device the white community manages to substitute patronage for power, and ensures that whatever political organization exists in the Negro community is dependent and subordinate to the old machine, leaving the community with an echo rather than a choice.

We face all three maneuvers in Mississippi. The first and most pressing in terms of immediate human needs is the economic squeeze, to which we simply have found no answer. Much of the movement's resources has had to be devoted toward the effort to find economic alternatives outside the white-dominated general economy of the state. Since 1961, food and clothes have been collected in the North for distribution in the state during the winter. But this, like the establishment of "Tent City" refugee centers, is a limited and temporary response, reaching only a bare fraction of the people affected. A grant of $1.6 million which was announced by the Office of Economic Opportunity last November for the purpose of distributing federal food surpluses in the Delta has not been used by the state as of this writing. Nor has the Department of Agriculture acted directly to initiate such programs because, as they tell us, they are waiting on local authorities to act.

Meanwhile the people struggle, and alternatives are sought. The organization of projects such as the Poor People's Corporation, the Mississippi Brick Co-op, sewing and farming cooperatives of all kinds, "freedom farms" to feed the families of strikers and evictees are expressions of this search for alternative sources of income. But these cannot be regarded as anything but a desperate holding action, a stopgap by people who have tried everything. Should these projects be successful beyond the expectations of the wildest idealist, they will still be inadequate in the face of the dimensions of the needs. Unfortunately ingenuity and desperation are no substitute for capital.

Early this year over one thousand people, most of whom were displaced, came to a conference on food, land, money, and jobs which had been called jointly by the MFDP, the Mississippi Freedom Labor Union, and the Delta Ministry of the National Council of Churches, which is, incidentally, the single institution of any stature in the country which has made any committed and sympathetic response to the conditions and aspirations of the people in Mississippi. After the conference a number of families who were without shelter in the subfreezing temperatures occupied a deactivated airforce base in Greenville, and were eventually evicted by the air force "for the protection of your own health."

Whatever happens, the changed economic conditions will be effective in reducing the Negro population in the Delta. But there is a grim and resilient tenacity in these very same people that Mississippi wishes to disperse. They have endured, and in the Delta this alone is an accomplishment. The community has had to develop traditions of sharing and interresponsibility which seem to deepen as conditions worsen. So, the state will discover that it is no simple matter to dispose of sufficient Negroes to eradicate their potential political strength.

Political Possibilities

It may seem inconsistent with what has gone before to say that at this point the potential for achieving a powerful, community-oriented, grass-roots political movement, embracing the majority of Mississippi's Negroes, is very real; but it is.

It is the MFDP's position that the route to effective political expression in Mississippi lies, at least in the immediate future, in *independent* political organization in the black community. For one thing, there are just no other possibilities. Behind its facade of moderation, the racist state Democratic party appears unable to moderate its actions or policies, or even to give a convincing appearance of having done so, in order to appeal to the Negro voter. So the newly registered Negro has little choice but to enter the MFDP. This is undoubtedly part of the reason that the Democratic administration indulges in its half-hearted, sparing, and almost nervous implementation of the Voting Rights Bill. It is not anxious to create a class of new voters in the South unless reasonably certain that they will gravitate into the ranks of LBJ's "great consensus."

As early as last spring before the voting bill was even passed, it became clear that as far as the national Democratic party was concerned the bill was intended to register not Negroes, but Democrats. The president and top officials of the national party played host to almost one hundred carefully selected Negro "leaders" from the Deep South. The largest single delegation at this carefully unpublicized meeting was from the state of Mississippi, and was comprised of the few figures in the Negro community who were not known to be active in or sympathetic to the MFDP. The group met with the highest level leadership of the party and the president, and the message was: Go home and organize your people into the Democratic party. They were also briefed on the War on Poverty, as though there was a relationship between organizing for the Democratic party and the Poverty Program. Nothing in the manner or speeches of any of the speakers indicated that they conceived of any role for their carefully chosen Negro "leaders" other than delivering the votes of the community and dispensing the patronage.

However, in Mississippi, it is a difficult task to organize Negroes into the party of Eastland and Ross Barnett, especially when this party maintains it doesn't want Negroes. So, when U.S. Attorney General Katzenbach is asked why there are only nineteen federal registrars in Mississippi, which has eighty-four counties, he is prone to mumble something about "giving the state time to reform." In the case of Mississippi and Alabama, the state means the local Democratic party. But, the fact is that there is a total absence of any element in the Mississippi Democratic party that can spearhead any kind of reform that the national party says it expects. And, ironically, so long as Washington holds the implementation of the voting bill to a pace just short of scandalous so as to minimize the independent effectiveness of the Negro at the polls, any incipient "moderates" within the white party who might be inclined to ally with us will remain well hidden. On the surface, the group that seems to gain most from this stalemate would appear to be the old line racists that control the state Democratic party now.

### Deepening Political Consciousness

However, while waiting for the vote to become a reality, we can use the time to strengthen and deepen the level of organization across the state, and develop the political consciousness in the community. Mississippi is the only state in which there is a statewide, active, and viable framework of organization in the Negro community. Our job now is to establish and entrench in every Negro community the tradition of active participation in politics, in which the people will understand that their involvement and control of *their own* political organization is their strongest weapon. By continuing to run candidates who are presently doomed to lose, by increasing the program of political workshops on the beat and precinct level, run by community leaders, we can change the old concept of political leadership in the community. We are deepening the concept of grass-roots democracy in which the community gets a chance to speak collectively, for itself, and when necessary to select its representatives. Conversely, a leadership is emerging which recognizes that any power to which it can aspire is nothing more than an expression of the unified and collective strength of the community, and that it is only to that base that its responsibility lies. In this way, the community will have a real choice, rather than being obliged to vote for machine candidates selected "downtown."

What is possible for such an organization? Of Mississippi's eighty-four counties, twenty-nine presently have outright Negro majorities, eleven are between 40 and 49 percent Negro, and twelve are between 30 and 39 percent Negro. At a minimum it is possible for a cohesive and unified political effort in the black community to elect candidates in twenty-nine counties and to determine the outcome of contests in twenty-three others. This would drastically alter the composition and politics of the state legislature. Municipal elections are also vulnerable. Of seventeen cities with over ten thousand population, five (Yazoo, Greenwood, Greenville, Natchez, and Clarksdale) have very slim Negro majorities. None of the other large cities has less than 20 percent Negro populations.

Our job must be, then, to continue organizing these black voters into an independent political organ capable of unified action on the state level. If this appears to "introduce racial politics and further polarize the state," as the national Democrats like to claim, that's all right. Once we have this organization functioning, white allies of all stripes, moderates, liberals, and even radicals, can blossom in the ranks of the white party, for ultimately no politician is going to ignore that kind of organized voting strength. But by the time these overtures come—when the majority of Negroes have the vote—the independent and democratic organization of the Negro community must be so established as to enable the community to negotiate with the white power structure from a *position of actual political strength* and in a unified manner. So, when this dialogue takes place, it will not be to individual Negroes on terms of patronage and prestige, but to the true representatives of the community and in terms of governmental power. It is only in this manner that the vote will become an implement for social change in Mississippi.

*1966*

# Toward Black Liberation

*With Stokely Carmichael*

ONE of the most pointed illustrations of the need for black power, as a positive and redemptive force in a society degenerating into a form of totalitarianism, is to be made by examining the history of distortion that the concept has received in the national media. In this "debate," as in everything else that affects our lives, Negroes are dependent on, and at the discretion of, forces and institutions within the white society which have little interest in representing us honestly. Our experience with the national press has been that where they have managed to escape a meretricious special interest in "Git Whitey" sensationalism and race-war-mongering, individual reporters and commentators have been conditioned by the enveloping racism of the society to the point where they are incapable even of objective observation and reporting of racial *incidents,* much less the analysis of *ideas.* But this limitation of vision and perceptions is an inevitable consequence of the dictatorship of definition, interpretation, and consciousness, along with the censorship of history that the society has inflicted upon the Negro—and itself.

Jes' as water seek the low places, power seek the weak places. Understand that, an' you understand why the young folk talkin' 'bout Black Power.

JUNEBUG JABBO JONES, Ways and Means address, Washington, D.C., 1965

Our concern for black power addresses itself directly to this problem: the necessity to reclaim our history and our identity from the cultural terrorism and depredation of self-justifying white guilt.

To do this we shall have to struggle for the right to create our own terms through which to define ourselves and our relationship to the society, and to have these terms recognized. This is the first necessity of a free people, and the first right that any oppressor must suspend. The white fathers of American racism knew this—instinctively it seems—as is indicated by the continuous record of the distortion and omission in their dealings with the red and black men. In the same way that southern apologists for the "Jim Crow" society have so obscured, muddied, and misrepresented the record of the Reconstruction period, until it is almost impossible to tell what really happened, their contemporary counterparts are busy doing the same thing with the recent history of the civil rights movement.

In 1964, for example, the national Democratic party, led by L. B. Johnson and Hubert H. Humphrey, cynically undermined the efforts of Mississippi's black population to achieve some degree of political representation. Yet, whenever the events of that convention are recalled by the press, one sees only that aversion fabricated by the press agents of the Democratic party. A year later, the House of Representatives, in an even more vulgar display of political racism, made a mockery of the political rights of Mississippi's Negroes when it failed to unseat the Mississippi delegation to the House which had been elected through a process which methodically and systematically excluded over 450,000 voting-age Negroes, almost one-half of the total electorate of the state. Whenever this event is mentioned in print, it is in terms which leave one with the rather curious impression that somehow the oppressed Negro people of Mississippi are at fault for confronting the Congress with a situation in which they had no alternative but to endorse Mississippi's racist political practices.

I mention these two examples because, having been directly involved in them, I can see very clearly the discrepancies between what happened and the versions that are finding their way into general acceptance as a kind of popular mythology. Thus the victimization of the Negro takes place in two phases—first it occurs in fact and deed, then, and this is equally sinister, in the official recording of those facts.

The "black power" program and concept which is being articulated by SNCC, CORE, and a host of community organizations in the ghettos of the North and South has not escaped that process. The white press has been busy articulating their own analyses, their own interpretations, and criticisms of their own creations. For example, while the press had given wide and sensational dissemination to attacks made by figures in the civil rights movement—foremost among which are Roy Wilkins of the NAACP and Whitney Young of the Urban League—and to the hysterical ranting about black racism made by the political chameleon that now serves as vice-president, it has generally failed to give accounts of the reasonable and productive dialogue which is taking place in the Negro community, and in certain important areas in the white religious and intellectual community. A national committee of influential Negro churchmen affiliated with the National Council of Churches, despite their obvious respectability and responsibility, had to resort to a paid advertisement to articulate their position, while anyone shouting the hysterical yappings of "Black Racism" got ample space. Thus, the American people have gotten at best a superficial and misleading account of the very terms and tenor of this debate. I wish to quote briefly from the statement by the national committee of churchmen which I suspect that the majority of Americans will not have seen. This statement appeared in the *New York Times* of July 31, 1966.

> We an informal group of Negro Churchmen in America are deeply disturbed about the crisis brought upon our country by historic distortions of important human realities in the controversy about "black power." What we see shining through the variety of rhetoric is not anything new but the same old problem of power and race which has faced our beloved country since 1619.
>
> . . . The conscience of black men is corrupted because, having no power to implement the demands of conscience, the concern for justice in the absence of justice becomes a chaotic self-surrender. Powerlessness breeds a race of beggars. We are faced now with a situation where powerless conscience meets conscience-less power, threatening the very foundation of our Nation.
>
> . . . We deplore the overt violence of riots, but we feel it is more important to focus on the real sources of these eruptions. These sources may be abetted inside the Ghetto, but their basic cause lies in the silent and covert violence which white middleclass America inflicts upon the victims of the inner city.
>
> . . . In short, the failure of American leaders to use American power to create equal opportunity *in life* as well as *law*, this is the real problem and not the anguished cry for black power. . . . Without the capacity to *participate with power*, *i.e.*, to have some organized political and economic strength to really influence people with whom one interacts—integration is not meaningful.
>
> . . . America has asked its Negro citizens to fight for opportunity as *individuals*, whereas at certain points in our history what we have needed

most has been opportunity for the *whole group*, not just for selected and approved Negroes. . . .

We must not apologize for the existence of this form of group power, for we have been oppressed as a group and not as individuals. We will not find our way out of that oppression until both we and America accept the need for Negro Americans, as well as for Jews, Italians, Poles, and white Anglo-Saxon Protestants, among others, to have and to wield group power.

Traditionally, for each new ethnic group, the route to social and political integration into America's pluralistic society has been through the organization of their own institutions with which to represent their communal needs within the larger society. This is simply stating what the advocates of black power are saying. The strident outcry, *particularly* from the liberal community, that has been evoked by this proposal can only be understood by examining the historic relationship between Negro and white power in this country.

Negroes are defined by two forces: their blackness and their powerlessness. There have been traditionally two communities in America. The white community, which controlled and defined the forms that all institutions within the society would take, and the Negro community, which has been excluded from participation in the power decisions that shaped the society, and has traditionally been dependent upon, and subservient to, the white community.

This has not been accidental. The history of every institution of this society indicates that a major concern in the ordering and structuring of the society has been the maintaining of the Negro community in its condition of dependence and oppression. This has not been on the level of individual acts of discrimination between individual whites against individual Negroes, but as acts by the total white community against the Negro community. This fact cannot be too strongly emphasized—that racist assumptions of white supremacy have been so deeply ingrained in the structure of the society that it infuses its entire functioning, and is so much a part of the national subconscious that it is taken for granted and is frequently not even recognized.

Let me give an example of the difference between individual racism and tionalized racism. But the society either pretends it doesn't know of this situation, or is incapable of doing anything meaningful about it. And this is an act of individual racism, widely deplored by most segments of the society. But when in that same city, Birmingham, Alabama, not five but five hundred Negro babies die each year because of a lack of proper food, shelter, and medical facilities, and thousands more are destroyed and maimed physically, emotionally, and intellectually because of conditions of poverty and deprivation in the ghetto, that is a function of institutionalized racism. But the society either pretends it doesn't know of this situation, or is incapable of doing anything meaningful about it. And this resistance to doing anything meaningful about conditions in that ghetto comes from the fact that the ghetto is itself a product of a combination of forces and special interests in the white community, and the groups that have access to the resources and power to change that situation benefit, politically and economically, from the existence of that ghetto.

It is more than a figure of speech to say that the Negro community in America is the victim of white imperialism and colonial exploitation. This is in practical economic and political terms true. There are over twenty million black people comprising 10 percent of this nation. They for the most part live in well-defined areas of the country—in the shantytowns and rural black belt areas of the South, and increasingly in the slums of northern and western industrial cities. If one goes into any Negro community, whether it be in Jackson, Mississippi, Cambridge, Maryland, or Harlem, New York, one will find that the same combination of political, economic, and social forces are at work. The people in the Negro community do not control the resources of that community, its political decisions, its law enforcement, its housing standards; and even the physical ownership of the land, houses, and stores *lies outside that community.*

It is white power that makes the laws, and it is violent white power in the form of armed white cops that enforces those laws with guns and nightsticks. The vast majority of Negroes in this country live in these captive communities and must endure these conditions of oppression because, and only because, *they are black and powerless.* I do not suppose that at any point the men who control the power and resources of this country ever sat down and designed these black enclaves and formally articulated the terms of their colonial and dependent status, as was done, for example, by the apartheid government of South Africa. Yet, one can not distinguish between one ghetto and another. As one moves from city to city, it is as though some malignant racist planning unit had done precisely this—designed each one from the same master blueprint. And indeed, if the ghetto had been formally and deliberately planned, instead of growing spontaneously and inevitably from the racist functioning of the various institutions that combine to make the society, it would be somehow less frightening. The situation would be less frightening because, if these ghettos were the result of design and conspiracy, one could understand their similarity as being artificial and consciously imposed, rather than the result of identical patterns of white racism which repeat themselves in cities as distant as Boston and Birmingham. Without bothering to list the historic factors which contribute to this pattern—economic exploitation, political impotence, discrimination in employment and education—one can see that to correct this pattern will require far-reaching changes in the basic power relationships and the ingrained social patterns within the society. The question is, of course, what kinds of changes are necessary, and how is it possible to bring them about?

In recent years, the answer to these questions which has been given by most articulate groups of Negroes and their white allies, the "liberals" of all stripes, has been in terms of something called "integration." According to the advocates of integration, social justice will be accomplished by "integrating the Negro into the mainstream institutions of the society from which he has been traditionally excluded." It is very significant that each time I have heard this formulation it has been in terms of "the Negro," the individual Negro, rather than in terms of the community.

This concept of integration had to be based on the assumption that there was nothing of value in the Negro community and that little of value could be created among Negroes, so the thing to do was to siphon off the "acceptable" Negroes into the surrounding middle-class white community. Thus the goal of the movement for integration was simply to loosen up the restrictions barring the entry of Negroes into the white community. Goals around which the struggle took place, such as public accommodation, open housing, job opportunity on the executive level (which is easier to deal with than the problem of semi-skilled and blue-collar jobs which involve more far-reaching economic adjustments), are quite simply middle-class goals, articulated by a tiny group of Negroes who had middle-class aspirations. It is true that the student demonstrations in the South during the early sixties, out of which SNCC came, had a similar orientation. But while it is hardly a concern of a black sharecropper, dishwasher, or welfare recipient whether a certain fifteen-dollar-a-day motel offers accommodations to Negroes, the overt symbols of white supremacy and the imposed limitations on the Negro community had to be destroyed. Now, black people must look beyond these goals, to the issue of collective power.

Such a limited class orientation was reflected not only in the program and goals of the civil rights movement, but in its tactics and organization. It is very significant that the two oldest and most "respectable" civil rights organizations have constitutions which *specifically* prohibit partisan political activity. CORE once did, but changed that clause when it changed its orientation toward black power. But this is perfectly understandable in terms of the strategy and goals of the older organizations. The civil rights movement saw its role as a kind of liaison between the powerful white community and the dependent Negro one. The dependent status of the black community apparently was unimportant since—if the movement were successful—it would blend into the white community anyway. We made no pretense of organizing and developing institutions of community power in the Negro community, but appealed to the conscience of white institutions of power. The posture of the civil rights movement was that of the dependent, the suppliant. The theory was that without attempting to create any organized base of political strength itself, the civil rights movement could, by forming coalitions with various "liberal" pressure organizations in the white community—liberal reform clubs, labor unions, church groups, progressive civic groups—and at times one or the other of the major political parties—influence national legislation and national social patterns.

I think we all have seen the limitations of this approach. We have repeatedly seen that political alliances based on appeals to conscience and decency are chancy things, simply because institutions and political organizations have no consciences, outside their own special interests. The political and social rights of Negroes have been and always will be negotiable and expendable the moment they conflict with the interests of our "allies." If we do not learn from history, we are doomed to repeat it, and that is precisely the lesson of the Reconstruction. Black people were allowed to register, vote, and participate in politics because it was to the advantage of powerful white allies to promote this. But this was the result of white decision, and it was ended by other white men's decision before any political base powerful enough to challenge that decision could be established in the southern Negro community. (Thus at this point in the struggle Negroes have no assurance—save a kind of idiot optimism and faith in a society whose history is one of racisim—that if it were to become necessary, even the painfully limited gains thrown to the civil rights movement by the Congress would not be revoked as soon as a shift in political sentiments should occur.)[1]

The major limitation of this approach was that it tended to maintain the traditional dependence of Negroes and of the movement. We depended upon the good will and support of various groups within the white com-

---

1   Prophetic.

munity whose interests were not always compatible with ours. To the extent that we depended on the financial support of other groups, we were vulnerable to their influence and domination.

Also, the program that evolved out of this coalition was really limited and inadequate in the long term and one which affected only a small select group of Negroes. Its goal was to make the white community accessible to "qualified" Negroes, and presumably each year a few more Negroes armed with their passports—a couple of university degrees—would escape into middle-class America and adopt the attitudes and life-styles of that group; and one day the Harlems and the Wattses would stand empty, a tribute to the success of integration. This is simply neither realistic nor particularly desirable. You can integrate communities, but you assimilate individuals. Even if such a program were possible, its result would be, not to develop the black community as a functional and honorable segment of the total society, with its own cultural identity, life patterns, and institutions, but to abolish it—the final solution to the Negro problem. Marx said that the working class is the first class in history that ever wanted to abolish itself. If one listens to some of our "moderate" Negro leaders, it appears that the American Negro is the first race that ever wished to abolish itself. The fact is that what must be abolished is not the black community but the dependent colonial status that has been inflicted upon it. The racial and cultural personality of the black community must be preserved and the community must win its freedom while preserving its cultural integrity. This is the essential difference between integration as it is currently advocated and the concept of black power.

What has the movement for integration accomplished to date? The Negro graduating from MIT with a doctorate will have better job opportunities available to him than are available to Lynda Bird Johnson. But the rate of unemployment in the Negro community is steadily increasing, while that in the white community decreases. More educated Negroes hold executive jobs in major corporations and federal agencies than ever before, but the gap between white income and Negro income has almost doubled in the last twenty years. More suburban housing is available to Negroes, but housing conditions in the ghetto are steadily declining. While the infant mortality rate of New York City is at its lowest rate ever in the city's history, the infant mortality rate of Harlem is steadily climbing. There has been an organized national resistance to the Supreme Court's order to integrate the schools, and the federal government has not acted to enforce that order. Less than 15 percent of black children in the South attend integrated schools, and Negro schools, which the vast majority of black children still attend, are increasingly decrepit, overcrowded, understaffed, inadequately equipped and funded.

This explains why the rate of school dropouts is increasing among Negro teenagers, who then express their bitterness, hopelessness, and alienation by the only means they have—rebellion. As long as people in the ghettos of our large cities feel that they are victims of the misuse of white power without any way to have their needs represented—and these are frequently simple needs: to get the welfare inspectors to stop kicking down their doors in the middle of the night, and the cops from beating their children, to get the landlord to exterminate the vermin in their home, the city to collect their garbage—we will continue to have riots. These are not the products of "black power," but of the absence of any organization capable of giving the community the power, the black power, to deal with its problems.

SNCC proposes that it is now time for the black freedom movement to stop pandering to the fears and anxieties of the white middle class in the attempt to earn its "good will," and to return to the ghetto to organize these communities to control themselves. This organization must be attempted in northern and southern urban areas as well as in the rural black belt counties of the South. The chief antagonist to this organization is, in the South, the overtly racist Democratic party, and in the North, the equally corrupt big city machines.

The standard argument presented against independent political organization is "But you are only 10 percent." I cannot see the relevance of this observation, since no one is talking about taking over the country, but only of taking control over our own communities.

The fact is that the Negro population, 10 percent or not, is very strategically placed because—ironically—of segregation. What is also true is that Negroes have never been able to utilize the full voting potential of our numbers. Where we could vote, the case has always been that the white political machine stacks and gerrymanders the political subdivisions in Negro neighborhoods so the true voting strength is never reflected in political strength. Would anyone looking at the distribution of political power in Manhattan ever think that Negroes represented 60 percent of the population there?

Just as often the effective political organization in Negro communities is absorbed by tokenism and patronage—the time-honored practice of "giving" certain offices to selected Negroes. The machine thus creates a "little machine," which is subordinate and responsive to it, in the Negro community. These Negro political "leaders" are really vote deliverers, more responsible to the white machine and the white power structure than to the community they allegedly represent. Thus the white community is able to substitute patronage control for audacious black power in the Negro community. This is precisely what Johnson tried to do even before the Voting Rights Act of 1966 was passed. The national Democrats made it very clear that the measure was intended to register Democrats, not Negroes. The president and top officials of the Democratic party called in almost one hundred selected Negro "leaders" from the Deep South. Nothing was said about changing the policies of the racist state parties, nothing was said about repudiating such leadership figures as James Eastland and Ross Barnett in Mississippi or George Wallace in Alabama. What was said was simply "Go home and organize your people into the local Democratic party— *then* we'll see about poverty money and appointments." (Incidentally, for the most part the War on Poverty in the South is controlled by local Democratic ward heelers—and outspoken racists who have used the program to change the form of the Negroes' dependence. People who were afraid to register for fear of being thrown off the farm are now afraid to register for fear of losing their Head Start jobs.)

We must organize black community power to end these abuses, and to give the Negro community a chance to have its needs expressed. A leadership which is truly "responsible"—not to the white press and power structure, but to the community—must be developed. Such leadership will recognize that its power lies in the unified and collective strength of that community. This will make it difficult for the white leadership group to conduct its dialogue with individuals in terms of patronage and prestige, and will force them to talk to the community's representatives in terms of real power.

The single aspect of the black power program that has encountered most criticism is this concept of independent organization. This is presented as third-partyism, which has never worked, or a withdrawal into black nationalism and isolationism. If such a program is developed, it will not have the effect of isolating the Negro community but the reverse. When the Negro community is able to control local office and negotiate with other groups from a position of organized strength, the possibility of meaningful political alliances on specific issues will be increased. That is a rule of politics and there is no reason why it should not operate here. The only difference is that we will have the power to define the terms of these alliances.

The next question usually is: "So—can it work, can the ghettos in fact be organized?" The answer is that this organization must be successful, because there are no viable alternatives—not the War on Poverty, which was at its inception limited to dealing with effects rather than causes, and has become simply another source of machine patronage. And "Integration" is meaningful only to a small chosen class within the community.

The revolution in agricultural technology in the South is displacing the rural Negro community into northern urban areas. Both Washington, D.C., and Newark, New Jersey, have Negro majorities. One-third of Philadelphia's population of two million people is black. "Inner city" in most major urban areas is already predominantly Negro, and, with the white rush to suburbia, Negroes will in the next three decades control the hearts of our great cities. These areas can become either concentration camps with a bitter and volatile population whose only power is the power to destroy, or organized and powerful communities able to make constructive contributions to the total society. Without the power to control their lives and their communities, without effective political institutions through which to relate to the total society, these communities will exist in a constant state of insurrection. This is a choice that the country will have to make.

*1966*

# Negroes with Guns

■ ■ ■ ■ ■

I F Sunday were not a "slow" news day, and if Americans—particularly white Americans—did not have an obsessional love-fear-guilt thing about guns, James A. Perkins, the president of Cornell University, would be resting more easily tonight. In fact he might have good reason to be downright pleased with himself and his administration. But for those two factors, Perkins would be able to point to the fact that Cornell was successfully weathering a potentially violent confrontation with its black students and their SDS supporters without large-scale destruction of property, massive police violence, or the "shutting-down" of the university's functions by dissident students—none of which Harvard, Columbia, or Berkeley was able to avoid.

But Sunday *is* a slow news day, and white America's guilt-ridden fascination with guns becomes paranoid hysteria when those guns are in the hands of young blacks. And the idea—greatly exaggerated by the way—that any part of the white society's governing institutions, even something as innocuous as a university, has "capitulated" or "surrendered" to those armed blacks evokes the beginning of the end, the specter of a black

All sho'nuff dialogue come from the barrel of a gun.

JUNEBUG JABBO JONES, Cornell University address, April 21st (day after the occupation of Willard Straight Hall)

If, as we are constantly being told, there is a white power structure at this university, then it had damned well better start acting like one.

VISITING PROFESSOR (White), Cornell University, May 1st

In 1969, one of the major issues in American education was the question of Black Studies Departments and Eth-

takeover, and blows white America's collective mind. So Perkins's regime, which was—until the appearance of the guns and what they refer to as "that damned picture"[1]—one of the most skillful exponents of the anticipatory compromise, has been shaken to the point where friend and critic give it no better than a 50-50 chance of survival. If the Perkins regime falls, it will be because the press said he "capitulated" to armed blacks—and to capitulate is unforgivable, even if the blacks were right and, as far as anyone could tell, quite determined to fight in dead earnest for their position.

The establishment has many strategies and tactics for dealing with dissent, but its ultimate weapon is violence. (There was no violence at Cornell, but nobody seems to remember that.) Short of violence, the establishment has minor ploys like transforming issues of principle into issues of etiquette (it is bad form for students to disrupt violently the vice president's speech, even though a rotten egg is not a fire bomb and the vice president *is* the spokesman for a policy of genocide in Vietnam). Another name for this is, of course, hypocrisy, and it is this process at work which has made the focal issue at Cornell the question of guns in the hands of the blacks. But the press in its foolish search for sensationalism has stumbled onto a question which may become crucial for the foreseeable future: *What if blacks and radicals generally refuse to concede the exclusive right to violence to the establishment?*

Traditionally, when the establishment calls for dialogue and negotiation, it means *limited* dialogue. That is, it will, as my students say, "dialogue with" you until it grows weary or impatient, at which point the language of dialogue becomes the language of the nightstick and the marines. This certainly has been the nature of all black dialogue with white America in

---

nic Colleges. At universities and colleges throughout the country, black students charged that the education they were receiving was white-oriented, and that it neither recognized nor responded to their special needs as black people. They demanded an acceleration in the recruitment of black students and the inclusion of black history and culture in the curriculum; paralleling the demands the black power movement was making in a larger social context, they called for power and autonomy over their educational life.

Universities were both unable and, in many cases, unwilling to respond to these demands, and confrontations between blacks and whites broke out on campuses across the nation. One of the most dramatic of these conflicts occurred in the staid Ivy League atmosphere of Cornell University, where black students finally armed themselves and occupied a campus building. The following selection by Michael Thelwell, who was a fellow at the Institute for the Humanities at Cornell during the crisis, is a case study of the black students' revolt at this school as well as a consideration of the broader question of violence on campus.—Eds.

1 A widely-published, dramatic picture of a black student wearing a bandoleer and holding a rifle.

the past. University administrations, despite their loud appeals to reasonable and civilized discourse, have reserved their right to "invoke cloture" by way of the machinery of violence that the system places at their disposal. It is only because the dissenters have tacitly conceded them this prerogative that the violence on university campuses has been "limited," if one considers broken heads and backs to be "limited" violence. Under the pressure of the situation, the Cornell blacks felt forced to take that option away from Perkins, and faced him with the necessity of choosing between equal negotiation or unlimited violence.

Negotiation from a position of equality becomes, in the language of the establishment, "capitulation." This is what got the trustees, the state legislature, the governor, and the conservative faculty uptight: the recognition that the rules had been changed and that their traditional position of paternalistic power supported by the threat of violence was not operative. For the first time in four months, the university had to *listen* to the blacks; all along they had been pretending to listen. Faced with the alternative of doing either a little "capitulation" or a little killing, they chose to negotiate for real—what is an appropriate response in Harlem, Watts, Newark, or Saigon is clearly inappropriate on an Ivy League campus. The black students violated not only the civilized proprieties but also the notion of aesthetic distance, the notion that white American violence should be kept as far as possible from suburbia.

It is ironic that—with the exception of an episode in which the occupied building was invaded by fraternity jocks intent on acting out their red-blooded white American male fantasies—the Cornell incident was totally nonviolent. To what extent was this due to the presence of those guns? It is not by any means *certain* that, had they not been present, Perkins, under pressure from trustees, faculty, and alumni, would have unleashed the cops to break black heads. That this did not happen at Cornell may not be due solely to the presence of those guns, but the black students feel that in this case, at least, the basic effect of the guns was to prevent violence. It is a sad commentary on the society and the university that they are probably right.

Given the relatively peaceful and nondestructive nature of the incident and the fact that the black students emphasized their intention to use their guns only in the event of physical danger to the black women in the building, and that they did not threaten, coerce, or intimidate anyone at gunpoint, the response of certain hysterics on the faculty (located interestingly enough in the upper echelons of the history and government departments) is significant.

These gentlemen claim to be hopelessly compromised, that the university is in ruins and chaos, and that "academic freedom" has been ravished—presumably by the phallic rifle barrels. Obviously they are speaking in terms of high and lofty principle, as they must be speaking symbolically when they say that the administration has surrendered and there is "no authority" at Cornell, since the school seems to be functioning no less efficiently than it was before. What does my colleague mean—he is a civilized and humane man—when he calls Perkins a "spineless jellyfish" and calls for the "white power structure to start acting like one"? Would they really have preferred a shoot-out? And to maintain what principle?— their own notion of their privileged class position protected by the coercive machinery of the state?

What exactly is the "trust" that they accuse Perkins of violating? That he did not swiftly and forcibly put the blacks in their place? How? None of these men have, as far as I can see, said a mumbling word against police violence at Harvard. Guns in the hands of the ROTC on this campus, on the hips of the campus cops, and in the hands of certain fraternities who had been arming themselves—this was a matter of public knowledge for weeks—do not seem to concern them. It is no wonder that "liberal" and "intellectual" have become dirty words in the minds of the young.

Given the peaceful nature of the confrontation, the agitation of these men is understandable only in the context of the entire controversy. The "trust" whose violation they bemoan is simply the racist principle that they and their class have the prerogative to run black people's lives. Because under-neath the labyrinthine swirls of red tape, due process, and rhetoric on both sides, that is what the ultimate issue is. The actual, specific issues that trig-gered the confrontation are quite trivial.

Here is an abbreviated version of how the issues developed. When James A. Perkins, a Philadelphia Quaker of liberal convictions and a man of humane conscience, gained the presidency in 1963, he took over a uni-versity that embodied, as do most American universities, the best and worst of American society. One thing it did not have was a race problem, since there were virtually no blacks (about six per class year or no more than twenty-four at any one time). Besides, the few Negroes who were present at that time, rather than preparing the university for what was to come, probably misled them. These were middle-class, "integrated" blacks who were upwardly mobile and who wanted to fit in and belong.

A committee was set up to finance and recruit black students at Cornell and in 1965 a group of thirty-nine arrived. Contrary to popular racist myth, the black students at Cornell were not "so badly prepared as to be unable to handle the academic load," which is a reason given by certain journalists for the agitation. Prior to the "troubles," this first group, which will graduate this year, had lost only three students, and only one for academic reasons. The psychological burdens are far greater than the academic ones, as we shall see.

What was expected, of course, was that these favored blacks would adjust, adapt, and integrate themselves into the life of the campus, happily, gratefully—and uncritically. At the end of four years, they would emerge with the skills, manners, and attitudes necessary to usher them into the middle-class world of affluence and gracious living. The only problems anyone visualized in that age of innocence were social ones, like what to do about fraternities that discriminate. (Cornell, with some sixty Greek-letter organizations, has not been quite able to shake its reputation as a winter playground for the sons and daughters of the eastern establishment.) But at first even the fraternities cooperated, sponsoring a "soul of blackness week" and setting up a committee to help black prospects cope with the intricacies of "rushing."

For a while, everything went according to script. The notion that this almost lily-white institution, which had been conceived, structured, and had functioned without any thought to the educational needs of the black community, would have to undergo very basic adjustments if it were to be really responsive to the practical and psychological needs of blacks, was apparently as unthinkable as any serious suggestion that God might be black. The fact that with three exceptions, and those in the professional schools, the faculty was lily-white and that no courses *at all* dealing *specifically* with the black experience were offered, seems to have escaped notice. Truly Cornell's small black community was without history or identity so far as the institution was concerned.

As the black population grew—it now numbers about 250—the sounds from the black community changed. Blacks began to perceive that integration was not liberation. Cultural integrity for the black community became a goal and instead of white tolerance and liberal sympathy, black folks were talking about black power, and not only that but by any means necessary.

Nationally the black community had stopped asking and started demanding. *They* would make the decisions affecting their lives, and *they,* for the first time in their history, would define the terms of their relationship to the white society. Junebug Jabbo Jones—may his tribe increase— the peripatetic black sage who is a legend in his own time, told a gathering of black Ivy Leaguers that "Harvard, Princeton, and Yale had ruined more good niggers than whiskey and dope together," and he received a standing ovation.

At Cornell, blacks began to examine their historical situation and the motives of their benefactors. What was the intent of the decision that had brought them to Cornell? Who had made it and who supplied the money? Had white folks suddenly got religion or did the riots have anything to do with it? Were black students in fact partners and beneficiaries in the exploitation of other blacks here and in the Third World? More important, would their education lead them to a never-never land suspended between the two communities?

They started talking about the role of a class-oriented, culturally chauvinistic, white educational system in dividing the black community and siphoning off and coopting its leadership. More than that, they saw the well-meaning but somewhat self-congratulatory publicity that the university was sending out (in fairness it was mainly to alumni for purposes of funding the project) as reducing them to laboratory specimens and evidence of the school's new morality.

They demanded an Afro-American studies program from the university shortly after the King assassination. It seems that the students had no clear idea of what the form and structure of such a program should be. But how in reality could they be expected to, given the educational system to which they were accustomed? Some faculty members, for reasons of politics, internal and general, expressed skepticism or outright hostility. But the administration, sensing the temper of the students, set up a committee to give shape to the idea.

This committee, under Professor Chandler Morse, set about its work in a methodical and cautious manner, genuinely concerned, I believe, with exploring all possibilities in order to set up a program that would not be vulnerable to sniping from the established departments nor offensive to even the most conservative sensibility, and that would also satisfy the blacks. This proved impossible, particularly since the no longer diffident blacks were definitely not interested in avoiding any of the first two contingencies.

Not much of a tangible nature had happened by November of 1969, and the blacks, suspecting that they were witnessing still another example of honky "tricknology," got restive.

They were simultaneously experiencing some guilt at either having "escaped" the ghetto or, in some cases, never having experienced it. This was exacerbated by a steady stream of black speakers and ideologically articulate students who challenged the group's presence on the white campus as opposed to "working" in the community or at a black school.

Thus the Afro-American studies program became very important as a tangible sign that they were not being "coopted" and seduced by the "man's" system. But to be that, the program had to be free of domination, control, and influence, overt or covert, from and by whites.

Within the Afro organization, sentiment for an autonomous black college developed; the group occupied the office of the committee chairman and declared the committee dissolved. This did not sit well with a great many faculty members.

In support of a number of political demands, the organization began a series of noisy, disruptive, and admittedly abrasive—but essentially non-violent—demonstrations. To emphasize the need for black courses and materials, they took a number of books from the library shelves and, finding them irrelevant, tossed them in a heap on the floor. To dramatize their demand for separate eating facilities, they danced on tables in the cafeteria at lunch hour. They disrupted the clinic in demanding a black psychiatrist. And when the promised building to house the activities around the program did not materialize, they took over a building and evicted the whites, giving them three minutes to leave. They still have that building, and when the university did not furnish it as rapidly as they wished, a task force "liberated" furniture from other campus buildings. Now faculty and students alike were murmuring that it was time to teach the blacks a lesson.

When a small group ran through the administration building and into Perkins's office brandishing toy guns (they were obviously on some revolutionary fantasy of their own), it was clear to many whites that they had gone too far. By this time black-white tension was quite high.

The demands were not what was at issue—since even critics had to admit that they were justified, and with each demonstration the speed of administrative implementation perceptibly increased. The sentiment among some whites, mostly faculty, was that the blacks had to be disciplined. Consequently, charges were brought against six brothers for the toy gun incident and the liberation of the furniture.

Despite repeated urgings, promises of merely "symbolic" punishment, and later warnings and threats of suspension, the six refused to appear before the disciplinary committee. Now all the time this committee was saying informally that the charges themselves were not too "serious" they were also threatening suspension for nonappearance. So the issue was clearly the validation of the judiciary by the appearance of the six, not the charges (especially since the committee's mandate provided a mechanism for judgment in absentia).

During this period there was a symposium on South Africa. Cornell did own stock in Chase Manhattan and several other companies involved in business in South Africa, and Perkins himself—a perfect liberal—was on the Chase Manhattan board. (He is also chairman of the board of the United Negro College Fund.) Because of these connections, the black students felt that Perkins was hardly qualified morally or politically to introduce the speakers in the final session.

They planned to disrupt the meeting, but one excitable student got carried away and seized Perkins by the scruff of the neck. (The brother was agitated at the prospect of his scholarship money possibly originating in South African slave labor. The contradictions for black people on a white campus are indeed great.) Anyway, that broke the dam and sentiment was now quite high for swift and irrevocable discipline for blacks. Meanwhile, the six brothers were still adamant.

At the point where the six were to be suspended, 150 blacks appeared before the committee and informed them that the miscreants were not present and would not appear because:

1. The actions against only six constituted selective reprisal and were clearly intended as political intimidation.

2. By insisting on their appearance and hinting at light penalties, the committee was acting out a charade, the purpose of which was a symbolic lynching to appease "racist" elements on the campus.

3. The committee, as an agent of the university, had no legitimacy to judge political actions directed against the university.

4. As a lily-white committee, it was not a jury of any black's peers and was thus illegitimate.

5. As long as black people were in the institution, it was necessary for them to reserve the right of political action as a group, and since the six were the agents of the entire body, the entire body was culpable. But they were not about to relegate to whites the right to control the political activities of blacks made necessary by "lingering vestiges of white racism."

The committee—a joint student-faculty affair—saw fit to make no judgment and passed the buck to the Faculty Committee on Student Affairs. This committee examined the Afro-American position and found no merit therein. The six were instructed to appear and did not. At this point, the issue became one of conflicts of autonomy. The blacks were trapped in a position of having to back up their statement and their definition of their "right to political action." The faculty committee—beneath B O M F O G[2] rhetoric dripping with words like "sensitivity," "understanding," and "sympathy"—was affirming its right to judge blacks for political actions. It is thus primarily responsible for creating the situation that the administration then had to deal with.

Pointing to the precedent of labor-management arbitration, the blacks said they wanted neither sympathy, understanding, nor sensitivity, but an objective judiciary committee made up of people independent of the university to judge political actions of blacks.

At this point, the action thickens—three white students are discovered beaten up on campus, one of them quite seriously. The allegation was made by one that his assailant(s) were black. The *Daily Sun,* the campus newspaper, printed a hasty and ill-advised editorial implying that their policy of collective responsibility for political acts made all blacks in the Afro-American Society responsible and that they should "ferret out" the assailants and hand them over. It is not clear that the assailants were in fact black or that, if they were, they were in fact students. But the editorial, hysterical in tone and quite vituperative, was a clear call to white vigilantism. No one on the faculty pointed this out, nor were any voices raised about the prejudicial nature of the *Sun*'s assumptions.

The blacks received word that some fraternities and individual white students were purchasing arms in Ithaca. The blacks followed suit. The matter of the six had now dragged on for over two months and, given the added tension of the muggings, the nerves of both blacks and whites were frayed. But the whites outnumbered the blacks 14,000 to 250. Both sides seemed unable to dismount from the principled positions which they were riding to what seemed an inevitable confrontation.

The judiciary committee suddenly discovered that suspension was not inevitable after all and that they *could* judge the six in absentia. Two months earlier, this decision might have averted trouble. But when they handed down the reprimands, which are purely formal anyway, the atmosphere of heightened tension made it a provocation to both black and white.

That night a cross was burned by person or persons unknown, at the black women's cooperative house.[3] When the campus police came, they

2  Brotherhood-of-Man-Fatherhood-of-God.

3  In the intervening years there has been the suggestion that this may have been the work of a few immature black women students. At the time no one had reason to imagine

were unable to stay because of a series of false fire alarms that were being triggered all over the campus. The blacks found both actions equally provocative. The cross speaks for itself, and the police action seemed indicative of a callous, even racist, disregard for the safety of black women.

This was Thursday night. The coming weekend was parents' weekend and the blacks moved to occupy Willard Straight Hall, which was to be the focus of activities. When the fraternity men forced their way in, and the blacks heard radio reports concerning five carloads of armed whites (which never materialized, however), they sent out and got their guns.

The rest is history—the arrival of the mass media, the picture of armed blacks leaving the building, and the agreement with the administration in which the reprimands were rescinded and promises of legal assistance and no criminal action were made to the blacks. It is this agreement that the faculty found so distasteful.

It is impossible to say for certain just which principles the faculty imagined themselves to be preserving. In the beginning, the black students would probably have settled for a lifting of the suspension threat. As the issue developed and frustrations increased, however, the question became in their minds one of their ultimate powerlessness and what they saw as the university's willingness and ability to assert its power over their lives arbitrarily, however veiled and mild the manifestation of that power. This appeared to them to be simply a new style of paternalism which their new-found concept of black independence forced them to resist. It is interesting that having resisted so successfully and with élan, they now evince a new spirit and unity that is much less uptight and beleaguered.

The Afro association has now become the Black United Front, and the American blacks are entering into negotiations with Puerto Ricans, American Indians, West Indians, and African brothers and inviting them to use the facilities of the liberated building which has now become the Third World Center.

The white students, as a consequence of the "dialogue" which followed the incident, are also much less uptight than before. It is interesting that while the administration, for reasons of public safety as they put it, made disarmament the first priority, the white students to whom I spoke felt that as long as the blacks pledged to use their guns only in self-defense, and as long as the university, as one administrator said, "could not be responsible for conditions in the general society" that might threaten blacks (some

---

anything of the sort. If true, and one profoundly hopes that it isn't, this would represent a most heartless victimization of a very tense and beleaguered community.

claim to be still receiving threatening phone calls), they saw no reason why the blacks should be forced to disarm. The generation gap again? But it is clear why the administration's priorities are different from the students'.

This is a division which is symptomatic of much more; as long as the universities continue to embody within themselves the best and worst aspects of the society, it will continue. At their best the universities, and particularly the private ones, have represented, however marginally, a tradition of decency and a principled resistance to know-nothingism, political orthodoxy, and repression in the general society. Witness the McCarthy era and the movement against Vietnam that was launched from American campuses. By expressing a perception of the possibility of man, they have been the incubators of a generation of audacious, impatient, morally committed and idealistic young radicals not committed to the excesses of folly, pride, greed, moral flatulence, and violent exploitation that mark their society's relationship to the poor and powerless at home and abroad.

But at their worst, the universities are the agents and beneficiaries of exactly these forces. Without the technical systems and personnel they provide, Vietnam would be possible but not easy. Too often the privileged and smug faculty mandarins are flattered to supply the intellectual underpinnings for economic and political imperialism, and are able to coexist with racism in the society and to perpetuate it in the curricula. They—the private universities—grow affluent and powerful by supplying tax and moral loopholes for the heavily burdened pocketbooks and consciences of the rich. And despite their frequent and loud appeals for reasoned discourse as the avenue to "orderly change," they are ultimately no less coercive, inflexible, manipulative, undemocratic, and elitist than the class which they serve and whose interests they maintain while professing to scorn its values. As long as this duality continues, the conflict can only intensify. And the society is certainly capable of more violence than the most revolution-intoxicated student can even imagine.

*1969*

# Black Studies

## A Political Perspective

ANY attempt to discuss the question of what has come to be called "black studies," or "ethnic studies" as they say in California, that incubator of meaningless pop jargon, outside of a political perspective is futile. The demands on the part of black students and their activist mentors are a response to political realities in the black community. The considerations out of which these pressures come are clear, so clear in fact, that there should be no need for an essay of this kind were it not for the apparently limitless capacity for the debasement of language and the obscuring of issues demonstrated by the mass media of the society. It is true that in this enterprise, the media has enjoyed the co-operation, witting or otherwise, of any number of hastily discovered "spokesmen" for black studies whose "revolutionary" fervor and extravagant rhetoric is equalled only by their mysticism and anti-intellectualism.

As if this outpouring of definition from the left which serves, more often than not, to obscure more than it illuminates were not enough, there is an attendant motion on the right flank of the black community which is equally uninformed, short-sighted, and dogmatic. This faction, which includes such

Education is something the blood need. But y'awl got to watch it. I believe Harvard University done ruined mo' good niggers than whiskey.

JUNEBUG JABBO JONES, Ivy League address, Cambridge, Massachusetts, May 1st, 1964

The two things that we black folk need most is a lot of patience and a sense of irony.

JUNEBUG JABBO JONES, Pool Hall address, "Don't Let White Folks Run You Crazy," Jackson, Mississippi, October 2nd, 1964

established Negro intellectuals as Andrew Brimmer of the Federal Reserve Board, Sir Arthur Lewis, the West Indian economist presently at Princeton, Kenneth Clarke who recently resigned from the board of trustees of Antioch College after it had yielded to student demands for a black residence hall, Professor Martin Kilson of Harvard, Bayard Rustin, Roy Wilkins of the NAACP (naturally), and a number of old guard Negro administrators from southern Negro colleges, seems to have become the cutting edge of the establishment backlash against the movement for black studies. The burden of their objections, which reflects very clearly a class position if not their political sentiments—they seem to have no discernible common political perspective save for an acceptance of the "one society myth"—is best reflected in Sir Arthur Lewis's comment that "black studies will not prepare a black student to be president of General Motors." Well, neither will it prepare him to be pope, but that hardly seems to be the issue since it is not clear that anything short of civil revolution on the one hand and divine intervention on the other will accomplish either.

Equally interesting, not to say informative, in what it reveals of the attitudes of the men currently entrusted (by white society) with the education of young blacks, is the story rather gleefully reported in a recent issue of the *New York Times*. This concerns a "joke" which circulated at a meeting of the United Negro College Fund. While most of the administrators present admitted rather sheepishly that their schools were initiating "some kind of black studies" programs to anticipate and forestall student militance, their attitude toward the undertaking was made graphically clear by the story reported by the *Times* as exciting great mirth among them. The essence of this story has to do with a student applying for a job and being told by a computer that his training in black studies had prepared him only to pick cotton. To quote Ralph Ellison's nameless protagonist, "Bledsoe, you ain't nothing but a greasy chittlin' eater."

That this story and the *Times*'s prominent and snide presentation of it was the greatest possible indictment of these men, the process of so-called education that produced them, and the alleged institutions of learning that they preside over at the command of racist southern legislatures was perhaps lost on them. But the Bledsoes[1] of this world are distinguished less for their sense of irony than by their ill-disguised contempt for the black community and its heritage and traditions.

1 From Dr. Professor Bledsoe, the autocratic yet servile college president in *Invisible Man*, who cooperates with the white managers of the society in destroying the spirit and emasculating the consciousness of his students. As used here it is a generic term for all of his too numerous tribe.

The most substantive objections coming from the Negro right—despite a certain intemperance of expression as when he sneers at "soul courses," a phenomenon of his own invention—comes from Rustin. His concern is that white colleges will attempt to cop-out of what he sees as their responsibility to the black community by the expedient of hastily manufactured and meaningless programs designated "black studies," taught by semi-literate dashiki-clad demagogues with nothing to offer but a "militant black rap." Rustin fears that white schools will accept this as an easier and less expensive alternative to providing the massive and costly programs of remedial education which are required. To be sure, there is little in the history of these institutions that would suggest that they are not capable of such a ploy. I know of very few isolated campuses where this is happening to some degree, and I suspect that there are at least some others which will not be inhibited by questions of principle, morality, or their own internal standards from attempting to follow suit. But the places where this can happen are not educational institutions in any but the most superficial sense and are at present educating no one, black or white. Besides which, it is inconceivable that such programs can survive, and even to exist they require the complicity of self-seeking and socially irresponsible black charlatans and careerists. Though few in number, such a type exists and their destructive potential is great. But it is the responsibility of the students and the adult black community to resist any such development in any institution where it becomes evident. It would be pointless to pretend that this danger does not exist in some small degree, but my impression of the basic good sense of this student generation, and their serious commitment and sense of responsibility to themselves and their community reassures me that this tendency will be a short-lived one.

Whatever unity there is to be found in the positions of the black establishment—figures mentioned seem to reside in a thoroughly uncritical acceptance of the methods, goals, and the educational practices of white America save for its traditional exclusion of black people. They are joined in this assessment by the overwhelming majority of white academics. There are other critical positions to the left of them in the black community, ranging from a nationalism impractical at this time: "The place for black students is in black schools" (consequently the establishment of black studies programs on white campuses is a delusion luring black students onto white campuses "to be coopted and corrupted by the 'devil' ") to militant activism: "All of whitey's education is bullshit; all black people need to know is streetology. Black students should come on home to the streets and take *real* black studies in the areas of judo, karate, demolitions, and assorted martial arts."

The second position speaks for itself; the first is more emotionally appealing until one checks some figures—of the 400,000 black college students in the country last year, fully one half were from the North and were in white schools, many of them as a consequence of "conscience" programs of recruitment and financial aid on the part of these white schools. Few of the black southern colleges can accommodate more students than are currently enrolled even if we ignored their chronic financial problems and the educational philosophy (political control, really) within which too many are forced to operate.

At this point in history, black students in increasing numbers will have to attend either white schools or no school at all. This being the case, certain problems arise: how can the almost inevitable psychological and spiritual demoralization of the small minority of blacks in an overwhelmingly white institution—which was conceived, created, structured, and operated so as to service an oppressive social order—be avoided? Are the educational needs, both psychological and practical, of the black student identical with the white? What elements of the society control these institutions and to what ends? What finally, when one cuts through the liberal rhetoric and the humanistic bombast, is the essential social and political function of these institutions? Is this function at all coincident with the necessities and aspirations of the black population as articulated by the growing nationalist consciousness of all elements of the community? Can anyone reasonably expect—in a situation where even the white student, the beneficiary and inheritor of the system, has begun to question its economic and political functions at home and abroad and to reject the yawning gap between its pious, self-justifying rhetoric and its viciously exploitative and murderous reality, and to question the role of the universities in this pattern—that black students who, for the most part have never been allowed the luxury of any delusions about the meaning of their relationship to this society and who are now quickening to a vision however tentative and problematic, of collective black possibility, will find it possible or desirable to make a smooth and easy adjustment to institutions with the historical record and contemporary posture of the universities? The answer must be, in Stokely Carmichael's cryptic phrase "Hell, No."

And even if they wanted to, the attempt at emotional integration into these institutions would necessitate a process of psychological and cultural suicide. (Last spring during the "troubles" at the City College of New York, an incident occurred which is significant. Black and Puerto Rican students came under attack for "vandalism" when they destroyed what was described as "a work of art." One had to read the press reports very carefully to discover that what was destroyed was a tapestry depicting

George Washington receiving the worshipful homage of a group of black slaves. A small incident, but symptomatic of a seemingly endless accumulation of gratuitous, racist affrontery.)

As the current academic year opens, there is some evidence that a reaction against the concept of black studies is beginning to take form from another and possibly more troublesome source—the faculty and administration of the universities. The two groups need to be considered separately for their interests, although congruent, are not identical. In every case with which I am familiar, the administration has adopted a posture that can best be described as interested neutrality. That is, they take no substantive position on the *issues,* being more interested in peacekeeping operations with the parties to the action, namely the black students and their supporters and conservative elements on the faculty which see the agitation for black studies as threatening their class prerogatives and traditional jurisdictions. In every case, the rhetoric coming from these pockets of resistance has been couched in terms of lofty liberal principles, and considerations of the highest academic and professional integrity, but the rhetoric barely conceals a most vulgar political and professional self-interest and occasionally an overt old-fashioned white paternalism. One canard, coming most often from the least informed members of the faculty, maintains that there is simply not sufficient material in the field to support and justify black studies as a major field of academic endeavor. This statement reveals more than the ignorance of its authors because were it in fact true, it would constitute the strongest possible confirmation of the covert racism and cultural chauvinism which informs the intellectual and scholarly establishment. And the patent absurdity of the "insufficient material" assertion does not really absolve the scholarly establishment because the existence of this basic research is due to the lonely and heroic efforts of past generations of black scholars and a few whites—Herbert Aptheker, Melvin J. Herskovits, Sidney Kaplan come to mind—in the face of the active opposition and indifference of the "profession." And in the case of the black scholars who had to endure the condescension, skepticism, and disparagement of their efforts by white colleagues and publishers, our indebtedness is beyond expression or recompense. It is some small consolation that some of these morally courageous and dedicated pioneers, men like C. L. R. James, Sterling Brown, John H. Clarke, George Padmore, Arna Bontemps, and many more whose works are only now being "discovered" and published are present to witness the turning of the tide and the recognition and vindication of their efforts. And we have inherited from such men as W. E. B. Du Bois, J. A. Rogers, E. Franklin

Frazier, Alain Locke, Edward Wilmot Blyden, James Weldon Johnson, J. Carter Woodson, Kelley Miller, Leo William Hansbury both a scholarly example and the legacy of a distinguished tradition upon which to build.

Let us, for the moment, ignore this tradition and pretend, as those who make the charge of insufficient material must be doing, that these men never existed and their work had never been done. Would this in any way affect the necessity of this generation of black intellectuals to engage and demolish the racist mythology and distorted perception and interpretation of the black experience, culture, and reality which constitutes the intellectual underpinnings of white racism in the society? The political struggle for liberation and cultural integrity must be accompanied by an intellectual offensive—and this is one of the tasks of black studies. The most obvious and pressing imperative is the reexamination and rehabilitation of our cultural heritage and political history—African and American—from the intellectual colonialism that has been imposed upon it. This is merely the first responsibility. The next level of responsibility accruing to black studies is related integrally to "issues" raised by its white academic opponents and has literally to do with the decolonization of education in this country. We need to examine these objections in the context of necessities and goals of the black community. There is the procedural objection to separate, autonomous departments of black studies. It is important to note that these objections come most often from white academics in those disciplines most clearly affected by what we are about, which is to say history, the humanities, and the social sciences. Frequently they come from the upper echelons of these departments and include the faculty mandarins, the men least involved in teaching, and whose reputations and prestige derive from their roles as advisers and resource personnel to the political, military, and industrial managers of the society.

Their style is as constant as is their approach. First they trot out their liberal credentials as friends of "The Negro." Then they proceed to the startling admission that there have been errors of omission on the part of the white scholarly and educational community. Next they demonstrate how little perception they have of the mood or aspirations of the black community by presenting an analysis and a solution based on the fallacy of an integrated society and of identical interests. Certainly, they say, black literature and history should be a part of the curriculum. (Two years ago this faction was denying that the concept of black literature or history had *any* validity. On the question of a distinctive black culture, they still are not sure.) In fact, they say, there should be courses dealing with the black experience in every relevant discipline. But, to set up an autonomous entity—be it department, program, or institute—of black studies is anti-thetical to everything we believe. It creates a false dichotomy, smacks of separatism, not to say black racism, creates a serious problem of stan-dards, and violates the concept of academic *objectivity*. Also, what as-surances will we have that what will take place within that autonomous entity will be *education* and not indoctrination? (This is said without ironic intent.) And besides that—these black instructors that you plan to bring in—what acceptable (to us) academic credentials do they have? We would not want to short-change these black students! (That this concern for the academic well-being of black students is a recent development and consequently suspect can be seen by the fact that few if any of these men ever expressed any concern at their absence from their institutions in the past.) How will you guarantee the ideological purity of this autonomous department? All of these questions are predicated on the assumption of a culturally homogenous society, the myth of scholarly objectivity, a rejec-tion of history, the denial of conflicting class interests within the society, and differing perceptions of necessities by the black and white community. The consequences of these objections, if followed, would simply be the perpetuation of their control over the education of black people and the imposition of their definitions of social and political reality upon the black community. This is precisely the issue, white cultural and ideological ter-rorism, and the right of black people to define for themselves the meaning of their past and the possibility of their future.

In order to deal with this position, it is necessary to remind ourselves of some basic history. The black experience in this country is not merely one of political and cultural oppression, economic exploitation, and the ex-propriation of our history. It also includes the psychological and intellec-tual manipulation and control of blacks by the dominant majority. The liberation of blacks requires, therefore, the redress of all of these depreda-tions. The relationship of the white community to the black has been and continues to be that of oppressor and oppressed, colonizer and colonized. To pretend anything else is merely to prolong the social agony that the society is currently experiencing.

Scholarly objectivity is a delusion that liberals (of both races) may sub-scribe to. Black people and perceptive whites know better. The fact is that the intellectual establishment distinguishes itself by its slavish acceptance of the role assigned to it by the power-brokers of the society. It has always been the willing servant of wealth and power, and the research done in the physical sciences, the humanities, and the social sciences has been, with very few honorable exceptions, in service to established power, which has, in this country, always been antithetical to the interests of black people. The goals of the research undertaken, the questions asked, the controlling assumptions governing it, and consequently, the results obtained have always fitted comfortably into a social consensus which has been, by definition, racist.

Look at two examples affecting black people in the history of the institutions of higher learning. In 1832, a young professor named Dew, at William and Mary College, published a widely circulated and praised pamphlet which was to propel him to the presidency of that institution. The thesis of this piece of objective scholarship was "It is in the order of nature and of God that the being of superior faculties and knowledge and therefore of superior power, should control and dispose of those who are inferior. It is as much in the order of nature that men should enslave each other, as that other animals should prey upon each other."

This example of objective scholarship and the attendant upward mobility which greeted it was not lost on a professor named Harper at the University of South Carolina. His work published in 1838 proclaimed that "Man is born to subjection. The proclivity of natural man is to domineer or to be subservient. If there are sordid servile and laborious offices to be performed, is it not better that there should be sordid, servile and laborious beings to perform them?" Professor Harper ended his career in the office of chancellor of his institution. Needless to say, the style as well as the issues have changed with history (witness Professor Jensen), but has the basic dynamic of "academic objectivity"?

The "let the established departments handle it" proposal is as specious as it is fraudulent. These departments have, over the years, displayed no interest in incorporating the black experience, a black perspective, or even Negro faculty members into their operations. What should now dispose us to trust them? And even if we should, how will they, after centuries of indifference, suddenly develop the competence and sensitivity which would enable them to do an acceptable job? Will they really undertake to adjust the entire intellectual ambiance, the total perspectives from which they have operated? This is not likely, and for our purposes nothing less will do.

Such an adjustment on the part of these departments, though quite improbable, is at least conceivable. But this approach—leaving the responsibility to individual departments to proceed at their own pace and in their own unique styles—will merely institutionalize and perpetuate the fragmented, incoherent approach to the subject which has been the only approach in the past. Besides which, this would deprive the black community of any effective organ within the structure of the university which would be principally directed to the educational needs in that community. It is important that we emphasize the two equally important considerations which are basic to the concept of black studies. The first requires an autonomous interdisciplinary entity, capable of coordinating its curriculum in traditional disciplines, to ensure an historical, substantive progression and organic coherence in its offerings. The second function, which is no less crucial, requires this entity be sufficiently flexible to innovate programs which involve students in field study and social action projects in black communities.

Another issue which is frequently raised is that of the "racial" and academic qualifications of the faculty for these programs. Some groups insist that the presence of white faculty contradicts everything that black studies represents, i.e., the freeing of the black community from the tyranny of white experts and their endless definition of black reality. *The fact is, however, that there are few academics, white or black, who are qualified by their training in "traditional" white-culture-bound graduate schools to undertake the aggressively radical transformation of their fields that is the purpose of these programs. In fact, almost the reverse is true: the cultural condescension and chauvinism that has dominated graduate departments, coupled with an absence of racial consciousness and cultural nationalism on the part of most traditionally trained black academics, makes them little more qualified than their white peers.* This means that an effective black studies faculty must be recruited from the handful of academics who have a particular radical stance toward the reevaluation of the treatment of the black experience in their disciplines, and from among the ranks of active black intellectuals with experience in the political and cultural battlefronts of this country and the Third World.

There have been attempts by affluent white schools to try to lure the most able and committed black scholars from southern Negro schools. The faculty in black studies programs on white campuses have the responsibility not to allow themselves to be used by white institutions to recruit blacks away from predominantly Negro colleges, and the prohibition of recruitment from this source should be a stated policy of every such program. The same conditions hold true for black schools in the Third World. The black academic community of this country must not participate in expanding the brain drain from these countries. Rather, what should take place is that exchange programs for students and professors should be established between black studies programs in this country and Third World universities. Thus will the academic community lead the way in the reaching out to the black nations of the Third World and reuniting the black community in American exile with the African and West Indian nations.

These alternatives are admittedly not a permanent solution to the problem of faculty. This lies in the establishment of institutions for the training of the kind of aggressive, culturally nationalist intellectual that is needed. Given the urgency of this need, established black studies programs should invest some resources in the creation and support of these institutes, in return for the privilege of sending their best students to these centers. An excellent start in this direction has been made by Dr. Vincent Harding of Atlanta and his associates at the Institute of the Black World. This is a crucial and timely development and promises to be of great importance in the creation of a national network of black educational institutions.

It is not possible to overemphasize the historical importance of this movement to control and define the quality and terms of black education in the nation at this time. It has been clear for some time that white educational institutions are in grievous default so far as black people are concerned. What we project is nothing less than a coordinated effort to secure our just portion of the educational resources of the country and make it over in our own image. The extent to which we are able to do this will determine the form, the reality, and the role of the black community for generations to come. If the black community is able to establish here—in the intellectual center of western technology—a series of institutions devoted to the training of a generation of dedicated, proud, and culturally liberated black intellectuals and technicians whose commitment and energies are dedicated to the service—in whatever way is necessary—of the international black community, then perhaps the travail of centuries, the dues paid in America by generations of our ancestors will not have been in vain. What is at issue is the cultural survival of a nation of people, a nation without borders, without land, and without government, but nevertheless a nation with a population greater than many European countries.

The present generation of black college students is perhaps the most important generation of black people ever to live in the United States. They stand poised between two cultures, their loyalties are being besieged, they must choose between a culture and a heritage they have been taught to despise and a social establishment that, having rejected and oppressed their parents, is now making a determined bid to dissolve history and obscure reality. The vision that this generation leaves college with, the commitments they espouse, the decisions that they take, will determine not only the future of the black community in America, but will affect the nature of the struggle in the motherland and other areas of the Third World. The obstacles are formidable, the opposition great, the goal, to some, perhaps quixotic, but history is full of surprises (particularly to bourgeois historians) and while the consequences of failure are dismal, it will be an unspeakable dishonor to this generation of black intellectuals if the effort is not made. We have, quite literally, nothing to lose.

*1969*

# On Literature

# James Baldwin

## "Native Alien"

■  ■  ■  ■  ■

A GEE'S statement occurs in a book that is one of the monumental literary achievements in the history of American culture. It is one great American artist's comment on what the grinding daily necessity in American society—possibly the most potentially lethal environment to an artist—means for his own creative existence.

In the twenty years since Agee wrote those words, this society has become neither better, nor more mature, and the wonder is not that we have so pitifully few *real* writers and artists, but that any are produced and manage to survive at all. Some are seduced by acceptance and adulation, some are smothered by the dollar-encrusted embrace of Mammon, others lured into esoteric irrelevance as the high priests of empty cults. But a few escape; those necessary enemies who continue to illumine the empty places in our contemporary culture and to force our collective consciousness back upon itself, into those dark and fearful places where we would rather not look. One of those who continue to "tell the truth, until we can bear it no more" is James Baldwin.

Much has been written about this little black man from that unguarded extermina-

A good artist is a deadly enemy of society; and the most dangerous thing that can happen to an enemy, no matter how cynical, is to become a beneficiary. No society, no matter how good, could be mature enough to support a real artist without mortal danger to that artist.

JAMES AGEE, *Let Us Now Praise Famous Men*

tion camp known as Harlem, and he, consequently, has a certain existence on the contemporary scene. It is the meaning of this existence that I am interested in here, because its significance is not that of some kind of "court-jester" figure where a "professional rebel" is tolerated so that he may be ignored. This is the role in which a large segment of the popular press, and the literary establishment would like to fix Baldwin—the figure who is expected to say daring, shocking, and *even* true things thereby proving the freedom that prevails in the establishment. But he is much more than that: in the words of Edmund Wilson, he is one of the country's few great creative artists. It is this role that I am interested in here.

Talking at Howard University last year, Baldwin perceived that, "insecurity is a condition of being an artist. . . . My problem is to tell the truth and survive with society, and as an artist, because there is the question of whether any society is prepared to have the artist speak the truth. . . ." It is important that he perceives his problem as "surviving with society, *and as an artist*" while telling the truth, because there is a real sense in which any artist may not survive *with* society, but outside of it.

This confrontation, or, as Agee rightly says, enmity, is not a literary conceit, but is a relationship of real and deadly implications. How is this? Any society, and especially the monolithic mass societies of our times, operates on certain assumptions and within the bounds of certain immutable purposes which are antithetical to those of the artist.

The artist's proper and only concern is with the dynamic of living, with vitality and motion and diffuseness. The society must proceed on the basis of reducing the human personality (or proceeding as though it had) to a series of constants. The artist is concerned with the infinite possibility represented by the human spirit; the society must so manipulate human personality as to render it predictable and controllable. The artist is concerned with the uniqueness and subjectivity of experience; the society must assume that all men are one man. The artist must re-create the truth he perceives, and he must do this from the privacy of a moral conscience whose source is himself; the society can abide no truth but that which is manufactured from the mythology that sustains the society. It is, in other words, interested not in truth but in plausibility.

This is the nature of the conflict which Baldwin and Agee are talking about: that the end of the society must ultimately be power and totality and a certain impulse toward order which is to say, conformity. The artist *must,* as artist, be the enemy of this order, and the creative will must be a generate and productive kind of spiritual anarchy. Baldwin expresses this: "the entire purpose of the society must be to create a bulwark against the inner and the outer chaos . . . the artist cannot take anything for granted, but must drive *to* the heart of every answer and *expose the question the answer hides. . . ."*

In discussing his own role, he makes this very clear.

One of the things about being an artist is that you are produced by a people because they need you. But the people who produce you cannot accept you. This is not a complaint, it is simply a statement of fact.

I suppose that the reason for this has to be something really bad and mysterious; that is in the same way a human being . . . any single human being, wants to know who he is, and wants to *become himself or herself,* wants to live, and one day to read his or her proper name . . . and at the same time wishes to be safe and therefore accepts and adopts all kinds of disguises, and begins to believe all kinds of lies in order to be safe. In this safety, this mystical, and unreal safety, he begins to perish. This is a war which is in everybody.

Americans want to believe a great many things about themselves that are not true. Negroes want to believe a great deal about themselves that isn't true, too. Part of the dilemma, I think, of being an American Negro, is that the Negro has been forced for a long, long time, in many, many ways—not only physically—to mantle himself on a society that has always been essentially incoherent. That is to say, one is mantling himself on someone who does not know who *he* himself is. This means, then, that the imitator—and for the sake of argument you may say that all Negroes in this country are imitators—finds himself in a very strange confusion. And, if the writer, me, Jimmy Baldwin in this particular case, is trying to find out where the truth is—where I begin and society stops—to try to tell the truth about my mother or my brother or the porter, and to try to find out how this truth relates to the American myth, how it relates to the situation of young people—black and white—who are lost, in despair, groping for values which do not seem to be present in the republic . . . Then, you have a fantastic kind of confusion. So, the role of the writer in this country, now, I think, is to begin to excavate, almost for the first time, the real history of this country. Not the history one would like to believe, but to find out what *really* happened here to get us where we are now.

In these deceptively simple and eloquent terms, Baldwin has outlined the formidable task he has set himself. It is nothing less than that of keeper of our emotional and moral history, and entails excavating through the accumulation of rubble, the accumulation of mythology and falsehood, the stereotyping of emotion and reaction, the sophistry, the image-making, the delusory witch-doctorhood of false prophets and physicians, who are themselves afflicted, to some usable bedrock of truth from which to start the tremendous job of moral and spiritual rebuilding that is necessary if we are to survive, if, in his own words "America is ever to become a civilization and not just a collection of Motels."

This is a task of truly daunting dimensions and one that might well be described as presumptuous. Also it is an undertaking in which success or failure is not easily assessed, and will not be even from the vantage point of historical distance. Indeed, these terms may not even be relevant, and what is important is merely that the attempt be in good faith.

But, we might, indeed, ought to, examine Mr. Baldwin's credentials, by which I mean those qualities which would enable him to set about the artistic purpose he projects. Baldwin's sincerity and seriousness are unimpeachable, as is his honesty. The scintillating and luminous vision, the power of his moral earnestness, the diamond hard incisiveness of his intellect—to which in combination we are indebted for countless and meaningful insights—are not disputed even by the most dedicated of his detractors. But these qualities alone, or even when displayed with a prose style of remarkable and breathtaking elegance, capable of alternating (almost in midsentence) between chilling and lucid objectivity, and sudden and breath-stopping passion, would not serve to sustain that purpose.

For one thing, no writer could come close to that kind of revealing and outspoken commentary for which we—all of us—stand in Baldwin's debt, without first having come to valid terms with the realities of his own emotional and social existence. This is the question of accepting the anguish of listening to, and forcing oneself, as fully as one is able, to accept the signals coming from one's heart. (One perceptive and word-clever commentator sees Baldwin as "standing at ground-zero of the heart.")

Baldwin does indeed stand there, and has done this thing of abandoning the armor behind which we all attempt to hide, and standing naked where fear and the urge toward safety would have one clothed. In short, he has said "Yes" to life, and what is significant, he has had the resources of honesty to do much of this publicly, and the grace to do it with dignity. On the flyleaf to his poignant and inclusive novel *Giovanni's Room* which is a testament of doomed love, and this love is doomed not because it is homosexual but because it is fearful, he has the inscription, "I am the man. I was there. I suffered." So, in a very individual and private way one exists, coexists really, with one's emotions.

In another way, one exists in terms of the society. If one is an artist, this

existence with the society becomes very important and special. This necessitates, it seems to me, a strange kind of paradox: to exist as a perceptive
and an aware consciousness *outside* of certain aspects of the movement
and flow of the society's forces, while maintaining sufficient of a passionate involvement as not to become irrelevant. I cannot see this, and it is
the really precarious balance that the artist must maintain, as being much
of a danger to Baldwin, as it is not to most Negroes in this self-consciously
white society.

My point is that Baldwin's relationship, and indeed any Negro's relationship, to the society, is structured very much in the pattern of what
I have described as the aesthetic paradox. The Negro is of this land, his
sweat and blood are here, and have been since the very beginning (Negroes
were with the French who explored the Mississippi Valley, and were
among its first non-Indian settlers) and he is what this country has made of
him, while having had a great part in moulding the form of what the
country is. Yet at the same time, he is thrust outside. It is as though, at
the same time, he was clutched to the breast, held at the very center,
smothered, trapped really, in an embrace not of his own seeking, the same
time that he was made witness, sometimes victim—for there is nothing
that Negroes and waiters may not hear—to all the shameful excesses of the
young nation, he was excluded . . . abused and despised. It was as though
"white" America (something this republic has never been) considered that
if it could repress the existence of the Negro in its consciousness it could
remove a people from existence. One had merely to look at TV as it went
about projecting the image that America has of itself, to believe that this
country was populated only by whites. Only four years ago this was true.

So this relationship, a curious amalgam of lover and victim, of shame
and glory, is at its roots a confused tissue of subliminal hatred and a
strangely incestuous love. I say incestuous for it is a love that is unnatural
and incoherent. How can any Negro articulate the nature of the community that unites him to his roots, his history, and, strangely, his sustenance in the black-mud cotton fields of Mississippi's Delta, the red-clay
hills of Georgia, or the concentration camp that is Harlem's streets? How,
I ask, is one to make real the bitter love-hate by which he is bound to that
past, for we *are* our pasts, and the fierce and terrible necessity, the hotly
visceral knowledge that he cannot and must not allow that past to live
further?

How can I affirm that this situation is real for James Baldwin, and predict
that it will preserve the artist in him from the beneficiary status of which

Agee warned us? Actually, apart from the testimony of his own words, and the fact of my personal racial alienation, I cannot. But an incident comes to mind. One of the crumbs of conscience that the mass media periodically purges itself by throwing to "art," took the form of a symposium of "leading" American writers, who, the libel laws being as vague as they are, will remain nameless. Baldwin was among them, and within a very few minutes, a depressing rift began to be evident. It became clear that of this distinguished gathering of best-selling authors, Baldwin was caught in an alienation that should not have existed. It became apparent that he was the only one still possessing anything of the certain fury that must be a condition of any artist's existence.

Even more depressing was the glibness with which these successful American authors mouthed (and seemed to believe) the clichés, the platitudes, the irrelevancies which pretend to describe the social, political, and emotional situation of America but, in reality, describe nothing. One realized with real shock that these protectors and shapers of our consciousness, for this is the responsibility of our artists, and life *does* sometimes follow art, *were in many basic ways ignorant of the state of the nation.*

I have told myself, and I do not believe, that I was shocked because they did not share Baldwin's (and my own) peculiar minority view of what was in reality happening here, but which I saw as a species of complacence, an uncritical acceptance of the superficial, and the absence of any willingness or motivation (which must be present in the artist) to pursue perceptions, however sacrilegious, profane, and unorthodox, to unknown and therefore dangerous conclusions. One author, and he was not joking, kept saying to Baldwin, "Ah, come on Jimmy, you can't be *that* angry anymore. You are big time now."

Later Baldwin, in a conversation, was to comment on that situation. He said,

> Writers who do this are not to my mind really writers. What they really do is to soothe people into believing what people would rather believe. And in order to do this the writer has to really believe it. Nobody writes down to anyone, you do the best you can.
>
> These people are respected as articulate and responsible spokesmen *for* society, and what they really are doing is saying nothing dangerous, saying nothing which would disturb anybody, and therefore are they writers? The image of America they have is nothing more than the popular image, and their role is simply to re-create and keep alive that image. There is nothing much

you can do about that except to know that it is perhaps the affliction of having too much money. You begin to be respected as a writer or composer or painter or whatever, and there are some changes. It does not mean that you have become any better, but usually that you have become a good deal worse, but because you have a bank account, you exist on the American scene in a way you never did before.

But this appears to be relevant mainly in terms of an economic security and does not fully approach the question of the fraudulent security accruing from accepting a manufactured identity imposed by the social order, and within which its members are embalmed. Baldwin, in his apocalyptic essay "The Fire Next Time," addresses this problem.

"The American Negro," he says, "has the advantage of never having believed the collection of myths to which white Americans cling: that their ancestors were all freedom-loving heroes, that they were born in the greatest country the world has ever seen, that Americans are invincible in battle or wise in peace, that American men are the world's most direct and virile, that American women are pure. Negroes know far more about Americans than that. . . ." In the same essay, he remarks on the anguish and confusion that is in attendance on being "born in a white country, an Anglo-Teutonic, anti-sexual country, black" and realizing that "the universe which is not merely the stars and the moon and the planets . . . *but other people,* has evolved no terms for your existence, *has made no room for you. . . .*"

This can be recognized as a statement of an existential alienation. It is perhaps overstated, for it is not that this society has not prepared terms in which a young Negro can be said to relate: it is that it has few terms within which any individual Negro who intends to be true to his impulses toward personal integrity can accept in order to make such a union. . . . The terms exist but one is charged with rejecting them and finding some way to force this hostile power complex to recognize you, *in terms of your own making.* This position in reality applies to all men, but the Negro sees this clearest. As soon as he recognizes that he is not what the society says he is, it becomes his necessity to discover and define, with pitifully little help, his real identity. (This is what our sit-ins are about.)

Baldwin admits to being forced into this posture of rejection and alienation at an early age. It was in his mid-teens that he realized that "white people who had robbed black people of their liberty and who profited by their theft every hour that they lived, had no moral ground on which to stand. They had the judges, juries, shotguns, the law—in a word, the power. But it was a criminal power, to be feared, but not respected, and to be outwitted in any way whatsoever. The moral barriers I had supposed to exist between me and a criminal career became tenuous. I certainly could discover no principled reason for not becoming a criminal."

It is a realization of this that Norman Mailer had when in his famous essay "The White Negro" he remarked on the real existentialism inherent in the situation of the American Negro. If one is forced to reject the establishment's version of your identity, then you cannot accept much else of its orthodoxy, for in the most important aspect of your relationship to that society you have caught it in a lie, and one which jeopardizes your sense of personality. You find out that you possess a dreadful kind of freedom which isolates you and places you in a cultural vacuum. The knowledge that you are not bound by the standards of the culture into which you were born, that you have no moral imperative to obey its laws, believe its history, honor its customs, praise its heroes, fight its wars, or love its God, represents a dubious freedom.

Because the society is at no pains to make its mythology even *appear* real for the Negro (few Negro children over seven years old have any illusions about the land being free, or the cops being their friends), he is forced outside. It is in this situation that Baldwin the artist was moulded, and from these pressures he was shaped, and his point of view is that of the alien who is somehow at the very center, the stranger who by some wild mischance finds himself firmly ensconced in the main-bedroom of the great house, and who has to know, if he is to survive, every movement and every action in that house. But he can in no way indicate how much he sees and hears.

It used to be, and still is in some places in this country, that if a white man asked a Negro if it was raining, the Negro would look into the questioner's face to answer the question. And if the face or voice did not indicate the nature of the answer that was desired then the only prudent answer possible was "Ah sho'ly doesn't know, Suh, Cap'n, boss, I sholy don't." And the white man would go away marveling at the childlike simplicity of this Negro who apparently could not tell whether it was raining, little suspecting that that shuffling, head-scratching darkie's "ignorance" was fathered by a profound intelligence of the true nature of white power, and of what that white man could accept, and was capable of doing. There is, in truth, a marvelously childlike simplicity present, but. . . .

I did not present this example to be "folksy," but because it is in a basic and exaggerated way typical of what has been occurring between the races in this country. This can best be seen in terms of (since it corresponds very closely to) a certain method of seeing and presenting social relationships used in his plays by the French dramatist Jean Genet. Genet presents social relationships as being determined by geography and ritual. People are situated in certain loci which have relationship to each other, and for each place there is a mask. One adopts one's position (knowing one's place) and dons the mask. The donning of the mask obliterates any possibility of a private personality, and the mask now dictates the personality while the "place" dictates the nature of what can pass between the actors. In other words, there can be no communication; one merely plays the role and conforms to the appearance.

This weird kind of ritualistic drama is precisely what has taken place between the races for the last three hundred years. It is most visible in the Southland, where a real dialogue is tentatively and traumatically trying to emerge after the silence of three centuries. In actuality there was sound, but people were silent, and the masks spoke. That which was sayable under these conditions was limited by the rigid protocol. The burden of the white mask, and it must have been an oppressive one, was the commitment to the mythical and innate superiority of the white skin, and to the entire complex image that the whites had of themselves with the attendant responsibility of acting this image out. The Negroes were also located in their place, bearing the burden of a Nigger mask, and of an also mythical personality created by the whites, which justified and complemented the role the whites had chosen to create for themselves, and was necessary for these reasons.

Baldwin, as have others, sees these masks and how they function. His importance lies in the way he attempts to excavate beyond the mere recognition of the appearances, and asks important questions, questions hidden as he says in the answers, about what is really happening here. He has been criticized in certain sections of the Negro community for "writing too much about whites." But this is extremely nearsighted and narrow criticism, because Negroes have few problems which do not originate in the ethnic and cultural confusion of allegedly white America, and one does not realistically write about where the Negro is, without writing as much again about where the whites are, or imagine themselves to be. Negroes can never establish their true identity here without helping the whites to establish their own, and, unless the false image that white America has erected to hide behind is laid to rest, the false public image imposed on the Negro will not be dismantled. It is in recognition of this that Baldwin's contribution to our consciousness of ourselves looms so important, and it is one reason why he is so potentially subversive to the "mystical and unreal" safety that is substituted for truthful communication.

Baldwin is saying "look at and understand the sources and the nature of those masks." Why, he asks, did America *need* to create the Nigger? "If a white person looks at me and sees a 'Nigger', and I know that I am not and have never been such a thing, then we both need to ask ourselves what it is that he is really seeing."

This is important. When images are projected around an object, the nature of this projection speaks more eloquently and revealingly of the attitudes and condition of the mind forming those images, than it does of the object around which they are projected. Negroes have traditionally been the objects rather than the perpetrators of these projections. Consequently, Baldwin says, if we examine the meaning of the "Nigger" to the white consciousness we will be rewarded by insight, of a special nature, to be sure, into the state of that consciousness. It appears to Baldwin that this Nigger image, volatile, razor-scarred, and dangerous, is an expression of those qualities in themselves—indeed in all of us—that white Americans are paralyzed and terrified of facing. The Nigger is that black beast within, who is invested with an uninhibited and insatiable sexuality, uncontrollable passions, a capacity for blind and reckless violence, an irresponsible and carefree sensuality, with animal grace and primitive rhythm, in effect, with all the vitality and emotionalism that is prohibited by the protestant ethic, and repressed because of the fear of the protestant hell which is so deeply ingrained in the cultural subconscious.

If whites see the Negro male as some kind of mobile phallus, and the Negro woman as the symbol of all kinds of prurient and salacious excess, then this is really indicative in Baldwin's words "of the poverty of the white chick's bed, and the white cat's bed." If this is true, my own suggestion would be that President Johnson extend his war on poverty to include this particular "pocket of poverty."

Despite that last frivolous aside, this is, in our time of rapidly shifting attitudes toward sexuality, a human issue of real seriousness. Baldwin has suggested that one of the primary concerns of the writer should be the honest exploration of the question of morality, responsibility, and the possibility of love and union in sexual relationships. In *Another Country,* his most recent novel, and in *Giovanni's Room,* he probes with a relentless perceptiveness the complex levels of love. In these pages, we follow the tortuous paths of a number of desperately earnest, but doomed, relationships. Relationships in which frightened and fragmented people, blindly fleeing the isolation that is our lot—we are born alone and die that way—

attempt to claw their way into some measure of security and permanence in the arms and persons of their lovers. We follow these sterile relationships into bedrooms, which are really grotesque battlegrounds where no victories are won, where people, acting from what are, in the main, decent impulses, inflict maiming wounds on each other, where spirits are mutilated but not comforted and what is called making love is emotional outrage and carnal exploitation.

In these novels, Baldwin "tells it" as we say in the streets, "like it is," with a stirring compassion and veracity. As we recognize ourselves in these pages, it becomes clear that no society that places such a crippling weight on the emotions of its young people, and where they destroy themselves and each other so voraciously and apparently inevitably, can, in humane terms (which are the only terms that ultimately mean anything) be accounted healthy.

There is no quick answer, but Baldwin's would be, I imagine, that the armor and the masks be removed from between lovers and the races, and that we begin again to see and listen and speak to each other in voices that come out of honesty, respect, and compassion. In short, that we re-create the possibility of love.

It appears to me imperative that this kind of honest confrontation begin rapidly, because just as there is a hooded Klansman lurking within the unconscious of the American white, there is a Black Muslim somewhere in each black. There will be, in the days to come, either the kind of dialogue of which I spoke, or ultimate and irreconcilable violence. This is one of Baldwin's real fears, and a fear intensified by his admission that "I should be caught in the middle, since I cannot make alliances on the basis of color." Until America reaches this point, we are none of us safe.

*1964*

# Baldwin's New York Novel

LATE in 1960, James Baldwin came back to America after a protracted period of European exile. He said on arrival that he didn't know if he was glad to be back, but that he needed to be, and that he had never really *seen* the country before. He said that he had two books in process, a collection of essays called *Nobody Knows My Name* and a novel called *Another Country*. What was the novel about, he was asked. He shrugged, impatiently, looked a little exasperated and said, "Look, it's over five hundred pages long . . . what's a novel usually about anyway, it's about five people in New York . . . now."

Naturally someone asked how New York got to be "another country" and he answered logically enough, "Well, that depends on where you are, does it not?"

The book appeared in 1962 to what is euphemistically called "mixed notices," but what actually happened is that the New York literary establishment, with only three notable exceptions, greeted it with some of the most fatuous, inept, and at times downright dishonest criticism that I had ever seen. A number of reviewers, for whatever reason, became so incensed at the book that, completely losing whatever tenuous grip they

To become a Negro man, let alone a Negro Artist, one has to *make oneself up* as one goes along. This had to be done in the not-at-all metaphorical teeth, of the world's intention to destroy you. This is not the way this truth presents itself to white men, who believe the world is theirs, and who, albeit, unconsciously, expect the world to help them in the achievement of their identity.

JAMES BALDWIN, "Black Boy Looks at White Boy"

commanded of the tenets of their craft, they gave vent to some of the most parochial, ill-tempered, irrelevant, and distasteful attacks on Baldwin's personal life and character. I remember reading these notices and becoming increasingly angry and perplexed at what I saw as either a near complete failure of vision, or displays of personal malice. Certainly, I could recognize little of the book I had read in these notices. So, when I was sent a copy for review, I spent much space reviewing the reviewers, because as I wrote then:

> Sometimes it chances that the critical response to a work of fiction will reveal as much about the society that produced that work, as the work of fiction itself. *Another Country* has proved to be such a work: too important to ignore and too cruelly honest and threatening to deal with objectively. At least this seems to have been the experience of some of our most prestigious critics.

I then proceeded to praise the book's strengths extravagantly, while ignoring its weaknesses. About this time I happened to see the author and asked how the book was doing.

"Very well," he said unhappily, "very well indeed . . . *outside of New York*. The notices *here* have been terrible, vindictive . . . I really don't understand it."

I suspect that if he ever was really confused by the critical reaction in New York, he is no longer. But at the time he seemed very hurt. Despite the fact that this was his fifth book, it was his third novel, and he was, in terms of his career under a kind of "second novel" pressure for a number of reasons. That is, his real second novel had been written in France, set in France, and had been widely conceded to be "delicately crafted, skillfully written, sensitively observed," but a *tour de force,* a kind of minor aberration. The second "serious" work was still to come, and this was of course *Another Country*.

In fact it appeared that the critical response did, at one point, succeed in shaking his confidence in the work. A TV interviewer asked him whether he agreed with the critical judgment that *Go Tell It On The Mountain* was his finest novel.

"I know some people are saying that," he replied, "and I am glad they like that book so much. But it *was* written ten years ago. No writer likes to feel that he is getting worse. This is a book I *had* to write. Now I can go on. I had to write this book."

The fact is, of course, that in terms of a purely formal and sterile graduate school kind of aesthetics, *Mountain* and *Giovanni's Room* may be better examples of a certain example of the *form,* but neither have the range, the power, the relevance, nor the passionate vitality and vision, of the later novel. And, significantly, neither early book speaks as explicitly of the relationship between white people and black people.

It must be said that by the term "New York establishment" I do not mean simply the magazines published in the geographic area of the city, but that area on the eastern seaboard that has as the focus of its literary activities New York, the area that would be within what Walter Lippmann would call "The New York sphere of influence."

The response was not of course at all of a piece in terms of what was said of the book. But whatever the conclusions, the *method* of approach showed remarkable consistency. The cleverer critics chose simply to discuss abstractions to do with the "form of the novel," the "concept" of the novel, the "structuring" of the novel, ignoring the comment that the novel makes on the contemporary New York experience. Most adopted tones of unctuous regret, "the fine gifts of Baldwin the essayist seem unfortunately to conflict with the novelistic sensibility," which being interpreted implies that the one way of ordering experience and perceptions is at irreconcilable odds with the other, which is nonsense. What it really *means* is "Stick with the essay boy, and leave the 'higher form' to us."

Most, as Norman Podhoretz pointed out, left sufficient space for "An earnest tribute to Mr. Baldwin's talents, calling him one of our very best writers, and voicing a pious confidence in his ability to do better in the future."

Different ones "of these critics of style" objected to all kinds of peripheral trivia, making sure that whatever element they chose to focus their indignation on was all but irrelevant in terms of the real vision and judgment of experience inherent in the book. For the most part that seemed to me to be the ploy, an escape into trivia or the aesthetic formalism that has the advantage, especially in a form as diffuse as the novel, of being arbitrary, and capable of serving any cause.

Another very common characteristic of this group was an ill-disguised tone of patronage, subtle but unmistakably present. The second group of critics, less clever and devious, made the error of doing battle with the vision of experience expressed. What came out there—mainly in the daily newspaper notices, joined on this occasion by the weekly *Village Voice* which surprised with the strident middle-class chauvinism and moral rigidity of its review—was a hysterical, threatened, shrill howl of heterosexual outrage and indignation. To anyone reading these notices, the urbane and sophisticated New York had in fact become "another country," one of repressive, white, middle-class babbittry which saw the

book as the spearhead of some insidious homosexual conspiracy to sub-
vert the sexual sensibilities and responses of the reading public, an attack
on marriage, on the virility of the white male and the sexuality of the white
female, and just about all of their accepted assumptions about human relationships. And, as has been pointed out, this was not generally true of the
reviews which came out of the West, Midwest, and even parts of the South.
Why?

An example of the first group is Paul Goodman, who defines his own
relationship to society in terms of a personalized and esoteric radicalism,
and who saw the characters as being without "social consciousness," and
complained about the city of the novel not being the city he knew, com-
plaints which even if true would hardly be important. The second is,
incidentally, less of a comment on where Goodman imagines he lives,
because Goodman's "*Empire City*" notwithstanding, this is *the* novel of
contemporary New York. I am convinced that this fact is part of the
explanation of the New York response, but more of that later.

Another critic saw the characters as "paper thin," an apparent protest
against the absence of convoluted Faulknerian family trees and psychiatric
case histories. The best example of the hysteria of the second group of reviewers appeared in the *Village Voice,* usually so self-consciously hip. This
man, the writer of the most tendentious and obtuse piece on the book, had
his sensibilities outraged because some homosexual relationships are
rendered as being no more destructive than heterosexual ones, because the
only sexual relationship between a white couple "which is graced by
matrimonial vows" is presented as being empty, and because the comments of a Negro woman character on white society, "is marked by a non-
feminine crudity." What this character (Ida) did say to her white lover
(Vivaldo) simply was "You is a fucked up bunch of people." A remark
worth two paragraphs to this reviewer.

In the middle of all this, Granville Hicks's intelligent and sensitive
review stood out as evidence that everyone was not rendered incapable of
honest and compassionate criticism by the book. Thank the Lord for that
old gentleman. If one believes that the book is flawed, but that its faults
become very insignificant beside its formidable accomplishments—the illuminating energy and passionate interpretation of experience and social
and emotional reality—the question becomes what happened to these
critics? Part, but only a very small part, of the answer, is the sheeplike un-
acknowledged borrowing of insights that this group is prone to. This
results in a situation where a few widely-read early reviews tend to influence the attitudes and vision of the writers who grind out subsequent

commentary, so an escalation of opinion takes place. For some reason, it is infinitely more *chic* to have panned a book that your friends liked than to have praised a book in print, when everyone else is disparaging it.

However, unless the state of book reviewing is even worse than its most trenchant critic admits, this does not approach an explanation of the critical reaction to *Another Country*. There must be other more significant answers.

Norman Podhoretz outlines the general dynamic of what I also suspect must have happened. In an article called "In Defense of a Maltreated Best Seller" published in *Show* magazine, he writes:

> But in spite of all this (the scattering of good notices and the enormous sales) I stand by the word maltreated. With few exceptions (*Newsweek* among them), the major reviewing media were very hard on *Another Country*. It was patronized by Paul Goodman of the *New York Times Book Review*, ridiculed by Stanley Edgar Hyman in the *New Leader*, worried over (with it must be said, genuine distress) by Elizabeth Hardwick in *Harpers*, summarily dismissed by the *Times'* anonymous critic, loftily pitied by Whitney Balliett in *The New Yorker*, and indignantly attacked by Saul Maloff in the *Nation*

Podhoretz finds "it hard to believe that these wrong-headed appraisals of *Another Country* can be ascribed to a simple lapse of literary judgment," especially in the cases of Goodman, Hardwick, and Hyman, whom he calls "first-rate critics." He is eloquently silent about the competence of the other three.

After fretting about certain explicit misjudgments on the parts of these "first-rate critics," Podhoretz guesses that

> all these critics disliked the book, not because it suffers from this or that literary failing, but because they were repelled by the militancy and cruelty of its vision of life. Granville Hicks was right when he called the book "an act of violence" and since it is the reader upon whom this violence is being committed perhaps one ought to have expected that many reviewers would respond with something less than gratitude.

This judgment is, I believe, accurate; the question that must be answered has to do with the *nature* of this violence, and the values that the reviewers felt to be threatened by Baldwin's version of our experience. Rather than risk doing violence to Mr. Podhoretz's explication of the impact of the book (those elements that the critics found dangerous), I shall repeat it in some detail.

Whites coupled with Negroes, heterosexual men coupled with homosexuals, homosexuals coupled with women, none of it involving casual lust or the suggestion of perversity, and all of it accompanied by the most serious emotions and resulting in the most intense attachments—it is easy enough to see even from so crude a summary that Baldwin's intention is to deny any moral significance whatever to the categories white and Negro, heterosexual and homosexual. He is saying that the terms white and Negro refer to two different conditions under which individuals live, but they are still individuals and their lives are still governed by the same fundamental laws of being. And he is saying, similarly, that the terms homosexuality and heterosexuality refer to two different conditions under which individuals pursue love, but they are still individuals and their pursuit of love is still governed by the same fundamental laws of being. Putting the two propositions together, he is saying, finally, that the only significant realities are individuals and love, and that anything which is permitted to interfere with the free operation of this fact is evil and should be done away with.

Now, one might suppose that there is nothing particularly startling in this view of the world; it is, after all only a form of the standard liberal attitude toward life.

. . . But that is not the way James Baldwin holds it, and it is not the way he states. He holds these attitudes with puritanical ferocity, and he spells them out in such brutal and naked detail that one scarcely recognizes them any longer—and one is frightened by them, almost as though they implied a totally new, *totally revolutionary conception of the universe.* And in a sense, of course, they do. For by taking these liberal pieties literally and by translating them into simple English, he puts the voltage back into them and they burn to the touch.

. . . *Another Country,* then, is informed by a remorseless insistence *on a truth* which however partial we may finally judge it to be, is nevertheless compelling as a perspective on the way we live now.

. . . But in the end, the failures of *Another Country,* however serious, seem unimportant beside the many impressive things Baldwin has accomplished here.

. . . I believe that *Another Country* will come to be seen as the book in which for the first time the superb intelligence of Baldwin the essayist became fully available to Baldwin the novelist, in which for the first time he attempted to speak his mind with complete candor and with a minimum of polite rhetorical elegance, and in which for the first time he dared to reveal himself as someone to be feared for how deeply he sees, how much he demands of the world and how powerfully he can hate.

It would be difficult to dispute Mr. Podhoretz's observation of that quirk of the liberal personality, expressed by an unreasoning terror of any thought of the implementation of their platitudes. And it is almost certain that much of the confusion surrounding the reception of the book is merely further evidence of this old truth, operating in precisely the manner that he describes. But the critical paranoia must have its roots in other equally significant reactions.

In terms of the literary culture, the book takes on monumental proportions as it represents a direct assault, not only on a few sterile sexual and social taboos, but on the cultural hegemony, the dictatorship of perception and definition, of the Anglo-Saxon vision as it operates through the literature onto the society. It presents a self-consciously and even arrogantly *black* consciousness refuting and demolishing certain cherished notions about the "quality of life" in society, presenting an unapologetic and relentless vision of white society and white characters as they are registered in a black consciousness. Here the critics are confronted by white characters, in roughly similar social positions and backgrounds, to themselves, and they do not like the image in which they are cast. This is a real world example of precisely the kind of inversion that is accomplished in the "class conscious" drama of Jean Genet, where masks are adopted, class roles reversed, and social relationships are viewed from the perceptions of the previously mute and oppressed. Baldwin's book represents a similar clash of sensibility and experience, and I am convinced that the reviewers were just not prepared to have their class prerogative of defining and interpreting the dynamics of their own social experience assumed by this black man from Harlem. They were not prepared to accept the Negro characters' comments on the white characters, simply because the identification between themselves and some of the whites in the book is too close. It is one thing for a precocious black boy to paint lyrical and moving pictures of life in Harlem, but it is, as the southern lady remarked, a "nigger of a different color" when this analytic vision is directed into their living rooms and bedrooms. It is one thing, in novels written by blacks, to have stock white characters carry the burden of white society's guilt re the Negro, the acceptance of which has become a perfunctory obligation of the liberal soul anyway, so it constitutes no real threat. It is entirely different to have them on terms of social and sexual equality with tough and commanding *Negroes* who expose gaping human and emotional inadequacies in these white characters, and openly attribute these inadequacies to cultural human bankruptcies within the white establishment. This irony is unacceptable precisely because it reverses the tradition coming from the very beginning of American literature, in which white perceptions and sensibilities, and a white consciousness interprets, defines, and gives form—hence a kind of reality—to all relationships of all characters within the society. It is because no previous novel by a Negro has ever appropriated this function so completely, probingly, and relentlessly that the white reviewers were constrained to ignore or disparage this vision. In this respect, the significance of *Another Country*'s being a *regional* novel cannot be overemphasized. The experience it describes is in many respects peculiarly New York, the conditions which operate are not to be found in quite the same way anywhere else in the country. This is the anxiety-ridden, abrasive, neurotic, and merciless world of the artistic underground. What the characters seek is not simply love, and an end to loneliness, but to "make it." They are seeking to force the society to come to terms with their own existence, that is to say, seeking their public identity. So the natural insecurity of the modern human situation is for them heightened by the competitive and spiritually destructive hustle of New York's talent jungle. There are among the major characters, two writers, one actor, a singer, and a TV producer. And as Truman Capote put it, "a boy's got to hustle." Their common enemy and the source of much of their neurosis, is anonymity and obscurity. They are all past the first flush of youth and some have begun to establish the basis of their fame and success. It is significant that the one character that seems to have established working terms on which to confront his own identity is Eric, the actor, who is "making it" on pretty much his own terms and without having done visible violence to his creative integrity. That he is also unrepentantly bisexual and appears to have made his personal peace with that reality also, is undoubtedly the cause of much of the heterosexual indignation that greeted the book.

The other successful characters are Ellis, the meretricious and exploitative TV executive, and Richard Silenski, who is a prototype of the typically middle-class white American male. He is presented as a well-meaning but limited man, hampered by the restricted vision and sensitivity of the white establishment consciousness, who is well on his way to being a successful writer for TV. He is the prototype of the objects of Baldwin's severest criticism. "The writers . . . who are not to my mind really writers. They are respected as articulate responsible spokesmen for society, yet the image they have of the society is nothing more than the popular image and their role is merely to recreate and keep alive that image." These are the only two characters who stand in the mainstream of contemporary success, so to say, and they emerge as the least sympathetic figures in the book. They also happen to be the people in the book with whom most reviewers would tend to identify themselves.

The other major characters, five in number, constantly struggle with more or less success, to avoid the stereotyping of identity and response, that the society demands, and the self-willed and deceptive "innocence" that Baldwin has said is the burden and insulation of white folks.

These must be the "five people in New York." They are Rufus Scott, a priapic and charismatic jazz drummer, his sister Ida, an aspiring singer who becomes the lover of Vivaldo Moore, an unsuccessful writer, Eric Jones, a white southern actor who is returning from France, and Cass Silenski, the wife of the writer Richard, who has a brief affair with Eric.

At the time the novel opens, this group, with the exception of Ida, is scattered after what was a period of great closeness and affection. Rufus is starving on the Bowery, Eric is in France, Cass is at home being a wife and mother, and Vivaldo, lonely and frustrated, is frequenting their old village haunts in the company of a bitchy and destructive woman painter. We learn that despite a deep mutual affection in the group, they were basically united, for reasons that are never made clear, by a deep, almost worshipful admiration for Rufus. They are also united by a number of factors including ambition, youth, and an optimistic and idealistic commitment to their various crafts.

They are reunited at the end of the first section by the death of Rufus who commits suicide after a painful and violent affair with a white southern girl. The dispersal and reunion is essential to Baldwin's central purpose which is the revelation of each character's, if not growth, then at least progression, toward insights, perceptions, and the recognition and acceptance of truths about themselves, a process which can be called the loss of innocence. So the difference between what the characters imagined themselves to be, and what they discover that they are, is revealed in conspicuous relief by the juxtaposition of then and now.

These five characters who find themselves in New York from Harlem, New England, the South, and Brooklyn are further united by having rejected their roots, and the identity imposed by those connections. They now face the responsibility of a dual and perhaps conflicting definition of themselves. The first responsibility is to shatter their social anonymity by achieving a "name," a public identity, by coming to terms, in a public sense, with the society. This pressure seems to be most insistent and demanding in New York. The complementary responsibility is to achieve coexistence with their emotional needs, which entails constructing an emotional identity which can only be done in intimate relationship with other people. Both of these urges are simply a response to the fact that human beings have no identity except in these terms, and are reactions against existential nothingness.

These five characters share this situation, but they do not start from the same place. Eric, for example, is aware of his isolation and the hostile posture of the general society toward him because he is an outcast and a refugee from the society of his youth. Thus, by demarking and defining the nature of his alienation, his bisexuality has done him a service, and he *knows* he must accept full responsibility for self-definition.

Similarly, the Scotts, being Negro, recognize that they must wrestle with the white-defined society for the right to self-definition—to be what you can be, to someday read your rightful name—in the teeth of a society that is quite ready with a gratuitous and shameful set of definitions for them. In this sense, they are never as "innocent" as Vivaldo, Cass, and Richard who begin with the assumption described here:

> This is not the way this truth presents itself to white men, who believe the world is theirs, and who, albeit, unconsciously, expect the world to help them in the achievement of their identity.

Rufus and Ida are presented as being beyond this *naïveté*. They are too familiar with the excesses of violence, the possibility of exploitation both sexual and spiritual, the gratuitous humiliation and denial of *lebensraum*, and the varieties of potential rape with which the society has surrounded them, to ever believe in society's myths in quite the same way as Cass, the New England aristocrat. But this knowledge is not, in practical terms, a liberating force, and is not even wisdom since it cannot easily be communicated or applied. For it has been gathered not merely at the price of "innocence," but at the cost of a bitterness and distrust which is so massive as to be insupportable. This knowledge, neither cerebral nor intellectual, but which as a function of experience, is almost pathological, renders the possibility of communication between the Scotts and their "*innocent*" white lovers difficult or impossible on any deeply significant level. Elsewhere, Baldwin has written that "people who strive to preserve their innocence after the justifiable time for that innocence has passed become monsters." Another and equally grim application of this aphorism must go, "people who are prematurely deprived of hope, illusion, and innocence become ruthless."

As this operates in the novel, both Rufus and Ida Scott have fewer discoveries to make, and fewer illusions to lose, than their white lovers. No less vulnerable, they are, because of their slum kid's gutter knowledge, somehow less surprisable. They both have white lovers who are committed to the attempt to create relationships grounded in respect, decency, and genuine and enduring love. This goal (though obsession may be more descriptive, since these characters seem to be motivated by a desperate and obsessive faith in the liberating possibility of love) ensnares Rufus and Ida too. They both at first resist and reject any possibility of that kind of a commitment, but are gradually led by their own needs to suspend this protective armor of earned cynicism, and to commit themselves to the attempt. Once they are "reached" by their relationships, they become victims of a new kind of vulnerability. Precisely because they do not have the "innocence" of a Cass, or the comfortable blindness of her husband, they must *will* themselves to participate, despite their dearly bought vision of the reality of pain, and hatred, of anguish and love as inseparable intertwine in the act of living, despite their knowledge that simply to live is a terribly dangerous thing, and that we "all must pay our dues." Instead of "innocent" victims, they are informed victims, because despite their "alienation" and their very hip knowledge of the protean shape of destruction within the society, they cannot escape it, and their choices and responses are defined by this fact.

Because many of his responses are conditioned by the process by which he received his knowledge, Rufus cannot control his increasing paranoia or the violence that is evoked in him. He looks at the body of his white lover and asks himself, "If she were Negro would I want her?" He finds that her body (the possession of which is allegedly the ultimate phallic triumph of the Negro man, and the ultimate insult to the white man, but this is a formulation of the white male mind made into a kind of social reality), her love, a physical and spiritual commitment which is so total as to be almost a capitulation, is not enough. But since he can neither accept and forget, nor completely reject her, the relationship moves from violence to violence, abuse to abuse, and ultimately to destruction and madness. He is unable to escape his emotional conditioning, received at the hands of society.

His younger sister Ida comes out of Harlem to do battle with the forces that she is convinced destroyed her brother. She *knows* the enemy and is not about to be seduced into lowering her protective isolation. She resists any but the most superficial relationship to Vivaldo, is not about to expose herself in the same way Rufus did, and will not be deluded into recognizing even a possibility of tenderness and compassion. When you run with the wolves, you howl like a wolf. So by maintaining her noninvolvement, she is able, by prostituting herself to Ellis's lust, to manipulate his attempt at exploitation to the advantage of her career. In so doing, she is acting out of her experience, that of the black woman in Harlem. But the burden is too great for her to sustain, and she ends up responding with compassion and tenderness to Vivaldo's earnest, if bumbling, faith in the possibility of communion. At the end of the book, she is going against the evidence of her experience, and is making a desperate commitment to the relationship. One gets the impression that she knows better, but must force herself to try.

One critic perceives all the characters as being "self-centered," and so they are, as who isn't? But their isolation, or alienation if you will, does not admit of so pat a dismissal, as I have been at pains to point out. They are—those that indicate any hope of positive development—involved in "making themselves up as they go along." They are isolated—but in the most existential and agonizing sense of the word. In their necessary rejection of the glib and ready-made, they are forced to construct a new reality, to impose their own order and definition on the chaos in which they move, if they can. This is the challenge which they accept, and their only resources are in their own tangled emotions, their own desires and needs (which they are forced to take issue with in their totality and there is, apparently, nothing as shattering as the encounter with our true image) and the depths of their own spirit. Baldwin writes of Eric, and it is true in large degree of them all, that

> He could not accept the hideously mechanical jargon of his age, saw no one around him worth his envy, did not believe in the cures, panaceas and slogans, did not believe in the vast grey sleep called security—and he had to make his own standards and slogans as he went along. It was up to him to find out who he was, and it was his necessity to do this, so far as the witchdoctors of his time were concerned, alone.

It is this character, Eric, who aroused most of the male chauvinist objections to the book. He is less tormented and uncertain than the other characters, and consequently strangely attractive to them. Many critics resented that this bisexual actor is presented as having attained a measure of peace in the acceptance of his own reality (as opposed to the identity that dominant conventions would impose), and that Cass Silenski is able to find with him a dimension of emotional integrity, that is not possible with her all-American writer-husband.

What this character represents is more subtle than simply an attack on
the virility of the conventional American he-man. His ability to discover
what and who he is, to accept this, and to be honest to his emotional
impulses, however socially unacceptable they may be, is an expression of
one of Baldwin's major insights. Perhaps more debatable and more interesting, however, are the emotional implications of bisexuality.

The tone of the writing is, as Podhoretz says, meant to deny any moral
significance to the categories homo and hetero sexual, since these are social
rather than natural distinctions. The point is not simply that there is
a sexual dualism of greater or lesser strength in each individual, and that
physical expressions of this are not *necessarily* perverse. The point is that
emotional responses between and across the sexes are determined by puri-
tan society's rigid (and arbitrary) separation of social functions and roles
into categories of male and female, and the attendant pressures on the
individual to repress and suppress natural responses which do exist. This
leads to an unnatural fragmentation not only of experience but of emotional sensibilities, and a rapidly approaching point at which the gap
between the "feminine sensibility, the feminine mystique" and the male
perspective will be unbreachable. Notice too, that while, thanks to the
feminist revolt, women are gaining access to experiences—not necessarily
overtly sexual—situations, roles, and styles of life which had been reserved
to men, there is no indication of a similar reciprocal broadening of male
possibilities. I once heard a young writer confounded by the question,
"How on earth do you ever hope to become a writer when you begin by
arbitrarily excluding yourself from a whole area of human emotional experience?" This question may be meretricious, but it expresses something
of the Tiresian quality that has been written into the character of Eric, in
that out of his own sexual ambiguity—a fairer word might be flexibility—
he is able to relate to vastly different needs in Cass and Vivaldo.

This is mentioned because I feel it has some relevance to the perceptions
of the author, who is able to illuminate and probe into areas of experience
and emotion convincingly and passionately, largely because of his awareness of emotional attitudes which are generally characterized as exclusive-
ly male or female. But I do not wish to belabor this.

Finally, although the book has its faults, and the most distracting of
these have to do with an uncharacteristic note of sentimentality and too
much of a self-consciously aphoristic and apocalyptic rhetoric, its accomplishments and its importance far outweigh these. Whether or not one
agrees with the vision of the *meaning* of contemporary experience presented, no one denies that the book is an accurate, perceptive, and truthful

expression of the texture, feel, and consistency of that experience. That is the first and major responsibility of the novelist. My own feeling and that of everyone I talked to when the book first came out was, despite anything else, "He is telling it like it is." I cannot remember anyone, white or Negro, who did not feel that the book spoke directly and fiercely to many aspects of his or her own particular experience.

Equally important in evaluating this book is a consideration of the place it represents in the body of Baldwin's work, and what that work represents in the flux of the American literary culture. Returning to New York with his perceptions sharpened, and with a vision that combined the freshness of the stranger with the knowledge of a native, he was able to excavate and display patterns, relationships, insights which had never been presented in quite the same way, with courage and candor. And this book, the book he was *compelled* to write more for truth and relevance than for "Art," is the one in which he confronts most fully the anguished issues peculiar to our age.

As Robert Sayre says "certainly one mark of his achievement, whether as a novelist, essayist, or propagandist, is that whatever deeper comprehension of the race issue Americans [presumably white Americans] now possess has been in some way shaped by him. And this is to have shaped their comprehension of themselves as well."

This revolution of consciousness that he has engendered is a social reality as much as a literary one. It is scarcely possible to write today on this issue without, consciously or not, making use of assumptions and relationships which first emerged as startling insights in Baldwin's work. He has single-handedly broken through a dead end of platitudes, sociological clichés, complacent white assumptions, and a monopoly of consciousness which had, since the thirties, just about lost their usefulness. How was this possible?

Mostly one only speculates, but certain things can be pointed up. Intellectual techniques and practices have a natural tendency to atrophy and stagnate, to *reinforce* themselves endlessly to the point where once useful truths became meaningless platitude. With this atrophy of language and concept, goes a limiting of vision and imagination. Generally, this had happened in America. One has only to read the Negro writers of the fifties to see how enclosed they were in the respectable terminology and analysis of the thirties, but it is hardly necessary to outline this vast canon of accepted American assumptions on the race question at this time.

Suffice it to say that these assumptions were based on a few meager studies by some Negro scholars and a Swiss sociologist, and heavily on the fact that whole areas of the real history of the country had been rewritten by whites, in service to the necessities of white political, economic, and cultural objectives. The basic cultural power-relationship, which decreed that the interpretation of the race question was to reflect only the whites' definition of themselves and the Negro, has persisted since the very beginning of literature in this country. A one way mirror.

The social ferment of the thirties did produce Richard Wright's and Ralph Ellison's magnificent efforts to balance this, but the very nature of the intellectual focus of that period—fervently political, predominantly one of class politics and economics—while establishing necessary and important horizons, could not incorporate other significant perceptions. When Baldwin left the country during the cultural and political depression which followed the economic depression, there was a need to go beyond the revelations and discoveries of the thirties. But how and to what?

I think the sojourn in France helped provide Baldwin with necessary analytical tools and a new way of seeing. Specifically, he was affected by the French existentialist sensibility, particularly that of Sartre, who while exploring the nature of the emotional warfare between one consciousness and "the other," concepts of alienation and emotional annihilation of the individual, never lost sight of certain Marxist concepts of class power and class influence. Genet's work, filled with revelatory insights into class perceptions and class subjectivity, and demonstrations of the transformation of relationships and situations that are caused by a simple shift in point of view, his work with the function of the "Mask" and the "Role" in determining social behavior (readily applicable to the American racial situation), affected the consciousness of the French intellectual generally.

The most meaningful of these insights in Sartre, Genet, and the French absurdists is their sophisticated understanding of the role of *power*, between individuals and between classes, the power to control language, and through language, expression and perception and thus even historical interpretation.

Baldwin's use of this insight is pervasive, beginning with the simple disclosure that the American Negro as the object of this kind of white power, had been defined in the public and indeed, his own consciousness, by white *needs*. This being so, the possibilities are overwhelming. First, an examination of the elements of the "image" of the Negro in the culture, literature, and public consciousness could reveal, albeit sometimes in disguised and inverted form, useful truths about the psychological needs of the white image maker and his culture.

From this it followed that if the image and identity of the Negro was in such large measure a product of *white cultural power,* then this condition could only be completely understood and changed by close and probing scrutiny of white society. "One can not understand where Negroes are today, without understanding twice as much about where white people are. . . . There is no Negro problem, there is a white folks problem. . . . The form and content of oppression are reflections of the fears and needs of the oppressor. To survive the oppressed must understand and use these. Why did the white need to create the 'Nigger'?"

If these are not new insights, at least the probing and sweeping application that Baldwin made of them resulted in vast breakthroughs, most important of which is the willingness, at least of some whites, to accept that those perceptions coming out of the peculiar history, experience, and vantage point of the Negro do have a validity and a dimension in describing contemporary social realities, which is not possible for the consciousness operating from "white" assumptions and perceptions.

Like the white rulers in Genet's *The Blacks* who were not prepared to be examined and discussed by the blacks, or the mistress in *The Maids,* also by Genet, who could not recognize herself as reflected in her maid's perceptions, America's dominant culture group was ill-prepared to cope with a Negro analysis of the culture. If he had done nothing else, Baldwin's determined insistence on interpreting events and attitudes affecting Negroes, both historical and contemporary, in terms of what they indicated about the initiators would be a major contribution.

Baldwin's *Another Country* is the first example of these sensibilities in operation *qua* "pure" literature. However the specifics are phrased, it is this fact that is at the base of much of the critical virulence that greeted the novel. But it is this fact also that will ensure its lasting significance. Its existence breaks the ground for the others that, one hopes, will follow.

*1969*

# Mr. William Styron and the Reverend Turner

■ ■ ■ ■ ■

W E know within certain general and stable (though they appear to be constantly expanding) boundaries what a novel is. We know also what a historical novel is, and the terms by which such works can be judged. But when a work of fiction is cast in the form of a novel, utilizes those techniques of narrative, situation, and structure that we associate with the novel, and which concerns an important historical event, but is declared to be "less an historical novel in conventional terms than a meditation on history," then what are we to make of it? Is its historicity more or less important than its meditativeness?

William Styron's *The Confessions of Nat Turner* straddles two genres, claims to be not quite either, and manages to combine the problems of both while to an extent reaping dual dividends as a novel which is in some way also "history." If the book were simply a novel, then there are things that could be said about its structure, characterizations, and language. But how is one to judge the proper and appropriate language of meditation? If it were simply history, then we would point to certain violations of the rules for reconstructing history, and point out that, on the face of any objective reconstruction of the evidence, it could not have been how the book says it was.

The fanfare with which the book has been greeted is largely based on the duality of its claims. It is hailed as a major novel with a significant theme. As a work which re-creates and significantly illumines a morally traumatic portion of the American past, it is held, *ipso facto,* to contribute to our awareness of ourselves and our subconscious postures toward present realities. In this context the work becomes a page in that sacred journal that marks the peculiarly American quest to master the truth of our past in a quest for historical and spiritual authenticity. This is doubtlessly an honorable and valid undertaking, but one which borders on absurdity on many sides. It is perhaps a function of this absurdity that I find myself writing in defense of a black rebel, dead since 1831, related to me neither by blood nor obligation, and whose shades, I suspect, have little concern with judgments of posterity as expressed through the person of Mr. Styron.

But my concern is less with the Reverend Turner's memory than it is with the future of his grandchildren—to whom he used to be a hero. And it is reasonably clear—if the notices with which the book was greeted mean anything at all—that Mr. Styron's book is being read as a kind of super historical novel by a public seeking what it seeks in all of its reading, the shock of mildly pleasurable outrage and, incidentally, information and insight.

Because the book is both "historical" and a "novel," a section of the public will invest it with qualities it does not necessarily possess. The facts and situations will be assumed to be accurate because by being "historical" it must of necessity be "true." And just as the facts of history are "true," so are, in a somewhat different sense, the insights of the novel. This is the great advantage of the form. By simulating a cosmos, its terms appear sufficient unto itself, its boundaries definitive and discrete, so that no further possibilities, no moral or philosophical dimensions, other than those existing within those boundaries, seem relevant to that cosmos. It is true, as Negroes are increasingly discovering, that what is excluded by historians is frequently as important as what they choose to record. This must be doubly true of the novel because of the cloak of self-containment which it wears, so that what is an extremely selective process takes on the illusory dimensions of being "the experience." So a book which according to its publishers "reveals in unforgettable human terms the agonizing *essence* of Negro slavery" can certainly be held accountable for what it selects and what it chooses to ignore. It is a solemn and rather prosaic truth that one cannot approach the essence by ignoring the *substance,* either in literature or in the laboratory. For an example, if it were true, or even suggested by the evidence—and this is not the case—that Nat Turner's first nineteen years were spent as a privileged and pampered house slave, favored (beyond all belief) by an ineffectually well-intentioned (beyond all belief) old master of vaguely liberal bent, this would be neither the essence nor substance of the experience of slavery. The substance of that experience, as we well know, was the deadening accumulation of event, the experience of the slave ship, the auction block, the torture of body and spirit, undernourishment, overwork, the violation of spirit and body, the deprivation of a culture, of language, and the overwhelming presence of the apparatus of white power, that is to say the power to coerce, to mutilate, and ultimately arbitrarily to kill. That, it seems to me, is the substance of reality out of which any "essence of Negro slavery" must be distilled. Those are the realities that have conditioned our present situation for both whites and blacks.

Despite the necessary secondary tasks which Styron undertakes in this book, i.e., the fleshing out of various contemporary positions on "the question," the evocation of a historical period, the reconstruction of a culture inherently morally schizophrenic, and so on, the theme of the novel, the central mystery that engages us and clamors for insight, is the personality and motivation of Nat Turner and the determined and desperate band of men who fought and died with him.

It is in this context that the questions which so plague our time become relevant. The question of the moral imperatives and consequences of violent rebellion, of its spiritual and political implications, the existential confrontation with the act of murder, and particularly the exquisitely painful responsibility of the instigator, who not only for himself must choose to resist—that is, to take the irrevocable step—but to be responsible for his followers taking it also. This is the ultimate revolutionary responsibility, and requires a certainty that approaches either love turned to desperation or madness. Styron's Nat Turner, in marked contrast to the historical Nat, has neither; lacking ideology or even the fervor of a prophetic fanaticism, he has only a pallid and unconvincing neurosis. It is perhaps, as one critic has proclaimed, that "only a white southerner could have written this book," this particular book. It is equally true that only a writer who is imaginatively familiar with the agonies of oppression and the morally convoluted dimensions of rebellion and who is in some measure liberated from that experience can do justice to this theme. Mr. Styron is not such a writer.

In selecting the subject and the strategy for this novel, Styron took certain calculated risks. In doing so—and one must assume a full awareness of the purely technical and creative problems they represented—he displays a *chutzpah* which borders on arrogance. First, by selecting Turner, Styron chose a personality with a reality in history, caught up in actual events, within a specific historical situation, about which and whom some facts are known. By so doing Styron placed on his creative imagination the responsibility of working within the facts and events as we know them. This he has not done, and his failure is at once significant and revealing.

Then, by deciding to render the novel through the mind, voice, and consciousness of Nat Turner, he undertook the challenge that finally ruined the book. Assume for a moment that a white southern gentleman could, by some alchemy of the consciousness, tune in on the mind-set, thought-pattern, impulses, feelings, and beliefs of a black slave in 1831. Having accomplished this miracle of empathy, since they lack common language or experience, he will still have the problem of creating a *literary* idiom in which to report his insights to his contemporaries.[1] And as the linguists are discovering, and novelists have always known, language is not only a medium of communication, but also helps shape and express consciousness. It not only functions to formulate attitudes but to create them, it not only describes experience but colors the perception of it, so that dialects and idioms are evolved by people to serve the necessities of their experience. This is one reason why people in Harlem do not speak like people in Bucks County.

When black people were brought here they were deprived of their lan-

---

1  It is a matter of considerable irony that at the time this was written, such a book had, indeed, been recently published. It is significant that it never received any of the publicity and literary awards that greeted Styron's novel and only came to my attention much later. The fact is that perhaps the finest—most serious, culturally and historically accurate—novel of the African experience of American slavery is by a white southerner, Mr. Harold Courlander. His novel *The African*—the story of a free-born Fon boy who becomes a slave in America— truly deserves the attention and superlatives ("captures the agonizing *essence* of slavery") that greeted *Nat Turner.*

Courlander, whose scholarship in black culture has been life long, came to the subject through an interest in Afro-American folklore. This led to a study of Haitian culture which led to the fascinating history of the religious cultures of Dahomey and West Africa.

Armed with a sensitive and profound understanding of Afro-American culture and history, *and* a clear grasp of its relationship to and evolution from the parent African culture, Courlander was able to create a powerful, compelling, and—in terms of capturing the nuances of language, imagery, and sensibility—remarkably convincing account of what the experience of slavery had to have been for an African. The novel is a major accomplishment in any terms; it is also a major classic in the Afro-American tradition. It should be better known and particularly in the black community. I have always regretted that I was not aware of this novel, published the same year as Styron's *Nat Turner,* at the time of the controversy.

guage, and of the underpinnings in cultural experience out of which that language comes. It is clear that they replaced it with two languages, one for themselves and another for the white masters. It is this latter that has been preserved, parodied is a better word, as the "Sambo" dialect in the works of southern dialect humorists (including Samuel Clemens at times)—to whom it was often simply quaint and humorous. The only vestiges we have of the real language of the slaves is in those spirituals which have survived. Mere vestiges though they are, most spirituals give a clue to the true tenor of that language. It is a language of conspiracy and disguised meaning, of pointed irony and sharp metaphor. It is a language produced by oppression, but whose central impulse is survival and resistance. It is undoubtedly the language in which Turner's rebellion and the countless other plots for insurrection were formulated. Anyone who has been privileged to catch the performance of a good black preacher in the rural South (or Martin Luther King talking to a black audience) understands something of the range and flexibility of this language. Lacking complicated syntactical structure and vast vocabulary, it depends on what linguists call para-language, that is gesture, physical expression, and modulation of cadences and intonation which serve to change the meaning—in incredibly subtle ways—of the same collection of words. It is intensely poetic and expressive since vivid simile and a creative juxtaposition of images and metaphor must serve (instead of a large vocabulary) to cause the audience to see and feel. It is undoubtedly a language of action rather than a language of reflection, and is as such more easily available to the dramatist than the novelist. Nevertheless it is some literary approximation of this language that the characterization of Nat Turner requires.[2] And Mr. Styron's Nat speaks or rather meditates in (as Spenser is said to have written in) no language at all. His creator places in his mouth a sterile and leaden prose that not even sizeable transfusions of Old Testament rhetoric can vitalize. It is a strange fusion of Latinate classicism, a kind of Episcopalian prissiness, and Faulkner at his least inspired. At times it would seem that Mr. Styron was trying, for whatever reason, to imitate the stodgy "official" prose of the nineteenth-century lawyer who recorded the original confessions. At other times Nat sounds like nothing so much as a conscious parody of the prose voice of James Baldwin, the Negro Mr. Styron knows best. This is not to say that the prose is not lucid, even elegant in a baroque Victorian way, especially in the functionally inexplicable pas-

2   Again, for a successful literary approximation of this language and its dynamics, see Harold Courlander, *The African* (1968).

sages of nature writing that continuously interrupt the narrative. But finally it is the language of the essay, heavy and declarative. It does not live.

This language combines with the structure of the novel to disastrous effect. Since the story begins after the fact, with Nat already in prison reflecting on his life, much of the book is in the form of long unbroken monologues, insulated in an inert prose. Even the most violent action or intensely felt experience seems distanced and without immediacy, strangely lumpen. Lacking the allusiveness of thought or the vitality of speech, and the quality of dynamic tension necessary to the illusion of the immediacy of the experience, the language reduces us to spectators rather than participants in the action.

Because the problem of language is inextricably caught up in the problem of consciousness, Styron's inability to solve this problem (and it may well be insoluble) is symbolic of, and operative in, his failure to bridge the gap of consciousness.

Nat Turner operates in this novel with a "white" language and a white consciousness. His descriptions of his fellow-slaves, for example, are not in the language of a man talking about his friends and family; they reveal, rather, the detailed racial emphasis best exemplified by slave-auction advertisements, or the pseudo-anthropological reports sent back from Africa by white missionaries in the nineteenth century. Lacking the idiom in which Nat might communicate intimately with his peers, and apparently any meaningful insight into what they might say to each other, Styron simply avoids this problem by having him spend most of his time in that paradoxically southern situation, close to but isolated from whites. This isolation in proximity becomes his obsession. And as his language is theirs, so are his values and desires. Styron's Nat Turner, the house nigger, is certainly not the emotional or psychological prototype of the rebellious slave; he is the spiritual ancestor of the contemporary middle-class Negro, that is to say the Negro type with whom whites and obviously Mr. Styron feel most comfortable.

Conspicuously intelligent—in their terms—he aspires hopelessly to the culture and status of his white masters, to break his isolation by being recognized on their terms. Witness his ecstatic joy when he is able to spell a word, thereby demonstrating his intelligence to his master's guests. Naturally, to Mr. Styron, and his white audience, he must despise and hold in contempt the society of his own people whom he considers dumb, mindless, unsalvageable brutes unfitted either for freedom or salvation. Hating the blackness which limits the possibilities which he feels should be his by right of intelligence and accomplishment he becomes a schizoid nigger-

baiter. That the speaker is supposed to be black merely obscures the issue.
In the historical context, it is impossible to imagine Nat Turner, a minister
to his people, teacher, and above all, a venerated leader, displaying the
kind of total alienation and contempt inherent in the following:

> A mob of Negroes from the cabins were trooping towards the house.
> Muffled against the cold in the coarse and shapeless, yet decent, winter
> garments Marse Samuel provided for them. . . . I could hear the babble of
> their voices filled with Christmas anticipation and loutish nigger cheer. The
> sight of them suddenly touched me with a loathing so intense that I was filled
> with disgust, belly sickness, and I turned my eyes away.

What this Nat Turner really wants is to become white, and failing that,
to integrate. This is the Negro whom whites, in the smug, nearsighted
chauvinism of their cultural and ethnic superiority, can understand. As
a type it certainly exists *today;* 1831 is a different question. What is
wrong with this characterization as applied to Nat Turner is simply that it
has sprung full-blown out of Mr. Styron's fantasies. It does not logically
derive from those facts of Turner's life that have come down to us. Indeed,
to develop this characterization, not only did Mr. Styron have to ignore
portions of this meager record, but he had to distort, in significant ways,
many of the portions he did use.

In an author's note at the beginning of the novel, Mr. Styron says that he
has "rarely departed from the *known* facts about Nat Turner and the
revolt of which he was the leader." "However," he continues, "in those
areas where there is little knowledge in regard to Nat . . . I have allowed
myself the utmost freedom of imagination in reconstructing events—yet I
trust remaining within the bounds of what meager enlightenment history
has left us about the institution of slavery."

One can only assume from this note that the author intends us to regard
this novel in a certain way. We must assume that it is an unbiased reconstruction of the events and probable motivations for the Nat Turner rebellion, true to the available facts. Where facts and events are missing, they
are imaginatively supplied, carefully based on the logical extension of
what is known. By virtue of this claim and the book's being titled *The
Confessions of Nat Turner,* thereby tying it to the event, we are led to
expect the greatest possible dispassionate, unprejudicial objectivity, and
accuracy. It is with these minimum expectations that we approach the
book, and they must affect how we react to it, and ultimately our attitudes
to the subject it illumines. While we cannot realistically expect the novel to
escape the influence of the author's private vision, his unique and subjec-

tive sensibilities and attitudes, we do expect it to be free of any kind of special pleading, fact-juggling, unsupported theorizing, and interpretations which answer not to the facts or logic of the events, but to an intellectual commitment to a version of history which is not only debatable but under serious question. We do not expect these specious qualities, because they are patently not the terms on which this work is presented to us. Yet Mr. Styron falls victim to all. If Mr. Styron presents his terms in good faith, we must conclude that he was betrayed by his own unconscious attitudes toward slavery, black people, and his ancestors whose myths, prejudices, and self-delusions are faithfully preserved in what must be one of the most touching examples of ancestral reverence outside oriental literature.

The primary source of information, of "known facts," is extremely brief, about four thousand words.[3] Why was it necessary, in this objective reconstruction, to depart from this source? In Nat's confession his formative years are deeply rooted in his family and within the slave society. His mother and father placed his first book in his hands and encouraged him in his efforts to read. His grandmother, to whom he claims to have been very attached, gave him religious instruction and predicted that he was too intellectually curious and intelligent to make a tractable slave. He taught himself reading and writing, and successfully deduced ways to make gunpowder and paper, being limited in these enterprises only by "the lack of means." The white lawyer who took his confession interrogated him about these processes and reports that he was "well-informed on the subject." From an early age, says Nat, he enjoyed the confidence of the "Negroes of the neighborhood," who would take him on their stealing expeditions to plan for them. What emerges from this is that Nat's character and attitudes in his formative years were molded by his family and peers. He becomes a leader and a plotter very early, and is involved with his black brothers in the clandestine resistance to slavery symbolized by stealing. Later he becomes a preacher, that is, a leader and a minister among the slaves. When he stops fraternizing with his peers, it is not out of any disdain or contempt, but for the very good political reason that "having soon discovered to be great, I must appear so, and therefore studiously avoided mixing in *society*, and wrapped myself in mystery."

It is Mr. Styron's inability or unwillingness to deal with the notion of a slave "society"—the presence of a black culture, that is, a system of social organization and modes of collective response—with its own

3  Gray's "Confessions of Nat Turner," reprinted in Herbert Aptheker, *Nat Turner's Slave Rebellion* (New York: Grove, 1968).

values, leaders, and rules, that more than anything else robs the novel of credibility. Because he cannot deal in convincing terms with the "culture" of slavery which produced and shaped Nat Turner, Styron, in contempt for the "known facts," simply isolates Turner from the blacks, places him among the whites, and attempts to create from that situation convincing motives and stimuli for his actions. If the case, historically, had been as Styron reconstructs it, it is difficult to imagine that a single slave would have followed Turner.

In Mr. Styron's "free ranging imagination," Nat's formative years are somewhat different. He has no knowledge of his father. His grandmother, a mute, catatonic, culturally shocked Corromantee wench, barely survives to give birth to his mother after disembarking from the slave ship. Nat's master, who is only mentioned once in his original confession, and then to say only that he was "religious," is elevated by Styron to be the major influence on Nat's life. Discovering Nat with a book stolen from his library (an occasion of great surprise since no nigger ever expressed interest in literacy), he has Nat tutored by his own daughter. Nat becomes a favorite, does light work around the great house, and observes the elegance, enlightenment, and moral superiority of his owners and strives to emulate and impress them. He feels superior to all other "niggers." Of his kindly and benevolent Master Nat reports,

> . . . I hold him in such awe, that I am forced to regard him physically as well as spiritually, in terms of such patriarchal and spiritual grandeur that glows forth from Moses on the mount. . . .

Such awe, indeed, that in his version rather than Styron's he is leading his fellow slaves in raiding his property.

This venerable patriarch is, as Styron is careful to report, educating Nat as an experiment to prove that Negroes are educable. After which presumably he will personally build schools and free them all since he feels that "it is evil to keep these people in slavery, yet they cannot be freed. They must be educated. To free these people without education with the prejudice that exists would be a ghastly crime."

Indeed, Marse Samuel does in due course reveal to Nat that, having educated him, he intends to free him. This contingency terrifies Nat, literate paragon among slaves though he is, since he simply is unable to conceive of assuming responsibility for himself. The wise and kindly master had, however, anticipated this insecurity and reassures Nat that he has devised a method to give him his freedom gradually, under his kind and paternalistic guidance. Nat is satisfied. (No explanation—except that time passes—is given in the novel of the process by which Nat moves from this abject dependence to the self-confidence that will allow him to accept responsibility for a colony of free rebels that it was his intention to start in the Dismal Swamps.)

This response (Please good Massa, dis yer Darkie ain't studyin' no freedom) is, of course, one of the favorite clichés coming to us from a certain school of plantation melodrama. Its inclusion here violates the evidence of history. This is not to say that it had no basis in reality, but there were other realities which are not shown. In order to make this response credible in Nat (remember he is the most intelligent and enlightened of any slave shown), Styron includes an image of "The Freed Slave" who is starving, confused, and totally incapable of surviving, and presumably this wretch, who is clearly worse off than the slaves, represents Nat's only experience or knowledge of freedom. This is misleading, since the fact is that every southern community and many northern ones had free Negroes, and at times whole colonies of them. These freemen worked as skilled artisans in many instances; some, to their discredit, even owned slaves. What is important here is that both masters and slaves knew this, and for the slaves these free Negroes represented a constant inspiration. What then is the purpose of this fanciful episode concerning Marse Samuel's plantation, Nat's fear of freedom, and the desperate straits of "The Freed Slave"?

The first figure is familiar: the gracious, courtly, humane, landed Virginia gentleman, wracked by conscience, solicitous of his chattel, and obligated by conscience to take care of his slaves who could not survive on their own. For him slavery is not a financial operation, it is the exercise of a moral obligation. (The example of the freed slave proves this.) His home, in which the First Families of Virginia "with names like Byrd, and Clarke" gather in elaborate carriages, rivals Tara in its gentility, charm, and benevolence. This is the Golden Age of Southern Chivalry, and what is being reconstructed for us is the enlightened benevolence of the "Old Dominion" version of slavery, surely the least oppressive serfdom in mankind's history. This only applies, as Mr. Styron is careful to indicate, to slaves fortunate enough to be owned by the enlightened gentry; it is the poor white overseers and small landholders who made the lot of slaves unendurable. Surely we have some right to expect serious novelists in 1967 to eschew this kind of fanciful nonsense? Especially if we know that it is precisely on these large Virginia plantations that the most degrading and debasing form of slavery was developed. Even as early as the 1830s, the Virginia land being increasingly exhausted by tobacco, these enlightened aristocrats had begun converting their plantations to breeding farms—

that is to say, the business of breeding black men and women like animals for the purpose of supplying the labor markets of the Deep South. That's one reality which is only fleetingly mentioned in this novel.[4]

In Marse Samuel's great house, Nat becomes "a pet, the little black jewel of Turner's Mill. Pampered, fondled, nudged, pinched, I was the household's spoiled child." Enjoying great leisure, he is enabled to lurk around for "a rare glimpse, face to face, of the pure, proud, astonishing, smooth-skinned beauty," of Miss Emmaline, one of the daughters of the household. It is clear that we are to be rewarded with some psychological insight into the emotional development of the young slave, and we are not disappointed. Nat, in his words, grows to "worship" Miss Emmaline, she who "moves with the proud serenity . . . which was good and pure in itself, like the disembodied, transparent beauty of an imagined angel," with a "virginal passion." For angels, what else?

Imagine then, the trauma of the poor youth who is raised in "surroundings where white ladies seemed to float like bubbles in an immaculate effulgence of purity and perfection" when he finds Miss Emmaline rutting with her cousin on the lawn and in her passion blaspheming God's name. When, having apparently enjoyed the act, she rushes with the inevitable "rustle of taffeta" into the house, she carries with her Nat's innocence and faith.

But for Nat, the experience, shattering as we are asked to believe it is, constitutes a form of emancipation. He had long rejected as too common the idea of sex with black wenches and substituted for it onanistic fantasies with faceless white women.[5] After his "Angel's" fall from grace, he says ". . . in my fantasies she began to replace the innocent imaginary girl with the golden curls as the object of my craving, and on those Saturdays when I stole into my private place in the carpenter shop to relieve my pent-up desires, it was Miss Emmaline whose bare, white full round hips and belly

4   In 1837, the Old Dominion exported to the death camps of the Deep South forty thousand black bodies for a net income of twenty-four million dollars.

5   There is some indication that the historical Nat, rather than being contemptuous of black women, was either married to one, or at least was the father of several children. Mr. Styron chose to discount this for several reasons. In the magazine *Per Se* (Summer 1966), he explains one of these reasons. "He was enormously unusual. He was an educated slave, and a man even of some refinement in a curious way. A man of that sort, I think, in a deep part of his heart would scorn the average, pathetic, illiterate colored woman, slave woman." It is unfortunate for the black woman of this country that Mr. Styron's ancestors, who were beating paths to the slave quarters after dark, were not of Turner's "refinement." This insult to black womanhood (wittingly or unwittingly) is an example of the kind of assumptions which underlie the novel.

responded wildly to my lust and who . . . allowed me to partake of all the wicked and Godless yet unutterable joys of defilement." Well, after all, that is what comes of all that "fondling, petting, and pinching." Nat becomes an inverted, frustrated, onanistic, emotionally short-circuited lecher after white women. Presumably, if he had given way to this secret lust and raped the white girl he is later to murder, the rebellion would never have occurred. The horror of this experience would probably have driven the young girl insane (almost a moral obligation for her in this tradition of southern literature) but some fifty-five white and two hundred black lives would have been saved. This moonlight, magnolia, and Freud view of history is presented as the basic motivation for the rebellion, a sexual desire (or love if you will) turned malignant in frustration.[6] Even if it did not come dangerously close to reiterating the infuriating sexual slander of the Negro male that is the stock-in-trade of the American racist, it would still be unacceptable as a theory of Turner's motives, because this kind of frustration-neurosis expresses itself in solitary, suicidal acts of violence, not in planned, public, political acts of rebellion.

The spare facts of Turner's life constitute grounds for a truly fascinating and illuminating meditation. Certainly more useful insight into Nat Turner's character and motives are to be achieved in the effort to reconstruct what it must have been like for the youth growing up in the influence of his family—two parents and a grandmother, his reacting to them and their attitudes toward slavery, his response to his father's running off, his early leadership in the stealing expeditions, his call to the ministry (while ploughing, not serving mint juleps), and his position among his fellows. Surely it is from these experiences that his personality and mission evolved.

6 To have this thesis seriously put forward is astonishing, and would be laughable if it were not for the easy acceptance that white reviewers have accorded it. It was, Mr. Styron tells us, suggested to him by the fact that the only murder that Turner admits to in his confession is that of a white girl. This is Styron's sole "evidence" for such a view. Along with millions of other Americans, we get another insight into Nat's character, here from the supremely authoritative and anonymous critic of *Time* magazine: "Nat must have been what the book makes of him . . . spoiled by the sweet taste of humanity some of his masters allowed. 'I will say this, without which you cannot understand the central madness of nigger existence,' he [Turner] explains, 'beat a nigger, starve him, leave him wallowing and he will be yours for life. Leave him with some unforeseen hint of philanthropy, tickle him with the idea of hope and he will want to slice your throat.' " This hodge-podge of cliché, stereotype, and *True Confessions* psychology would be disappointing from a novelist of Mr. Styron's accomplishment, whatever the context. To have it accepted and disseminated as wisdom and insight is a reflection of a certain failure of intelligence that in a less polite journal I would call "racism."

Turner tell us, through Gray's, not Styron's, "Confessions," that as he grew to young manhood, the memory of what had been said about him as a child by "white and black"—that he would never be of use to anyone as a slave—began to obsess him, "finding I had arrived to man's estate and was a slave." But he says he is consoled by the spirit of prophecy which indicates to him that there is a preordained role for him in that position. He begins his ministry and continually exhorts his people who "believed and said my wisdom came from God." He obviously occupies a place of some importance among them on his own merit, not from being the favorite of a paternalistic master. That he is a man of charisma and magnetism is evident. He seems totally preoccupied with his God and his people and the only mention of any white person at this time is of an overseer from whom he runs away and is at large for thirty days. He returns voluntarily because the Spirit orders him to return to his "mission," the exact nature of which he does not yet know. Upon his return the "negroes were astonished and murmured against me, saying that if they had my sense they would not serve any master in the world." This incident either did not impress Mr. Styron enough to be included, or else was at odds with his "interpretation." For one thing their unequivocal condemnation of Turner for returning establishes his peers' attitudes toward slavery, and it is different from the one generally found in the book. This is, significantly, one of the few cases on record of any slave returning voluntarily to slavery. What did it mean? Did Turner return out of a sense of solidarity with his black brothers, out of a sense of divine mission? Was it simply another case of nostalgia for the irresponsible security of slavery, did he get hungry? Subsequent events, and his own explanation, suggest some glimmering of a deliberate motive.

His given reason (at the time) for returning must stand as a masterpiece of irony. He simply quotes one of the Biblical texts best loved by slave owners: "he that knoweth his master's will and does not do it, shall be beaten with many stripes and flogged with a rod." To the slave master, this must have been gratifying indeed, evidence further of the faithful darky well steeped in the acceptable slave morality. To Nat, knowing that his master is God, a terrible, vengeful God, who has selected him for a "mission," it meant quite something else. He may even have undertaken the episode simply to establish his trustworthiness, thereby getting the necessary mobility to organize.

Let us examine how this omission serves the "interpretation" presented in the novel. While the historical Turner is trying to regain the confidence of his fellows, who are angry, incredulous, and suspicious at the idea of a man returning voluntarily to slavery, Styron's Nat Turner is fuming and fulminating endlessly at the spiritless subservience and servility of his fellow slaves who are presented as totally lacking in the will or imagination to change their condition. There can be no question that "Uncle Toms" existed, but it is also equally clear that these types and the attitudes they represented were seized upon by apologists for the institution and publicized and exaggerated, out of all proportion, while militance and rebelliousness were played down. Who can doubt this after hearing any contemporary southern sheriff mouthing his eternal platitude, "our niggers are happy"? History testifies that the desire for freedom among the slaves was a constant problem to their owners.[7]

The reality of slavery was that the slaves were constantly resisting and rebelling, whether by sabotage, malingering, escape to the north, physical retaliation to attack, plotting insurrection (with a frequency that caused the masters to live in a state of constant apprehension and under conditions of continual vigilance and security), running off to join Indian tribes, or else to form small bands of armed guerrillas operating out of swamps and remote areas. It is difficult to imagine why, if the majority of slaves were inert "sambos," broken in mind and spirit as Styron's Nat suggests, southern governors filled the official record with so many requests for federal troops to guard against insurrection. Why were meetings of slaves so severely proscribed? Why were they required to have passes permitting them to use the roads? Why were curfews so rigidly maintained? Why were armed patrols abroad in every slave community at night? Why were firearms considered a necessary part of the overseer's equipment? Is it perhaps because the "Sambo" type was the product of "enlightened" Virginian slavery that no suggestion of this massive machinery of coercion and control is found in the novel? What does its absence do to the "essence of the experience of slavery" that the publishers boast about? It is rather like trying to capture the experience of the Nazi concentration camps without mentioning the barbed wire or armed guards.

Two examples of incidents reported in the original "Confessions" and transformed by Mr. Styron's imagination are worthy of mention, as they are indicative of the pattern of interpretation that runs through the book. Turner tells of converting and baptizing a white man, an event unprecedented in Tidewater, Virginia, of the time, and which would probably cause an equally great furor were it to happen today. The two men are refused access to the church and repair to the river for the ceremony, where they are mocked and threatened by a white crowd.

7 For the testimony of slaves, see B. A. Botkin, ed., *Lay My Burden Down: A Folk History of Slavery* (Chicago: University of Chicago Press, 1958).

In Styron's version, the white convert is a drunken, degenerate, child-molesting pederast who is about to be run out of the county anyway, and is shown as the typical subhuman, white trash "cracker" that one might find in Erskine Caldwell. Again the logic dictating such an interpretation is not clear, but this is what happens in this novel to the only white who is shown associating with slaves on anything that looks like simple human terms, outside of the paternalism and implied superiority of the social categories of the time.

The second instance of arbitrary and derogatory "interpretation" concerns a slave called Will, who invited himself to join the insurrection. He is different from the other conspirators by virtue of this fact: Will was not recruited, he volunteered. In the original confession, Turner reports finding Will among his men when he joins them on the day of the insurrection.

> I asked Will how he came to be there, and he answered his life was worth no
> more than others, and his liberty as dear. I asked him if he thought to
> obtain it? He said he would or lose his life. This was enough to put him in
> full confidence.

In the subsequent violence, Will is identified specifically as "dispatching" a number of people, while most of the other murders are not attributed to members of the band. The most that can be said of Turner's references to Will is that they show him operating with a single-minded efficiency in carrying out the work at hand, which is, after all, the extermination of whites. In the context of Turner's narrative, there is no suggestion of dementia or frenzy in Will's actions; like Joshua, he is simply engaged in the destruction of the Lord's enemies. There is one probable explanation for Turner's specific references to Will other than his being particularly impressed by his murderous efficiency. This is simply that Will, being the last of the original band recruited, may have felt it necessary to stay close to the leader so as to demonstrate his sincerity, thus causing Turner to remember his actions more vividly than others in the group.

In the novel, Nat sees "the demented, hate-ravished, mashed-in face . . ." whose "wooly head was filled with cockleburrs. A scar glistens on his black cheek, shiny as an eel cast up on a mud-bank. I felt that if I could reach out I could almost touch with my fingertips the madness stirring within him, a shaggy brute heaving beneath the carapace of a black skin." Will is "streaked with mud, stinking, fangs bared beneath a nose stepped upon and bent like a flattened spoon." His eyes shine "with a malign fire" and he bears a hatred "to all mankind, all creation." We learn that Will has been reduced to this condition of bestiality by the unen-

durable cruelties of a sadistic master so that his is not the "natural depravity" that another generation of southern writers would have evoked.
But even so, this characterization, this portrait of an evolutionary marvel,
half-nigger, half-beast, is surely familiar to anyone who knows such clas-
sics of southern literature as Dixon's *The Klansman*. His has been a long
history. He has been constantly and conveniently evoked for any number
of purposes, to frighten children with or to justify lynchings. And as he
sidles into the scene, stinking and licking his fangs, we recognize his
function: like the others of his type who have preceded him, he will rape
a white woman. And thirty pages later, despite Nat's injunctions against
rape (no sexual incidents are mentioned in the record of the trial), an in-
junction all the nobler in light of his own perennial, frustrated cravings, we
find this scene:

> There deserted of all save those two acting out their final tableau—the tar
> black man and the woman, bone-white, bone rigid with fear beyond telling,
> pressed urgently together against the door in a simulacrum of shattered
> oneness and heartsick farewell. . . .

and it looks as if Nigger-beast has struck again. One had hoped that this
particular stereotype had served his time in the pages of southern fiction
and could now be laid to rest. It is, to say the least, disappointing to see him
resurrected by a writer of Mr. Styron's unquestioned sophistication—and
to what purpose?[8]

8   William Wells Brown, a Negro whose book on the Negro in the American Revolution
appeared in 1867, mentions the Nat Turner rebellion. His version does not in any way
contradict the meager record that is the original "Confessions," but it adds information not
included. One may speculate as to the source of this information—possibly newspaper
accounts of the time, or the testimony of black survivors of the incident—but the account is of
interest, representing as it does an early account of the insurrection by a black man. About
Will, Brown has this to say: "Among those who joined the conspirators was Will, a slave who
scorned the idea of taking his master's name. Though his soul longed to be free, he evidently
became one of the party as much to satisfy revenge as for the liberty he saw in the dim
future. . . . His own back was covered with scars from his shoulders to his feet. A large scar
running from his right eye down to his chin showed that he had lived with a cruel master.
Nearly six feet in height and one of the strongest and most athletic of his race, he proved to be
one of the most unfeeling of the insurrectionists. His only weapon was a broad axe, sharp and
heavy." Brown then quotes from the "Confessions" of Will's path of carnage and describes
his death in the final skirmish. "In this battle there were many slain on both sides. Will, the
blood-thirsty and revengeful slave, fell with his broad axe uplifted, after having laid three of
the whites dead at his feet with his own strong arm and terrible weapon. His last words were,
'Bury my axe with me.' For he religiously believed, that, in the next world, the blacks would
have a contest with the whites, and he would need his axe." No sociological comment is

In addition to these (and other) examples of pejorative "interpretation," there is finally the major invention that gives color to the entire novel. Mr. Styron, on no historical evidence, has Turner's final defeat coming as a result of the actions of loyal slaves who fought in defense of their beloved masters. That these slaves are identified as "owned by the gentry" further underlines the book's emphasis on the benignity of "aristocratic slavery" which was able to command the loyalty of these slaves who were in one white character's words "living too well." Asked about this in the *Per Se* interview, Mr. Styron, who really talks too much, said: "The slaves in many of these houses—and not at gun point either, but quite voluntarily— were rallying to their masters' defense. . . . I'm sure the cliché liberal of our time would ask for proof that this is true. But there are a lot of motives, quite real ones, that would cause a Negro to defend his white master against other Negroes. One was to preserve his own skin. He was shrewd [at all other times in the novel, with the exception of Nat, he is loutish and stupid] and he figured that if he played his cards right he'd get off better. And also I think that there was quite frankly often a very profound loyalty in those days. The fashionable historians can't convince me otherwise, because there's too much evidence."

He never, however, cites any of this evidence. Mr. Styron simply *knows,* like a Mississippi planter of my acquaintance, that "them old time darkies were loyal and true." This is an item of faith. Apart from the fact that there is no evidence of this having happened, is it logical? Can one really believe that a group of outnumbered and frightened slave-holders discovering themselves in the midst of a slave revolt would have armed other slaves, who might themselves have been part of the conspiracy?

This thing which did not happen is made into one of the central motifs of the book. Turner broods on the memory of "Negroes in great numbers . . . firing back at us with as much passion and fury and even skill as their white masters." When his lieutenant, Hark, falls, Turner recalls "three bare-chested Negroes in the pantaloons of *coachmen* . . . kick him back to earth with booted feet. Hark flopped around in desperation, but they kicked him again, kicked him with an exuberance not caused by any white man's urgings or threat or exhortation but with rackety glee. . . ."

This invention makes it possible for a white lawyer at the trial to "revise certain traditional notions about Negro cowardice," because "whatever

---

necessary. But from a purely literary standpoint, it should be clear that Will, lifelong rebel and archetypal destroyer, presents possibilities which Mr. Styron simply ignored in favor of the "ravening, incoherent black beast" stereotype.

the deficiencies of the Negro character—and they are many, varied and grave—this uprising has proved . . . that the average Negro slave faced with the choice of joining up with a fanatical insurgent leader such as Nat Turner, or defending his fond and devoted master, will leap to his master's defense and fight as devotedly as any man and by so doing give proud evidence of the benevolence of a system so ignorantly decried by Quakers and other such morally dishonest detractors." The "bravery of those black men who fought bravely and well" at their master's side is to be recorded "to the everlasting honor of this genial institution."

It is true that those lines are meant to be read as special pleading and polemical defense of the institution *by a single character*. But it was not that character who invented those black loyalists, it was Mr. Styron, and much in the novel—the picture of life at Turner's Mill and Turner's own reflections on the event—support this general position. It is built into the architecture of the novel.

When Gray, the lawyer who is taking Turner's confession, says to Nat,

> . . . you not only had a fantastic amount of Niggers who did not *join* up with you but there was a whole countless number more who were your active *enemies* . . . they were as determined to protect and save their masters as you were to murder them. . . . All the time that you were carrying around in that fanatical head of your'n the notion that the niggers were going to latch onto your great mission . . . the actual reality was that nine out of ten of your fellow burrheads just wasn't buying any such ideas. Reverend, I have no doubt it was your own race that contributed more to your fiasco than anything else. It just ain't a race made for revolution, thats all. Thats another reason why nigger slavery is going to last for a thousand years.

we are clearly meant to read it as one taunting rationale of an apologist for slavery. Because of the emphasis in the whole book, it is none too clear that this *is* a qualifiable position. Quite literally *nothing* that we are shown in the novel denies the fictional Gray's conclusions. Quite to the contrary, as I have indicated, characters and events which in fact support them are invented in a systematic way.

Turner himself acquiesces in this interpretation. Dispirited and broken, he sits in his cell feeling himself betrayed by his people and his God. He thinks "it seemed . . . that my black shit-eating people were surely like flies, God's mindless outcasts, lacking even that will to destroy by their own hand their unending anguish. . . .[9]

9  Brown's version makes it clear, as does the court record, that Turner's defeat came at the hands of whites. No black loyalist mercenaries are mentioned, but he does give an

A pathetic and almost obscene figure, Nat broods and sulks in jail await-ing his death. The night before his execution he is comforted by fantasies of a sexual encounter with the white girl he murdered. In the original "Con-fessions," Turner shows no such uncertainty or ambiguity. When asked if he could not see that the entire undertaking was a mistake, he answers simply, "was not Christ crucified?" Gray's final description of him is significant: ". . . clothed with rags and covered with chains: yet daring to raise his manacled hands to heaven, with a spirit soaring above the at-tributes of man: I looked on him and my blood curdled in my veins." This is the Nat Turner of historical record: the rebel whose "calm deliberate composure" and unshakeable defiance in defeat so troubled and puzzled his white captors. Unfortunately Mr. Styron has not escaped their fate; that is why his Nat Turner is such a grotesque reduction. If this novel is important, it is so not because it contributes anything to our awareness of the Negro's experience and response to slavery, but because of the demonstration it presents of the truly astonishing persistence of white southern myths, racial stereotypes, and derogatory literary clichés even in the best intentioned and most enlightened minds. Its largely uncritical acceptance in literary circles shows us how far we still have to go, and what a painfully little way we have come.

Its almost wholly favorable reception, up to now, is in some respects more significant and revealing than the book itself. Why, for example, in a book that alleges to deal with important themes and events in Negro his-tory, was no black writer asked to comment on it in any major journal? Is it not a form of cultural condescension and indirect racism that only one

---

instance of a master's life being saved by a slave. That, too, is instructive. "On the fatal night, when Nat and his companions were dealing death to all they found, Capt. Harris, a wealthy planter, had his life saved by the devotion and timely warning of his slave Jim, said to have been half brother to his master. After the revolt had been put down, and parties of whites were out hunting the suspected blacks, Capt. Harris with his faithful slave went into the woods in search of the negroes. In saving his master's life Jim felt he had done his duty, and could not consent to become a betrayer of his race; and, on reaching the woods, he handed his pistol to his master, and said, 'I cannot help you hunt down these men: they, like myself, want to be free. Sir, I am tired of the life of a slave: please give me my freedom or shoot me on the spot.' Capt. Harris took the weapon, and pointed at the slave . . . The Capt. fired and the slave fell dead at his feet." I do not claim that this incident necessarily took place in exactly the way that Brown relates it. But it also seems too specific to be pure invention by Brown, who was, after all, writing history and not fiction. It seems most probable that this was one of those minor incidents which become part of the "folklore" surrounding any major event; it is discussed, passed on, almost certainly distorted in the telling, but for some reason not included in "official" records. In this case, moreover, the nature of the incident suggests a reason for its exclusion.

white critic bothered to check its historical accuracy? Would a book similarly interpreting the history of any other cultural minority be so uncritically accepted? Would the fate of this novel have been the same had it appeared in 1964, before the liberal literary intelligentsia had begun to feel estranged from the movement for black independence? These are, admittedly, sociological rather than literary questions. But forcing these questions upon us may ultimately prove to be this novel's real contribution to our awareness of contemporary realities.

*1968*

# The Turner Thesis

D R. Robert Coles's review of William Styron's *Confessions of Nat Turner*[1] dismisses certain very real problems presented by this work which, according to Styron himself, is "less an historical novel . . . than a meditation on history." Dr. Coles regards questions about this book's "psychological accuracy or historical inaccuracy" as irrelevant, and does not believe that "it is the validity or historical accuracy that count all that much," yet goes on to predict that "the book will make history" and finds "it all valid." But Dr. Coles cannot have it both ways.

The contradictory nature and strangely defensive tone of the review seem to derive from Dr. Coles's determination to endorse at least the effort if not the accomplishment of the novel. While he appears to be aware, as earlier reviewers were not, of certain racial issues raised by the book, he never discusses them. As a psychologist who has worked with southern Negroes (the anecdote about the Mississippi sharecropper which comprises the first third of the review establishes his credentials) and who presumably knows the "Negro mind," he simply pronounces the book "valid."

But the question of historical accuracy can-

1 *Partisan Review*, Spring 1968.

not be lightly dismissed since in the terms the author sets up and in which the book has been generally accepted and is being read, one of the major claims made for the book is a responsibility to "the essential truths of history." And this is precisely the issue, not the changing of one or two of the known facts of Turner's life. What is objectionable in the novel is the entire process of selection, invention, and emphasis in the use of materials surrounding Turner's life, and the clear manner in which these distortions cumulatively serve to present a peculiarly southern view of black history not supported by the known facts.

Why is it that most black readers find the characterization of Nat Turner in the novel unacceptable, while most whites, to judge from the reviews, find him perfectly credible and perhaps even comforting? The answer to this question lies in the very differences in attitude, world-view, and self-definition so glibly glossed over by the currently fashionable terms "black consciousness" and "white consciousness." Part of this response does have to do with what Christopher Lasch calls the blacks' search for "a usable past." But this does not mean that American history is being subjected to "the meatgrinder of black nationalist historical revision" with its implication of reckless invention and ideological rewriting. The question is more one of revising and expanding certain orthodox white assumptions, and adding to the currently limited arsenal of terms, categories, and definitions through which white historians have structured black history. *Black necessity has less to do with manufacturing a history than with the excavation, articulation, and legitimization of what has been ignored or misrepresented in our history.*

Assume that it is possible for a twentieth-century white southern writer to tune in on the thought patterns, beliefs, impulses, and world-view of a black slave in the 1830s. There are undoubtedly literary terms in which such a psychological and historical leap is possible, and there are many instances, from Shakespeare to Tolstoy, of seemingly successful recreations of a remote or alien experience. But for a white southerner writing from a black point of view, this kind of leap necessitates disengagement from that pervasive accumulation of white mythology about black people, and from that vast tradition of literary cliché, racial stereotype, and the romantic and sentimental version of history that is his own particular cultural heritage. It also requires his acquiring a sensitivity to aspirations, sensibilities and attitudes, to black cultural and linguistic tradition which is at odds with most of his class assumptions.[2]

2   For a demonstration that this is neither impossible nor unthinkable, see Courlander's remarkable novel, *The African.*

That Mr. Styron was not oblivious to these problems can be seen from his brilliant and candid essay "This Quiet Dust" (*Harpers*, April, 1965). (There is an interesting, but tangential, problem implicit in the way in which Mr. Styron was able in his essay to engage questions which he could not in his novel, and it is perhaps because the novel is so much more intimate, less detached, and less rational than the essay.)

"My boyhood experience," he tells us in the essay, "was the typically ambivalent one of most native southerners, for whom the Negro is simultaneously taken for granted and the object of unending concern. . . . My feelings seem to have been confused and blurred, tinged with sentimentality, colored by a great deal of folklore, and wobbling always between a patronizing affection . . . and downright hostility. Most importantly my feelings were completely uninformed by that intimate knowledge of black people which most southerners claim as their special patent; indeed they were based on almost total ignorance."

This knowledge, he writes, came from a distance, "as though I had been watching actors in an all black puppet show." He concludes that "one of the most egregious of southern myths" is that of the white southerner's boast that "he knows the Negro." A major factor in this distance is the effect of "the sexual myth" which he says "needs to be reexamined." "Surely a certain amount of sexual tension between the races continues to exist," he writes, "and the southern white man's fear of sexual aggression on the part of the Negro male is still too evident to be ignored. . . . While it cannot be denied that slavery times produced a vast amount of interbreeding . . . it is impossible not to believe that theories involving a perpetual sexual 'tension' have been badly inflated." (Later in the essay when he discusses the Turner insurrection, Styron says he finds it interesting that "the Negroes did not resort to torture, nor were they ever accused of rape. Nat's attitude toward sex was Christian and highminded, and he had said: 'we will not do to their women what they have done to ours.' ")

The southerners' ignorance of the Negro, Styron notes, has its effect on his literature. "Most southern white people cannot know or touch Negroes," a gulf reflected even in "the work of a writer supremely knowledgeable about the south as William Faulkner, who confessed a hesitancy about attempting to 'think Negro,' and whose Negro characters, as marvellously portrayed as most of them are, seem nevertheless to be meticulously *observed* rather than *lived*." (Faulkner, in retrospect, proves the wiser, as we shall see, and Styron should have given a great deal more thought to the reasons behind the canny Mississippian's "hesitancy.")

And, in the essay, Styron summed up the political nature of Nat's insurrection: "That the insurrection was not purely racial, but perhaps obscurely premarxist, may be seen by the fact that a number of dwellings belonging to poor white people were pointedly passed by."

Significantly, his comments on Turner's place in the slave society is quite different from that found in the novel: "His gifts for preaching, for prophecy, and his own magnetism seem to have been so extraordinary that he grew into a rather celebrated figure among Negroes of the county, his influence even extending to whites, one of whom—a poor, half-cracked, but respectable overseer named Brantley—he converted to the faith and baptised in a mill pond."

Styron assumes the white southerner's ignorance of blacks to be a recent phenomenon. But the evidence is that slave masters and overseers had no more intimate an understanding of blacks than do their descendants. As the first real leisure class produced in this country, and under the pressure of its morally ambivalent position, the slave-holding South devoted much energy to rationalizing and justifying its situation. The resulting elaborately articulated regional mythology—a guilt-generated, intelligence-perverting, self-serving view of race—limited the perception and evaluation of experience. With a few concessions to changed social realities, this system still provides the basis for white racism in the nation.

In the portrait the South created of itself, slaveholders were much maligned, benevolent Christians whose concern for and services to their chattel far outweighed, they felt, the labor they extracted in return. Their slaves were simple, childlike subhuman types of limited intelligence and potential who were basically happy and contented with their lot. But it is clear from the most cursory look at plantation records that only the most obtuse slaveowners ever really believed this. What emerges from these documents is that the more perceptive whites recognized that they were almost totally ignorant of what really went on in the minds of their property.

Kenneth Stampp's *The Peculiar Institution* cites many texts which indicate the extent to which slaveholders were aware of the blacks' concealed loyalties, values, social, legal and moral codes. The question is: how does what we know of the historical Nat Turner fit into a framework of a slave culture and society which was zealously protected from white scrutiny. As Stampp reports, one Virginian observed his slaves to have "sharp faculties" and "extremely fine and acute perceptions." Another found his to be "so deceitful" that he could never "decipher their character" or "get at the truth." According to an overseer, any white man who trusted a

Negro "was a damned fool." In 1851, a slave master bemoaned the "notorious fact that on every large plantation of Negroes, there is one among them who holds a kind of magical sway over the minds and opinions of the rest; to him they look as their oracle. . . . The influence of such a Negro, often a preacher, on a quarter, is incalculable." Clearly, these indications of a black community response to slavery are important, not only to blacks in search of their true history, but to any understanding of what must really have taken place in Southampton County in 1831.

All available historical sources indicate that Nat Turner's roots and his support came from the organization and the culture of the slave community. His brief confession, recorded by a white lawyer in 1831, hardly mentions whites until the passages where the violence is described. (The other source to which Mr. Styron appears to have resorted is *The Southampton Insurrection* [1900], a book written by one William S. Drewry, an unabashed apologist for the "benign" institution. Styron does not appear to have considered two earlier accounts, one in 1867 by William Wells Brown, a black historian, or that of Thomas Wentworth Higginson, a white abolitionist, whose account appeared in the *Atlantic Monthly* in 1869.)

However, despite Drewry's clear conviction—repeated again and again—that Virginia's slaves were "faithful and affectionate" and represented "the happiest laboring class in the world," he reveals much that contradicts his basic position. While triumphantly citing cases of slaves hiding or protecting their masters, he is baffled by the fact that most slaves apparently knew of the planned uprising yet failed to denounce it. Though insisting that Turner was motivated by a "hideous fanaticism" and that his followers were "weak, misguided and ungrateful," Drewry never denies the political basis of the rebellion, which he attributes to abolitionist agitation and the blacks' knowledge of the Haitian revolution, refugees from which were in the county. Another factor, according to Drewry, was the presence of 1,745 free blacks in a county with a slave population of 7,756. These freemen were "prosperous, many owned land" and their presence "encouraged the slaves to the possibility of freedom." Drewry notes that "news travelled among the slaves rapidly and mysteriously," as it did among "natives of the Congo." He believes that the insurrection plot extended to neighboring counties and into North Carolina. (In his jail cell, Turner denied all implication in the North Carolina plot.)

Drewry's comments on Turner's personal history are instructive. Turner's education he attributes to his master, "assisted by his parents who were intelligent Negroes." Nancy, Nat's mother, came "direct from

Africa" and was "so wild" that she had to be tied to prevent her murdering Nat at birth. (Infanticide committed by African-born mothers who preferred to see their children dead rather than slaves seems to have been frequent.) His father, described as "highspirited," ran away when Nat was a boy and was never recaptured.

Nat was a youthful strategist and leader of stealing expeditions. But Drewry attributes Nat's importance in the slave community mainly to his charlatanry, reporting that "he spat blood at will" having previously filled his mouth with dye, and that "he wrote hieroglyphics and prophecies on leaves of grass, which subsequently being found according to his prophecies, caused the slaves to believe him a miraculous being." Higginson reports that as late as the 1860s, there were traditions among Virginia slaves of the "keen devices of Prophet Nat." "If he were caught with lime and lamp black conning over a half-finished county map on the barn door, he was always 'planning what to do if he were blind' or 'studying how to get to Mr. Francis' house.' "

Despite Drewry's impulse to disparage the abilities of Turner's lieutenants, he does describe Hark as "a black Apollo" and as "the most intelligent and enthusiastic conspirator." He claims that this slave had taken the name of "a famous Negro general named Hark who served under Saood II . . . and who about 1810 carried his arms across the Euphrates and threatened Damascus." In a similar vein, William Wells Brown mentions a slave Will who joins the rebellion as being "a lifelong rebel who scorned to take his master's name" and whose last words after committing great carnage with his axe were "bury my axe with me." "For he religiously believed," Brown explains, "that in the next world, the blacks would have a contest with the whites and he would need his axe."

Aside from the origins of Nat Turner in the self-image and world-view of slave culture, the search for a credible Nat Turner and an objective reconstruction of his rebellion must certainly include the effects of his young mind on his "militant" family. What passed between the young Nat and his "wild intelligent" African mother? What was the legacy of his "highspirited" father who successfully escaped? Or did he have nothing to say to his son before leaving? To what extent was the slave "society" that Nat refers to sustained and structured by memories and legends of Africa? Is no glimmering of the slaves' understanding of their situation to be found in their quick acceptance and adaptation of the Book of Exodus as both a metaphor of their condition and a promise of deliverance? By what devices did news circulate "rapidly and mysteriously" among the "surprisingly well-informed" but "passive and inert" Sambos? Was that haunting, dirgelike melody with its not quite "civilized" melodic patterns and antiphonal scheme the words to which were "Steal 'way, Steal 'way, Lord, ah ain't got long to stay heah," just more evidence of the darkies' simple faith?

We find no answers in Mr. Styron's meditations. Indeed, these questions, which must surely have comprised a large part of the historical Turner's consciousness, are not raised, and Styron's black people, having lost the African heritage, are by the implications of this void in the novel in danger of being deprived of the tragic, grim, yet infinitely moving and inspiring heritage created for us by those "many thousands gone" who found ways to endure and myths and ideas by which to comfort and sustain themselves.

What does it mean, for example, that the Nat Turner of the novel speaks in a highly literary, convoluted, latinate prose reminiscent of one of Charles Dickens's Victorian pedagogues? Mr. Styron has said that the language was in part determined by his desire "to make him every bit as intelligent as I possibly could."

The language that the real Nat Turner must have spoken, preached, exhorted, and plotted in still exists in the rural South. The true tenor of that language—apocalyptic, poetic, richly allusive, and moving—can be seen in the spirituals and bitter blues poetry—which is a familiar part of the national culture. It is a language coming out of suffering and oppression, a language of subterfuge, of sharp metaphor and parable, which implies a world-view. It is a functional, living language, rather than a formal literary one, depending on vivid similes, effective juxtaposition of images and contrasts rather than large vocabulary for its range and flexibility. It is capable of communicating incredibly subtle nuances of meaning through variation of rhythm, cadence, and intonation. A credible characterization of Nat Turner demands some literary approximation of this language, and not only because many black readers feel that there is an implicit insult in Mr. Styron's giving Turner an abstract "white" language to make him "intelligent."

In the act of giving Turner a white language, Styron invests him with a white consciousness. Styron's Nat is removed from the slave cabins and installed in the great house from which, isolated from his peers, he observes blacks from a distance "like actors in an all black puppet show." He is constantly observing "lines of Negroes etched against the sky," or in coffles going south. The most striking characteristic of this figure is the extent to which he operates within the context of nineteenth-century plantation owner assumptions about blacks. The voice and consciousness which operate in this novel as Turner's, perceive and define black existence in terms which black people *have never accepted*. The underlying racism may be no more virulent than that of Faulkner, but in Faulkner's characters one recognizes a self-justifying class rhetoric quite unrelated to black consciousness.

Styron's black preacher, teacher, and revolutionary sees his "black shit-eating people" as "flies," "God's mindless outcasts, lacking that will to destroy . . . their unending anguish." He describes field hands as "a disheveled ragged lot" whose voices "babble, with loutish nigger cheer" and fill him with "a loathing so intense it was akin to disgust and belly sickness." From his position in the great house, he regards "Negroes of the mill and field as creatures beneath contempt." He describes an old slave as being "simple headed and in a true state of nigger ignorance." He is revolted by a group in church who are "picking their noses, scratching, sweating and stinking to high heaven" with "faces popeyed with nigger credulity." Nowhere do his descriptions and reflections on his fellow slaves escape the exaggerated, parodic, pseudo-anthropological language of the slave-auction announcement. The only slave of any accomplishment, with any psychological integrity and purposefulness that the young Nat mentions is a driver, and his very occupation means that his sense of self-worth is a gift of the whites.

On the other hand, all of the inflated, self-congratulatory, sentimental white myths about their own genteel and chivalric past are accepted by Styron's Nat, who views his master "in terms of such patriarchal and spiritual grandeur as glows out from Moses on the Mount." To him white ladies possess "the disembodied, transparent beauty of an imagined angel," and appear to float "in an immaculate effulgence of purity and perfection." His master's household (in which it is not clear that the historical Turner ever set foot) where the First Families of Virginia gather for formal balls and feasts, and where he is "pampered, fondled, nudged, pinched" and educated as the "black jewel" and "spoiled child" is presented to us through Turner's eyes as a virtual temple to the "lost" elegance and gentility of the golden age of southern chivalry, a world peopled by patriarchs, demigods, and angels. (That southerners wish to think that their slaves viewed their masters in these terms is clear, but that the slaves in fact did so is highly questionable. The young Nat Turner was not too awed by his master's patriarchal grandeur to organize raiding forays against his property.)

It is this mythic version of southern history that forms the ideological skeleton of the novel, and all incidents and detail flow logically from it. Turner is isolated from blacks, and influenced and motivated by "white" considerations. This denies the tradition of independent black leadership reported by Stampp and typified by Turner, since in the novel his authority is based on his master's favor and preference, and those attributes coming from his exposure to white influences. Turner hates and despises his blackness and aspires to the culture and enlightenment of his masters. His rebellion is a consequence of the inevitable frustration of these aspirations.

The old sexual myth, which Mr. Styron himself questioned in his piece in *Harpers,* becomes a dominant theme. Turner is an onanist who scorns women of his own race, and represses his lust for white women. In his case, it is not white "blood" that generated his militancy—the standard explanation of earlier generations of southern writers—but his exposure to white "culture," and his sublimated sexuality.

General Hark, the "black Apollo" and "the most enthusiastic and intelligent conspirator" who Drewry believed took the name of an African warrior, becomes a dumb, shuffling darkie, reduced to quivering paralysis by the sheer presence of whites, and terrified by a white woman and boy.

Brantley, the "respectable" overseer converted by Turner, becomes a retarded, child-molesting pederast, which apparently is the price he pays for abandoning his class position and violating the protocol which decrees that normal whites do not relate to blacks in terms of genuine respect and equality.

The slave Will who "scorned to take his master's name" and who is reported by Turner to have joined the insurrection because "his life was worth no more than others and his liberty as dear" and who was "resolved to obtain it [liberty] or lose his life" becomes another figure borrowed from plantation melodrama. He is a ravening, demented, hate-maddened monster who "sidles" into the scene stinking, licking his fangs, driven by blood lust to rape white women. In this case, the bestiality of the figure is attributed to the abuses of a cruel master rather than natural depravity, but the figure is a familiar one from a certain school of southern writing.

The rebellion is defeated by loyal slaves, armed by their masters, who attack the insurrectionists with, in Turner's words, "as much passion and fury and *even* skill" as their white masters. When three black coachmen maul the rebel Hark with "exuberance and glee," it is another indication of the benevolence of the enlightened, aristocratic Virginia gentleman, whose slaves were contented, loyal, and believed themselves superior to "field niggers." Not only did no such confrontation take place, but all the evidence suggests that the majority of slaves placed more importance on their standing in the slave community, with its own rules and values, than on the goodwill of their masters. In general, the emphasis on the slaves' worshipful affection for "the quality" is at odds with the radical implications of the "obscurely premarxist" forces Mr. Styron mentioned in his *Harpers* essay.

There are many other instances of the influence of prevailing myths on Mr. Styron's historical re-creation. For example, Nat's doubts about his ability to cope with the freedom promised by his master (who is presented, with no discernible irony, as being inhibited from freeing all his slaves only by his fears for their survival in that unaccustomed condition) are inexplicable in light of what Drewry reports about the free black population of the county.

It would be too optimistic for blacks to expect the white literary and scholarly establishment to abandon the comfortable myths, traditions, and habits of many lifetimes to undertake the reassessment of black historical and cultural contributions and realities. But we must insist—a burden no other minority appears to have—in our prerogative to define this heritage in *terms* of our own choice. This is necessary not only to black needs of the moment, but to fill a vacuum in the total history, consciousness, and sensibility of the nation. By glossing over the vacuum and denying by implication the very existence of our own terms, this novel reinforces the foolish and dangerous notion that the black community participates in the myths of its oppressors and shares the same perceptions of historical experience. It is in this sense that the novel is "reactionary."

*1968*

# Contra Naipaul

■　■　■　■　■

*New York Times Book Review*

TO THE EDITOR:

Had the brothers Naipaul not existed, would you have had to invent them? One suspects so. For how else would it have been possible for little brother Shiva to pontificate in your columns [Shiva Naipaul's "North of South: An African Journey" reviewed by John Darnton] that "the African soul is a blank slate on which anything can be written, onto which any fantasy can be transposed." That was May 6. In your May 13 issue, senior brother Vidiadhar compounds the nonsense by intoning dramatically, to the quite evident titillation of interviewer Elizabeth Hardwick, that "Africa has no future."

Enough already! What Elizabeth Hardwick understands about the real world has always been questionable. "Crippled cultures," indeed. But Irving Howe? [Mr. Howe reviewed V. S. Naipaul's "A Bend in the River" May 13.] Should we not expect from him at least some understanding of the ironies of history and its devious little sister, literature? Why then does he have such difficulty in recognizing and discussing the emotional need that the Western literati has for the Naipauls of the world?

Times and fashions change, but needs are constant. This is why the role of the Conrads and Kiplings of the imperial age—that of caricaturing and disparaging the societies and cultures of Africa and Asia—has had to devolve to native replacements. That these *assimilados* display an even greater zest and inventiveness at this task is a minor irony, tribute not only to the slumbering intelligence of the native, newly awakened, but to the inspirational example of their colonial mentors.

Today, Gunga Din no longer serves up cold beers and comforting toddies in the officers' mess. In his contemporary incarnation he distills cultural reassurance. Shiva and Vidiadhar, with their white alter ego Paul Theroux by their side, range like restless, deracinated, malevolent spirits through the Third World, their insatiable scavengers' eyes seeking signs of sickness, rot, or anything that they may mock, parody, and patronize. They have made careers of wallowing in the travail and pain of the black world. And to what end? Nothing more honorable or valuable than feeding the cultural smugness and reassuring the historical insecurity of the Western literati, that historically irrelevant class which is their only constituency.

But then, Gunga Din in whatever incarnation, is always a pathetic creature to his own people, his virtues being apparent only to the other side. As a writer he is without historical memory, outside of community, without kinsmen, ancestors, or gods. He lacks roots, culture, responsibility, obligation, or commitment to anything more substantial than his own alienated ego. To Irving Howe this in a writer is a strength? Since when . . . the time *he* left his father's house? No wonder the vision is so bleak, corrosive, lifeless, and ultimately self-hating. Gunga Din, in a clown mask, dhoti flapping round his spindly shanks, dances on his ancestors' graves, while the cold smiles of the Pukka Sahibs applaud his antic agility.

*Les Arbres musiciens,* a novel of political and religious conflict by the distinguished Haitian author Jacques Stephen Alexis, engages precisely this issue.

A poor but ambitious peasant woman—herself a traditionalist—struggles to educate her three sons. The reward of her sacrifice is that one son becomes a military officer, the second, a lawyer, and the third, a Catholic priest. The priest in a fit of assimilationist zeal and pious intolerance leads a crusade against the shrines and priests of his mother's religion. Finally, he leads his zealots against the great holy shrine *La Remembrance* only to find it already set aflame by *Bois D'Orme* the old keeper of the shrine who is dying. The High Priest of Voudou—ignorant old peasant to be sure—greets the Catholic priest with these words.

"The *Loas* [Gods] have not allowed your sacrilegious hands to defile the

ancient shrine of Remembrance. Though it is now flames and ashes, the
*Loas* live. . . . The ancient shrine will rise again, greater, higher, more
beautiful, eternal like the *Loas* of eternal Africa. I go to my death. You—to
your misfortune—will survive, but there will be more dead than you. . . .
*Go, son of no father. Go, man of no race, man of no land, man of no na-
tion, the hands of the Gods are upon you*" [italics added].

That Africa and the Third World face formidable and intimidating
problems, not all of them of Western devising, is true and distressing, but
the sneers and insults of the Naipaul collective notwithstanding, it is not
Africa and its people that have no future. It is the literary Gunga Dins and
the class whose cultural insecurities they so meretriciously and cynically
serve.

With every good wish,

I beg to remain, your obedient servant,

MICHAEL M. THELWELL
*Associate Professor*
*W.E.B. DuBois Department of*
*Afro-American Studies*
*University of Massachusetts,*
*Amherst*

IRVING HOWE REPLIES:

Michael Thelwell's eloquent letter—which shows he may have learned
some skills from that "historically irrelevant class," the Western literati—
drops a number of writers into roomy ideological bins, pastes on those
bins the label of "deracinated," and then declares them enemies of the
Third World. But please, not so fast.

I didn't review "the brothers Naipaul," or discuss the politics of V. S.
Naipaul, with which I might well disagree. I reviewed his novel "A Bend in
the River," a gifted, reflective, and by no means totally unsympathetic
portrait of the ordeals of an imagined African country. I quoted passages
indicating that Naipaul, though hostile to military demagogues and their
intellectual apologists, writes with some warmth about ordinary Africans.
About such mere details Professor Thelwell can't, apparently, be bothered.

Suppose, however, Naipaul were to seek "signs of sickness and rot," not
in Third World countries, but in the Western countries? Would Professor
Thelwell still be so passionate in his attack? I think not. I'm reasonably
sure he would then be celebrating Naipaul as a caustic critic of a decadent,
indeed "historically irrelevant" society.

A good number of Third World countries, about which high hopes were held a decade ago, have turned out to be ruled by brutal and rapacious dictatorships. The agonies and absurdities this leads to is one of Naipaul's major subjects. Professor Thelwell seems, however, to feel that it's a betrayal for a writer born in Trinidad to find in the Third World countries an abundance of the inhumanity, injustice, and cupidity that is abundantly present everywhere else. Were Naipaul to follow Professor Thelwéll's line, he might turn out tracts but he could not write honest novels.

If we look at the brutalities associated with Third World dictatorships, whether mere old-style military or bespangled with "leftist" ornament; if we consider what the gangsters of Amin and Mobuto, the political cadres of Cambodia, Ethiopia, and Guinea have done to their own bloodied people, we have the right to ask: why should not this historical phenomenon be as open to scathing criticism as anything that our writers have attacked in the West?

There remains Naipaul's novel, with imaginings and nuances far beyond the reach of Professor Thelwell's anger. Nor is there a spot of evidence that the professor even read this book before sending off his letter. Given his prepared certainties of opinion, he didn't have to read it.


The Editors
New York Times Book Review
229 West 43rd Street
New York, NY 10036

GENTLEPERSONS:

Surely a careless editor must have misattributed the reply to my letter that I have just read. Can this trivializing of issues, this pedestrian, though admirably evenhanded belaboring of both the obvious *and* the irrelevant be the issue of Professor Irving Howe's finely tuned literary sensibility? The product of that vaunted critical intelligence so attuned to the ferreting out of literary nuances and subtlety? The "socialist" critic, who once so roundly cudgeled Ralph Ellison for the dual sins of undue literariness and insufficient political consciousness, now wraps himself in the threadbare vestments of new critic aestheticism, and in the same breath presumes to lecture us on what constitutes an "honest novel" on Africa? *Oy Vey!* "Son, if you live long enough you will see everything." When my mother said that it was a warning. She was, I fear, more right than she knew.

It seems the good professor may be regretting that rather than following

as he elected to do, literary fashion, he did not in his review pursue the
vague "uneasiness" that the novel prompted in him. It is a great temptation to say of Howe and Naipaul, simply, that they deserve each other and
to let it go. But there are issues here, beyond perhaps the reaches of Prof.
Howe's bumptious cultural ethnocentricity, which are real enough and
should be discussed.

First, Prof. Howe's straw man: since no one, certainly not I, ever suggested that the "failures" of Africa or the stupidities of certain of its leaders
should not be examined and criticized, Prof. Howe's trotting out of his
shopworn, totalitarian liberal's laundry list of these "failures" is as transparent as it is absurd. He succeeds, despite his pious expressions of regret,
only in sounding like your common or garden *Broederbonder* on the question of African independence. Unlike the Boer, Prof. Howe, to his eternal
credit, once "held high hopes" for these poor benighted nations. Like the
Boer, however, he conveniently forgets that both Amin and Mobuto, those
scourges of Africa which he so readily conjures up, are in very real ways
creatures of Western creation.

The real issue with Naipaul's work is not that he discusses these questions which, presumably, I would like to sweep under the rug, but that he
doesn't. He merely exploits them. Naipaul is, on the evidence of his latter
work, a bitter, barren, venomous, possibly disturbed, perhaps disillu-
sioned, and certainly tragic figure. He is, and has always been, an excellent craftsman of distressingly limited intelligence. His writings and
utterances display that fundamental, self-immolating stupidity best expressed in the Ibo story about "the lizard that spoiled his own mother's
funeral," thereby willfully ensuring his own spiritual doom. A few representative pronouncements, culled at random from memory, will illustrate.
Naipaul on his native West Indies: "The West Indies are the Third World's
Third World." Or, "History is built around achievement and creation, and
nothing was created in the West Indies." Naipaul of his ancestral land and
his literary constituency: "I do not write for Indians, who in any case do
not read. My work requires a civilized and liberal audience. It would not
do in a primitive society." Naipaul on Africa: "Africa has no future."

What is sad about these is not merely that they are calculatedly offensive, but that they are so pompously sophomoric and so demonstrably
false. Given his posture of aggressive regurgitation of Western bias and
animus, who, except Prof. Howe, expects "honest novels" on Africa from
Naipaul's pen?

But sad though it be, his situation is instructive. Because, "barbed
satires," "classical cadences," "nuanced imaginings" notwithstanding,

Naipaul is as disastrous a product and implement of Western cultural imperialism as are Amin and Mobuto of its political interference. Here is an Indian who does not address Indians, who, in his words, accepted apparently uncritically by Ms. Hardwick, "in any case do not read." A West Indian who does not address West Indians and abhors the West Indies. Nor does he address Africans. And rightly so because they are not his audience; they are his victims. His rather questionable goal is the acclaim of the arbiters of bourgeois literary fashion. And, if the gushings of Ms. Hardwick, the uninformed fulsomeness of Howe and Updike, himself a literary carpetbagger in the African landscape, or the double-edged approval of the British right ("Dashed clever for an Indian, what? Always knew those bloody kaffirs, wogs, and coolies would one day regret deserting the flag, eh?"), is any indication, he has succeeded richly. No one envies him this pathetic celebrity. One merely wishes he could find a way to achieve it other than at the expense of the black world.

It is in this regard that Prof. Howe's silly question, or rather a reversal of it, takes on a certain significance. *Were* Naipaul to turn his arid and alienated vision to the manifold sins, wickednesses, follies, decadences, and excesses of the West, whose creature he so obviously is, I would neither praise nor damn him. The interesting question is, would the Howes and Hardwicks continue so fulsome in their admiration?

In his wisdom, Prof. Howe knows that I have a "line," the pursuit of which would result in, dare I say that forbidden word, "*tracts.*" I do, in fact, have a position on this question, but Irving Howe quite obviously does not know what it is. For his benefit, therefore, I will respectfully suggest what the rudiments of an "honest" African novel might be.

It does *not* distort the experience of a people by imposing on it the outmoded, discredited, supercilious, and alien point of view of the colonial novels of Cary, Kipling, and Conrad, a tradition in which Africa and its people are mere backdrops for whatever nonsense they care to impose. Rather, it proceeds *organically* and *naturally* out of the sensibilities, cultural traditions, and linguistic styles and resources of the people who are its subject.

It does not take a mocking and scornful glee in parodying the real sufferings of the society, nor does it blink at or excuse any excesses and brutality of the leadership, but is, rather, resolutely and courageously critical in a principled way. Honest African writers have paid high prices in personal suffering for doing this. They have gone to jail or into exile. Naipaul's work is a mockery of their commitment and sacrifice.

An "honest" novel cannot proceed out of a glib, fashionable, coffee-house cynicism and unearned despair in which everything is beyond human effort. It is, rather, predicated on the assumption that there is a future for which to struggle; that conditions however grim are not beyond the reach of the peoples' decency, will, and intelligence, and that the writing and reading of such novels are not only testament to that faith, but an *integral part of that struggle.*

An "honest" African novel seeks to contribute to a peoples' evolving perceptions of their historical and cultural identity and the shared sense of national purpose. To the extent it is successful it will in part create its audience. This is a challenge and an honor denied contemporary Western writers. Any Third World writer who forgoes this wealth of possibility in favor of posturing to the Western bourgeoisie is condemned not by egotism and vanity, but by damned stupidity.

Finally, an "honest" novel about Africa seeks to make a contribution to the evolving form and to the content and purposes of a vital and modern tradition of African literature. It does not seek to latch onto the tail end of a moribund and thoroughly discredited colonial tradition which serves only to exploit and mutilate those cultures for frivolous, if not sinister purposes.

If such novels be "tracts," then I salute such tractarians as Chinua Achebe, Elechi Amadi, Ngugi Wa Thiong O, Kofi Awoonor, the splendid Buchi Emechita, and their embattled colleagues who are producing the most exciting and purposeful body of novels in the English language today.

With every good wish,

I beg to remain, Sir, Your Obt. Svt.,

MICHAEL M. THELWELL
*Associate Professor of Literature*
*W.E.B. DuBois Department of*
*Afro-American Literature*
*University of Massachusetts,*
*Amherst*

P.S.: Prof. Howe should be informed that I come from a long line of eloquent people, not a one of whom, thank God, ever got close enough to the Western literati to learn anything from them.

*1979*

IRVING HOWE REPLIES (1986):

I am content to let Prof. Thelwell have the last word in this exchange. I would only add that if I correctly surmise V. S. Naipaul's political outlook, I have serious disagreements with it. But that, in my judgment, does not affect the matter under dispute, which is the differing estimates Prof. Thelwell and I have of Naipaul's novels.

# "The Gods Had Perished"

## *Tutuola's* Palm-Wine Drinkard  ■ ■ ■ ■ ■

I T happened in the Yoruba town of Abeokuta, somewhat more than sixty but less
than seventy years ago, on a night just before
the second Ogun festival. The sound of singing and joyous cries rose from behind the tall
mud walls of the compound of the *Odafin*
Odegbami. It was the sound of the midwives
praising the gods (*Orishas*) and ancestors and
proclaiming the birth of a boy.

The boy's father, the firstborn son of the
*Odafin*, known as *Tutuola*—"the gentle one"
—received the news calmly (this was not,
after all, his first son). He uttered the traditional words of thanksgiving, rewarded the
midwives, and then made his way through the
complex of rooms and passageways to the *obi*
or receiving room of his father where he informed the old man.

The *Odafin*, the spiritual leader of his clan,
subchief, and administrative ruler of a section
of the city of Abeokuta, was a figure of power
and authority, as befitted the head of a large
and influential compound. His name, Odegbami, meant "Gift from Ogun," or alternate-
ly, "It was hunting that saved me," for the
Yoruba language is subtle and flexible and the
same combination of phrases can be variously
interpreted. His strong name indicated that

the *Odafin* was favored by the great *Orisha* Ogun, lord of fire and iron and therefore father of technology and political power and patron of smiths, warriors, and hunters. He was "one of Ogun's children."

Anticipating his son's message, the old man would have had ready to hand kola and palm-wine with which to offer thanks and libation to the ancestors. Then he whispered into his son's ear the name already selected after divination and consultation with the elders. "His name shall be Olatubusun," the old man pronounced gravely. Tutuola thanked him for the name.

At sunrise the *Odafin* and his heir apparent would go to offer the proper and necessary sacrifice of thanksgiving in the upper room where the great ancestral mask or *egugun,* the visible symbol of the clan's power, resided. Then they would go to the *ile-Orisha,* the house of the *Orishas,* where the images of the gods were enshrined. But for the moment Tutuola took his leave and made his way back to the birth chamber where the grandmother waited to whisper the name and *irike* or birthpoem into the ear of the newborn, thus setting the new spirit in its appropriate place in the world of mankind, society, and history.

If Tutuola was disappointed at the name, he was not surprised. Looked at in one way, the name was almost a cliché. In its most obvious meaning Olatubusun could mean simply "wealth increases," which was, among the Yoruba and all African peoples, true of the birth of any child, particularly a son. He might have wished for a name more powerfully portentous, more resonant with omen. But a birth was not extraordinary in this household. The *Odafin* had six wives and more than twenty children and he himself had three wives and was already the father of a number of sons. Yet, like every father, he would have welcomed a name of unique power and promise, something that would mark even so junior a son for special prominence. Not that there was anything wrong with this name Olatubusun. For all wealth was not the same and no wealth was bad. The boy might be the bringer of a special kind of wealth, perhaps in ways not yet contemplated in the councils of the elders. For was not the world changing before their very eyes? Had not the great oracle under the rock foretold such change? By its very lack of specificity this name could suggest that the boy was specially chosen. This fourthborn son will see things that we have never seen, mused the gentle and thoughtful Tutuola as he went to look upon his son.

According to local legend a small band of refugees, fleeing the destruction of their town during a war of slave-taking, were guided by a spirit to a

cave in the side of a hill that was capped by a spectacular granite forma-
tion. There in the cave, "under the rock," or in Yoruba "Abeokuta," they
found refuge. The cave became their most sacred shrine—the seat of an
oracle—and the place where festivals of sacrifice and thanksgiving, ritual
reenactments of the salvation of the town's founders and the ongoing
covenant with the protective spirit, were performed.

Secure in the covenant, the town prospered, and indeed, spread so widely that the king had to appoint surrogates for different sections of the city.
These *Odafins*—an appointive rather than a hereditary position—were
responsible under the authority of the king for the administration of local
government, the collection of taxes, and the observance and enforcement
of law and tradition, both religious and secular. To be effective these
appointees would have had to be figures of recognized worth; men of substance, respect, probity, and virtue within the terms of the traditional
values of the culture.

The fortunes and prominence of the family had reached its zenith with the
appointment of the "father," Odegbami, as *Odafin* of their sector. Ironically, this rise in the family fortunes coincided with a serious erosion of the
primacy of traditional values and practice. As befitted his civic status and
influence, the *Odafin* had taken additional wives and expanded his compound. His son Tutuola, next in succession for head of the clan, did like-
wise. As was proper, the *Odafin* commissioned the finest artists of
Abeokuta to create a new and elaborate *egugun*. This new ancestral mask,
ornate and imposing in its awful beauty and authority, was consecrated
and enshrined in an upper room specially built for that purpose. The
elaborate mask was at once a symbol of the family's spiritual foundation
and an expression of its material prosperity. So too was the *ile-ere* of
the compound, the large room in which imposing images of important
*Orishas—Shango, Oya, Ogun, Obatala*—were carefully tended and min-
istered to by the *Odafin* himself as part of his responsibility as spiritual
head of the household. All of this was no more than what tradition required and was supported for a time by produce from ancestral lands and
the revenues and entitlements of office.

What was not anticipated was the way in which the integrity of the
indigenous Yoruba institutions of Abeokuta would begin to feel an unprecedented and unassimilable pressure. This is not to say that the region
had been culturally insulated. At the time of Odegbami's appointment
(circa 1900–10), Islam had long been present and mosques were not unknown in the city. Islamic culture and doctrine and Yoruba belief and

practice coexisted relatively free of tension for Islam in West Africa went back many centuries and each system had had time and pressing reason to adjust, however uneasily, to the peculiar character of the other.

The new pressure came at this time from an intolerant, bumptious, and vigorously proselytizing European Christianity, a new dispensation that was not to content itself with the harvesting of souls and the elevation of the spirit, but which increasingly set itself the task of transforming societies. The missionaries—courageous and mostly doomed—frequently brought, or possibly had to bring, to their civilizing mission that narrow self-righteousness that is so often the sword and shield of the religious idealist.

More significantly, hard on the heels of their chapels, mission schools, and hospitals had come new laws and moral codes which were enforced by native courts, a parallel civil service buttressed by police and military forces, a mercantile economy accompanied by a different system of currency, and a new and mysterious system of land tenure, all of which in combination represented during the transition first a parallel government and then a superseding one. The cumulative effect of this challenge on all the traditional institutions of religion, culture, education, commerce, and government was the growing devaluation of native conceptions of identity, authority, and value on civic, moral, and personal levels alike.

It was during this period of transitional confusion—a chaos of values and moral authority—that the birth of Olatubusun was celebrated according to custom and tradition, in circumstances themselves emblematic of this tension.

The child was born into a powerfully traditional household—to Christian parents. From his earliest memories he recalls that "I met my father and mother as Christians." Though nearly all of his children adopted the new faith, the *Odafin* never did. While he lived, he was master of a traditional household in which all the *Orishas*'s festivals were celebrated, ancestral feast days observed, and the spectacular dancing *egugun* regularly received the petitions and offerings of women wanting children. Every Thursday the household awakened to the sound of ritual drumming and the chanting of the *babalawo* or sacred drummer. On Sundays the Christians went to church. But in that house, young Olatubusun remembers, "in a large room I met all the gods, Ogun, god of iron, Shango, god of thunder, Oya, Oshun, Obatala . . . all of them." This was an encounter certain to make a lasting impression on the young boy. As Robert Farris Thompson, our most inspired Africanist, has observed, "A child growing up among the Yoruba is exposed daily to one of the finest traditions of sculpture produced by any people." And the pantheon of gods, the *Orisha* system, was considered by Frobenius to be "richer, more original, more rigorous, and well-preserved than any of the forms coming down to us from classical antiquity."

But the youthful imagination was fed not only by the awesome images looming in the dim, sacred *ile-ere*. Ritual, spectacle, song, dance, drumbeats, mystery, and power surrounded him. Poetry, pageantry, and history combined in the luminous presence of the *egugun* as the ancestor became flesh and danced among his children. The boy was attracted to the art of the storyteller, a tradition of oral literature that had reached a very high level of complexity and diversity among the Yoruba. But to call these expressions of the culture "stories" is reductive. As developed in this culture, their elaborate narrative line incorporated elements of theater, music, mime, ritual, magic, dance, and the linguistic elements of proverb, poetry, riddle, parable, and song. They were not told so much as performed, dramatically reenacted, so that the accomplished taleteller had to be master of a range of skills. He was at once actor, mime, impressionist, singer, dancer, composer, and conductor, using his range of artistic skills and even the audience and environment to create a multidimensional experience that has no obvious equivalent in Western culture. A more elaborate expression of this form—most often with a strictly religious reference, being ritual re-creations of sacred myths—was performed by costumed dancers to the accompaniment of religious music, and became known to Western observers as "folk operas."

It was in this dynamic, powerfully dramatic, and evocative, yet extremely *ordered* environment that the boy's formative sensibilities developed. At about fourteen years old, a new Christian, he left the traditional compound for the Salvation Army School, literally a new world. The death of the distinguished grandfather, followed a few years later by that of the father, brought further changes. The family yielded to new realities and Europeanized their name. Mostly in deference to the great man—now a respected ancestor—who had brought them prominence, they took the surname *Odegbami*. Only the boy Olatubusun, junior though he was in the lineage, dissented. He either chose or was given the Christian name Amos for the fierce old prophet of righteousness ("Justice shall come down like a mighty water. . . ."). And with filial loyalty he took his father's praise name, hence Amos Tutuola.

Change was rapid. The grand household of the *Odafin* could not be maintained. In this transition period, there appear to have been the usual prob-

lems of succession, inheritance, entitlement, and questions about which
lands belonged to the family (who in any case had now neither the power,
prestige, or revenues of former times) and which to the office. The family
dispersed to make their way in the strange world where 2,000 cowries,
a substantial sum in traditional exchange, translated to sixpence in British currency. Amos Tutuola attended the Anglican Central School in
Abeokuta while his father, now living on some family lands a short distance from Abeokuta, was alive. Upon his death the "junior" son had to
end his formal education. He went to Lagos, became apprenticed to a cop-
persmith, and joined the British army, occupations that must have brought
a smile to the face of the dead grandfather since both were under the jurisdiction of his patron *Orisha,* Ogun.

At the war's end he was demobilized with thousands of other young men
and thrust upon his own devices to make his way in the world. He secured,
in his own words, "this unsatisfactory job" as a messenger in one of the
civil service departments in Lagos. There he might have lived and worked
in modest circumstances and obscurity save for a fortuituous accident.
One of the Commonwealth information journals that the British used to
circulate in their colonial territories and at home caught the eye of
Mr. Tutuola. His attention was attracted to the cover, an impressive full-
color reproduction of a sculpture of an *Orisha.* The section on Nigeria
contained many such "portraits" of gods, artfully photographed in color,
and his mind rushed back to the *ile-ere* of his grandfather's compound. He
bought the journal.

> Well, it happened that since I was young and I was in the infant school
> which we call nowadays primary, each time I went to my village I learnt many
> tales and I was much interested in it so that later when I could read and write
> I wrote many of them down. And as much as I had great interest in these, I
> took myself to be one of the best taletellers in the school for the other children.
> Later, having left the school, one day I bought one magazine. I was working
> then. I had joined the army and left the army. I was engaged as a messenger by
> the Department of Labor. One day I got one magazine published by the
> Government of Nigeria Information Service. It carried all the festivals, Oya,
> Ogun everything. It was a quarterly magazine, so I bought the magazine and
> started to read it. It contained very lovely portraits of the gods. When I bought
> the magazine I read it to a page where books which were published were
> advertised. Well . . . I had read some of those books when I was at school.
> Then I saw that one of the books which were advertised here was about our
> tales, our Yoruba tales. "But Eh! By the way, when I was at school I was

a good taleteller! Why, could I not write my own? Ooh, I am very good at this thing." The following day I took up my pen and paper and I started to write *The Palm-Wine Drinkard*. Well, I wrote the script of *Palm-Wine* and kept it in the house. I didn't know where to send it to.

Again, the following quarter I bought another magazine of the same type. Fortunately when I read it, I got to where it advertised "Manuscripts Wanted" overseas. Well then! Immediately I sent my story to the advertiser. When my script got to them they wrote me in about two weeks saying that they did not accept manuscripts which were not concerned with religion, Christian religion. But, they would not return my manuscript. They would find a publisher for me because the story was so strange to them that they would not be happy if they returned it to me. By that I should be patient with them to help me find a publisher. Then a year later I got a letter from Faber & Faber that they got my manuscript from Lutheran World Press. Faber & Faber said that the story . . . uh they were wondering whether I found the story fallen down from somebody because it is very strange to them. They wondered because they were surprised to see such a story . . . they wanted to know whether I had made it up or got it from somebody else . . . and they would be happy if I would leave the story for them to do it as they want. I reply that I didn't know anything about book publishing and so on, so I leave everything for you to do as you see is good. . . . Then after about six months now they publish the book in 1952 and sent a copy to me. That is how I started to write.

What was in my mind? Well. Oh . . . the time I wrote it, what was in my mind was that I noticed that our young men, our young sons and daughters did not pay much attention to our traditional things or culture or customs. They adopted, they concentrated their minds only on European things. They left our customs, so if I do this they may change their mind . . . to remember our custom, not to leave it to die. . . . That was my intention.

Appearing unannounced and without fanfare in the British edition in 1952 and in the Grove Press American edition in 1953, the book has had the kind of career of which publishing legends are made. I cannot say to what extent the lineage's "wealth increased" as a consequence, but certainly the book has continued in print ever since. It has been translated into fifteen languages, European and non-European as well. It seems to enjoy a respectable and steady circulation and to have attracted a loyal following worldwide. It is frequently to be found on syllabi of university courses in religion, anthropology, psychology, and even literature and has been followed by *My Life in the Bush of Ghosts* (1954) and *The Brave African Huntress*.

I shall not speculate—intriguing though that prospect be—on precisely which chords of modern literary sensibility are set resonating under the stimulus of *Drinkard's* unique vision. Certainly one can see where certain Jungian and Freudian critics could, with barely compatible assumptions, find much to engage them in its world. So too can surrealists and devotees of magical realism find within it hospitable territory on which to plant their respective standards. It is, however, more important to attempt to identify the cultural and intellectual provenance of the material, and to determine its specific relationship to the traditions that produced it.

This novel is a cultural hybrid, the child of the clash of cultures I have been describing. The stories in it are translations—more accurately, trans-literations—of conventional folktales into the idiomatic "young English," as Dylan Thomas mistakenly called it, of the Nigerian masses. It is clear from the reading, and even more so when one listens to the author telling a story, exactly how difficult the translation process really is. This is not simply "young English" but *new* English, an English whose vocabulary is bent and twisted into the service of a different language's nuances, syntax, and interior logic. The result is original and often startling.

Apart from the aesthetic distance between rhetorical devices, linguistic traditions, rhythms, puns, repetitions, cadences, nuances, metaphors, and idioms, the total poetic sensibility of one language and culture and that of another, there is a further consideration. We are looking at only one element of the form. The other inclusive aesthetic dimensions of the tradi-tion—dramatic voice, expression, pantomime, song, and rhythm—are necessarily absent in the purely literary form. To that extent it is a new form. And if the form is new, what survives presumably must be "sensibility."

It is usual to hear that these tales express the "traditional sensibility" of an "African" world view and offer a window into the inchoate and fright-ening world of the primitive imagination. So general a statement would be quite misleading. The stories and the narrative and visionary techniques reflect one particular and identifiable aspect of a complex and sophisti-cated tradition.

The central Yoruba tradition—that of the sacred myth describing the creation, evolution, and jurisdiction of the deities and historical heroes—represents a remarkably rigorous cosmology of intellectual coherence and elegance. It is a universe of elemental forces both natural and social which finds metaphoric expression in a pantheon of deities, whose complicated interrelationships, jurisdictions, and necessities are rationalized into an architectonic system of knowledge. The sophisticated world view embodied in this myth has as its central value the balancing and harmonizing of powerful forces—natural, numinous, and social.

Out of the interplay of deities, ancestors, and humanity, through a process of mutual obligation expressed in language, ritual, and protocol as handed down by tradition, society became possible. A universe of history, stability, morality, and order was achieved.

But bordering on this system of stability was terra incognita: the evil forest, the bad bush. Here was the home of chaos, where random spirits without name or history, of bizarre forms and malignant intent were to be found. This was the domain of the deformed, the unnatural, and the abominable. The Sunufo, distant cousins of the Yoruba, have a mask that expresses this. It has the snout of an alligator, the tusk of a boar, the horn of a rhinoceros, and the ears of a zebra. It represents an animal that existed before order was imposed on the world.

In the oral tradition the folktale—a moral and cautionary story but clearly recognized as fiction and entertainment—had free range of this random and arbitrary world. Because they were intended for entertainment and instruction, these tales could be as horrific, frightening, and bizarre as the imagination could render them. They required the willing suspension of disbelief.

Many of Tutuola's motifs and even complete tales and images are drawn from this genre. But the structure and cumulative effect, the vision, is the creation of this sensitive and pensive man. To what extent this overriding vision, one of constant suffering, danger, insecurity, and struggle is the product of the cultural trauma, uncertainty, and psychic alienation through which that generation passed is hard to say. But that this generational experience of wrenching transition has been vastly influential on the book's language, sensibility, and architecture is quite evident. In the same way that the book's prose occupies a cusp where two languages intersect, so do Tutuola's sensibilities inhabit dual realities. More accurately his is a traditional imagination wandering—much like his narrator in the Land of the Spirits—through the cultural chaos of modern urban Nigeria.

The sensitive boy, whose earliest perceptions are indelibly imprinted with the ritual language and imagery of the ancestral compound, whose young manhood occurred during the disruption of postwar urbanization, now inhabits a present in which the technological artifacts and institutions of the twentieth century jam up hard against stubborn ghosts of ancient tradition.

He carries with him then the burden of a certain psychic sorrow and loss; the weight, so to say, of time and change, which is not to suggest that there is in his presence any mournfulness of spirit, but rather a quality of dividedness, of a spirit looking both backward and forward. It is a spirit of quiet, of reflection, and solemnness that one recognizes also in black elders in rural Jamaica and the American South. Tutuola, however, has recourse to a rich literary tradition. "In those days we did not know other money, except cowries, so that everything was very cheap and my father was the richest man in our town." This is the third sentence of the book. It is not only nostalgic in tone but quite autobiographic and very soon thereafter we read "then my father dies suddenly," and the strange adventure among terrible creatures begins—an adventure given shape and content by an imagination which is a profoundly literary one, but with the literariness of the oral tradition and its poetic images, rendered in English. Tutuola calls on that mythopoetic tradition to capture the uncertainty and dangers of the time.

In his words to evoke a lost luminous past: "I wrote to tell of my ancestors and how they lived in their days. They lived with the immortal creatures of the forest. . . . But now the forests are gone. I believe the immortal creatures must have moved away." Immortal creatures, which he as a youth remembers meeting at sunrise on his way to the fields. So too are gone the domestic symbols and expressions of this relationship between man and spirit.

Some years ago he returned to the ancestral compound, photojournalist in tow, in order to visit *ile-Orisha*. The compound was ruinate, the giant *egugun* mask was not to be found and in his words, "The gods had perished."

*1984*

# Modernist Fallacies and the Responsibility of the Black Writer

■  ■  ■  ■  ■

RESPONSIBILITY, of any sort, is not a term having much currency in the fashionable gibberish of our age. It clearly is not a concept with which the modernist mood is comfortable in any context, save perhaps, where it finds expression in those tiresome and redundant formulations of bourgeois egotism, for example, "one's responsibility to one's self," "to one's inner being," "to one's private vision," *ad nauseum*. On these rare occasions of uncomfortable association, we are almost certain to hear of the writer's paramount responsibility to his private *vision* and to his *Art,* quite as though both had, in splendid isolation, sprung full-grown from his fevered genius like Athena from the forehead of Zeus, untouched by human society, history, politics, or culture. "Art," in this usage, has a meaning not unlike God in another, somewhat older usage: at once mystical and transcendent, it is all-demanding, all-consuming, the object of ultimate concern yet displaying a charmingly paradoxical democratic aspect in that it is quite willing to assume whatever arbitrary and eccentric form the peculiar needs and obsessions of its worshiper and creator may dictate.

The subject of this chapter, however, is pre-

Yea, even though I speak with the tongues of men and of angels, and have not compassion, I am become as a sounding brass and a tinkling cymbal. . . . I am nothing.

I CORINTHIANS 13.1

In America when I was younger the term black literature referred to only one country. . . . America. Talking about black literature today one is really talking about the world . . . about Brazil, Nigeria. . . . We had been dealing with, controlled by really, a vocabulary coming out of an arbitrary invention called Europe, where the frame of reference has always and only been Europe itself. That frame of reference has shifted and a new vocabulary is needed.

JAMES BALDWIN, *New York Times* Interview, 1979

A writer dies inside when he betrays, like a paid spy, the rhythm of his race.

DEREK WALCOTT

cisely responsibility—a responsibility neither private nor subjective which all black writers share, whether they choose to recognize it or not. This responsibility seems to me so clear, so unambiguous, so historical, so self-evident, and so absolute that failure to recognize it would necessitate either willed blindness or egregious stupidity on the part of a writer who is black. In addition, such a failure of perception and consciousness calls into question not only the writer's intelligence and seriousness, but also causes us to doubt fundamentally the value of the entire literary undertaking. The question is inescapable: Why would any black person, representative by definition of a culturally oppressed people, espouse the obsessively subjective and private reasons that modernists give as their motivation, aesthetic concerns, and literary preoccupations? And given these preoccupations and purposes, should anyone read the results, much less regard them seriously?

Surely, our increasingly narcissistic world abounds with ways and means of exorcising personal trauma short of writing them down and boring the public. "A little sincerity is a dangerous thing," said Oscar Wilde, "more bad poetry having been created out of sincere feeling than from any other source." I am a firm believer that if one suffers from guilt or insecurity one should undertake psychoanalysis; if haunted by ghosts and demons, see a priest; if beset with sexual inadequacies of any sort, consult the encouraging variety of therapists, professionals, and experts which now exists. If the problem is marital in origin, one can, depending on its seriousness, get a divorce, buy a whip, or establish separate bedrooms; for naked self-expression I am given to understand that a loud scream in the night is far more immediate and satisfying than scribbling endlessly; and if the problem is one of repressed aggressions, one can always either get drunk and wreck the bar or join the armed services, thereby with a single act improving both the nation's defenses and its literature.

I should make it clear that the following discussion is devoted specifically to the novel, although much of my argument has implications for drama, despite the marked differences in the material requirements, ancestry, and potential of the two forms. Modernist poetry is not included, that phenomenon having advanced entirely too far into the upper reaches of arbitrary subjectivism, preciosity, and privatist aestheticism to be considered anything other than therapy. I am unable to perceive in that particular thicket much evidence of the shared conventions of meaning, form, purpose, communication, and intention which would make it accessible to rational and productive discussion. Undoubtedly the failing is mine, because a similar imaginative failure prohibits me from seeing anything but an ink

blot in one of Rorschach's cards. Yet, I am told that there are those to
whom these ink smears are profoundly and wonderfully meaningful. And,
indeed, my aesthetically more advanced colleagues are able to fill volumes
with eloquent and closely reasoned explications of the mysteries of modernist poetics. To my poor benighted mind, alas, these explications shed,
not a dim or feeble light, but no light at all upon the explicated. Just as the
latter seems beyond poetry so the criticism hovers on the outer fringes of
prose, having passed into those rarified altitudes of semantics and sensibility to which a poor, culturally deprived West Indian Negro such as I, is
quite incapable of venturing. Thus, I can offer no useful discussion of modernist poetry: the widespread practice of explaining the already sufficiently obscure by means of the more obscure is one that I gladly concede to my
modernist colleagues. But, this is the only concession that I am prepared to
make . . . willingly.

You may well be wondering exactly what all this has to do with the culture of the Black World and its novelists? Unfortunately, as I hope to
show, a great deal too much, in far too many cases, for the health of our literature. But since it would be unseemly of me to commit here the very sins
of self-indulgent assertion in the absence of evidence or history for which I
have been berating the modernists, I had best turn first to some basic questions of definition and cultural history.

The movement in European culture (which my good friends on that excellent Pan-African journal *Okike* love to characterize as "Euro-modern-
ists obscurantism") is the result of developments among elements of the
European bourgeoisie between the wars. It is important to take some time
to understand precisely what modernism was and was not in its origins because both cases are at some distance from the picture that is generally presented today. Modernism patently and emphatically was *not* a spontaneous response of mainstream European artists to a new historical reality.
That is to say it was not some spontaneous and inevitable historical expression of Western cultural necessity, as claimed by its proponents, unless
*all* of Western culture was more spiritually depleted, morally bankrupt,
and creatively exhausted than can conceivably have been the case. It was
and is an expression of bourgeois literary style and fashion: the capricious
and arbitrary creation of a small, identifiable, and recondite element of the
bourgeois avant-garde, whose neurotic egotism, distressing and unhealthy
personal lives, and political conservatism it expressed. For example, quite
apart from their work, one does not have to study at any length (I have not
and have no interest in doing so) the biographies of T. S. Eliot, Ezra Pound,
Marcel Proust, André Gide, Gertrude Stein, James Joyce, Sigmund Freud,
and Virginia Woolf (to name only those luminaries of the modernist

movement who come readily to mind) in order to conclude that collectively they were as self-obsessed, unpleasant, and eccentric a group of people as one could hope to avoid having to meet. So, even though, it seems to me, the modernist movement represents a capricious minority that became inordinately influential, its rise and its dominance over European art and letters suggest that there might indeed be some grounds for arguing that modernism was an expression of some deep malaise in European bourgeois culture.

It is perhaps a simplification, but for our purposes a necessary simplification of a complex and ambiguous development, to say that the modernist revolt was essentially one of style, or more accurately, of content disguised as style—an open and unabashed call to an aesthetic elitism of bourgeois sensibility. Its influence manifested itself in music, painting, and the theater, as well as in poetry and prose. While there were at times flurries of progressive and humanist expression—most usually in painting and theater—modernism was more characteristically the excuse and justification for a general retreat from the wide-ranging engagement with social and moral questions which had characterized the best of nineteenth-century European literature. In the novel, modernism generally rejected realism and the broad and humane social vision and moral concern that had characterized the great Russian, French, and English novelists of the previous century, in favor of formalist experimentation for its own sake, a celebration of aestheticism, the cult of the individual consciousness and sensibility, and the internalization of experience and concern. While it contributed a number of technical innovations—which when put to serious purpose could and did add to the arsenal of technical devices available to the novelist and thus to the flexibility and capability of the form—modernism was not in its essence either a progressive or regenerating development. It was a retreat into emptiness.

When the novel abandons realism—that is, the obligation to re-create, crystallize, sharpen, and illumine human experience in ways that are recognizable and realistic, against a setting of accurate social and political detail; the obligation to capture credible and convincing psychological and class motivation and responses in its characters—when it in effect abandons history and cultural reality, what is left it? It has but three avenues: (1) a turning inward to private fantasy and the exploration of the sores and lesions of the novelist's psyche; (2) experimentation with form, in which complexity of language and structure become their own ends and stylistic eccentricity is substituted for content; (3) related to that, a literariness, the cannibalization of the past, the picking over of the corpses of earlier works. Instead of dealing with the world, the novel must turn to writing about writers and about writing—composing elaborate literary puzzles replete with allusions, references, borrowings from and parodies of earlier works. "Art" becomes the subject of art.

All these developments represent a truly monstrous abandonment of the artist's responsibility as it had been conceived in the humanistic traditions of Western art. I would remind you that one central evidence of decadence in a literary tradition is the arrival of that historical moment at which the creation of new and vital formulations and interpretations of cultural reality becomes secondary to the parody and cannibalization of earlier works.

This cannibalizing tendency of literary modernism has generated an attendant impulse of quasi-religious, vaguely fetishistic character, one that goes sufficiently far beyond traditional ancestor veneration as to approach a species of relatively harmless necrophilia. Having exhausted the corpus of the late master's work, the attention of the devout must needs turn to the *relictus vitae*. Usually at the onset of summer, when school is out and particularly in those years when the dollar is strong in Europe, one can observe bands of devout literati jetting across the Atlantic. In Europe they will search out the house, garret, desk, café, inn, park bench, and grave where the late guru was born, lived, wrote, caroused, took meals, simply sat, and finally was eaten by worms.

Having recapitulated this journey, the pilgrims return, brandishing murky photographs, grave rubbings, and an air of spiritual fulfillment and accomplishment. "This is the interior of the little atelier in the Rue la Princesse where such and such was written. See that," they point with an air of breathless and reverent discovery, "baroque chamberpot. Well, standing in *that room*, looking at it, I had this *feeling*, amazingly strong. . . ." And one immediately recognizes from the glazed eyes that one is in the presence of epiphany—yet another of those interminable, obligatory, pointless, and utterly banal epiphanies, the achievement of which is the entire point of the pilgrimage.

This corpse-veneration syndrome is curiously paradoxical in a movement so self-consciously avant-garde and contemporary. Perhaps it is what comes of the deification of the "artist." It is also a syndrome that invites parody, as in Philip Roth's *Professor of Desire*. Roth's protagonist, after literally recapitulating the cradle-to-grave passage of Kafka through the streets of Prague, has a dream. "Do you wish," asks his tour guide, "to meet the whore Kafka used to visit?" He then produces a disreputable crone, ancient and arthritic, who babbles in Czech. "She wishes to know," the apparatchik translates solemnly, "whether you would like to inspect her pussy?" Well, after all, true relics don't grow on trees.

Marxists argue that these developments were the inevitable consequences of a backlash among a self-centered, morally bankrupt bourgeoisie that, politically threatened and traumatized by events in Russia, consciously turned away from any engagement with the irresolvable class contradiction and social injustice implicit in bourgeois privilege. That thesis may be a trifle too schematic; I am not sure. But what is absolutely clear is that the emergence and rise of modernism in Europe represented a rather abrupt turning away from what had been the first responsibility of the novelist—that of *communicating* generally shared and accessible truth and perceptions, which implicitly must mean socially and culturally derived insights and knowledge. In the celebration of the individual consciousness, communication became secondary to "self-expression," no matter how arcane, private, and neurotic in its inspiration. Similarly, the emphasis on literary allusion (cannibalism), elaborate structural invention, and private reference as cnds in themselves is obviously not geared primarily to communication. James Joyce, a celebrated pioneer down these literary cul-de-sacs, is alleged to have boasted that only four people fully understood *Finnegans Wake* and that two of them were dead. While the story may be apocryphal, the reverence in the voice of the teacher who told it to me was not—and that is significant. It was also said of Joyce, by no means the worst offender among the modernists, that it used to be that novelists were men of wide learning and broad interests in human events. What Joyce demonstrated was that all a novelist needed to know was himself. Regrettably, that lesson is *not* lost on many among my brothers and sisters.

Unfortunately the story does not end there; there is a related development that has had an even greater impact on the literatures and cultures we are interested in. Under well-deserved attack from a public that felt, with excellent reason, that it was being put upon, patronized, and ripped off by the self-centered and arrogant effusions of modernism, this movement generated a gang of critical fellow travelers—the priests and proselytizers for the new dispensation. These rascals developed—as priests will—an elaborate critical gospel in defense and explanation of the faith. Although these explanations made no more sense than the art they were intended to explain, significant elements of the doctrine and dogma invented by the clerisy lurk to this day in the dark crevices and corners of the academy, just waiting to pounce upon and infect the susceptible minds of the young. These are the influences that are infecting black modernists, for I suspect that most of them do not read the Torah; instead they only receive the commentaries.

These critical justifications are, however, much more insidious than the works themselves. They seek to render what should really be considered aberrations of false consciousness and egotism as necessary and inevitable expressions of "the modern condition" and "the state of the culture." The style and content of modernism, they argue, was appropriate to the times, for the conventions of realism could no longer express the alienated condition of man in modern society (they were too coherent and made too much sense). Nor could the traditional modes of realism any longer adequately express the fragmented, self-conflicted psyche of modern man, living as he does in a state of high anxiety, emotional isolation, and spiritual desolation. It is the peculiar arrogance of the bourgeois intelligentsia to generalize a universal from their own neurotic dysfunction: the ills of the bourgeoisie becoming, in their assertion, the very essence of the human condition. Thus, the basic issue became not the creative exhaustion of the avantgarde, not their intellectual arrogance and self-celebration, not their moral aberration and lack of artistic discipline and political vision—in a word, their decadence of mind and spirit. No, it was *human existence* itself that was blighted, suddenly inchoate, and void of value and meaning. Where once human beings had walked, robots, ciphers, and humanoids now rattled aimlessly around the mechanistic wasteland of an industrial mass society shrouded in gloomy and suffocating existential smog.

Thus, modernist art was *necessary;* all the artist was doing was struggling to escape the grasp of dead convention to create those necessary new forms, devices, and structures by which this grim new reality might be apprehended and expressed. This has to be the most outrageous and transparently self-serving excrement ever served up in the interest of justifying decadence. And not only that, if one failed to recognize just how splendidly the modernist mode—through a triumph of the individual will, the anguished visions of alienated geniuses—had forged the language, forms, and modalities to reflect the disjointedness of the age, one had only one's own undeveloped sensibility to blame.

This aesthetic shell game traded on bourgeois insecurity. It was not any newer than the emperor's spring outfit, but it worked wondrously well at intimidating bourgeois audiences who demonstrated that they would endure any boredom, accept any insult to their intelligence, rather than be found out of step with intellectual fashion or be thought deficient in taste or sensibility.

The working classes were having none of it, however. They knew what they liked, and modernist excretia was not it; they stopped reading the stuff. There is evidence that the European working class once participated to a surprising degree in intellectual life, had actually read and been instructed by serious novels in the nineteenth century. (The London poor, for example, are said to have devoured the serialized novels of Charles Dickens, recognizing therein a faithful depiction of their lives and social circumstances.)

Over time, literary modernism—once shocking and controversial—became the orthodoxy of our time. Once "daring and experimental," it passed rapidly into cliché, then to doctrine and now into sacred dogma, so enshrined in the hearts and minds of the Western literary establishment that its tenets are not even critically examined anymore. It would be of little concern to me that modernist dogma lay over the West like a toxic cloud impoverishing the literature and reducing the phrase "critical thought" to a hollow mockery. The problem, however, is that, like other of the West's toxic wastes, it seeps out of Europe and America and poisons the wellsprings of the Black World—a most insidious form of cultural colonialism. As a result of modernism's effect, our literature is in danger of bypassing maturity and plunging directly from infancy to decadence.

First, let us attempt a description of literary modernism in its contemporary incarnation.

In the contemporary modernist novel, the emphasis is on fragmentation rather than coherence. Elements of experience never coalesce into meaning, and the part is frequently greater than the whole. Its style runs to pastiche, collage, and willful and eccentric distortion rather than organic and intelligible meaning. The contemporary modernist novel is a function of shattered mirrors and refracted images, a mockery of purposeful intelligence and communication in favor of glib and easy effects. It is quite useless for the projection of political and moral vision or statement. Its tone is parodic and its impulses contemptuous—both of the reader and of observable reality. It essays contempt and succeeds only in being contemptible.

The mood of modernist fiction: gloomy, fashionably cynical, sneering at all save its own preoccupations with obscurity of allusion and gratuitous structural complexity—all for no discernible artistic reason.

Its literary preoccupations: images of sickness and perversion; physical deformity and grotesquery as emblems of moral deficiency. It lacks the passion to be erotic and is only pornographic; a pornography of the spirit. Where it occurs, sex is either mechanical, grim, and joyless or violent, perverted, and exploitative.

The rendering of character: originality is much evoked, by which the authors seem to mean that a character who acts in ways previously consecrated by human behavior is insufficiently original. This view leads, ironically, to a predictable aberration: modernist characters must not obey any recognizable pattern of human motivation and response. Yet, it *is* possible to predict certain things about these modernist originals: there will be no discernible reason for their actions. Given a choice, they will choose the sensationally perverse, the morally disgusting, the degrading, but these choices will be so arbitrary and eccentric as to have neither meaning nor effect. But they will be *original*.

Another modernist value: inventiveness, a facility for creating new forms of perversity. To take some examples from recent black American fiction: a mother douses her sleeping son with kerosene and roasts him; a woman bites off her lover's genitals. Even inventiveness has its conventions: thus, any young black woman in certain kinds of fiction must be sexually abused during adolescence by an older male relative. Inventiveness is shown by the choice of relative, the circumstances in which the act occurs, and the ingenuity with which the act is rendered as painful, humiliating, and traumatic as is humanly imaginable.

Now, let us turn to the processes by which modernism is diffused into the cultures of the African world, Black America, and the Caribbean. This diffusion takes place as a result of myth and institutions. Young black writers frequently find themselves in Western institutions of higher education whose departments of literature have long been hotbeds of modernism. (An African or Caribbean university is a Western institution.) Here at the hands of the clerisy the young writer learns the catechism and, unless the student has a highly developed sense of literature and of his or her national cultural imperatives, that student emerges like the previous generation of colonized intellectuals: a zealous convert to the inevitability of Western literary fashion. The second institution is the bourgeois publishing establishment. Unless the young black writer is from a country that has made a decisive break with the practices and traditions of its colonial past and also established a national publishing house or indigenous industry, he will find himself seeking publication in the West, as many of us are forced to. This is unhealthy because the Western publishing establishment is effectively in the hands of the disciples of modernism. These editors generally have no concept of the Black World, and see no reason why their own inclinations and preoccupations should not be perfectly adequate for expressing the experience of these countries. They are not inhibited by judgment, modesty, or humility from imposing their literary taste on the young black's work, or at least trying to do so. Moreover, they have no political or economic interest in black novelists who wish to address their own people. To them, the black novelist is to function as a kind of foreign correspondent for the West, their novels being nothing more than literary dispatches sent back to titillate the bourgeois audience and to reaffirm its preconceptions of the Black World. In their defense it should be said that these editors are only serving their own household gods and cultural constituencies—their class interests, if you will. Too many black writers refuse to see that these interests are not and cannot be the same as ours.

Closely allied to the publishers is the Western critical establishment, long since the captive and tool of the modernists. Literally all of the influential journals of literary opinion in the West are firmly in the control of some coterie, cult, or sect of the modernist dispensation. These organs tend to seek out and bring to prominence those writers of the non-European world who best demonstrate that they have ingested and can regurgitate modernist style and dogma in their work. Seeing this situation, young black writers begin to think that the path to literary success lies in imitating those of their number who have won the accolades of the bourgeois press. Thus, the modernist movement—which at this point has exhausted any limited contributions it could make to literature—appears all-encompassing, authoritative, pervasive, and inevitable. It represents "high" literature. To some of us one is not a respectable and respected writer until the *New York Review of Books* and the two *Times*es (London and New York) have certified that fact. This attitude has consequences that are quite unhealthy for indigenous literary development. Consciously or otherwise, one responds to the pressure to address one's work to the critics of these organs, rather than to one's own people, unless one is very clear about one's purposes in writing and the responsibilities incurred in doing so.

Any black writer who writes about black peoples, societies, and cultures but who addresses his work not to the people who are his subjects but to the Western literati is nothing but an exploiter of his own. Such a writer accepts and perpetuates the colonial mission in literature begun by the Kiplings and Conrads of the imperial age.

This phenomenon raises another very important and troublesome question. How is it that so many writers of the Black World—men and women who in their private and public discourse seem wondrously clear on questions of history and imperialism, who seem sophisticated and clear-eyed, even militant, in their nationalism, whose economic analyses are impeccable—seem to become totally recolonized when they sit down to write fiction? Why, in so many cases, do they either not see an alternative or not feel a need to avoid adopting Western modes, Western perspectives, even Western biases.

One can only conclude that the literary recolonization of black writers—a colonization of style, purpose, implied audience, literary concern, and intention—is possible only to the extent that we do not subject Western literary myths and assumptions to the same searching scrutiny we give to their political motives, interests, actions, and rhetoric. Yet, in fact, the relationship between the two areas is close—even symbiotic—and certainly their ancestry is the same.

What, for example, are the fundamental cultural assumptions that lurk behind all the uncritical prattle about "the Artist" and "the Universal"—concepts that are among the most sacred of the cows in the herd of Western literary pieties. When we are told (as I was as an undergraduate by a charming Irish lady who taught "the humanities" in a black college) that all literature has the same audience—"the international community of educated men and women"—what assumptions are implicit in that apparently innocuous vocabulary? I doubt the good lady professor had any notion precisely how Europocentric, culturally chauvinist, and reductive that formulation really was.

When black writers accept the mission consciously to act as "universal artists," as so many of them do ("I don't want to be merely a black writer, I want to be a writer"), what are they in fact agreeing to? Does the term "universal" describe anything in reality? Who today dismisses Aeschylus or Sophocles as parochial and limited simply because they created only Greek characters, worked within a narrowly hellenistic cultural and religious frame of reference, and addressed only a Greek audience? Or Faulkner because his characters are all narrowly regional and from the backwaters of America?

But a black editor of that bumptiously avant-garde, Third World journal *Yardbird* asked Chinua Achebe to describe the nature of his interest in creating a particular character. Significantly, the editor seemed interested only in Obi Okonkwo, the one of Achebe's characters who had traveled to Europe, the brother. "I am working on the notion that he [the character in question] becomes a mythic figure and a person who tests the limits, not only of a tribal person, or a person with a *national* identity, but in fact he becomes a kind of universal figure and tests *human* limits" (editors' emphasis).

Chinua answered mildly as to how he hoped elements of universality might be embodied in the particularity even of an Ibo tribesman. Under the circumstances, Achebe's restraint was exemplary, perhaps too much so. For, two pages later, apparently not satisfied that he had made himself clear, the brother returns to worry the issue: "But were you thinking of him as reflective of broad universal human characteristics? You didn't just aim this for a *Nigerian* audience?" (emphasis mine). Perhaps, I reflected upon reading this passage, the broadest, most universal human characteristic is stupidity.

Similarly, what exactly—especially in modernist parlance—is meant by "Artist"? Does the term still describe anything useful, and is it a description to which any self-respecting black honorably can aspire? What was otherwise an extremely intelligent, articulate, and culturally informed review of *The Harder They Come* by a black academic concludes with the following language: "Thelwell views himself as a political writer, a cultural nationalist, an activist. But what this novel admirably demonstrates is that he is first of all a consummate artist." First of all? Hardly. Of course I think I know what was intended, but is the unexamined dichotomy really inevitable? Are the categories "artist" and "cultural nationalist," or "political writer," truly incompatible? To the modernist mind they clearly are. To my thinking, however, any black novelist who is not consciously and purposefully a cultural nationalist is an aberration. If modernists insist on the dichotomy, our choice is clear. As effective as are the institutions in literary colonization, that is, the universities, publishers, and critical journals, they would be ineffective if we ourselves were not so uncritical of certain fundamental assumptions about literature, culture, the role of the novel, and the purposes of the novelist which underlie the mythology.

Because, even if modernist perceptions of the state of Western culture and the role of the novel therein were accurate, so far as the West is concerned (I suspect they are not and have succeeded only in rendering the novel quite irrelevant as a serious force in cultural and social life), they certainly do not describe the situation in the Black World. To accept them is to suggest that the West and the Black World are at the same historical point in cultural development. They are not. We are evolving, forming, and creating a vital cultural and literary tradition while similar traditions in the West are clearly degenerating.

The cultural and historical situation of the Black World demands entirely different aesthetic, artistic, and literary imperatives and purposes at this time. Among our people the novel has not exhausted its usefulness, has not run its course. In the nineteenth century when European nationalism was emerging, the great novelists of Europe played a signal role in defining national character and a shared sense of cultural and national identity. In our lifetime the Black World has decisively begun the process of seizing unto itself the essential elements of our own identity from the distortions and obscurities of alien interference and control. We face the awful yet exhilarating task of recording, exploring, clarifying, understanding, articulating, of making accessible and therefore potent the force and presence of our history—the struggles of our ancestors.

The black novel has not yet given to our people those unifying images of their historical experience and identity. Their lives, their culture, their national experience and consciousness, the struggle and travail of their forefathers—they have yet to see these things clarified, distilled, crystallized, made available and accessible through serious, realistic, artistically responsible political novels. We owe that to our people and to history. If ever a generation of writers had a clear, inescapable historical responsibility, it has to be the generation of black writers coming to maturity at this point in the black struggle for cultural autonomy, national identity, and integrity in the world.

We stand face to face with the necessity to continue the work, begun in earnest in our generation, of adding to that body of works which forge and articulate enduring metaphors embodying the spirit and meaning of our passage and presence in this world. We, in the Black World, still have before us the challenge to shape emerging national consciousness out of the deeply held and ancient values and moral perceptions of our cultures and to express this in a literary idiom fashioned from the myth, metaphor, and language which has evolved out of the collective experience of the race.

This is for me—and I would imagine to any thinking being—the most transcendently inspiring human process at work in the world today. This motion—however tentative and uncertain at first, but every day growing in clarity and purpose—includes the effort to apprehend the past, define the cultural future, and to engage and control the immediate and fiery passions of revolutionary change and the chaos of transition. Surely there is a role, indeed even a demand, in these turbulent and uncertain times for what might be called the novel of national consciousness—novels of national resonance of serious historical exploration and purpose, of moral and political consequence; rooted in the national struggle and experience; inspirited and informed by styles, traditions, and resources of indigenous popular and literary cultures. Novelists conscious of this duty, like the artist in traditional African culture, operate not out of any alienated, fevered, individual genius. They are the conduits through whom the collective force and experience of the people is reflected, shaped maybe, refined a little perhaps, and given back. In this endeavor one can, in Amilcar Cabral's words, "Tell no lies. Mask no difficulties. Claim no easy victories and hide nothing from the masses of the people." I would add, and play very few ego-indulgent games.

What are and are not the rudiments of engaged, responsible, and honest novels?

They are not the creatures of every passing whim and trendy fashion of the Western avant-garde, but are firmly rooted in the bedrock of our people's being. They do not distort the experience of a people by imposing on it the discredited, supercilious, and alien point of view of the colonial novels of Cary, Kipling, and Conrad, a tradition in which the Black World and its people are mere backdrops upon which any nonsense can be imposed. Rather they proceed naturally and organically out of the sensibilities, cultural traditions, moral imperatives, and linguistic styles and resources of the people who are their subject.

They do not take a mocking and scornful glee in parodying the real suffering of a society; nor do they blink at excesses or brutality of the leadership, but are resolutely and courageously critical in a principled way. Honest black writers have paid high prices in personal suffering for this, having gone to jail or into exile. Work like Naipaul's is a mockery of this commitment and sacrifice. An honest novel cannot proceed out of a glib, fashionable coffee house cynicism and unearned despair in which everything is beyond human effort. It is, rather, predicated on the assumption that there is a future for which to struggle, that conditions however grim are not beyond the reach of the people's will, intelligence, and decency, and that the writing and reading of such novels are not only testament to that faith, but are an integral and effective part of that struggle.

Such novels seek to contribute to a people's evolving perceptions of their historical and cultural identity and a shared sense of national purpose. To the extent that it is successful it will in part create its own audience. This is a challenge and an honor denied by history to contemporary Western writers. Any black writer who forgoes this wealth of possibility in favor of posturing to the Western bourgeoisie is condemned not by egotism and vanity, but by a fundamental stupidity.

Finally, an honest novel of black culture seeks to contribute to the evolving form, to the content and purpose of a vital modern tradition of black literature. It does not seek to latch onto the tail end of a moribund and thoroughly discredited colonial tradition which served only to exploit and mutilate those cultures for frivolous if not sinister purposes.

If such novels are tracts, then I salute and take my position with such tractarians as Chinua Achebe, Ngugi Wa Thiong O, those splendid women Buchi Emechita, Kofi Awoonor, and their embattled colleagues on the continent. And it is happily a growing company including Albert Wendt of Samoa, Andrew Salkey, Roger Mais, and V. S. Reid of Jamaica, and the Afro-American lineage of the extended family very important but too numerous to mention here. It is out of the ferment and travail of these evolving worlds that come the most exciting and purposeful body of novels in the English language today.

*1983*

# A Contemporary Perspective

# "God Aint Finished with Us Yet"

## Jesse Jackson and the Politics of the 1980s

DISSENT is a journal distinguished mostly by a self-conscious tone of high political seriousness, grave editorial responsibility, and analytical rigor, almost to the point of fussiness. How then to understand the curious editorial lapse represented by its printing of Julius Lester's eccentric and capricious assault on the personal and political morals and intelligence of the Reverend Jesse Jackson and his distortion and misrepresentation of the character and meaning of his campaign?[1] The piece is so patently unfair and perverse in interpretation, so transparently contemptuous of fact and reason as to invite, indeed demand, speculation as to the editors' motives and the author's compulsions, both political and psychic. It is difficult to identify a central, sustained argument in the essay, and were it possible to pronounce a piece of writing neurotic, it surely should be done in this instance. Trailing clouds of invective and moral indignation, it charges boldly off in all directions, nervously asserting about seven theses (and as many minor motifs), each of which is clearly incompatible with at least one other, demonstrable fact, or simple intelligence: Consider.

Member y'awl. When you gits to Atlantic City grab them Democrats by they delegate count and they hearts and minds will follow.

JUNEBUG JABBO JONES, Curbside address to the delegates of the Mississippi Freedom Democratic Party boarding the bus to Atlantic City at Jackson, Mississippi, August 1964

1 "You Can't Go Home Again," *Dissent* (Winter 1985).

We are first informed that the Jackson candidacy was invested with its apparent significance only by the "enthusiastic paternalism" of the white media, which, because of "the inherent intimidation factor" of Jackson's race, "took [the candidacy] far more seriously than it might have been because he was black." Ultimately it pronounces that "paternalism was nowhere more evident than in *how well* the press *allowed* Jackson to survive his Hymie/Hymietown gaffe and his association with Louis Farrakhan" (my italics).

In fact, it gleefully reveals, the campaign was an expression of Jacksonian ego and "opportunism" gone mad. A cynical and elaborate shell game—"a race for *power*, disguised as a presidential candidacy"—masking Jackson's real ambition to be "President of Black America." Happily, this cynical ploy was doomed to failure because "Jackson's political acumen could be considered as questionable as his morality . . . his radicalism put him to the left of the black electorate and the Democratic party" whose leadership "did not regard him as a political peer to be invited into the Party's inner circle, which is *what Jackson wanted*." Not only was the aspirant "President of Black America" to the left of the black electorate, he was "curiously out of touch with the black mood"; most blacks—according to the author's polls—preferred Mondale or Hart.

But even though blacks had rejected it outright, Jackson's candidacy and its rhetoric were still a despicable exploitation of the desperation of the black masses, "a cruel raising of hopes to a people for whom hope is the last lifeline" because it dangled before them the illusion of "Messianic deliverance."

Similarly, the Rainbow Coalition was "a romantic phase with overtones of the 60's—Woodstock, Peoples' Parks and a perpetual March on Washington, . . . pots of gold and Judy Garland. . . ." The attempt to form a multiracial, multi-issue coalition was doomed to failure because "no coalition of rejected groups ever brought about social change. . . ." Indeed, the "Rainbow Coalition had racial overtones" and "the very concept limited its appeal, ensuring Jackson the black vote and nothing else." While ". . . Mondale and Hart made the mistake of appealing primarily to the white middle-class, *Jackson's mistake was ignoring that same middle-class*."

In this mass of contradiction, there is a single clear, resonant, and unambiguous chord—that of Jackson's alleged anti-Semitism. He is presented as an Arafat-embracing, Farrakhan tolerant anti-Semite who demonstrates that he does not appreciate "the depth of his moral confusion about Judaism and anti-Semitism," which indeed may be the cue and motive for all this persiflage and its publication by *Dissent.* Given the article's barely concealed tone of patronizing contempt for the intelligence and political morality of the black community, one wonders how the editors would have responded had its author been a white writer. Undoubtedly it would and should have been dismissed as an example of a peculiarly dumb kind of racist polemic. But that is *Dissent*'s problem. The issue remains of the meaning of the Jackson campaign in the black struggle and American politics—what it meant to the vast majority of black Americans and what it revealed about the political condition of the white electorate and presidential politics in the 1980s.

The campaign was neither the spontaneous creation of unbridled Jacksonian ego and opportunism nor the messianic escapism by desperate and politically naive blacks that Lester and *Dissent* assert. It was, rather, the logical result of a period of discussion and analysis among many elements of the national black community distressed by the mixture of overtly racist policies, predatory social Darwinism, narrowly fundamentalist Christian intolerance, and chauvinistic military adventurism coming from ideologues of the extreme right who had captured the Republican party and the White House in 1980.

It seemed clear that their continued tenure in Washington was inimical not only to the well-being of racial minorities and the poor but to *all* the humane and civilized values that have been so hard won and vital a part of the American social contract. As the real political agenda and awesome political incompetence (particularly in international affairs) of the Reagan administration revealed themselves, elements of the black community were certain that the American people had to be appalled by the content of the political package they had purchased with Reagan's election in 1980.

So, faced by an administration whose stated economic policy was to further enrich the wealthy (it was, in David Stockman's candid and memorable phrase, "feeding time at the trough") and whose supply-side "trickle down to the poor" rhetoric was, again according to Stockman, only a cynical selling point; an administration unmoved by the lines of jobless that its policies had helped create and that the media broadcast nightly into the living rooms of America; a regime that combined the mortgaging of the nation's future in a reckless paroxysm of fiscal irresponsibility with wasteful military expenditure and the evisceration of the social and educational programs that had created from waves of immigrants the American middle classes, we waited for the pendulum to swing back. In the off-year congressional elections of 1982 we thought we saw the beginning.

Surely, therefore, in 1984 the forces of civility and compassion, social

and economic fairness and fiscal realism, religious tolerance and international restraint could be expected to reemerge in national political
discourse. Expressing their wisdom, better instincts, and long-term self-
interest, the American people would certainly turn the rascals out.

But what we saw, beginning with the Thatcher "landslide" in Britain
and an attendant heralding by the media of "a conservative tide sweeping
the West" was a most craven rightward sidle by aspiring Democrat standard bearers. It was apparent that the Democratic party lacked the nerve
or the vision to challenge the tenets of Reaganism, so as to expose its
dangerously untested, doctrinaire fantasies disguised as economic policy
and to outline clearly to the American people the basic ugliness of the
society implied by the social attitudes and pronouncements of the regime
and its supporters.

That was when the discussion of a possible black candidate began, apparently spontaneously, at many different points in the national black
community. I became aware of it early in 1983 during that terrible winter
of apparent official indifference to lines of cold and unemployed workers
applying in the hundreds for jobs advertised in tens. I witnessed a near
riot in a welfare office in the South Bronx. It was a Friday afternoon and
the office was closing. A young mother who had waited all day became
hysterical because, as she screamed, her children would have to pass
a weekend without food. The police removed her forcibly. The large
crowd responded with anger as did the harassed staff. Everyone—staff,
clients, and cops—was either black or Hispanic. A middle-aged black
worker explained tearfully that the tension had become daily more unbearable. Staff, she said, was being laid off and benefits cut while the
numbers of the jobless were constantly swelling. The poor were at each
other's throats.

None of the emerging Democratic candidates was addressing these
realities in a forthright way. Among a widely scattered group of former
civil rights activists a tentative, even wistful, discussion of the possibility
and potential effect of a black candidacy began. Harold Washington's
mayoral campaign lent energy to these discussions, not simply because it
had managed to defeat the fabled Cook County machine, but because of
the way in doing so it had mobilized the energy and commanded the passionate involvement of elements in the Chicago community that had never
participated in electoral politics before. Evidently that campaign had
struck a sensitive chord elsewhere because a number of nationally syndi-
cated columnists began to devote space to demonstrating the "political
futility and racial divisiveness" of such a candidacy. At that point the issue

began to seem less fanciful and quixotic, and when the NAACP leadership was prominently quoted in the important white media as strongly opposed to a black candidacy, the idea fairly glowed with new luster. There were reports that the Black Congressional Caucus, elected officials, and elements of the "national black leadership family" had examined and rejected the strategy of running a black candidate.

The received wisdom was that Vice President Mondale's juggernaut with its armies of volunteers, banks of telephones, batteries of computers, regiments of political professionals and media experts, a state-by-state game plan, and PAC swollen coffers had reached critical mass and was unstoppable. This being so, "best you git an early reservation, Jack, and hop onto the band-wagon with a low number on your ticket." This was more than a year before the convention and months before the first primary.

What was most troubling about all this was its atmosphere of anonymous corporate sterility. It was, and grandly so, equipage, technology, organization, logistics, and endorsements, but oddly without spirit or passion. Apparently intimidated by media assertions of Reagan's extraordinary—and quite mystifying—hold on the imagination and affection of middle America, Mondale and the Democrats embarked on a desperate search for a way to campaign for the presidency without running against the president. And what a president! One who publicly demonstrated only the most tenuous grasp on the activities of his administration—an administration that seemed intent on heating up the cold war; that believed American workers were grossly overpaid and was intent on correcting that social ill; that was directly responsible for a major recession; that had declared its intention to open up the wilderness to corporate exploitation and was in open and comfortable collusion with industrial polluters; that included the architects of a foreign policy, the incoherence and incompetence of which had resulted in spectacular embarrassments and whose single great success was represented by the invasion of a poverty-stricken Caribbean island the size of Martha's Vineyard. The mystique surrounding this presidency did not extend into the black community.

To us, Reagan's was, and is, the first openly racist administration in recent history. Forget for a moment its open class biases and assaults on the meager entitlements of the poor. Black interests clearly were the special targets of a president who began his 1980 campaign in Neshoba County, Mississippi, talking about "states' rights" and whose subsequent policies were entirely consistent with that beginning. This administration supported an end to the Voting Rights Act; sought and has pretty well succeeded in destroying the Civil Rights Commission; sought tax exemptions for avowedly racist private schools; and was using the legal resources of the federal government to attack state policies of affirmative action. By their deeds shall ye know them, and this was racism. In alliance with the lunatic fringe of the far right and the moral majority (so called), this president, beneath a benign "ah shucks" smile and homespun geniality presided over an administration that was cynically and consistently exploiting and exacerbating the baser racial instincts of the white majority.

We felt this administration to be both shameful and dangerous; thus there was a deep-seated need in the community, an almost visceral need, to oppose it publicly and effectively. But from all appearances, if the Democratic leadership had its way, the campaign would take place on territory chosen by the Reaganites, a misty, fog-shrouded terrain right of center and in the intelligence-numbing idiom of double-talk, newspeak, and buzz words, which had become the currency of political exchange. (By some sudden alchemy of language "special interests" were no longer malefactors of great wealth and large concentrations of capital seeking hegemony over natural resources; the phrase had come to designate those organizations representing the workers, minorities, and the poor.)

In such a scenario it was not clear that the very justified black outrage at the incumbent could cut through the haze of Democrat blandeur to find its way to the polls. And if it did, the black vote would again be a distant appendage choking in the dust and jackass droppings at the rear of the Democrat bandwagon, which, in truth, has been our history. Indeed, there was something in the courtship very much as though they would prefer that on election day we sneaked secretly before dawn into some back room of the polling station for a shameful consummation safely out of sight of respectable white America.

In spring 1983 a few friends—widely dispersed veterans of the civil rights movement with some access to the black media—entered into a minor conspiracy. We would seek every opportunity to agitate in the black media for a candidate. It seemed quixotic and unachievable at the time, but why not?—if only to tweak the beard of the leadership. As we discovered, the notion was percolating upward across the length and breadth of the black nation quite independent of our efforts.

In July 1983, for example, I suggested such a strategy in *Essence* magazine, a journal read by half a million black women. I argued that:

> Under this administration . . . the black community is losing even the minimal
> and hard-won gains of the sixties and seventies. Which of the present five

Democratic candidates is speaking out forthrightly and powerfully of our sufferings and dangers? What is clear is that if we do not speak out loudly and
persuasively in our own interests then no one will. . . . The candidate must
articulate our issues, interests and views eloquently and effectively. . . . And
what will give our candidate's voice the power and resonance that will bring
results? Can we win the presidency? No, but what emerges from serious
analysis is that it is entirely possible that a skillful, intelligent, well-organized,
purposeful black candidacy, supported by a unified and enthusiastic black
community, can determine who the Democratic nominee and the next president will be.

   . . . Look at the numbers. The first thing is that the campaign has begun so
early that we have six months to organize. Remember also that we are not
talking about winning a national election, but about a series of Democratic
state primaries which could not have been better selected to showcase black
political strength had we selected them ourselves. In the last year a black won
the Democratic nomination for Governor of California. Blacks have won
mayoralities in Detroit, Chicago, Philadelphia, Atlanta, and Birmingham,
Alabama, and hold it in Newark, New Jersey. All these states have important
primaries, as does Washington, D.C.

In the piece we argued that in the large industrial states and in the South
our candidate would be a real presence. In the depressed industrial states
the voters of other minorities and the white unemployed, who could well
respond to the social and economic issues raised by the candidate, might
also enter significantly into the equation.

   Moreover, we thought, our candidate would not need to go to the expense of campaigning in all sixteen states. On the basis of campaigns in
eight to ten major states with large black populations and high incidences
of unemployment, we optimistically projected that with five candidates
splitting the white vote, our candidate could enter the convention with two
to four hundred delegates on the first ballot. And if "the candidate succeeded in activating the community in those primary states in the way
Washington had in Chicago and this enthusiasm and interest were accompanied by massive voter registration wherever black people lived" we
could be a decisive force in a close convention (and subsequent election)
determining, if not who the nominee was, then at least who it would not
be. Almost as good.

   "Then," I wrote, "our candidate could stand up before the Convention,
the nation and the world and say, 'I stand here representing the hopes,
dreams, aspirations and sufferings of a sizable bloc of voters, and during

this campaign we have registered X millions more. We control two to four hundred delegates . . . now let us reason together.' "

"This moment would mark a new level in the political history of the race and the nation," I argued. "We would be represented in the councils of the Democratic party no longer as orphans, supplicants or stepchildren but as a powerfully organized constituency, with legitimate interests to advance, and the power from which to begin to do so. It was an opportunity to change forever the way the political leadership of the nation regards us and the way we see ourselves, that might not soon come again."

Although that appeal was couched in terms of fairly narrow group interests there were larger dimensions envisioned. The kind of candidacy we hoped for would inevitably widen the range and sharpen the tenor of the political debate. It would, in Martin Luther King's phrase, "subpoena the conscience of the nation" and dramatically remind the Democratic party of the honorable historical role it seemed to be abandoning so cravenly and short-sightedly. It would restore balance and sanity to the campaign, especially on the questions of the consequences for the nation of the new cold war; the incoherence and adventurism of foreign policy; the rape of the environment and the evisceration of social programs. By forcing these issues, we would give the Democratic party back its guts whether it wanted them or no.

Also and important—to the extent it rekindled anything like the passion and excitement of the civil rights movement, it would inspire the active participation of many of the four million adult black people who had *never* been involved in the political process, thus increasing our strength in local politics while broadening the base of American democracy.

At that time we felt certain that the president had to be vulnerable. We simply could not conceive of a campaign capable of selling the administration's record to the American people, the vast majority of whom, we felt, were neither wealthy, stupid, nor born-again zealots of the right. Believing Lincoln's dictum about the impossibility of "fooling all the people, all the time," we felt the election might at worst be close, and the passionate and mobilized black vote could be, clearly and demonstrably, the margin of victory for the Democrats. And, given the Reagan administration's scarcely disguised contempt for the political effectiveness and intelligence of the black community in particular and poor folk in general, this would be a consummation, as Hamlet said, devoutly to be wished.

A splendid scenario, but was it realistic? Theoretically it seemed quite possible, but as a practical matter, unlikely—the idle and wishful speculations of armchair theoreticians without a computerized mailing list, much

less a P A C, to call their own. The political fantasy life of the powerless everywhere must be something like that: a succession of boldly conceived
schemes of surpassing clarity, strategic elegance, and possibility that are
always thwarted, with the approximate worth in the political real-world
of John Nance Garner's "bucket of warm spit."

First a candidate had to be found. He would have to combine unusual—
even incompatible—qualities. He must have national "stature" but not
the caution that doth attend it. To even entertain the idea, he'd have to be
imaginative and bold, but he couldn't be seen as reckless or adventuristic.
He must be in very practical terms "political," but not a "machine" politician. Indeed, a paragon having on the one hand vision, charisma, and
energy and on the other the *gravitas* and credibility that would compel
our—and the country's—serious attention. No poolipops need apply.

Our desultory speculations continued late at night and by long distance.
With a cavalier disregard for the brute fact that collectively we had no
material organizational resources with which to persuade anybody, we
flipped through lists of our own devising. Andy Young? He's a national
figure! Nah, too inherently cautious and besides he's got Atlanta to worry
about. Yeh, besides, the Carter administration had left him holding some
unfortunate political baggage on the P L O thing. (The irony of that was yet
to come.)

Pity Harold Washington just got a good job. Yeah, he seems to have
great style on the stump, witty, cool, seems smart, pity. Who else? Ron
Dellums? Yah, he's tough, flamboyant, good politics and track record.
. . . Impressive physical presence, too. Think he'd go for it? Who can we
get to talk to him. . . ? Oh man, where's Adam Clayton Powell now that
we need him? Yeah, ol' Adam'd go for it . . . "audacious Black Power," as
he used to say.

My own thoughts stayed on an old "Snick" colleague, Georgia State
Senator Julian Bond. Julian was cool, highly articulate, politically credible,
very seasoned, and—very important—probably available and, as they
say, "media compatible." (Not to laugh, friends; in what presidential politics have become, a full head of hair and a good make-up artist are crucial.
Recall the fates of the only baldies in the race, Cranston, Glenn, and
McGovern, out in the early going.) Oddly enough—so much for our political prescience—at this stage the name of Jesse Lewis Jackson came up only
peripherally ("Yah man, but Jesse is a *preacher*. What we need is a politician), and the reasons for that were interesting.

We had known him in the civil rights movement, but not closely. He had
come fairly late into the S C L C, so S N C C veterans, not knowing his prior

credentials as a CORE student leader, felt ourselves his senior in the struggle. To us he was another of the brash, mouthy young Baptist ministers around Dr. King who were always wearing suits and praying. In the largest sense brothers and allies in the struggle, but still—the competition. And Jesse—like Caesar—was said to be "ambitious." Aha, but when the poor hath wept. . . .

It should not have been lost on us that, unlike most of those having these discussions, Jesse had not, after the southern movement, gravitated into the comfortable anonymity of the professoriat. Rather, he had moved his ministry north into the bleak landscape of the urban ghetto, stayed the course, and been effective. However, I did not then associate him with electoral politics.

Julian's still seemed to me the best credentials. Although serious, he had the irreverence, the wry impudence that might recommend such a scheme to his imagination. Besides, he had practical political experience, media smarts, and well-developed political views on the hard issues. His "youthful charm" and coolly rational delivery would sweep the debates. Benjamin, a coconspirator, demurred, "Julian'd be great with the college kids and white liberals, man; but if we talking about stirring up black folk —getting to the blood—it's gotta be a preacher. Jesse'd be better for that." I have recapitulated here the discussions to which I was a party. As I was to discover, very similar and equally wishful discussions were taking place around the national community, and for much the same reason: a frustrating sense of exclusion from the process by the confluence of conservative Republican hostility buttressed by Democrat timidity, coming at a time when we perceived there to exist scattered pockets of black electoral strength of real national potential. If only they could be united for some powerful demonstration of effective black power. But the likelihood then seemed increasingly remote.

But, as they say in that cradle of resistance, the black church, "Only wait on the Lord." And, indeed, the Lord did "raise up" a candidate. My doubts about the political skills of the Rev. Jesse Lewis Jackson evaporated mistlike in the brilliance of the initial campaign by which he tested the waters, prepared the ground, and ultimately preempted the territory. It bears recounting here, for it converted many a skeptic into a believer.

In the political climate of the fall of 1983 that I've been describing, any black seriously intending to run for president had to accomplish more or less simultaneously three tasks which were close to being mutually contradictory. The first was to impress the viability of such a candidacy into the imagination of the black public while avoiding the appearance of an unseemly self-promotion—by no means simple, given the communities' justifiable cynicism and alienation from the process.

To accomplish this would involve the second problem—that of attracting an unprecedented level of *serious* but nonprejudicial attention from a national media that even then already seemed quite prepared to project the winner. Any movement toward effecting the first two tasks would inevitably elicit responses from the black political establishment. These responses, at this point not necessarily to a *candidate* but simply to *the idea*, were not only natural but necessary. But they had to come in a context that, if not compelling support, would render open opposition at least difficult.

Too early a declaration, one made before the idea had rooted itself in the community's imagination, would have been a certain and easy target for charges of adventurism. And, indeed, outside of a ground swell of popular support and serious discussion and planning, those charges would be merited, the media dismissive and the politicians worse. But without a declaration—nothing. An ancient, recurrent yet infinitely tricky political circumstance. How to stimulate and sustain discussion of, and engineer a "spontaneous" wave of support for what does not exist?

Jackson's answer was a masterly exercise in political foreplay, deft in execution, unerring in timing, and with a surpassingly light and skillful touch. No American politician in my memory ever played so weak a hand to so remarkable an effect and with such apparent effortless skill and sureness. It is difficult now to say exactly when or how it was started—the delicately dangled, infinitely deniable rumor, whisper, suggestion of a possible candidacy that took care of the media in a far more effective way than a declaration possibly could have.

Faced with smiling Jacksonian inscrutability, the media embarked (for what seemed weeks) on an orgy of "Will he?" "Won't he?" and "What does it mean if he do?" "If he don't?"—leaving the five already declared candidates fuming in a state of benign semineglect. Naturally and swiftly the issue reached the bars, barber shops, beauty parlors, and other important arenas of political decision making in the community. It couldn't lose; the audacity of the idea was as appealing as the discomfiture of the media was delicious. Quite naturally, the media sought clarification from the usual black spokespersons, thus providing the Jackson camp with valuable political intelligence.

But the media has the attention span of a moderately intelligent kindergarten class. How could this interest be sustained? Should it? And for how long, before it became redundant and counterproductive? Certainly

Jackson had to avoid any appearance of coyness and manipulation on one hand, and indecision on the other.

Like all suitors since the world began, the media is at its most attentive when its courtship is not sought. And the Reverend ignored it and went diligently about the Lord's work, his father's business, so to say. He went into the South, seeking the constituency of the cloth and the platform of the pulpit. And so from the Baptist network in Dixie, from the ahmen corners and the threshing floors of the Lord, from the sanctuaries of the oppressed after the handsome young visitor had finished his sermon, the cry went up, spontaneous and unrehearsed with a resonant and fervent sincerity. "Run, Jesse, Run." But he never said a mumbling word. Merely waved, smiled, and headed for the next pulpit trailing clouds of media as he went.

> "Hey, the Brother gon' do it, Man?"
> "Gon' do it? Shoot Jack, he already doin' it—Jesse running lak a big dowg."

Discussions were held, opinions sought, readings taken. The idea, chimeric and quixotic at first, the merest glimmering of possibility delicately planted, began to take on the flesh and substance of reality. A nice irony. But just the same, the time was rapidly approaching when even a clerical gentleman must, as they say in the street, deposit something solid or get off the seat.

(At about this time I was asked quite casually if I would be willing to serve on "Jesse's Advisory Committee on Issues." I allowed as how I'd be honored and thereafter heard never a word further about "issues." That was the kind of campaign it was to be. But I gathered then that a decision had indeed been made. . . .)

The Campaign

It is a phenomenon of politics—certainly, anyway, of American politics—that the mantle of candidacy usually imparts to the wearer a certain aura—a patina, if you will, of personal luminescence. This gift, although always in some degree present, is by no means equally bestowed. Much depends on the office sought, the character of the campaign, and, of course, the style and presence of the candidate.

Many years ago in a movement office I first heard the syndrome wryly explicated during a conversation among some shrewd and experienced activists, the products of the hurly-burly of New York City reform politics and of campaigns for offices ranging from district leader to the presidency. One of them was describing something she called "Goodman's theory of the phallic mystique of candidacy," which indicates the extent to which it antedates the women's liberation era and the Geraldine Ferraro phenomenon, though in a certain way it does indeed describe the latter. "Have you noticed the change that sets in the moment some guy becomes *the candidate?* Could have been the wimpiest little nerd the day before. But the instant he gets the nod—the entire persona, or at least the public perception of it, changes. Suddenly there is a mystique—you see it most clearly among women supporters and campaign workers—he is the standard bearer—*our* candidate."

I forget now exactly which campaign of which Kennedy brother had triggered the discussion that went on at great and humorous length, the collective political experience of the women producing numerous examples of the syndrome. No one had ever, in my presence, accused the Reverend Jesse Lewis Jackson of any previous condition of wimpiness, but in November 1983, when he took the floor before a gathering of supporters and the assembled media of the nation and the world, an elegant, virile, supremely confident figure, the powerful unmistakable *aura* of candidacy, perhaps even *serious* candidacy attended him.

The press by their numbers would seem to affirm it. As did the accoutrements of candidacy—not the least of which was the security—a detachment of hawk-eyed Fruit of Islam arrayed pretorianlike around the room, soon to be replaced by the more official, no less cold-eyed secret service men.

Also there were other auguries of things to come. The campaign's strategy and purpose was reflected in the range of supporters on the platform: representatives of the black church and elected officials, Indian nations, Latino, Arab, and Jewish communities, as well as the antinuclear, peace, and environmental movements and the unemployed: the Rainbow, a coalition of the periphery and the excluded of American politics.

His announcement made it explicit: he was a candidate for the presidency of the United States. To that end he was seeking the nomination of the Democratic party and would contend in every state primary and caucus and would take his candidacy and delegates into the national convention in San Francisco.

There was nothing extraordinary about that—it was no more or less than some five or six white men had previously said. Yet some representatives of the media appeared at first oddly discomfited, unable, it seemed, to assimilate the familiar words into any intelligible pattern previously consecrated by human use. What did he hope to accomplish? Was he simply the candidate of black America? No. He was seeking the support of all the American people everywhere, like any other candidate, but he did hope and expect that his candidacy would appeal to and motivate the millions of Americans—including but not limited to blacks and minorities—who have been alienated from political participation, thus strengthening and deepening the democratic process.

Wasn't there the real danger of dividing the Democratic party along *racial* lines? The extent to which the Democratic party was divided racially—or at least was involved in racial politics—would later become clear. But this cannot fairly or *intelligently* be attributed to the Jackson campaign. No other candidacy seemed to present the media with the same discomfiture (although when the ill-fated Ms. Ferraro appeared, something similar in character if not kind became apparent).

Jackson's unflappable refusal to accept any definition of his candidacy as "symbolic," "therapeutic," or merely tokenistic seemed to offend— profoundly so—the media's most cherished notions of social order and propriety. Jackson, after all, did not seem actually crazy or of diminished faculties, and even less so to be clowning. Yet he stood there, unmistakably black in pigment, manner, and style, serenely insisting that he was indeed the candidate for a major American party's nomination to the office of the presidency.

What could they be missing? A stalking horse, perhaps? If so whose man was he, Hart, Glenn? Surely not Mondale's, who could hardly be expected to welcome any defection of the black vote. Maybe the Machiavellian hand of Kennedy kingmakers hoping for a dead-locked convention and a desperation draft? One even remembers the extraordinary speculation that Jackson was "consciously" or "objectively" the agent of Reaganism—the only obvious beneficiary of the oft-evoked, much to be dreaded "white backlash" which was certain to emerge from Jackson's candidacy, particularly if it were perceived to be doing too well. How well was "too well" and for what or whom remained unclear, but the idea is interesting.

Significantly enough, none of this confused speculation appeared in the black press, where the political columnists were very clear on the strategy, possibilities, and limits to the candidacy, and where most of them urged massive and passionate support cushioned by realistic expectations.

By the time he announced, the brother had accomplished more than could possibly have been expected a mere three months earlier: in that short time his southern pulpit strategy had worked splendidly in engaging the attention of the folk to the point that the declaration, when it came, was a response to the closest approximation of a genuine grass-roots draft as anything in recent presidential politics. The confident, sure-footed execution of the strategy had commanded the admiration and support of activists and particularly younger black politicians, a combination that rendered overt opposition by establishment black Democrats—nearly all of whom were pledged to Vice President Mondale—very difficult indeed. Yet even their temporary difficulty and estrangement from the base during the primaries could have its rewards. *Were* Mondale to be nominated *and* elected, these good soldiers could point to their toughing it out in his hour of need. The Jackson candidacy thus lent new value to what had been almost *pro forma* endorsements.

With the Jackson presence in the field, his candidacy became one of the central issues of the Democratic campaign. The black vote—indeed, the very existence of black America—took on a new political reality, at least for this campaign. We shed our invisibility; our vote could no longer be maintained in obscurity as the Democratic party's dirty little secret. Certainly it was no longer to be brokered and delivered quietly to Vice President Mondale whose vaunted credentials as a civil rights champion seemed rather less than met the eye. (Many of us remembered him quite vividly from 1964 in Atlantic City, when his national career began. There, as chairman of the Credentials Committee, he had frustrated the effort to bring the Mississippi Freedom Democratic party challenge to the convention floor.)

In three months Jackson had, in short, elevated the notion of a black candidacy from wishful pipe dream to reality, or at least, in the admittedly ephemeral ways such things occur in the media-defined and deformed politics of the times, to a *species* of reality. All of which—intoxicating though it was—had an alarming insubstantiality to it, the fleeting quality of last night's evening news or tomorrow's headlines.

The tough questions remained, and already there were those—in the media, in the Party, and in some elements of black leadership—who were asserting that the campaign had peaked. The campaign had, they sneered, no media experts, no pollsters, no experienced staff, no national organization, no endorsements, no war chest, in short, no visible means of support. The campaign could not sustain itself through the early going and would dissipate long before even reaching the southern primaries.

Except on the last point they were of course quite right. A quality of hand-to-mouth improvisation haunted the campaign, creating a host of avoidable problems, right up to the convention. But it is hard to see, in the nature of things, how it could be expected to have been otherwise.

At the point that we were scrambling to slap together a semblance of a campaign staff and a national organization amidst intimations of early mortality, the Lord, moving in his mysterious way (with Reagan by his side), sent a sign. Nothing too startling or portentous at first and a man less sensitive than the Reverend to the devices of the almighty might have missed it entirely.

Given its track record in that troubled region, it was in no way extraordinary that the administration would, in its wisdom, intervene militarily in a Middle Eastern civil war of truly byzantine complexity and ambiguity, *and* do this on behalf of a minority government of questionable antecedent and little popular support. Nor, in such circumstances, was it surprising that one of its war planes would be shot down bombing targets in a country with which the United States was not at war. That the sole survivor, however, should be a youthful black airman from New Hampshire seemed to move beyond probability into the neighborhood of the portentous. (Divide the number of fliers in the navy by the number who are black. Multiply that by the number of whites in New Hampshire and divide the result by the number of blacks, then calculate the odds against the result being in the Bequa Valley, surviving the crash, and ending up a prisoner in Syria almost on the eve of Christmas. . . . a month before the New Hampshire primary. "Signs and portents chillun, signs and portents. . . .")

And, in the face of the administration's reluctance or inability to negotiate his release, the Lord called Jesse—even as he had once called Saul—to Damascus. Those—myself among them—of little faith and rational bias saw in the mission signs of hubris and great and needless political risk. We also heard an ominous grinding of steel coming from the long knives of the political press. Perceiving the brother finally to have misstepped they would now gleefully take his legs at the knees. Our Ibo ancestors say "As a man dances, so are the drums beaten for him." And the brother had led them a furious dance.

But it was not to be . . . yet. He returned in triumph with a sadder, one hopes wiser, Lieutenant Goodman in tow and, to the great joy of black America, delivered him like an ironic Christmas present to the White House and a president wearing a grim and labored smile.

For the long knives the time had not yet come. The blades had to be discreetly returned to scabbard. Their time was coming, but for the moment, it was the cover of *Time* and *Newsweek;* the network evening news; Ted Koppel's "Nightline"; and the front pages of every metropolitan daily in the country and much of the world. There was a heady atmosphere of unreality best expressed by the conservative *Le Figaro* of

Paris which pronounced gravely that Jackson had in one swoop moved "from marginal candidate to major contender." Not quite. At least not in our America.

Objectively nothing but its perception had changed, but the campaign was now seen to have gained momentum, and Jackson himself attained a degree of credibility with, or at least attention from, his white compatriots.

The extent to which the media—especially the electronic media—has the power not merely to report but also to create and define in the public's mind the parameters, form, and meaning of political reality is greatly lamented. For example, we understand, or think we do, the unprecedented degree to which the present incumbent of the White House has been created—the consequence of a media-transmitted image, the product of arbitrary composition, artifice, and illusion—in much the same way that good fiction is made. Early in the campaign we got an intimation of that media power.

About a week after his return from Syria, on two-days' notice, word went out that western Massachusetts could "have the candidate." All the schedule permitted was an hour in the middle of a working day. It was January, snowing, a windy fifteen degrees and we were in a college town that is white though of liberal tradition. School was not in session so the town was empty of students. We had had reports of other Democratic hopefuls preceded by impressive deployments of advance men beating the thickets to turn out a few hundred voters. We arrogantly scheduled a church with a capacity of 1,200 and prayed to avoid being embarrassed, only to be more deeply so by the line of white folks four deep and half-a-mile long standing in the snow—some 5,000 potential voters and contributors—who could not be admitted.

What did it mean? What had brought those people out; was it curiosity, entertainment-seeking, the attraction of media celebrity, or a more profound political need that could be translated into votes? Would this response be typical of white America? If so, we and the country were in for some, as my students would say, "very heavy shit." Anyway, the answers would soon be forthcoming; the campaign would tell.

The campaign answered some questions, left others still obscure, and posed a great many new ones which not even the most prescient among us could have anticipated. Problems of structure and staff remained in what was essentially a volunteer operation throughout. But the candidate—with the exception of one deplorable and costly blunder—was superb. He did everything we had wished a candidate would do, and he did it with consummate style, grace, and charisma. The campaign strategy he defined expanded the appeal from the black community to other constitu-encies of conscience. He transformed a perfectly legitimate attempt merely to harness black voting strength into an organized and visible force in national politics to a broader coalition—the Rainbow. This would cen-trally include progressive whites, feminists, environmentalists, antinuke activists, pacifists, students, workers, and the poor—as well as those tradi-tionally excluded racial minorities—Asians, Latinos, original Americans and, of course, the black base.

For such a coalition to be effective requires, in the context of American ethnic division and alienation from one another and the political process, much more time for purposeful organization than a hastily put-together campaign allows. But the seed was planted and, given the pressure of time, scarcity of funds, and the quickly assembled national network, the wonder is that it worked as well as it did. One problem was that many white ac-tivists and their organizations which philosophically had no other natural resting place in the Democratic party appeared uncomfortable in a coali-tion with a black base and leadership. On the other hand, some of our state campaign directors seemed less committed to broadening the base than they should have been. Their reasons—scarcity of funds and a natural skepticism about the effectiveness of such an effort—were quite cogent. But the gamble should have been made and more resources committed. The campaign, given its volunteer aspect, could not be tightly controlled from the top. Nevertheless, enough was accomplished to show the Demo-cratic party the potential of the still largely untapped ethnic vote; unfor-tunately, the lesson seems to have escaped them.

In California, for example, the cooperation and spirit between pro-gressive whites, Asians, Chicanos, and blacks was truly impressive and heartening. In New York City, the alliance between the black and His-panic communities as well as the West Indian precincts, which was new, encouraging, and spirited, resulted in unprecedented registration and vot-ing in those communities.

Just before the New York primary, I talked with Alice Childress, the distinguished author and playwright. Her voice conveyed her passion.

"Oh," she said, "we just owe *so* much to that young man. In the super-market where I shop, the youths—mostly black and Hispanic—who bag groceries were talking politics this afternoon. Usually they are so brittle and unconnected! But today they were excited, passionate even, planning to go in a group to register. We just owe Jesse so much."

The roots of the campaign lay in the black South, Beulah Land, and it was there that one saw in stark and unforgettable scenes its meaning and justification. Here Jesse's campaign was in many ways the consummation of that bitter, brutal, heroic, and dearly won struggle for our peoples' right to vote. And the signal of a new stage.

—On caucus Sunday in Tidewater, Virginia, when church was over, lines and lines of black folk marched out in their hundreds, proud and determined, to the Democratic caucuses, packing the halls in numbers so unprecedented as to overwhelm the caucus machinery.

—In the Mississippi Delta, where attendance at precinct caucuses averages less than a hundred, organizers talked in awe of the turn-out in black precincts, "Man we had close to a thousand and next door in the white precinct about fifty." Both elected the same number of delegates, however.

—Mondale, feeling Hart's cold breath at his heels, desperately reaching out for black support, stood in an Alabama church and pledged to be, if elected, "The best president for black America in the history of the country." This, in full view of the media, was a promise he clearly had wished to avoid having to make.

I remember my last visit with Mrs. Fannie Lou Hamer, just before her death. Very ill and, though I did not know it, with only a few months to live, she showed me her new concrete house, part of a project built since the movement. It seemed cramped, too small for the great spirit of the woman, but she was proud of it. She sat surrounded by the many awards, so richly deserved, painfully won, and yet somehow so totally inadequate. I had known her in the full power of the movement. I looked into her eyes, those luminous brown eyes, so indescribably haunting and expressive.

"What is it, Mrs. Hamer, tell me?" I coaxed.

"Mike . . . you know. . . ." She stopped and a look of pain and confusion came into her face. When she continued it was in a hoarse whisper, almost inaudible as though she were about to reveal something of which she was deeply ashamed. "These young folk . . . you remember how *haaard* we had to fight . . . jus' to get the *right* to vote? . . ." She shook her head, a gesture of misery and disbelief. "Wal . . . the young folk, y'know they don't care *nothin' 'bout voting?* You *believe* that Mike?"

I regret she could not have lived to be in Jackson, Mississippi, on that spring morning of 1984 to see the line a thousand strong of young Jackson State University students following Jesse down to the registrar. She might have felt better about her life of struggle.

Jesse's entry into the primaries was, in many ways, *the* story of the campaign, and the media recognized that, even if it initially had difficulty *understanding* what it meant. In the early stages, amid the chorus of doomsaying, the candidate maintained a spirit of poised and determined confidence which inspired courage and commitment from thousands of otherwise cynical and alienated people. This is all the more impressive when one remembers the atmosphere of harassment and potential violence that was being generated then toward the candidate and his family. In light of recent history and the character and persistence of these threats, even Reagan's Justice Department assessed the danger to be serious enough to warrant secret service protection before the other candidates received it.

Yet one looked in vain for any sign of faltering purpose, hesitancy, or fear from Jesse. Knowing that the risk he was taking had dimensions far more tragic than mere political embarrassment, my respect for his courage grew immensely.

And so did my respect for his vision and character as it was reflected in the nature of his campaign. According to the press, he was the most "charismatic" of the Democrats. What exactly does this mean? For one thing it meant there was not only passion in his voice, but clarity and directness in his language. Platform ambiguity and nonspeak is not a medium that lends itself to either projecting or evoking feeling, much less passion. Partly, therefore, it was Jesse's refusal to obscure his position in clouds of code words—it was, in short, simple honesty and sincere conviction—that was perceived as "charisma." The other part was black style, a tradition of spoken language distinctly Afro-American with resonance of the pulpit, a tradition in recent times shared in some measure by people as diverse as James Baldwin, Malcolm X and, of course, Martin Luther King, Jr. In the best possible sense of that term he *was* a *black* candidate, articulating a higher vision of American reality and moral possibility, a vision sorely tested and tempered by the fires of generations of struggle, disappointment, and persistent hope for this nation. His forthright attack on the principles of Reaganism was not a liberal position or a left position—it was fundamentally a black critique of the intellectual contradictions, macho posturing, great power fantasies, racial chauvinism, and social and economic predatoriness that deforms the American Dream as dreamt by white men. The vision he articulated was one shared by me and millions others—of a land ruled by justice, decency, and tolerance, at peace with its neighbors and with itself. A powerful force for good in the world. A world power—not because of the brute fact of a great economy and intimidating strength of arms, but by virtue of its visible and even-handed deployment of this power in the service of democracy, social justice, and respect for human rights—in short for the dreams and needs of the world's people. America's best and only defense, in the long term.

Also moving was the effect he had among the wretched of the nation.

The citizens of the ghettos, rural as well as urban—from the barrios of the South Bronx, to the hollows of West Virginia, to the cottonfields of the Delta—responded to the campaign and to the candidate because, I think, they could see and feel the depth of his concern, compassion, and determination. His was an empathy that could not be simulated, and people recognized that. He was the moral presence in that dismal campaign, naturally and genuinely.

That is why the "Hymie" remark was so painful to so many, so unexpected and so damaging. It was tasteless and inappropriate, especially for him. And, having uttered it, he should have followed his instinct rather than his advice, admitted a mistake and apologized immediately and publicly. Not because it was politic to do so, but because it was right. This failure of judgment and principle was undoubtedly more damaging to the public perception of his character than even the initial remark. And of course the long knives had their chance, which they gleefully exploited, worrying and belaboring the issue all the way to the convention.

During those tense times, I was most moved by the effect on those of our volunteers who were Jewish. One must remember that the campaign was just beginning to gather momentum, and people working for it tended to be passionate in their commitment, an intensity factor generally not present among the other candidates' supporters. A number of Jewish volunteers came in—some in tears—to say they could no longer work. I sympathized. Others came in and, before one could say anything, said, "You don't have to explain. I know Jesse's no anti-Semite—it's a false issue." I was again moved, especially when some volunteers and members of the local Jewish community organized "Jews for Jesse" groups and began discussion of the issue. Because the erosion of the relationship between the black and Jewish communities in recent years is a real issue, it is an ironic and tragic development that requires discussion, at length, honestly, and in detail. But that discussion must take place between responsible black and Jewish leaders and representatives, not in the public media.

What I will say to Professor Lester is this. He more than most should understand that it is indeed possible, natural even, that a great many blacks cannot help identifying with the experience of the Jews in the modern world. While sympathizing with the suffering, we even more respect the struggle and understand very clearly the need for the dignity and security of a nation and a homeland. Given our history how could we not?

But for those same historical reasons, how can any conscious black person of the Americas fail to see that the Palestinian people also have rights, do also suffer, and no less have aspirations? And that until this reality is accepted and discussed, there will be no real progress toward peace and security for any of the bloodied peoples in that unfortunate region? And to say this, even as Jackson has done, does not make one anti-Semitic or an enemy of Israel.

We have been allies once and will be again; the logic of our similar histories and that of America decrees it. But an alliance must begin with mutual respect and the kind of free and honest discussion that cannot take place in the pages of *Dissent* and in tones of such rancor and malice. Perhaps, also that time too, will come.

I said then that if I remotely believed the candidate to be anti-Semitic, I would not continue to be associated with the campaign. The question was a serious diversion of energy, a sower of confusion, and it badly tarnished the perception of the campaign's moral authority. But the sense of political possibility and a most heartening mass response to that possibility was still evident and would remain present until Mondale achieved the votes for a first ballot nomination. After that an atmosphere of anti-climax, inevitably descended, distracting attention away from the Rainbow's real accomplishments.

The real goal of most of us was the drama and possibility of a meaningful convention, something almost forgotten in American politics. It would be one in which the Rainbow delegation—the stone that the builders rejected—would hold the key to nomination. We wanted that with a visceral intensity. It would have been the successful culmination of the most long-shot, quixotic political gamble, one unimaginable only a year earlier. It was, of course, the last thing the Democratic leadership wanted to see. In the received wisdom of that leadership, the frenzied cut and thrust of that kind of convention in the full glare of the television cameras, which is to say the American people—*and* with black and minority people at its center—would be the kiss of death. (Maybe, but could it have been more fatal than the Mondale-Ferraro debacle? So much for received wisdom.)

And why did we want such a result so passionately? Egotism? The vindication of strategy and a wish to be included? The opportunity to cut deals and peddle influence? Not really. Though, as in all presidential campaigns, there was a "pork-chop" element present, looking for the main chance. But precisely because of this campaign's origin and content, this element was negligible. In fact, to locate this element of the black political community one had to look to the Republican convention where it was to be seen shining with cupidity and opportunism, and, one hopes, some considerable embarrassment.

There were substantive reasons. In a convention in which real interests and ambitions were to be decided—and in which we were strategically placed—we could force the Democratic party to confront the traditional Democratic issues it was trying to avoid, to recognize the real nature of the Democratic coalition and particularly the place and future of minorities and progressives in it. Such a convention would have forced the Party to abandon its courtship of what's been described as the national "redneck" vote, and to face the electorate from a dramatically different posture—a posture that would have made it necessary for it to cultivate, deepen, and strengthen habits of political participation among blacks, Asians, Indian, and Hispanic communities in the way earlier generations of Democrats cultivated the white immigrant vote. It was this process that we had hoped to force. We would undoubtedly have heard cries from the Democratic right that "you are hurting the Party." So what's new? In 1984 the Party carried only three of its traditional constituencies, black, Hispanic, and Jewish voters. We could hardly have hurt them more than that.

Mondale's early victory rendered all that "nonoperative." What is not generally known is how painfully close we came. Not only did we get to San Francisco, but we also received three and one half million votes en route. The black community was unwavering, giving the Rainbow 85 percent of its vote, and this in the face of a strong establishment attempt for Mondale. But the black vote was only 60 percent of the vote we received. Twenty-one percent was white, 10 percent Hispanic, and 9 percent Asian, native, and Arab Americans. Moreover, and this has profound implications for the House of Representatives, we won sixty-one congressional districts. The numbers of black local officials elected, particularly in the South, was unprecedented.

A campaign conceded between 100 and 150 delegates at most by the experts ended up with 465 delegates in San Francisco. This is significant because a study published after the election concludes that if delegates were apportioned fairly in relationship to popular vote, the Rainbow would have gained a further 400 delegates. Mondale would have been short of nomination by that number, and Hart would have remained the same, some 300 short. What a convention that would have made!

It is remarkable how very close we were. What is distressing is that the Democratic party seems to have learned nothing from this entire demonstration. A Gallup poll taken in 1985 reports that 60 percent of Jackson voters are willing to follow him out of the Democratic party in 1988 if necessary. Let us hope the Party does not make that happen. After eight years of Reagan, this nation does not need his heirs, even for only one term. The Democrats would be well advised to begin rebuilding their coalition with precisely those elements that Jackson mobilized and led into San Francisco. To do this, however, requires that the Party decide exactly what it stands for in this nation's life. At the moment, alas, it seems uncertain. And the nation is much the poorer thereby. But "God aint finished with us yet."

*1986*

Library of Congress Cataloging-in-Publication Data

Thelwell, Michael.
   Duties, pleasures, and conflicts.

   1. Afro-Americans—Civil rights. 2. Afro-Americans—
Fiction. 3. United States—Race relations. 1. Title.
E185.615.T49   1987      973'.0496073      86–14607

ISBN 0–87023–523–0 (pbk. : alk. paper)